The House by the River

J. William Hauck

The House by the River

Copyright © 2015 by J. William Hauck

eBook ISBN: 978-0-9904348-5-6
Paperback ISBN: 978-0-9904348-4-9

White Ladder Books

ALSO BY J. WILLIAM HAUCK

The Sheep Rancher's Series

The Sheep Rancher's Daughter

The House by the River

Chronicles of the Watchers Series

Elijah's Awakening

Elijah's Quest

The Sojourner Series

The Sojourners

The Soul Seekers

The Searchers

To those searching for happiness.
May their journey be complete.

THE ARRIVAL

Boise, Idaho
October 1919

*I*t was a lovely day in Boise for early October, with white billowing clouds to the east and red and orange-leafed trees lining the road. Mildred Read had a hard time pulling her enchanted gaze from the handsome young man dressed in a suit and tie as they motored down the street. That Bill Kane, the man she had for so long written to and fallen in love with, was beside her in the flesh, was almost more than she could believe. Mildred, whose light brown hair was pulled back in a bun, breathed in Bill's scent as she leaned into him. He had a manly muskiness mixed with burned tobacco that was both compelling and disappointing to her.

"How was your train ride?" asked LaVerda, in the back seat beside her sister. Six years younger than Mildred, LaVerda was the one responsible for their meeting, and studied Bill with curious eyes.

"It was long," nodded Bill, smiling at the giddy Mildred, her arm wrapped around his.

"Where did you stop?" called back Mr. Read at the wheel over the drone of his car's engine.

Bill gulped. Mr. Read's bony features and dark, bushy eyebrows reminded him of an officer in the Army. "Quite a few places I can't remem-

1

ber." He looked down a passing side street, then added. "I spent a day or so in Chicago."

"That's where you're from, isn't it?" asked Mrs. Read, half-turned and looking back from the front. A hat and scarf held down her pulled-back hair, and her slightly beaked nose gave her a look of forgotten elegance.

Bill nodded. "Yes, ma'am. Chicago."

"Did you visit your kin there?" asked Mr. Read.

Mildred's brow tightened as she watched for Bill's response. She knew his sad story better than anyone else, but had many questions herself.

"No," Bill sighed. "There wasn't anybody left."

Mildred rubbed Bill's arm, then leaned forward and said, "If you remember, Bill's mother died when he was young and his father when he was sixteen." Her eyes flashed to Bill, uncertain if she should have shared the story.

"I'm sorry to hear that," said Mrs. Read with a loving smile.

"What about your other family?" asked a saddened LaVerda.

Bill shook his head. "I don't know. I couldn't find them. We lost touch after I joined up." He looked down at his hands. "It was my fault, really. I should have tried harder to keep in touch."

"Well, we can be your family now," beamed LaVerda.

Bill glanced at Mildred and smiled.

AFTER DINNER, the rest of the family had retired to different parts of the house to read or play the piano and sing when Mildred led Bill out onto the front porch. "I bet you're exhausted with the train ride and all the questions at dinner."

Bill turned to Mildred and smiled. "I don't mind."

They sat on the bench outside the front door, and he took her hand. Mildred's face brightened as she snuggled up next to him.

"You have a lively family, and they all seem to get along."

"Not always," shrugged Mildred.

"But you have each other and love each other."

Mildred nodded and leaned her head on Bill's shoulder. "I'm sorry you don't have your family anymore. It must have been tragic losing your mother at such a young age. And then your father. And now you've lost contact with your brothers and sister. I'm sorry," she sighed.

Bill's brow tightened.

"Do you remember much about your mother?"

"Some," said Bill, his gaze fading across the yard.

"Your father, though. He was around much longer. I'm sure that was nice."

Bill drew in a ragged breath. While his memories of his mother were few, they were warm and happy. Bill's recollections of his father were not the same and caused his jaw to tighten.

Mildred lifted her head from Bill's shoulder when he reached into a pocket for a cigarette.

"Do you mind if I smoke?"

Mildred's brow gathered, and she forced a smile. "Okay." But the truth of the matter was, she considered smoking a horrible and dirty habit, although so many did it.

Bill put the cigarette in his mouth and felt for his matches.

"How long have you smoked?" Mildred asked as he lit up.

Bill took a drag, then shrugged. "I don't know. I tried it a little as a kid, but it was the thing to do in the Army."

"Do you like it?" Mildred asked as he blew a gray puff of smoke away from them.

"It calms my nerves," Bill shrugged. "The doc says it helps with digestion too." He turned to Mildred and said, "You wanna try it?"

Mildred sat back and shook her head.

Bill noticed, and his brow tightened. "Doesn't your father smoke?"

"No," said Mildred, eyeing the cigarette's plume. "It's a church thing. We don't smoke or drink."

"Oh." Bill pulled back in thought, then mashed the cigarette on the bench. "I won't smoke then."

Mildred smiled, but in her mind, she wondered how many other things she would learn about him. She told herself none of that mattered, even Bill's smoking. After dozens of letters, she felt she understood his heart, and it was good, and that was all anyone could ask for, including God.

"Thank you for writing all those letters. They kept me going. So did your pictures," said Bill.

Mildred smiled. "Well, it was all that stinker LaVerda's doing, really. She was hot to trot for writing the war boys. I don't know how many of those poor fellas she had on the line."

Bill laughed, but then grew contemplative. "I'm sure she helped a lot of scared and lonely boys."

"How is your friend, Bill Sharp? He was the one who put the advertisement in, wasn't he?"

Bill grinned and chuckled at the memory of Sharp's desperate move to get girls to write to them: an advertisement in the *San Francisco Chronicle*. "Yes, he was. We all thought he was crazy, but look how things turned out." Bill's grin faded. "I don't know what happened to him."

Mildred nodded in thought. She knew many had died during the war, and it was sometimes better to not press. Even those who had come home were often scarred both inside and out. She knew more than a few boys who had a terrible time dealing with their war memories.

"I'm glad you made it through that influenza pandemic okay. It sounded like you were in pretty rough shape for a while."

Mildred sighed. "I don't remember much of it. Mother says I was delirious for days. I'm grateful I made it through to be with you."

Bill sat back on the bench and looked across the street. The sun had set, and the neighbors' lights were glowing through their windows. His content gaze moved to the fading skylight as Mildred tightened her shawl and nestled in close to him. Bill wrapped his arm around her.

"What are you thinking about?" she asked, looking up from his shoulder.

"I'm thinking it doesn't get much better than this. Watching the sunset after a delicious meal of chicken and dumplings and holding a beautiful girl."

Mildred blushed. "Do you really think I'm beautiful?"

Bill looked down at Mildred and nodded. "Yes, I do." He leaned his head down and kissed her.

Mildred sighed contentedly as she licked her lips. "I think you're very handsome."

Bill smiled and kissed her again, more passionately this time.

"My!" gasped Mildred, pulling back with wide eyes. "You are a good kisser."

Bill laughed.

"Have you kissed a lot of girls?"

Bill shrugged. "A few." His thick brow gathered, and he looked down at Mildred. "Have you kissed a lot of boys?"

Mildred looked away coyly and said, "Wouldn't you like to know?" Then turned back and laughed. She looked into Bill's eyes then said. "A few, but I enjoyed none as much as I do yours."

Bill nodded approvingly, and they kissed again. This time, Bill's hand reached around Mildred and pulled her into him.

"My goodness! I see how this can get out of hand!" gasped Mildred, breaking away for air.

"Don't you like it?"

"A little too much!" said a wide-eyed Mildred.

Bill sat back, uncertain if he had offended her.

After a composing breath and sigh, Mildred flattened the front of her dress and turned to Bill. "I thought we could talk a bit about...us."

Bill nodded and took her hands. "What about us?"

"Well, you've come all this way and, well, I was wondering what your intentions are."

Bill's brow gathered. "To be here with you," he said, not understanding. "I love you."

Mildred blushed. While they had expressed the sentiment many times in their correspondences, it seemed a different matter, saying it in person. "I-I love you too," she said with a nervous smile.

Bill leaned in and kissed her again. He would have kept kissing her, but Mildred gently pushed him away.

"So, we've established that," she smiled. "Now, what does that mean?"

"That we love each other?"

Mildred nodded.

Bill studied Mildred, not sure what he was missing. "Well, I guess that means we get married."

Mildred's face lit up. "You meant it then!"

"Of course, I meant it."

Mildred's face filled with concern. "There are some who would say we don't know each other except for our correspondences."

"Your parents," concluded Bill.

Mildred gulped and then shrugged. "Them and others."

"But I'm not in love with them or others, just you."

Mildred's eyes widened, and her shoulders raised with the thrill of the notion.

Bill studied her for a time, then asked, "What do you think we should do?"

"I suppose...I suppose we should do what we feel is right. We're pretty well grown up, after all! We're both twenty-three. You've been around the world, and I came back from the brink of death! We should know what's good for us!"

Bill nodded. "I agree."

Mildred sat back and eyed him expectantly.

"What's wrong?"

"I'm just waiting."

Bill cocked his head in confusion. "Waiting for what?"

"For you to ask me to marry you."

"Oh!" Bill straightened up in his seat and gazed across the yard in thought. With a gulp and a serious look, he got to his knees.

Mildred clutched her breast in a giddy spasm.

"Nancy Bushelbasket," he began, using the fictitious name Mildred first used in her letters, "will you be my wife?"

Mildred lowered her hands with a look of disappointment. "I'm talking about for real."

"Sorry," Bill grinned. His face grew serious again. "Mildred Read, will you marry me?"

"I'll have to think about it," she said, looking away playfully, before turning back and exclaiming, "Yes, I will!" After falling to her knees, Mildred wrapped her arms around Bill and they kissed.

When they sat back on the bench, Mildred flattened her dress, then brushed back her bangs, trying to regain composure.

"Well, now that we got that out of the way, I suppose we need to talk about when," said Bill, the finality of marriage settling in.

"My mother says when you know something is right, there's no sense in putting it off." Mildred shrugged, then said, "Maybe in a couple of weeks?"

Bill nodded, both eager and frightened by the notion. He took Mildred's hand, but his gaze was past her. "I suppose I better find a job first. That's the respectable thing, anyway. I have to be able to provide for us, especially if..."

Mildred's brow raised, waiting for him to finish the sentence. "Especially if?"

Bill gulped. "You know, babies and all."

Mildred sat back, and her face emptied. The idea of being a wife excited her, but the responsibilities of motherhood were entirely different. The idea of her getting pregnant and having a child made Mildred feel strangely old. She wondered if she was responsible enough for such a thing. "I suppose that's right." Her face brightened when she remembered her father's job offer. "You can work for my father!"

Bill scratched the back of his neck. "I don't know much about sheep, but I am a fast learner."

"There! It's settled!"

Bill sighed. "What about a house? A place to live?"

"Well, we'd live in Oreana, of course. It's a lovely place." Mildred's brow gathered, and she shook her head. "Oh, who am I kidding? I despised it growing up, but that's where the sheep are and...well, it would be different living there with you! We could live at the Z-Bar and even build a little cabin close by. There is a lovely place near the creek that I used to dream about. We could do that, don't you think?"

Bill looked a little pale as he nodded.

Mildred sighed as the possibilities flooded her mind. She looked into the now dark sky and pulled her shawl a little tighter. When she turned back to Bill, she saw his apprehension. Mildred gulped, then said, "It's getting late, and I'm sure you're exhausted. I know I am. Maybe we should retire and talk about it more tomorrow?"

Bill met eyes with Mildred and nodded. "Where am I to sleep?"

"In Jack's room. I'll show you."

Bill nodded and took Mildred's hand.

BILL DIDN'T KNOW what time it was when he came back out onto the front porch, bundled in his coat. The half-moon was over the trees when he looked around the bench for his discarded cigarette. After finding it, he lit a match, then inhaled the calming nicotine. Bill sighed as he eyed the moon and considered all that had happened. He had loved Mildred from her letters and wasn't the least disappointed in her now, but he wondered what the right thing to do was. A part of Bill told him to leave. To get back on the train and go back to his home in Chicago. But then he reminded himself he had no actual home. Even the Army, his constantly changing home for the past six-plus years, was gone. Bill took another drag and calmed his nerves a little more. But he still felt like a stranger in a foreign land.

After finishing his cigarette, Bill stepped on it and went back inside. He knew things had a way of working themselves out, and a good night's sleep would be a start.

IT WAS the rooster crowing that woke Bill up. After pushing aside the covers, he pulled on his shirt, pants, and shoes, then opened the door to the hall. The smell of bacon and eggs greeted him like a warm embrace. Bill went down the creaking stairs, wondering what the day would bring. He was tempted to go out for a smoke, but when he saw Mildred standing near the kitchen with hair neatly pulled back wearing an apron, he smiled and said, "Good morning."

"Good morning," Mildred glowingly replied. She moved closer, as if to kiss him, then stopped, thinking better of it with her parents and six younger siblings watching.

"How did you sleep?" asked Mrs. Read at the stovetop.

"Darned well," said Bill, rubbing his eyes. "I'm still half-asleep. Nothin' a good cup of joe won't fix."

Mildred's brow tightened, and she glanced at her father reading the paper.

"We don't have coffee, Bill, but we've got some Postum and orange juice," smiled Mrs. Read.

Bill wanted to ask, "What the hell is Postum?" But nodded and said, "That sounds quite tasty."

Mr. Read raised his eyebrows and returned to the paper. Despite the Church's prohibition on coffee, he, for one, would have welcomed a cup.

It was halfway through breakfast when Mildred flashed a loving glance at Bill, then said, "Bill and I were talking last night."

"And?" Mrs. Read asked, pretending to be unworried by the notion of her daughter falling so quickly for a stranger.

Bill looked up, a spoonful of oatmeal suspended halfway to his mouth. He felt the entire family's eyes on him. Even two-year-old Forrest, with mush running down his chin, was watching.

"And…" Mildred turned to Bill. "Why don't you tell them?"

The color emptied from Bill's face. He thought they were going to talk about marriage some more before telling the others. Bill set down the spoon, glanced at Mildred, then cleared his throat. "Well, we were just talking about…what to do next."

"What do you mean?" frowned Mr. Read.

Bill's uncertain gaze moved from Mr. Read to Mrs. Read as Mildred waited and LaVerda held back a snicker.

"I think what Bill is referring to is the job you promised him," said Mrs. Read.

Mr. Read nodded. "Oh, yeah. So, you think you want to be a rancher, do you?"

Bill shrugged. "I've never done it before, but I should probably get a job if I'm gonna…stick around."

Mr. Read glanced at Mildred, looking down at her plate. "I can use another hand. You could even help John build the new house there. That is if you don't mind living out in the sticks. City folk don't take to that sometimes."

"I lived in the jungle on an island in the Philippines," said a more confident Bill. "That's about as far away from Chicago as you can get."

Mr. Read nodded approvingly.

Mrs. Read saw Mildred stirring uncomfortably, then said, "What's the matter, dear?"

Mildred sighed and glanced at Bill, urging him on.

"Oh, well," Bill turned to Mr. Read. "I wanted to talk to you about this directly, sir."

"And what's that?" asked Mr. Read as LaVerda gave an excited squeal.

"LaVerda, did you get something caught in your gullet?" asked Mrs. Read.

"No, ma'am," LaVerda squeaked with a grin.

Mildred shook her head.

Bill forced a dry swallow down his throat, then squared up to Mr. Read. "Well, sir, I was going to ask for your permission to marry your daughter."

"I knew it!" cried LaVerda, but she clamped a hushing hand over her mouth when she saw her mother's glare.

"Oh, I see," said Mr. Read, taken aback.

"We've come to love each other and…" Bill turned to Mrs. Read. "And, well, Mildred said you thought it might be best."

"How so?" asked Mrs. Read. She had a hunch talk of marriage was coming, but wasn't ready for it yet.

"Mildred told me you always say if you know something is right, you should do it and not wait," said Bill.

Mrs. Read's gaze moved to Mildred. "Is that right?" she asked, her voice squeaking.

Mildred gulped, then nodded. "We love each other. It's the same thing you and Father did."

"Well, we knew each other for more than eight hours," said Mrs. Read with a forced smile.

"Mother! We've known each other much longer than that!"

"Through letters!" exclaimed Mrs. Read as Mr. Read watched, dumbfounded.

"And it's all because of me," said LaVerda, proudly.

"Yes, it is," glared Mrs. Read.

Bill pushed back from the table. "I'm sorry. I should go."

"Where are you going to go?" asked Mrs. Read, her compassion overcoming her surprise.

"You're not going anywhere," said Mildred firmly. "We're getting married, and you'll soon see what a marvelous husband Bill Kane is!"

Bill forced a smile, then said. "I do love your daughter. She was a beacon of light to me during some of my hardest times." He turned to Mildred. "You've raised a wonderful daughter, and I would be a fool to let someone like her get away. I know I can make her happy. And even though I don't have much to my name, I'm a hard worker. I'll take care of her and our children. If you think it best we wait, I'll do that. A month, three months, a year. Whatever it takes for you to be happy with her marrying me."

Mildred wilted in her chair, her loving gaze fixed on Bill.

Mrs. Read turned to her husband, staring at the table, and sighed. "If you know something is right, you should do it. But it doesn't hurt to wait to know for sure."

Bill nodded.

Mr. Read, still staring at the table, shook his head, then said, "Ah, hell, Mother, we did the same thing. We were hot for each other, and your mother didn't like me a whole lot when we were courting. And look, we done okay."

Mrs. Read smiled at her husband, then turned to Mildred, who had slid her chair beside Bill. "You two are going to have to decide. Just be wise and understand that your futures and the futures of your children are at stake."

Bill turned to Mildred, and they gave each other loving smiles.

OREANA

31 October 1919

*B*ill grimaced and rubbed his back as the stagecoach bumped and rolled along the dusty road. "How much longer do we got?" he grumbled as the endless sea of sagebrush and the occasional juniper passed by.

"Maybe another half-hour," shrugged Mildred, still bubbly from the day before.

The wedding was a simple one. In the front room of the Read's Boise home, with the children huddled on the stairs and Mr. Read holding his teary-eyed wife, Elder Orson Rawlins pronounced Bill and Mildred husband and wife. Mildred's dress was a hand-me-down—and a simple one, at that—but she didn't mind. Nor did Bill, whose grin was ear to ear. Mildred's five-year-old sister, Carol, was perhaps the most concerned, as Mr. Read had told her the bride and groom would have to jump over a broomstick to get married. After hugs and kisses, followed by ice cream and cake, the celebration was over.

Mildred glanced fondly at the cake box and the last piece saved for them. She wondered how long it would keep on the shelf as a memento of their special day.

After a bored huff, Bill reached for a cigarette but then pulled back his hand, irritated by the dust, jarring ride, and nicotine withdrawals. He swallowed some of his annoyance and turned to the humming Mildred. He wondered how she could be so cheerful. A faint smile grew on Bill's face from her barely contained delight, and he asked, "How does it feel to be Missus Kane?"

"Pretty good," Mildred blushed.

Bill nodded, but his smile faded with a jarring bounce of the coach. "Does he have to hit every hole and stone on the road?" Bill fumed. "And how old is this thing? I feel like I've gone back in time fifty years!"

"Ralph Prichard is the only coach driver Oreana has, but his crossed eye does get in the way sometimes, I admit," said Mildred, as positive as she could be.

Bill sighed and shook his head. The train ride from Boise was long enough, but the twenty-mile coach ride was proving to be his undoing. Another jarring bump knocked Bill's hat off, and it was all he could do not to release a blue streak of Army profanity. "I think I'd just as soon walk at this point!"

Mildred's smile faded as she tried to understand Bill's irritation. She wondered how long Bill would hold up in the country. "It's not too much farther," she said, turning to look out her window with some concern.

It was a few bumpy miles more when a farmhouse came into view, and Bill leaned out his window. "Thank the Lord! There are signs of life."

"Good," chuckled Mildred. "That's the Patterson's place. We're almost there."

.

IT WAS late afternoon when they finally arrived at the Z-Bar Ranch. Bill carried his and Mildred's bags as they approached the old farmhouse, nestled in a valley with a creek, meadow, and leafless cottonwoods. Added onto twice, the house had grown from its humble origins, but had not been well maintained and badly lacked a coat of whitewash. Bill set the bags down twenty feet from the front door and surveyed the homestead. A cow grazed near an orchard, and chickens roamed near a tattered barn. A neighing horse turned Bill's head, as he hadn't been on one since Corregidor. His sourness faded as he pictured him and Mildred building a life there, just the two of them.

When a dark-haired young man in a hat and bib-overalls rounded the side of the house carrying a load of two-by-fours, Bill straightened up, and his brow furrowed.

"Mildred," nodded the man, setting down his lumber.

"Hello, John! How are you?" beamed Mildred, hugging the handsome man.

Bill's eyes narrowed.

"I'm fine, Mildred. How are you?" said John with a restrained smile. When he noticed Bill, his face emptied, and he said, "Howdy. Who's this?"

"Oh! John Young, allow me to introduce you to Bill Kane, my husband!"

John looked at Mildred as if she were joking.

"I'm so excited to finally say that!" beamed Mildred.

Bill gave a manly nod and reached out his hand. "Bill Kane, pleased to meet you."

Not one to mince words, John turned to Mildred as he shook Bill's hand and asked, "Did you really get hitched?"

"Why, yes, we did!" Mildred said proudly, wrapping her arms around Bill. "Isn't he adorable?"

Bill tried to hide his scowl, unsure if John was a former beau.

"Oh! This is the fella you were writin' to," said John in realization.

Bill nodded, still not sure where he stood compared to the young man who was taller and arguably more handsome.

"John is courting LaVerda," explained Mildred, "And if that little sneak is right, I think we may hear wedding bells pretty soon!"

Bill's brow lifted, somewhat relieved.

"So, when did you get married?" asked John.

"Last night," said a still giddy Mildred.

"Huh," John's confused gaze moved to Bill. "So, when did you get out?"

"About a month ago."

"And when did you get here?" asked John, doing the math in his head.

"Just over a week ago," smiled Mildred.

"Well, that was mighty fast," said John, his brow bent in thought.

"Yes, well, Mildred and I love each other and figured there was no point in waiting," said Bill, somewhat defensively.

"Well, congratulations is all I gotta say," said John, shaking Bill's hand again.

"Thank you," Bill nodded, glad to be past all of that.

"Say, you don't happen to have any carpentry experience, do ya? I could use a hand on the Read's new house over yonder."

Bill turned to the framed structure nestled between the trees across the meadow, then shook his head. "No, but I'm a fast learner. I figure I can do the same as any other Joe."

"He's even willing to help Father ranch the sheep," said Mildred.

"Well, that's just fine," nodded John. "A willing hand is the best kind to have." He glanced back at Mildred, then said, "I'll let you two new-wedded folks have at it and see you in the morning, Bill."

Bill watched John pick up his lumber and head across the meadow.

Mildred moved to the front door, then glanced back at Bill and said, "I think that's the most I've ever heard John Young say in the time I've known him! LaVerda does the talking for both of 'em!"

"Seems like a nice enough fella," said Bill, glancing back across the meadow.

Once inside, Bill followed Mildred with their bags in hand past the front room and the small kitchen, his curious eyes taking in the worn yet cozy ranch house. It was somehow just as he imagined.

Mildred pushed open a bedroom door, then turned to Bill with large, expectant eyes.

Bill looked back down the short hall, then said, "We're all alone?"

Mildred nodded as she backed into the bedroom with a sly grin.

The smile on Bill's face grew as he set down the bags and followed Mildred inside. "I think that damn coach ride might have been all worth it," he said as he closed the bedroom door.

10 January 1920

BILL STOMPED the snow off his feet as he came in through the back door with a load of firewood. "It smells good. What's cooking?"

"Chicken and biscuits," replied Mildred. She tried to hide her sickly scowl as she cleaned and cut the chicken. Mildred had felt more than a little nauseous the past week, and with food the last thing on her mind, it was all she could do to cook. "How is the house coming?" she asked as Bill set the stack of wood beside the fire-burning range.

"Pretty well done," said Bill, straitening up and giving Mildred a peck on the cheek. "John and your dad are headed back to Boise for the last few things. Then I suppose your folks will be moving in."

Mildred glanced at Bill. She knew he had mixed feelings about living in the country. While he often missed the bustle of city life, he had enjoyed the solitude and alone time with Mildred. But that would soon end with her family moving into the new house across the meadow. Bill had seemed mostly content while keeping busy and helping John with the house, but had grown increasingly restless as the work had slowed. There wouldn't be much to do with the sheep until spring, and she wondered what he would do to occupy his time.

Bill sat at the table and drummed his fingers as Mildred fought a wave of nausea.

"What's Harry doing?" asked Mildred, forcing a swallow. Harry Brandeberry, her cousin, had helped around the ranch for years.

"He had to go to Murphy," said Bill, who thought little of the scrawny young man who he sometimes referred to as "dim-witted."

"Oh, I see," said Mildred, wiping her brow. She took a sip of water from a tin on the counter, then asked, "Who's going to milk Lavy tonight?"

Bill's brow gathered in thought. "I suppose I can do it."

Mildred turned back to Bill. "Have you ever milked a cow before?"

"No. But how hard can it be if Harry can do it?"

Mildred turned back to the stove and chuckled.

Bill sat up, slightly riled by Mildred's response. "Where are the damn milk buckets? I'll do it," Bill huffed.

"Buckets? You only need one," said Mildred, glancing back.

"That's 'cause they don't do it right. Just you watch. I bet I can fill up two," said Bill with a confident nod.

"Well, that would be swell. They're under the counter."

Bill snatched the buckets and started out of the kitchen.

"Don't be too long. Dinner will be done in about fifteen minutes."

"I shan't take that long!" Bill called back.

Mildred chuckled, but when another wave of nausea overcame her, she set the chicken aside and sank into a chair. She looked down at her belly through her apron and sighed. Mildred hadn't told Bill yet, but they would have a baby by the end of summer.

Mildred had just pulled the biscuits from the oven when Bill pushed through the back door. She could tell by his huffs and sighs that the milking hadn't gone as he had hoped. Mildred fought off a grin when Bill set a bucket with barely a cup of milk on the counter.

"There's something wrong with that damn cow. I think he's all dried up," snapped Bill.

"Lavy's a mother cow. She's a *she*," smirked Mildred.

"I knew that," scowled Bill.

"Oh, Billy, I do adore how you're so willing."

Bill sank onto the chair by the kitchen table. "Well, someone's gotta do the work around here."

"Yes, they do," replied Mildred, setting a plate of chicken legs and biscuits and gravy before him.

Bill looked down at the plate and nodded his approval as Mildred set a tin of water before him, then bowed his head and mumbled, "Thank you, God, for this meal we are about to partake, amen."

Mildred sat at the table without a plate as Bill took a bite of chicken. When he noticed she wasn't eating, he wiped his mouth and said, "Aren't you hungry?"

Mildred shook her head.

Bill set the chicken leg down and studied Mildred. "What's wrong? Don't you feel good?"

Mildred gulped. "Yes, and no."

Bill's brow gathered, unsure what she meant.

"Billy, we're going to have a baby," whispered Mildred, tears welling in her eyes.

Bill's shoulders slumped and his jaw slackened. "What? We are?"

"Yes," Mildred beamed, pushing tears down her cheeks.

Bill gulped and looked across the kitchen, slightly pale. "What does that mean?"

"It means we're going to have a baby," shrugged Mildred.

"When?" asked Bill, trying not to panic.

"This summer. I think August," replied Mildred, not prepared for his bewilderment. "Aren't you happy?"

Bill looked at Mildred with round eyes. "Yes," he said, his face white, his jaw hanging.

"You'll be a fine father," smiled Mildred.

Bill gulped. His heart sank when he thought of his father. Robert Kane was many things, but in Bill's mind, he was not a fine father. Bill pushed those thoughts away. They had burdened him too much already, he told himself. He would be his own man, not like his father.

"We're going to have a baby!" exclaimed Mildred.

Bill nodded, still unsure what it would mean. His brow tightened.

"What's the matter, Billy? Aren't you happy?"

"No. I mean, yes, I am, it's just…I'm going to have to find work."

"There's work here," said Mildred, her joy fading.

"Not really. Not with the house done."

"But the ranch."

Bill shook his head. "Your dad and Harry have that handled. I'm a third wheel. John said he could use me on a job in Boise."

"Boise," Mildred sighed. "That's so far away. I want to be with you."

"And I want to be with you. But I'm barely making any money. If it weren't for your parents giving us a place to live, we'd be out on the streets!"

"Billy. It's okay. We can live like this," insisted Mildred.

"On nothing?"

"We have each other."

Bill shook his head, fighting off the panic. "I have to be able to care for you—and our baby!"

"You can," said Mildred, reaching for Bill's hand.

"Mildred, you don't understand! Things cost money. We can't live off your parents forever! I'm going to have to find a real job!"

Mildred sat back, her face full of concern, and sighed, "Billy."

"I want to be able to buy you nice things! To be a good husband! A responsible man!"

Mildred's heart sank when Bill got up from the table and stormed from the kitchen. She put her head in her hands and cried.

May 1920

Mrs. Read was hanging laundry on the clothesline when she spotted Mildred sitting in the tire swing across the meadow. She eyed Mildred, brooding back and forth in the swing, then hung the last shirt with clothespins. With a sigh, Mrs. Read walked across the meadow to the tall, leaning oak flush with spring leaves, then said, "Hello, dear."

Mildred lifted her head and sighed, "Oh, hello, Mother," before hanging it again.

"I'm glad to see you can still fit in that swing."

Mildred rubbed her protruding belly. "Who are you kidding? I can't fit in anything anymore. Pretty soon, Billy will have to widen the door for me to walk into the house!"

Mrs. Read gave her daughter a warm smile and stepped closer. "Now dear, what are you to expect when you're carrying twins?"

Mildred sighed.

"How have you been feeling? Besides mopey?"

"Like someone has taken over my body."

Mrs. Read laughed. "Someone has, dear. Two of them, in fact."

"How did you do it, mother?"

Mrs. Read shrugged. "You just grin and bear it, dear. It will all be worth it when you're swaddling those little sweethearts in your arms."

Mildred glumly nodded. "I suppose so."

Mrs. Read eyed Mildred. She didn't have the heart to say she'd get twice as big in the coming weeks. She looked across the valley to the hill where she could barely see Bill and Harry tending to the sheep. "How is Bill doing with it all?"

"Billy? He's a nervous wreck. I'm surprised there are any cigarettes left in Owyhee County!"

Mrs. Read put a hand to her mouth.

"He was shocked enough by one, but two. I'm afraid that's gonna do him in!"

"Now, dear, I'm sure he's stronger than that," smiled Mrs. Read.

Mildred sighed.

Mrs. Read's brow gathered. She considered saying nothing, then asked, "You two are doing okay?"

Mildred shrugged. "I suppose so. I guess I imagined being married would be different. That all of my worries would be gone. But I guess that was just a fairytale."

Mrs. Read's brow raised. "Well, dear, sometimes marriage is like that, but mostly, it's hard work. Both of you have to work double duty to make it work."

Mildred nodded.

Mrs. Read studied her daughter for a moment, then asked, "Is Bill holding up his end?"

Mildred nodded.

"You're feeling a little blue?"

Mildred sighed. "Bill has a sour side that I didn't know about."

"Of course he does. He's a man."

Mildred gulped.

"Is he rough with you? Does he hurt you?" Mrs. Read asked warily.

Mildred looked up at her mother and said, "Oh, no. Billy would never do that. It's just…It's just that he's angry a lot."

"At you?"

"At me, at the sheep, at the weather." Mildred sighed. "I thought I could make him happy."

"Dear, your Bill has been through a lot. He grew up in a different place with a different upbringing. He's been in the Army—that's enough to sour most any man to good, wholesome living. He's been through a war. We know what that can do to a man."

"He never went to France. He only trained other men."

Mrs. Read shooed a bee away and said, "I read about survivors' guilt. Soldiers who came home when their friends didn't sometimes have it bad. Do you think it's that?"

Mildred shrugged. "I think it's more than that. The other day, I asked him about his mother. He had the sweetest memories of her, and he was only a little tyke when she died."

"That's sweet," nodded Mrs. Read.

"But when I tried to get him to tell me about his father, Billy got mad and stormed out of the room!"

"Hmm." Mrs. Read scratched her head. "It can be tricky with boys and their dads. I can't say I understand why, but I know plenty who struggle with it. Your father had his differences with Grandpa Read."

"But he didn't hate him. Daddy talks about Grandpa all the time."

Mrs. Read nodded. "I don't know, dear. Men are complicated creatures. They give us a hard time 'cause we get so emotional, but they're just as bad 'cause they hold it all in—maybe worse!"

Mildred nodded and looked up at her mother, strangely comforted by the notion.

"At the end of the day, we're all just trying to figure life out and make amends with our past. That's all the good Lord expects of us. That and to be a little better each day."

Mildred pulled out of the tire swing with a groan. "I suppose that's the last time I'll be able to do that for some time," she said, rubbing her backside.

Mrs. Read laughed.

"Thank you, Mamma," said Mildred, moving to embrace her mother.

"What on earth for?"

"For making me feel better, of course. Maybe I'm not such a sad sap after all."

"You're nothing of the sort, dear." Mrs. Read said, kissing her daughter on the forehead.

Mildred watched her mother go back to her laundry, then turned to the sheep on the hill and sighed.

WELCOME TO BOISE

Six Years Later
October 1926

*B*ill blinked as he stared at the darkened ceiling above him, the glimmer of a dream fading. Somewhere a rooster crowed. Its call was loud and crisp in the chilly morning air. Bill sighed. He ran a hand through his wavy brown hair, then sat up in the bed and swung his legs over the side. Bill reached for the pack of Lucky Strikes on the nightstand, shook one free, and put it in his mouth. *Today is a big day*, he told himself, striking a match. He lit the cigarette, then shook out the match. He had looked forward to Mildred and the children finally joining him in Boise for some time and hoped it would turn out as he expected. But Bill had dealt with enough disappointment to recognize it might not.

Bill knew he was a wanderer. All of his life, he had searched for something to bring him peace. He didn't find it in his childhood home in Chicago, nor in the Army. Even playing baseball, which Bill dearly loved, didn't make him whole. He wondered if the elusive peace and happiness he craved were even real or if they were just the things of fairy tales and movies. Bill felt an inkling of that happiness when he fell in love with Mildred through their letters. It grew even more when he finally met her and they married. But that sense of completeness faded, and Bill wondered if the ghosts of his past would ever let him be content.

The past seven years and the realities of life had strained their fairytale love affair. Inking out a living as a sheep hand while Mildred toiled to care for an ever-growing family was not what he had imagined their life to be. Bill still loved Mildred; there was never a question about that, but he was not content, and Mildred knew it.

It wasn't that Bill despised caring for the sheep—he found the work mostly relaxing, but it gave him time for soul-searching. Bill wondered if that was the worst part. He didn't like to consider his past. There was too much pain there. Bill preferred sweaty and body-aching labor that left no time for such introspection. Life was about getting things done, he told himself. Whether that meant working or playing baseball on the Oreana ball team, Bill preferred staying focused and punishing himself.

But the hardest part of working for his father-in-law, Alva Read— arguable the kindest man Bill had ever known—was just that. He was completely dependent on Mr. Read to support his family.

The birth of twin boys, Alva and Alma, changed things for a time as new babies do. But Bill's sense of responsibility and worry that he was not man enough to lead and care for his family only grew. A year and a half later, Mildred gave birth to a beautiful blue-eyed baby girl. As Bill first held little Helen Irene and watched his two boys crawl across the floor, he lamented they were still in Oreana and finding it increasingly difficult to make ends meet. Bill had traveled as far away as Oregon and Utah to find work, but it was still not enough. Bobby came next. But it was with Patty's birth that Bill knew he could wait no longer. Random, unpredictable work was no way to provide for a family.

Despite Bill's sometimes gruff and impatient way, Mildred knew he loved her and their growing family, but Bill seemed increasingly troubled. As they sat on the porch at the end of the day, sipping lemonade or cider as the children fell asleep, she would ask him about his hopes and dreams for their future and wonder if they would ever be.

Mildred was an insightful woman. She knew Bill yearned for the city. He had even spoken fancifully of moving the family back to Chicago, an idea Mildred had cleverly steered around. But when Bill mentioned the corre-spondence course to become an electrician, she knew that was their chance for change. She hoped Bill having a trade and steady work would provide for their growing family and give him the sense of self-worth he craved. While a sizable cost was involved, she encouraged him to take the course.

The correspondence course was not easy for a man who had not finished high school. But Bill's stubbornness once again proved the conqueror, and he soon found himself with a certificate of completion and a job in Boise working for Idaho Power.

Bill set his cigarette on the end table as he pulled on his worn wool slacks and white cotton shirt. He put on his socks, careful to keep his big toe inside the expanding hole, then his bent and cracked leather shoes.

After finishing his cigarette, Bill moved to the washbasin and poured some day-old water into the large ceramic bowl. After splashing the cold water onto his face, he pushed back his brown, wavy hair, then lathered up shaving cream and spread it across his angular jaw. Bill's striking blue eyes followed the straight blade in the mirror as it scrapped and cut along his cheek.

While Bill had been on the job in Boise for nearly a month, today was a special day. His family was coming. It would be a new start for the Kane family, and Bill was ready.

It was a lovely fall day in Boise, with a vibrant blue sky, white billowy clouds, and colorful foliage. It reminded Bill of the day he met Mildred seven years before. Bill hummed happily as he drove his new Ford toward the train station. Wearing a gray tweed coat and Irish cap, Bill grinned proudly as the black open-topped Model T sputtered and popped down the road. Even though the car was nine years old, it was a step up from the miserable clunker called Old Kate he had wrestled with for years. With his arm resting atop the car door, Bill was singing when he passed another motorist and gave a friendly wave.

> *"Oh, what became of Hinky Dinky Parley-vous?*
> *And what became of all the friends that Hinky knew?*
> *They all got drunk and got in jail,*
> *And had no one to pay their bail,*
> *Hinky, Dinky, Parley-vous."*

After parking his car, Bill hurried up the steps to the platform. It had been weeks, and he was eager to see his family, but especially Mildred. His brow gathered, surprised the train was already there. As Bill slipped through the crowd, he searched for his wife's lovely features. It was that same station where they had first met, and even though it had been seven years since, he could still remember the excitement he felt. It was as though his entire future was laid out before him for the picking that day.

The air at the train station was thick with the smell of burned coal and burning cigarettes. Bill half-heard the hiss of escaping steam from the train's engine and the excited chatter of arriving travelers, but it was a child's call, "Daddy! Daddy!" that caused him to spin to his left. Bill kneeled as a dimpled four-year-old girl in a pale blue dress and an open coat the color of chocolate rushed toward him with wide, eager eyes.

"Helen! How are you, my little bug?" Bill asked as he swept up the curly-haired girl and placed a kiss on her petite lips.

"Do you have a new house for us, Daddy?" Helen asked, her blue eyes wide.

"Why, yes, I do," Bill grinned proudly. "Where's Mommy?"

Bill followed Helen's outstretched arm across the platform to a somewhat overwhelmed Mildred. Bundled in coat and hat with a baby in one arm and a bulging carpetbag in the other, three wide-eyed boys followed her. "Let's help Mommy." Bill lowered Helen to the wood-planked platform and, holding her hand, started toward his family.

Mildred's harrowed look changed to one of relief as she spotted the disappeared Helen and Bill approaching. "There you are!" Mildred gasped, shifting the baby in her arm as she looked from Helen to Bill. "Well, we're here," Mildred announced, any smile lost in her frustration.

"You're early. How was the train ride?" Bill asked, pleased his family had arrived but still not picking up on Mildred's exasperation.

"Long," she said, pushing a fallen strand of her brown hair back under her hat.

Bill took in her familiar features and smiled. He had missed her.

"Do you—" Mildred paused as the train's whistle sounded, followed by the spinning of massive wheels on iron tracks.

Bill glanced past Mildred at the train as it began moving.

"Can you help me with the bag or Patty?" Mildred asked with pleading eyes.

Bill looked at the baby with some hesitancy and reached for the bag.

Mildred repositioned the baby as a thin-faced, sandy-haired three-year-old boy stepped up and said, "Did you get a new house for us, Pa?"

"You better believe it, Bobby," Bill beamed. "A nice one too."

I hope not too nice, Mildred thought as she forced a smile. She was happy to see her husband, but tired from the journey and anxious over their financial situation. They had never had money in their years together, and while she was excited about Bill's new job and the security it would bring, she worried it might still not be enough for their expanding family.

"Say, have you grown some?" Bill asked the three-year-old Bobby.

Bobby's proud nod caused his bobbed blonde hair to flop.

"Hello, Pa," said Alma, one of the redheaded twins standing a few feet away beside his brother, Alva.

Bill's gaze moved to the two bashful boys dressed in matching blue suits. "It's good to be all together again," he smiled. But Bill's smile faded when Patty began to fuss. His brow gathered with the realization his simple life of going to work and coming home to quiet was now over. Bill shook off the thought, rubbed his hands together, and said, "Well, let's pile in, and I'll give you the grand tour!"

"Yay!" Bobby exclaimed, with Helen joining in.

Mildred shifted the fussing Patty in her arms and said, "Billy, can we just go to the house? I need to feed Patty and put her down."

"Sure thing," Bill said, seeing her frustration. "Is this all you have?" he asked, hoisting the over-filled carpetbag.

"No," Mildred said as she looked around and then at the twins. "Alma, where is that bag I asked you to carry?"

The eyes of the already sheepish Alma widened, and he turned back to the platform across the tracks. Before anything else could be said, the six-year-old darted toward the bag. Mildred didn't notice the approaching train with her back turned, but Bill did.

"Alma! Wait! There's a train coming!" cried Bill as his son jumped off the platform and started across the tracks. But the tumult of churning iron drowned out his warning. The shrill whistle of the approaching train came next, standing the hair of everyone on the platform.

Not realizing what was happening, Mildred turned back in time to see her second oldest son frozen on the tracks, the mighty black locomotive bearing down, its brakes squealing. "NO!" she screamed, her cry lost in the train's whistle as it sped closer.

Bill had already dropped the bag and was racing toward his son when the train rumbled past, leaving Alma nowhere to be seen. Standing at the edge of the platform, his chest heaving, his eyes bulging, Bill watched and waited for the train to pass as Mildred called out frantically, "Alma! ALMA!" her words drowned out by the thunderous noise.

Both watched agonizingly from the platform, looking through the gaps in the passing cars to see if their son was alive.

The rear of the train was just in sight when Mildred handed the baby to the wide-eyed Alva, hiked up her dress, and climbed off the platform, ready to cross. Still on the platform, Bill watched, his body knotted as the caboose passed. When he spotted his son standing frozen on the other side of the tracks, Bill's shoulders relaxed, but his brow tightened.

Furious over the boy's poor judgment, Bill leaped off the platform and bounded past Mildred toward his dazed son. When he reached Alma, he grabbed him by his shoulders and yelled, "What were you thinking? Why didn't you look? You could have been killed!"

The white-faced Alma looked up at his angry father with teary eyes. "I-I was getting the bag," he whimpered.

"You could have been killed!" scolded Bill. "Do you understand that?"

"I'm-I'm sorry, Pa," Alma stammered as a panic-stricken Mildred and a conductor in a black suit arrived.

"You okay, boy?" asked the breathless, mutton-chopped conductor, looking from father to son. "You gave us quite a scare."

Alma sobbed as Mildred pulled him away from Bill and embraced him. "Don't be so hard on him. He's scared to death."

"He wasn't thinking!" chided Bill.

"He's just a child!" Mildred replied as she guided Alma back across the tracks.

"Close call," sighed the conductor, pushing back his hat.

"I'm sorry," Bill huffed, seeing the crowd that had gathered. "I thought he had more sense than that."

"He's a boy. You gotta watch 'em," shrugged the conductor.

"Yeah," Bill muttered as the conductor started back for the train. *Nobody watched me as a boy*, Bill thought as he retrieved the forgotten bag.

Alma was still crying and leaning against his mother when the Kane family arrived at their new car.

"Well, this is it," Bill said anticlimactically as he pointed to the black Ford. He hoped for it to be a surprise, but was not in the mood now.

Mildred blankly stared at the car, then asked, "What happened to Old Kate?"

Bill turned to his wife. "She was old and unreliable. So I got rid of her. This one's a beauty! Don't you think?" Bill said, frustrated that things were not going as he had planned.

I guess I better not get old or unreliable, thought Mildred.

"Do you like it?" asked Bill.

"Well, I guess so. How much was it?" Mildred daringly asked as she bounced the crying baby.

Bill hesitated, then said, "Seventy-five dollars."

Mildred would have normally never challenged Bill's judgment, but the emotions and fatigue were too much. "Billy, how are we going to pay for it?"

"You don't need to worry about that," Bill muttered. But when he saw the concern on Mildred's face, his brow softened, and he said, "I have a job now, a good one! We deserve something nice for once. *You* deserve it!"

Mildred's brow raised. "But I don't drive!"

"Just think how nice you'll feel riding in it," said Bill as he ran a proud hand across the car's hood.

"*I* like it," said Bobby, hoping to please his father, but Bill didn't respond.

Mildred tiredly shifted the crying baby in her arms, forced a smile, and said, "I like it too."

Bill grinned as he looked from his wife to his children. But his grin faded when he noticed Alma's red and puffy eyes. He stepped to Alma and put a hair-ruffling hand on the boy's head. Despite the day's turmoil and his now shattered peace, Bill was happy they were together again.

One by one, the children piled into the back seat of the black Ford as Bill helped his wife into the front. He then moved to the crank starter below the radiator, bent down, and turned the crank until the engine barked to life. After climbing in behind the wheel, Bill turned to Mildred, bundling up the crying baby, and sighed. Then, with a push of a pedal and a flip of a lever, they rattled down the street.

~

THE PEARL DIVERS

A week had passed since Bill's family had joined him in Boise and moved their hard-earned belongings and hand-me-downs into the small white clapboard rental house. With the move came change. The serenity of the Z-Bar Ranch, with its grazing sheep and gurgling creek, had been replaced by the bustle of city life, the clatter of passing cars, and demands of an eight-to-five job. Mildred's days were long as she cared for their five children. Being raised in a home that knew how to make do, she had all the cooking, sewing, and mending skills needed to care for their growing family while Bill spent his days working as a lineman for the power company.

The sun was low in the sky as the black Ford clattered up to the front of the house. Bill stepped out of the car with his lunch can in one hand and a smoldering cigarette in the other and started up the walk. It had been a long day. When he noticed a woman coming down the walk, Bill gave a polite nod and continued to his front door. When he realized she was following him, he paused and turned. She held a small basket of fresh-baked rolls.

"Hello," said the large-eyed woman, who whore a green hat with a bow. "Allow me to introduce myself. I'm Mabel Browning. We live just across the way," she said, pointing to her home with a tilt of her head. "We wanted to welcome you to the neighborhood," she added, presenting the basket to Bill.

Bill stepped on his cigarette, then took the basket from her and said, "Well, thank you very much. They smell delicious."

"Oh, and there is also some marmalade—of my own making, of course."

Bill looked from the basket back to the pleasantly smiling woman and said, "Thank you," as he wondered what she wanted.

"I'm also the Relief Society president here in the ward," she added with searching eyes. "Would your family happen to be Latter-Day Saints?"

Here it comes. Bill glanced back at the house. "My wife is—and my kids, but I'm not. I'm Catholic," he added, matter-of-factly.

"Oh, how nice," Mrs. Browning said politely.

"I'll let you talk to my wife," Bill said as he backed up to the door and pushed it open.

"Oh, how nice," Mrs. Browning repeated, her large eyes brightening.

A burst of warm air was the first to greet Bill as he opened the door, followed by his four-year-old daughter. "Daddy's home!" Helen exclaimed as she wrapped her arms around his leg. Then, looking past him at the woman in the doorway, she asked, "Who's that?"

"Oh, please come in," Bill said, waving the neighbor in. "Mildred, you have a visitor!"

Alma and then Alva poked their heads around the corner. Then, like twin red-haired turtles retreating into their shells, bashfully disappeared.

"Yes, hello," an aproned Mildred said warmly as she came into the front room drying her hands.

"This is our neighbor," Bill said, "Missus…"

"Browning," she smiled. "Please, call me Mabel."

"Pleased to meet you," Mildred nodded.

"She brought these," Bill said, holding up the basket.

"Oh, how thoughtful of you," beamed Mildred.

Bill set the basket down, shed his hat and coat, then watched and listened as the two ladies chatted like old friends. Part of him felt like an outsider looking in, and a tinge of resentment filled him as the neighbor spoke about their ward and "sisters" and the activities planned. Mildred's interest in it all caused his resentment to grow. It was the first time Bill and his family had lived outside Oreana, where there were few Mormons besides his in-laws, and he wondered if such visits were common among church-goers everywhere. He supposed one of the men from the ward would visit him next, but then he reminded himself he was not one of them.

"What a delightful visit," Mildred said, closing the front door.

Bill, who was leaning against a bureau and pretending to read the evening paper, nodded.

After picking up the basket of bread, Mildred moved toward her husband, who was still in his off-white work shirt and navy pants, and said, "How lucky we are to have such fine neighbors, don't you think?"

Bill shrugged. "She seems nice enough. Are they gonna come around like that all the time?"

"And bring you fresh-baked bread and other goodies? I don't doubt it," Mildred said playfully as she drew closer. "How was your day?" she asked as she pecked a kiss on his cheek.

"It was fine," Bill said, following her into the kitchen, which was rich with the aroma of a roasting brisket.

"She was just being neighborly," Mildred said as she went back to work on the stove. Then, without looking at Bobby climbing up the back of a chair, she snapped her fingers and warned, "Bobby, get down before you fall and get hurt!"

The bobbed-haired three-year-old sighed and climbed down.

"Are you sure it wasn't a church visit?" Bill asked, sitting at the table beside the twins, drawing pictures.

"What difference does it make? Being a good neighbor is all God's work. I dare say even Catholics take fresh-baked rolls to their neighbors."

With a huff, Bill shook out the newspaper and started reading.

"How was your day at work, Pa?" Alma asked, looking up from his drawing.

Bill looked from the paper to his son, whose auburn hair was smoothed over to one side, and said, "It was a good day. I'm working with a good crew."

"Oh, that's nice to hear," Mildred said as she pulled the steaming brisket from the oven.

"Did you climb up any poles today?" Bobby asked, climbing back on the chair.

"Yes, I did. Clear to the top," Bill nodded, returning to his paper.

"Daddy, is this your first *real* job?" Helen asked, her voice young and sweet, her blue eyes curious.

"Helen, tending to the sheep and helping Grandpa Read was a real job too, you know," Mildred clarified.

"But you're getting paid for this one, aren't you?" Alva asked, wondering if he should have.

Bill snickered. "Boys," he said, looking from the twins to Bobby, who was climbing back up the chair. "I got my first job when I was six."

"Six?" Alma asked with wide eyes, "That's how old I am."

"Me too," added Alva.

"*Six* years old?" Mildred questioned, looking over her shoulder from the sink.

"Well, maybe a little older," Bill grinned as he folded the newspaper.

"Was it mending sheep?" Bobby asked, standing the chair.

"*Tending* sheep," corrected Mildred.

"No," Bill laughed. "The only sheep in Chicago were for dinner or coats. I worked on a steamer. It was a *real* job. A *man's* job, in fact," he nodded, his gaze distant.

"But I thought you was just a kid," Alma frowned.

"I was, but that didn't stop us from going out looking for work."

"What did you do?" Alva asked with growing interest.

"I told you, we worked on a steamer on the Great Lakes. I still remember that day," Bill grinned. "I was with my best friend, Harry, and his brother..."

Summer 1907

"Here we are, fellas," Bill announced with gleaming eyes as he and his two friends came down the stairs from the elevated train station.

"Wow. It's even busier than last time!" Harry Mandel exclaimed as he took in the surrounding bustle.

"There it goes," Max Mandel pointed as their train rumbled on down the elevated tracks.

Down the center of the cobbled Lake Street was a forest of massive iron girders that supported the "L." Ferrying its passengers twenty feet overhead, the elevated trains traversed the modern city. On the ground level, running in between the sturdy iron legs, were the crisscrossing rails that guided streetcars throughout the downtown district. Running east and west was the even more congested State Street. Tall brick buildings with colorfully painted signs and advertisements lined the crowded streets. Striped awnings shaded the first-floor windows above the wide sidewalks where sharp-suited businessmen moved in timely fashion past vendors peddling their wares and drunks begging for beer money. In the streets were coaches and carriages of all kinds, some carrying people, others crates or barrels. A few wagons sat parked with their horses, patiently waiting to stretch their legs as streetcars with long arms reaching up and arching along the over-head lines rang their bells to move the commuters from the tracks.

To the three boys, downtown Chicago was the center of the universe. While they lived only thirty minutes away in the Westside suburb of Oak Park, the expense of the train ride made their excursions infrequent. Even though each trip into the city was an adventure, Bill hoped this one would top them all.

"Hurry up, you two! We don't want to be late!" yelled Bill as he bumped past a tall man in a bowler hat.

"We're coming," said Harry, dodging another man.

Bill's eyes swelled when he spotted two nuns approaching. He darted behind a man in a hat and suit and walked the edge of the sidewalk between a newsstand and a beer wagon with the skill of a tightrope walker to avoid being seen by the sisters.

"Bill, hold your horses!" cried Harry as he pushed through the crowd.

"What's your hurry?" asked Harry's brother, Max, who tipped his Irish cap as the nuns passed.

"Because it's their first day of hiring, and we don't want to miss out!" Bill insisted, still eyeing the nuns.

Harry looked at Bill oddly and said, "Why are you so scared of nuns, anyway?"

"I have my reasons," Bill glared. "Come on, fellas. You don't want to be hanging around Oak Park all summer! This is our big chance! We can see the world and get paid too!"

Max Mandel, the older of the two curly-haired brothers, was bent forward, pulling his socks up to his knickers when he righted himself and exclaimed, "See the world? The lines don't even get out of the Lakes!"

"Those lines go all over!" Bill insisted. "I've heard stories of excursion boats getting lost and going all the way to *China*."

"Yeah, me too," Harry nodded. "There was one that was even attacked by Pirates!"

"Pirates?" Max scoffed. "There ain't no pirates 'round here."

"Not here, ya silly," Bill frowned, wiping the sweat from under his Irish cap. "Down in the Crab-ee-in by Trip-o-lee."

"Who told you that?" Max laughed.

"Ernie," Harry said.

"Hemingway? That kid's just a big talker," Max scoffed.

"Well, that's what he said," Harry insisted as the three moved through the crowd.

"Well, he's telling stories. And this is all a waste of time. They're not gonna hire three kids to work on a ship!" Max huffed.

Harry squared up to his older brother, who was two inches taller and a dozen pounds heavier. "You know, you don't have to come with us if you're *chicken.*"

"Are you kidding? Someone's gotta keep you two outta trouble. Besides, Mother would have kittens if I came home, and she found out you went off like this."

"She's gonna have kittens either way," Harry laughed.

"Yeah, but *I'm* not gonna be the one to tell her," Max replied.

"What about your dad, Bill? What does he say?" Harry asked as the three of them crossed a cobbled street in front of an approaching horse and buggy.

"He don't care. He's so busy at work, it'll be the end of summer before he even knows I'm gone. And by then, we'll be back home and *rich*," Bill said with sparkling eyes.

"That's right," said Harry, greedily rubbing his hands together.

Passing a sign, Max pointed and read, "Carberry Carpet, where the happy feet go. Did your dad really make that up?"

"Sure as sure can be." Bill nodded proudly.

"So, you gonna work in a carpet store when you grow up?" Max asked.

"No," Bill scoffed, "I'm gonna be a pitcher for the Cubs."

The trio continued down the busy street, but stopped when a policeman on a horse appeared. Bill tried to look innocent as the officer's penetrating gaze skimmed over them.

"Wow," muttered Harry as the mounted officer clip-clopped down the street.

After watching a black man in overalls shovel manure into a small wagon, the three boys continued past an old, wrinkled street vendor holding a wooden tray of cigarettes against his chest. The old man eyed the boys warily as they passed, knowing from his youth the pranks he had pulled.

Lock-eyed with the street peddler, Bill bumped into Max just as several women in long, colorful dresses, protruding rumps, and broad, feathery hats swanked past, their chatter giddy and pretentious at the same time.

"Look at that hat, will ya?" Harry said, loud enough for all to hear. "How many birds you have to kill for that hat?"

The women paid no attention to them but smiled coyly as a passing man in a pin-striped suit with a mustache curled at its ends tipped his straw hat.

Max shook his head at the display and, with his thumbs in his suspenders, said, "Boys, someday the dames are gonna look at us like that."

"Why would you want 'em to?" Harry scowled.

"Yeah," Bill added.

"Someday, you'll change your tune," Max replied, echoing words he had heard his uncle say.

Bill considered Max's comment and said, "Maybe when we're good and rich. The dames love the dough."

"Hey, that's funny," Max chuckled, "The dames love the dough."

Down the street, the boys came upon another street peddler with a cart of apples.

"You fellas ready for lunch?" Bill asked, eyeing the merchant who wore a long, tangled beard and a sagging gray apron over his faded coat.

With a wink and a nod, the boys spread out, approaching the unsuspecting vendor from two sides. Max was the first to reach the cart, picking up a pair of apples to examine.

"Two for penny," grunted the vendor in a thick Slavic accent.

"Two cents? They're not worth one!" Max countered as the merchant's overripe body odor caused his nostrils to flare.

"No, I say two. Two apple for *one* penny," the bearded peddler clarified, wondering how they could have misunderstood.

Standing across the cart from his brother, Harry reached for another apple only to have the smelly merchant turn and slap his hand. "Hey, what was that for?" Harry whined.

"I know you boys try steal my apples! Do not take!" the peddler scolded, his eyes shifting between the two brothers. "Buy only!"

By this time, Bill had already passed the cart and doubled back behind. Before the vendor had finished his sentence, Bill's grubby little hands had snatched three ruby reds and slipped them inside his coat.

"Well, I was gonna buy a whole dozen, but not if you're gonna be like that," Max scowled. "Come on, let's scram."

After leaving the perplexed vendor, Max and his brother caught up to Bill, who then casually divvied up the looted apples.

Before the apples were half finished, Bill raised his hand, bringing his small band to a halt, and then pointed across the street to a black six-panel door with a sign that read: GRAHAM & MORTON LINE.

"Here we are, boys," Bill declared. "The end is near."

"What's that supposed to mean?" Max asked.

"I don't know. I heard it from some street preacher a while back." Crossing the street, Bill paused before the tall black door. After looking it over, he fed his apple core to a shiny black mare, then wiped his sticky hands on the front of his coat. "All right, fellas, here we go."

Harry tugged on the back of Bill's coat as he reached for the door and asked, "You think they'll give us a job?"

"Sure, they will," Bill replied, surprised by his friend's doubt.

With a shrug, Harry entered behind Bill, but Max was less convinced, shaking his head as he followed them into the building.

Inside the dark-paneled office, a fan whirred as it moved the hot, damp air. Cigar smoke swirled around the ceiling corners until the fan pulled it down. The shadow of the company name painted on the large window was perfectly cast on the hardwood floor to the side of the massive desk and left Harry tilting his head to read the reversed words.

"So, you boys are looking for work, eh?" the wide-faced, balding man asked in a deep, resonating voice, a stub of a cigar dangling from the corner of his mouth.

"Yes, sir," Bill respectfully answered, sitting on a hard chair across from the desk.

The fat man looked mildly amused as he eyed the three young boys. After rubbing the middle of his three chins, the lowest of which disappeared into his barreled chest, he leaned forward and asked, "So how old are you boys, anyway? Fourteen? Fifteen?"

"Ele—"

Bill jabbed an elbow into Harry's side. "Fourteen. Max here is almost sixteen, ain't ya, Max?"

"Uh, yeah," Max replied with sideways eyes.

"Hmm." The fat man placed his thumbs under his suspenders and asked, "What kind of experience do you have?"

"Experience?" Harry asked with a raised brow.

"We got lots of experience on the river," Bill replied, thinking of their hours playing on the shore watching boats and barges float past.

"We do?" Max asked under his breath.

"What ships you worked on? What's your seaman rating?" the cigar-chomping fat man asked, holding back a grin.

"Well…" Bill started, his eyes searching. "We were on the *Teddy Roosevelt* and—"

"You were on the *Roosevelt*? You must know Gilbert Danbury then."

"Oh, yeah, we know Gil," Harry joined in.

Bill gave his friend a sideways glance, then said, "Say, is he the big tall fellow with the whiskers?"

"No," the fat man said, scratching his head in pretended confusion. "He's short and wears a patch over his eye."

"Oh, him. Sure, you betcha," Bill said with a remembering nod.

"That's funny," the fat man said, pulling his suspenders away from his belly, "because Gilbert Danbury isn't on the *Roosevelt*. He's on the *United States*."

The boys' eyes were as wide as silver dollars as the fat man rose from behind his desk and said, "All right, boys. This has been fun, but I gotta get back to work now. So, get along with ya."

"But, mister, what about a job?" Bill insisted.

"He's not gonna give us one," Max muttered, already up from his chair.

"Boys, how old are you, anyway? Ten? Eleven?"

"No, sir. We're older than that," Bill said as convincingly as possible.

The fat man exhaled, then pulled the cigar from his mouth and mashed it into an ashtray on his desk. "You boys really want a job?"

"Yes, sir," Harry and Bill said in unison, with Max close behind.

The fat man studied each of the boys. "I have an opening for a couple of pearl divers on one of my excursion ships. You wouldn't be interested in that, would you?"

"*Pearl divers*? Yes, sir!" Bill exclaimed.

"You know what that is?" the fat man asked, eyeing Bill.

"Yes, sir," Bill lied, glancing back at his two friends, who were nodding unconvincingly.

"You would be gone for a few weeks at a time. It goes up to St. Joe and Benton Harbor. Is that what you're looking for?"

"Yes, sir!" Bill replied, the other two giving enthusiastic nods.

"It's okay with your folks?"

"Yes, sir," Bill nodded.

"Are you kidding? They can't wait to get rid of us for the summer," Harry laughed.

"Well, you get word to them just the same. I don't want them worrying none."

"Yes, sir," Max nodded.

"All right then. It pays four bits a day and includes meals and board."

"Wow!" Harry exclaimed, hardly believing his ears.

"When do we start?" Max asked.

"Today." The fat man leaned over his desk, pulled a paper from under a stack, and scribbled out a note, pausing twice to dip his pen. After blowing on the ink, he handed it to Max and said, "Take this down to the side-wheeler on Dock Seventeen. Give it to Bubba O'Neal. He's the first mate on the *Liberty*. He'll put you to work."

.   .   .

"Wow! You were a pearl diver?" Alma asked, his eyes wide.

"Yup, we were pearl divers," Bill chuckled

"Did you find many pearls? Did you find buried treasure?" Alva asked, his eyes just as wide.

"Did we ever," Bill grinned as Mildred brought a platter of sliced brisket to the table.

"Don't let your father fool you," she smiled. "A pearl diver is a fancy name for a dishwasher."

The twins turned to their father in confusion. It was Alva who asked, "You *washed dishes?*"

"A lot of 'em," Bill nodded. "I made twenty-five dollars that summer. And that was a lot back then!"

"Wow!" Alma exclaimed, still impressed.

Mildred set the last of the plates at the table then said, "Well then, that makes you a professional dishwasher. I'll let you show me a thing or two after dinner."

"I can do that," Bill winked.

"I meant washing the dishes," replied a blushing Mildred.

Bill smiled and hummed "My Wild Irish Rose" as he eyed Mildred, dishing up the meal.

$\sim$

O CHRISTMAS TREE

*W*ith only a week before Christmas, Mildred still had much to prepare. Besides her daily cooking, cleaning, and caring for their five children, she had gifts to purchase or make, and they had not yet put up a tree. Bill had promised her a Christmas tree, but with his busy work schedule, he came home exhausted each night, and the front room's corner space stood bare. With not another weekend before Christmas, Mildred feared they would have no tree and wondered how their children would deal with the disappointment. It was Mildred's sister LaVerda and her husband John Young who came to the rescue with a freshly cut pine, perfect for her front room.

LaVerda and John had been married six years now, but unlike the Kanes, who had struggled to make ends meet all their married lives, the Youngs had done well with John's construction work. While once friends, Bill's relationship with John had become stained. Even though Bill claimed to be unbothered by the Young's success, Mildred could tell her competitive husband felt outdone by him.

Mildred and the twins were putting the final touches of tinsel on the tree when she heard the squeal of the Ford's brakes as it pulled up to the house. "Your father's home!" Mildred announced as she turned to Helen, who was holding Patty and watching from the rocker.

Helen's eyes widened as she exclaimed, "Won't Daddy will be surprised?"

"Hurry. Let's get this all cleaned up off the floor," Mildred said, directing the twins to the task. "Bobby, father's home!" she anxiously called back to the kitchen as she strung the last of the tinsel and straightened a crooked candy cane.

By the time Bill pushed open the front door, Mildred and the children were standing in front of the decorated tree with wide grins. Mildred's brow gathered when she heard a strange swishing sound as her husband backed in through the door. Her heart sank when she realized what he was struggling with.

"Surprise!" the children cried as Bill backed into the front room where Helen hopped up and down, and Bobby stood on his toes.

"Oh, shoot," Mildred breathed when she spotted the green branches of another pine tree coming through the door.

Just inside the doorway, Bill stopped and looked back at his welcoming family with a proud smile. But when he saw the already decorated tree, his face emptied.

"Yippee!" cried the still bouncing Helen. "We get to have two trees!"

Bill turned to Mildred, standing with her hand over her mouth. His wounded look turned to anger. "You already got a tree?"

"I'm sorry, Billy. I didn't think you'd have time to get one."

"Who brought it?" Bill seethed, ignoring the eager looks of his children. Mildred gulped.

"Uncle John and Aunt Birdie brought it," Helen gleefully exclaimed.

"Wasn't that kind of them?" Mildred asked, but she knew the damage was already done.

"We're not a charity case," grumbled Bill as he pushed his tree back out the front door and pulled it closed behind him.

"Aren't we going to have two trees anymore?" Helen asked, looking up at her mother.

"I don't think so, dear," Mildred whispered as she looked sadly at the closed door.

WHILE PROHIBITION HAD DRIED up saloons across the nation, some found ways of staying open serving food and watered-down ales known as "near beer." Other establishments went underground and became known as speak-easies selling illicit liquor. While Pengilly's saloon was not a speak-easy, the shadowy tavern, which had a history of quenching the locals' thirst for over thirty years, had gotten around the prohibition laws by serving still legal "home brews."

Bill sat at a corner table nursing a brew and his pride when a few others from his work came through the thick front door and hung their coats on the pegs along the wall. Bill looked up and nodded at Tom Tanner, his vest-wearing and pipe-smoking foreman.

"Hey, Bill," called the man walking in behind Tanner, "I thought you were getting a tree for your family?"

Bill looked up at the thin-faced Sylvester Schmig, whose long nose spent a good deal of time in other people's business. "Sylvester," Bill muttered.

"Kane, I wouldn't have let you off early if I knew you were just coming here," said a wary-eyed Tom Tanner, gesturing with his pipe.

Bill shook a Lucky Strike from its pack and put it to his lips. "It's not like that, Tom. I got the tree and everything, it's just..." He paused to light up.

"What?" Sylvester asked, sitting across from Bill.

Bill's brow gathered as he shook out the match. "When I got it home, she already had one."

The men chuckled. Tom Tanner shook his head and said, "She took matters into her own hands, eh? Just who wears the pants in your family, Kane?"

Bill looked down at his beer and sighed.

"Who gave her the tree?" Sylvester asked, waving for a beer.

Sylvester was the first friend Bill made after joining the company, and while almost everyone considered him an annoying buffoon, Bill still felt obliged to consider him a friend. "My brother-in-law."

"The rich, goodie-two-shoes brother-in-law?" Sylvester asked.

"My *only* brother-in-law," Bill shrugged.

"What gives him the right to go into your house like that?"

Bill glanced at Sylvester as he pulled the cigarette from his lips. "I wanted to..."

"Wanted to what?" Sylvester pried.

"I wanted to surprise them, that's all," Bill grumbled. "I went to all that work to get that damn tree, and she goes behind my back and gets one from her sister."

"It's not right," Sylvester said, taking a drink and wiping the beer suds from his mustache. "It's your house. No one should do nothin' without askin' you first."

Bill frowned.

"What's his name?"

"John Young."

"Let me guess; your brother-in-law is one of them good-doer Mormons. Probably one of Brigham's hundred kids!"

"Well, no," Bill said, looking through his glass. "He's not, but his wife—my sister-in-law—is."

"Uh, huh. I'll wager dollars to dumplings she put him up to it. Trying to make you look bad," Sylvester said, shaking his head.

"It don't take much," Tom Tanner smirked from the next table.

"Don't you see? Them churchy folk do all that to prove they're better than we are," Sylvester sneered.

Bill considered his friend's words, then said, "You may be on to something. All their good deeds do is make me feel low…every time."

"See? What I tell ya?" Sylvester shrugged. "They wear you down and then try to get you to join up with 'em. You know that, don't ya? They just butter ya up with their goodness."

"Well, they've tried, believe you me, but I ain't budging," glared Bill. "There's just too much Irish Catholic in me."

Sylvester's eyes narrowed. "You a Catholic, Bill?"

"You knew that," Bill said, finishing his beer.

"Huh, I pegged you for a Protestant."

Bill frowned. "The thing that bothers me the most is that Mildred's family doesn't think I can provide for her! I've busted my butt over the years! Now I got this job, and they still don't think I can do it. Her sister's husband is a foreman for Morrison Knudson. He builds houses and makes good money. How am I supposed to compete with that?"

Sylvester shrugged.

"I don't know what to do. Just keep bustin' my butt, I guess."

"That a boy. Prove 'em wrong," Sylvester nodded. Lighting up, he watched Bill gaze dejectedly across the bar, then leaned forward and asked, "Say, Bill, what you gonna do with that extra tree?"

Bill's eyes narrowed as he turned to his conniving friend.

"I mean, I'd hate to see it go to waste with Christmas just a week away and all," Sylvester shrugged.

"You don't have one either," Bill scoffed.

"No, and my mother has been on me about it for a month."

"Why don't you go home and look? Maybe she got one too," grumbled Bill.

Sylvester shook his head. "Nah, I don't got a rich brother-in-law."

. . .

BY THE TIME Bill got home, the house was dark but for a dim porch light. As he approached the house, he glanced angrily at the discarded tree, stepped on his cigarette, and pushed open the front door. After hanging up his coat, Bill listened for the sounds of his children, but heard only silence. With a tired sigh, he moved down the creaky hall to the kids' bedroom and looked inside. Crowded in one bed were the twins, Bobby, and Helen, with Patty bundled in a trunk Bill had converted to a crib. Helen raised her arm in a tired wave as he pulled the door closed. After moving to his small bedroom, Bill quietly opened the door to the glow of a bedside lamp. Kneeling beside the drawn bed was Mildred in a long flannel gown, her hair let down and braided for sleeping. He hesitated, then went to the clothes cabinet and began undressing.

"You didn't come home for dinner," Mildred said softly as she climbed into the bed and pulled up the comforter.

"I got something at Pengilly's," Bill sighed, pulling on a nightshirt.

Mildred hated it when Bill went to the bar. She thought it was no place for a good family man, which she believed Bill was, and certainly no place for a good church-going husband, which he was not. While Bill never came home stumbling drunk, Mildred could tell when he was "feeling good," and she feared their boys would one day lose respect for him. "The children wanted to surprise you with the decorations."

"Hmph. I wanted to surprise them too—with a tree." Bill moved to his side of the bed, slid under the comforter, and offered a perfunctory, "Night."

Mildred, who was still sitting up, turned to him and said, "I'm sorry, Billy. I know it was your place to get the tree. I should have waited, but John came by and said he had one for us and...well, I thought I was doing you a favor."

Bill sighed.

"I should have waited for you to get home," Mildred whispered. "The children missed you tonight." Seeing her efforts were getting nowhere, she turned off the lamp.

After a few minutes of staring at the wall, Bill said, "It's not just that."

"What do you mean?"

Bill sighed. "Sometimes..."

Mildred turned to Bill. "Yes?" she gently coaxed.

"Sometimes I don't think you trust me—that I'll take care of you and the family, I mean."

"Why would you say that? You've always cared for us."

"It's just that…I'm the man of the house, and sometimes it feels like you and others have it in for me. That you don't think I can do it."

"Who?" Mildred asked, placing a hand on his arm.

"Your family. Your church people. I don't like being judged. Just 'cause I'm not a Read or a Mormon doesn't mean I'm not a good person."

Mildred's face filled with concern. "Of course not, Billy. Everyone loves you. You know that."

"Sometimes it doesn't feel that way," Bill said as he turned on his side and closed his eyes.

~

SNOW ANGELS

*I*t was a gray, wintery day. A soft layer of New Year's snow blanketed the farmland. To the side of the rutted road, rising through the pristine snow, stood occasional mailboxes and lines of fences that divided the endless fields of white.

Bill was at the wheel of the black work truck, peering through frosty windows, his breath billowing in the cold cabin air, while Sylvester Schmig sat beside him, rubbing his hands to keep them warm.

"The other crew should be just up around the bend," Sylvester said, his narrow-set eyes peering out from under a red flannel cap as they followed the line of snow-plastered power poles.

"I think I'm gonna do it," Bill said, intently eyeing the road.

"Do what?" Sylvester asked, lighting up a cigarette.

"I'm gonna talk to Mr. McCracken. I'm gonna ask for a raise."

Sylvester chuckled.

"Why shouldn't I?" Bill asked. "I've been on almost six months."

The sight of another power truck off of the side of the road caused Sylvester to point and say, "There they are."

Bill let the truck slow as they drew closer, careful to not slide on the compacted snow, but when a serious-looking Tom Tanner stepped out into the road in front of them, Bill pushed on the brake harder than he wanted, causing the truck to fishtail as it came to a stop.

"What's going on here?" Sylvester frowned, seeing a lineman lying in the snow with another standing above him. "What happened?" Sylvester asked with wide eyes as he pushed open his door to a waiting Tom Tanner.

"It's Buckwalder," Tanner said, shaking his head.

Sylvester's thin face grew longer still as he looked at the lifeless body of their coworker lying in the snow. "What happened?" he asked, getting out.

"It shouldn't have been hot!" cried Ed Sorensen, a large, strapping man standing in the snow over the body.

Bill turned off the truck and stepped out into the frigid morning air. His gaze went from Tom Tanner to the lifeless worker, then to Big Ed Sorensen, who was crying. "What happened?" Bill asked, already knowing the answer.

"Twenty thousand volts is what happened," seethed Tom Tanner. "You got room in the back of your truck?"

Bill looked up at the smoldering transformer at the top of the power pole, twenty feet away, and nodded.

"I never seen nothin' like it," Big Ed blathered. "It was like he was blown from a cannon."

Tom Tanner shook his head and said, "I want you to take his body back to town."

"Sure thing, Tom," Sylvester said numbly.

Bill's nod was barely noticeable as he eyed the lifeless and blackened Buckwalder whose body was smoking.

"Help us carry him," Tom Tanner said.

Bill followed Sylvester into the eight-inch-deep snow, his gaze never leaving the blackened face of his dead coworker.

"Everyone take an arm or leg," Tom Tanner ordered.

Stepping up to the body, Bill saw Buckwalder's eyes were open and disjointed. He reached down for an arm, then paused and said, "Shouldn't we close his eyes or something?"

Tom Tanner removed his glove and pulled down Buckwalder's already stiff eyelids. Bill gulped and reached for an arm.

"Watch out for his shanks," Tom Tanner warned as he nodded to the metal spikes on Buckwalder's snow-covered boots.

Big Ed Sorensen was still crying as they lifted the body from the snow. Bill felt a sickening feeling in his gut as the dead man's head rolled back and hung limply. It was not the first time Bill had seen death, but it disturbed him just the same, and he tried not to think of the other dead men he had seen as they carried the burned body through the snow. Gently, they placed the body in the back of Bill's truck, and the four men looked at each other, uncertain of what to do next.

"Should someone say something?" Bill asked.

"No, that's when you bury 'em," Tom Tanner grunted.

Bill nodded.

Tom Tanner turned to Big Ed, who was still sobbing, then said, "We'll gather up his tools and meet you at the office."

THE SNOW-GLAZED power truck was a mile down the road before Bill broke the silence by asking, "Did he have a family?"

"Yeah. A wife and five kids," Sylvester muttered, gazing dully out the window.

Bill shook his head sadly.

"First time seeing a dead man?" Sylvester asked.

"No," Bill muttered. "I wish it was."

Bill's mind went back to his twelfth summer. After he and his friend Harry had spent most of it working on a steamer, they were on their way to Detroit and the state fair when they ran out of money. While in Flint, they met a railway section boss looking for workers for the new Pere Marquette Railroad. Eager to make some money before heading on to the fair, they signed on for nine dollars a week as section hands. While Bill had visions of running a locomotive, he instead worked a rocker arm on a rail cart carrying water to the dry and thirsty men and cleaning up around the camp.

Bill could still see the swath of scrub oak and black walnut trees, chokecherry, and steeplebush the workers had cut away, making a flattened corridor through the woodland from which they had come. The way they were going had men with axes and shovels, wheelbarrows and picks, cutting and clawing a path through the trees and brush.

Bill could hear the thump of heavy wooden ties being dropped into place on the cleared and level ground followed by the *clang-clong* of iron rail being laid down on top and the incessant ping-ping-ping and *tink-tink-tink* of the rails being pinned together and the iron spikes being hammered into the ties. Long hammers wielded by large men with thick arms and shoulders beat the track into submission, and their chorus of grunts, gruff commands, and cursing gave the backbreaking work a certain harmony and rhythm.

Bill was taking water to the men when it happened. One of the massive supply cars had rolled over a worker's legs, crushing them. Bill could still hear the man's agonizing cries and see the helpless looks of men staring with horrified faces as the trapped man's blood stained the surrounding earth.

What was his name? Bill strained to remember. *O'Reilly...*

Summer 1908

THE YOUNG BILL, horrified and yet gripped by the carnage, slipped between the stunned workers to better see the trapped man. He watched as two men frantically cinched their belts around his severed legs, but it was all in vain.

"Do sumpin' for him!" shouted a man.

"He's still bleeding!" cried another.

"Make it tighter!"

"They're cinched up all the way," the foreman replied, his eyes wide and searching. "There aren't a blessed thing we can do for him now," he groaned, his hat pushed back, his ruddy face a pasty white.

"Sit him up!" called a man.

"Someone get'm whiskey!" yelled another.

The foreman nodded and said, "Get some whiskey," as he propped the still howling O'Reilly up.

Bill was again fighting for position when O'Reilly's crying and moaning stopped. He looked at O'Reilly, expecting to see him dead, his eyes open wide and staring back like the cat he had seen trampled by a team of horses; but Bill saw the dying man looking past the foreman and through the men.

Bill watched as the dying man looked around. His cries of agony stopped, his face suddenly at ease. He saw O'Reilly's lips move as if in conversation, but heard no words.

"What's wrong with him?" a man asked.

"He's dying," said another.

Bill watched the dying man with wide eyes and gaped mouth. At one point, Bill thought he even saw a smile just before the man's face relaxed and his eyes lowered to the blood-soaked ground. Bill was watching and waiting for O'Reilly to say something when the foreman gently laid him back in the dirt, pulled off his coat, and laid it over the top of O'Reilly.

That night, the mood at the camp was somber, and Bill stayed close to hear the men talking at dinner, wanting to understand what had happened to O'Reilly in his final seconds.

"He'd plum lost his mind," said one man. "All that pain and his blood gone—that's what done it."

"No, that weren't it at all," said another. "He was seein' angels."

"What?"

"Them were angels that come to fetch him. When he quieted all down, just before...you know...when he was talkin' like. He was seein' angels then."

"Angels," scoffed the other man.

"I'm a-tellin' ya. Them was angels come to get him. Happens all the time."

"It don't happen all the time," the other man sneered.

"It do if you're goin' ta heaven."

BILL GLANCED from the icy road to Sylvester, who was nervously puffing on a cigarette, and asked, "How about you? You seen a dead man before?"

Sylvester nodded, his gaze a mile down the road.

Bill had seen that look before. "You were in the war, then?"

Sylvester nodded again, more slowly this time.

A mile passed, then Bill asked, "What do you think happens?"

Sylvester shrugged and said, "They'll tell his family and bury him."

"No, I mean..." Bill searched for the words. "What do you think happens after you die?"

Sylvester glanced at Bill and said flatly, "You die. You're dead. Nothing. That's it."

Bill swallowed, and his brow gathered. "So, you don't think angels come to take you to heaven?"

"Heaven?" Sylvester scoffed. "I was in France right up 'til the end. I lived in a hole in the ground and waded through mud and dead bodies for six months. I know there's a hell, 'cause I was in it, but a heaven? No, sir. No such thing. You die, and then you're gone. There ain't no winged angels or clouds or harps. That's all just kiddy tales."

Bill's eyes were on the snow-packed road, but his thoughts were years in the past when he was just a small boy of four. He remembered the flickering light of candles dancing across the dark paneled walls of the bedroom. Bill remembered the people gathered around the bed, which was too high for him to see over the top. He remembered the crying and words of comfort that had no meaning to him. Bill remembered someone lifting him and seeing his mother's still body. He didn't know what it meant. Bill didn't understand why his mother wouldn't wake up. He wanted to go to her. He wanted her to hold him, but she couldn't.

Bill had often wondered where his mother had gone. He wanted to believe she was in heaven. He wanted to believe she was an angel always looking down on him, but the notion seemed somehow childish now, just as Sylvester had said.

Bill thought of the nuns who had tried to teach him in school. They had told him about such things, but he had forgotten it now. *What was it they had said?*

Large flakes fell as Bill looked down the snow-packed road. He remembered looking out another window back in Chicago. It was his schoolroom window, and they were the largest snowflakes he had ever seen, gently settling to the earth and creating a thin blanket of white over the playground…

Winter 1905

"Now, class," the nun started, her jaw tight and the corners of her mouth bent as she stared down the group of boys. "I require your attention if you wish to frolic in the snow later—and I do know how you adore the snow—otherwise, you shall remain indoors," she finished, her eyes on Bill.

It was no secret the nuns disliked the mischievous Kane boy. It may have started with his incessant wisecracking or his ongoing pranks, but Bill was not content with the usual thumbtacks on chairs, taped signs on backs, or honey in books. He set his sights higher. On one occasion, he had placed a stray dog and a tomcat in the corner broom closet and laughed with the other boys as Sister Charlotte chased them around the class. On another, he had released rats in the classroom, and while that was great fun for the other boys, it caused great panic for the Benevolent Sisters of the Holy Family. Bill sometimes joked his ears were larger than normal due to the nuns so often leading him by them to the schoolmaster's office. But on this day, young Bill was up to no such misbehavior; he was simply staring out the window at the falling snow.

"William, your eyes up here," glared the nun, her puffy, red face standing out against the white coif. "I'll have your attention," she demanded. Then, after adjusting her spectacles, she turned back to the board and, with her pointing stick outstretched, said, "Class, repeat after me: 'So shall it be at the end of the world: the angels shall come forth and sever the wicked from among the just.'" She paused, looked back over the group, and said, "I didn't hear everyone, and it would be a shame for you to have to stay in for recess with that lovely fresh snow outside."

All but Bill's eyes were on the nun who stood at the board, dimly illuminated by two oil lanterns.

"William!" she growled.

Bill turned forward to the nun, but his attention was soon back on the magical light of the falling snow.

"Again, after me, 'So shall it be at the end of the world: the angels shall come forth and sever the wicked from among the just.' "

The glistening snow bathed the darkened classroom in light, and it was all Bill could do not to be pulled through the window by it.

He saw the teeter-totter was already blanketed. A kickball too. The snow was falling harder now and having to sit in a classroom and watch was more than a nine-year-old boy could stand.

Bill carefully planned what he would first do once outside. There was so much. Snowball fights, snow angels, a snow fort—he had to outdo Harry's from last year! "OW!" Bill cried as the nun cracked her stick across the back of his hand.

"William Kane!" the angry nun bellowed, her face betraying her satisfaction. "You haven't been listening to a word I've said!"

"Yes-yes, I have!" Bill protested, trying to hold back the tears as he clutched his welted hand. "You were talking about angels."

"And what did I say about those angels?" the nun demanded.

"That…that…" Bill's teary eyes shifted to Harry, four rows away, who was looking back with the anguish of a forever-lost soul.

"Let me help you!" the red-faced nun snarled. "When the day of reckoning comes, and the angels come down to pluck out the wicked, they won't have any trouble deciding on you, WILLIAM KANE!"

BILL SLOWED the truck as they neared a turn. He thought again of his mother and wondered if there really was a heaven. He didn't understand such things, but wanted to believe there was. Bill glanced out the back window at the body of Walter Buckwalder, glazed over by a thin dusting of snow. He wondered if angels had come to get him. Bill wondered whether angels would come for him if he were to die.

THE SHANTY IRISHMAN

*B*ill breathed in the warm spring air as he carried the last of the boxes into the kitchen of their new home. "Well, what do you think?" he asked, setting the box on the dining table.

"It's very nice," Mildred smiled, trying to hide her hesitancy. "Are you sure we can afford it?"

"We can since Old Man McCracken promised me a raise," Bill said proudly. "Besides, we need the space. The kids aren't getting any smaller, that's for sure. Where do you want this?" he asked, pointing to the box.

"Oh, leave it there for now," Mildred said, preoccupied with the placement of her hand-me-down china. Tilting her head, she slid the stack of plates a little to the left. "I have to say, I adore the cupboards in here. It gives me a fine place to display my china that was packed away in the other house."

"See? You like it," Bill grinned as he started for the stairs. "I'm going to get the beds put together."

"*When* will you get your raise?" Mildred asked, still eyeing her china arrangement.

"Next payday, I suppose," Bill said, disappearing up the stairs.

Mildred glanced at the contentedly playing Patty in the corner near an empty apple crate, then returned to her china. She carefully placed the last of her dinnerware onto the shelf, slid a platter a few inches to the left, then stood back, picked up the crawling Patty, and admired her display. "That should do nicely, don't you think so, Patty?"

The dark-eyed Patty looked at her mother as if trying to understand, then reached for the crumpled newspaper on the floor and let out a wanting cry.

After setting Patty back down, Mildred gathered up the leftover newspaper that had protected the china, placed it in the empty box, and started into the front room, leaving Patty looking for the missing paper.

When Mildred discovered more cabinetry on the wall opposite the kitchen, she set the box down and eagerly moved to the newfound storage space. Mildred tugged on the painted-over cabinet doors, but they remained closed. Again, she pulled, but still, the cabinets would not open. Not about to be outdone by a sticky cabinet door, she gave one last tug, and as she did so, the stuck doors flew open. Stumbling backward, Mildred tripped over a box and tumbled to the floor. More embarrassed than hurt, she looked up at the open cabinets in confusion, wondering how her china had gotten into them. By the time Mildred realized it was the backside of the same cabinet, it was too late. She gasped as the shelves sagged and then tilted. "Oh no!" she cried as the shelves collapsed, emptying her china onto the hardwood floor with a shattering crash.

"OH NO!" Mildred exclaimed as she looked at the pile of broken porcelain and glass. "MY CHINA!" In no time, her look of shock turned to disbelief, and then grief. "My chiiinnnaaa!" she wailed as a startled Patty, who had waddled into the room, burst into tears.

Upon hearing the crash, Bill rushed down the stairs, and his eyes widened at the pile of the broken china. Staring at the shattered plates, his mind flashed back to another time. It was a buried memory from his teenage years, and like most buried memories, it brought pain and regret. Bill blinked away the memory and turned to Mildred, who was comforting the frightened Patty. "What happened?"

"That shelf let loose when I opened the door!" cried Mildred.

Still fighting the memory, Bill stepped over the broken china, lifted the empty shelf back into position, and pushed the cabinet doors closed. "You shouldn't have opened this side," he grumbled, more annoyed than angry.

"Well, that's what doors are for, aren't they?" Mildred replied.

Bill shook his head as he painfully eyed the broken china.

"We're both okay," Mildred muttered. "Thanks for asking."

"I could tell you were," mumbled Bill. Kneeling, he examined the pile of dinnerware, then announced, "I can't fix this. They're all broken."

"I know," groaned Mildred. "They were my grandmother's."

Bill's shoulder's slumped in despair, but his body tightened when he turned and snapped, "Just don't slam the door!"

"I didn't. They fell when I opened it!" cried Mildred.

Bill looked back down at the irreplaceable china, fighting against the memory that had now come into full view. "I'll clean it up when I get done upstairs," he said in a putout sort of way.

"It was my fault," Mildred fumed. "I'll clean it up."

"Suit yourself, stubborn English," muttered Bill.

"Shanty Irishman," replied Mildred under her breath.

Bill turned to the stairs where the twins and Helen were looking down with wide eyes and said, "It's just broken china! Get back to work unless you want to clean it up for your mother."

The children turned and trudged back up the stairs.

"And nobody break anything else! I'm not made of money!" Bill hollered, but he heard the harshness in his voice and gave a frustrated sigh. When he looked back, he saw Mildred and Patty comforting each other and said more calmly, "I, uh. I better get back to work on those beds, so we have a place to sleep."

Mildred's sad eyes never left the broken china as Bill went up the stairs. After a moment, she let out a defeated sigh, then set Patty down and started for the broom.

Closing the bedroom door, Bill sank onto the floor and stared at the half-assembled bed as his recollection brightened. It was a memory that brought him more pain than any other.

February 1913

"SEE YA LATER, HARRY!" yelled the sixteen-year-old Bill as he threw one last snowball, causing his friend to duck. Harry Mandel responded with a snowball that slammed harmlessly against the porch column. Bill laughed and waved as his friend continued down the snowy lane. After stomping the snow from his boots, Bill pushed open the door to his home and stepped into the warm, musty air. He had closed that door thousands of times before, each time with a heavy thud that rattled the china on the shelf in the front room. But this time, as Bill pulled off his hat, he watched in horror as two plates teetered and fell to the hardwood floor with a crash. Bill's face was pale and drawn as he stared at the ivory and blue fragments spread on the floor beside a rug. He looked at the other plates, saucers, and cups still on the shelf. They were not ordinary plates. They had been his mother's and meticulously cared for by his sister for as long as he could remember.

"What was that?" barked Bill's father from the kitchen.

Bill stood frozen as he stared at the china fragments, his coat still on, puddles forming from the melting snow around his boots.

"I said, what was that?" Mr. Kane demanded, coughing as he entered the front room with a dishtowel in hand. He lurched to a stop when he saw the broken plates. Robert Kane was a lean, handsome man who normally wore his dark hair combed to the side and his mustache long and curled, but he had been ill of late, and his face was drawn and tired, his hair tangled and messy. His dark brown eyes, typically relaxed, were now piqued with anger. "How many times have I told you not to slam the door?" he scolded before bending over in a deep, barking cough.

"I closed the door the same as always," Bill bristled.

"Look what you did!" Mr. Kane exclaimed, tears forming in his dark-ringed eyes. He lurched to the fragments and got to his knees, but hesitated to disturb them further. "Those plates were your mother's! Rest her soul," he said, coughing. "She loved them!"

"I know, Father," Bill said, both saddened and angered.

"They have been here all of these years until you—*you* come here and-" again he coughed. "You break and wreck and ruin! That is your way! You don't listen to me, your father! You never take my counsel!" Coughing, Mr. Kane looked up, tears streaming down his face. "Why do you have to be like this? Why can't you be like your brothers? They are respectful to me! They are respectful to their mother! They are respectable!"

Bill's face was red. He no longer cared about the plates. "What do you want me to do, Father? You're never here! You're always at work!"

Mr. Kane brought a hand to his mouth, overtaken by a cough. "*I'm* never here? What about you? I have to work! You-you go gallivanting around like some—some damn gypsy!" he coughed and wheezed. "I work to support you, you ungrateful..." again he coughed, turning his head, his arm outstretched, his finger still pointing at his son in scorn.

"If you would have been home more, maybe Mother..." Bill paused, his face torn with emotion.

"Maybe Mother what?" Mr. Kane cried. "Maybe she would still be here? Do you think my providing for my family killed her? You didn't even know her! If she would have lived—raising you—with all the trouble you caused

—that would have killed her just the same! You're a delinquent and a vagabond!"

Bill's eyes were red, his face contorted as his father doubled over, coughing. "That's not true! Damn you, Father! That's not true!"

"You-you have been nothing but a worry to me!" Mr. Kane coughed and sputtered, red-tinted saliva foaming at the corners of his mouth. "You-you would have broken her heart just as well!"

"No, I wouldn't! If she were here, I'd be different! She'd love me! She'd be here for me! I'd *want* to come home!" Bill cried.

Mr. Kane wiped the blood from his mouth with the dishtowel and angrily threw it to the floor. His face trembling, he pointed to the door and exclaimed, "Get out of my sight! I have no place for such an ungrateful son!" He wheezed and coughed up more blood. "Get out and don't come back until you are on hands and knees!"

BILL COULD STILL SEE his heartbroken sister Iliene standing at the top of the stairs with tears streaming down her face as he pulled open the door and stormed out of the house.

Bill stared past the half-assembled bed, his chest rising and falling as he tried to push the memory from his mind, but the pain lingered. He remembered the wounds from that day, but even more troubling, he saw himself in that memory. Bill had become his father, something he swore he would never do.

∾

LITTLE DEVILS

The three-day Fourth of July visit to Mildred's parents in Oreana was a welcome escape allowing Mildred to relax, the children time to explore, and Bill the chance to lead Oreana's baseball team to victory over Murphy. But the long and dusty ride back to Boise (usually a three-hour journey that had taken six because of two flat tires and multiple overheating stops) was made worse by four quarreling children and sweltering summer heat, undoing any relaxation they had enjoyed.

When the dusty black Ford finally arrived home with Patty and Bobby wailing in the back seat and the twins bouncing to contain their bladders, Mildred pushed open the door like an escaping prisoner. The panicked twins were close behind with the shrieking Patty and sobbing Bobby following. But Bill stayed glued to his seat, still gripping the wheel, as the realization that their horrific journey had finally come to an end.

"Hurry!" Alma cried, dancing as he held his crotch at the front door. "Hurry!" Alva echoed, doing the same.

"I told you boys not to drink so much," Mildred reminded them as she hoisted the wet and tired Patty. "Billy, will you get Helen? She's asleep in the back seat."

"How can she be asleep?" Bill muttered, still staring straight ahead. "We're never doing that again."

"Now, Billy, you loved that trip, and you know it. You even got to play baseball. That was worth the trip by itself!"

"Hurry! I gotta go!" cried Alma.

"Oh, find a bush and hush up," Mildred called back.

The twins wasted no time and hobbled around the side of the house to relieve themselves. They didn't notice the beady eyes of Guy Whitney behind a shrub near the shabby house next door. Guy and Paul Whitney were a year older and younger than the twins. Mildred had some concern about the mischievousness of the boys, and on more than one occasion, had blamed their influence on her two oldest sons' misdeeds. Bill didn't share her concerns. He was happy the otherwise milquetoast twins were showing a heart for adventure.

Bobby, whose golden hair was going this way and that, was rubbing his tired eyes as his sobbing subsided.

"Everyone take something into the house," Mildred directed, as she waited for Bill and the key.

Bill pushed the car door closed and gave the black Ford a questionable look as he walked around its front, its hot engine still spitting and sputtering.

"I need to water the flowers," Mildred said to herself as Bill approached with the key. He wasn't yet at the door when Alma pulled it open from the inside.

"How'd you get in there?" Bill asked, his brow gathered.

Alma looked at his father as if he had done something wrong, then pointed back through the house and said, "The back door."

"Was it unlocked?" asked Mildred.

Alma nodded.

Bill pushed past Alma and marched through the house to the open back door. He looked around for a moment before noticing the hole in the screen door.

"What happened?" Mildred asked as she moved beside him.

"Someone broke in," Bill growled.

Mildred gasped. "Someone broke into our house?"

"Someone small," Bill said, pointing to the opening in the screen door, then to the dusty handprint on the floor just inside. "And look here," he added, pointing to two sets of footprints leading out the same door.

"You don't think it was *them*, do you?" Mildred asked, wide-eyed.

"The Whitney boys?" Bill frowned. "Why would they want to break in?" He turned back to see Alva sheepishly holding an empty mason jar that served as his piggy bank.

"My money's gone," Alva muttered in dismay.

"Mine's empty too," Alma whined, coming down the stairs.

"How'd they know about your money?" Bill glared.

Alma looked down, shamefaced, and said, "I showed Guy my bank before we left."

"Well, you're askin' for trouble then," Bill grumbled. "You don't show people where you keep your money!"

Alva glanced at Alma with some hesitation, then said, "We showed them Mama's play money too."

"Play money?" Bill frowned.

Putting a hand to her mouth, Mildred went into the kitchen and discovered someone had moved a chair against the cupboard. After opening the cupboard, she pulled out a cigar box that held their rent money and gasped when she saw it was empty. "Oh, those little dickens!" she exclaimed as she stomped out of the kitchen to the back door. "They took the rent money too! I'm going to march right over there and—"

"No," Bill barked. "I'll handle this."

"What-what you gonna do?" Alma asked with round eyes.

"Why, I'm going to get the sheriff!" Bill fumed.

Mildred nodded approvingly.

"After I beat the tar out of 'em!" he added, pushing open the back door and leaving Mildred and the twins looking on in bewilderment.

Stomping through the backyard, Bill ignored the scattering chickens, which had once again gotten out of their coop, and hastily marched past the pile of wood the twins had yet to organize, through the garden and its patch of knee-high corn. After hopping over the teetering picket fence, Bill stepped into the Whitney's yard, which was in even worse repair. He felt a pair of eyes looking at him through a window, but they quickly disappeared when he turned his head. His face red, his blood boiling, Bill marched to the front door through the weed-infested and overgrown front lawn. He raised his clenched fist, his eyes intent, his lip snarled, and rapped a knuckle on the peeling green paint of the front door. Bill's loud knock rattled the door, and he heard the hurried patter of fleeing footsteps through the open window to his right. Bill knocked again, then looked through the dirty window into the darkened house. "I know you're in there!" he bellowed. "Come out now and face the music, and I won't get the sheriff!"

"Billy, shouldn't you just get the sheriff?" a worried Mildred called from across the teetering picket fence.

Bill flashed a glance at his wife, then angrily pounded on the door with the side of his fist. "He's in there! I heard him!" Bill paused and listened, but heard only the sound of his quickened breathing. Shaking his head, Bill checked the door latch. It was unlocked. Against Mildred's protests, Bill pushed it open and stepped inside.

Bill's nose wrinkled at the stale smell of cooked cabbage and unwashed clothes inside. Determined to reclaim what was his, he started through the shadowy front room past a cluttered card table and a couch, losing its stuffing. His first steps were quick and heedless, but he slowed when he realized his situation. Bill considered leaving and calling the sheriff, but he knew the little thieves were in there, and so was his money.

Bill stepped into the messy kitchen, where pulled-closed draperies left uneasy shadows, then paused and listened as the wood floor creaked above him. *There you are!*

Spinning, Bill left the kitchen and moved to the stairs. "I know you're up there!" he yelled, his anger lessening. "Come down and talk to me, and I won't call the sheriff!"

"No!" whimpered a high-pitched voice, followed by another yelling, "Shut up, dummy!"

They're both up there. "All right then!" Bill bellowed as he stomped up the stairs.

"Mister, we got a gun!" cried the younger brother, Paul, in a high-pitched voice.

Bill paused as he considered the threat. He looked down at the open door. Then, defiantly shaking his head, he turned and stomped up the stairs. There were only two doors on the second level, and it was easy to tell which room the boys were hiding in from the noise they were making. As Bill pushed open the door, a burst of sunlight through the window blinded him. Wincing, he raised his arm to block the light. Inside the wood-planked bedroom was an unmade bed and a chest of drawers. The face of one drawer was missing, with clothes hanging from it. A sliding sound moved his searching gaze to the unmade bed, where he noticed two small feet sticking out from underneath. Bill shook his head at the feeble attempt to hide and, with hands on hips, barked, "All right, hand it over!"

"Hand what over?" came the muffled voice of the older brother, Guy, from under the bed.

"You know what!" Bill growled. "Everything you took from our house!"

"We didn't take nothin'!"

"Is that so? Maybe we should have the sheriff decide. I saw your footprints, you little crook!"

Paul, who was still trying to push himself under the bed, finally gave up and whined, "Aw, give it back; we don't wanna go to the lockup."

"Shut up!" snapped Guy.

"Come on. Get out of there," Bill ordered, pleased by his detective work.

"We didn't take nothin'!" Guy insisted.

Shaking his head, Bill reached down and grabbed the smaller brother by his ankles, drug him out from under the bed, and pulled him to his feet by his collar. Bill glared at the pug-nosed six-year-old with two buck teeth, and barked, "Where is it? Where's the money you took?"

Refusing to make eye contact, the squirming Paul reached into his pocket and pulled out a fistful of coins. "This is all I got, Mister Kane," he muttered, his head lowered in shame.

"That's what you took from my boys' banks?" Bill asked sternly.

Paul nodded.

"All of it?"

Paul hesitated, then shook his head.

"Where's the rest?"

"Guy has it."

"Shut up!" snapped Guy from under the bed.

"You! Come on out from there!" Bill demanded.

"No!"

"Maybe I should wait for your pa to get home and talk to him," Bill said, catching Paul's eye with a sideways glance.

The threat caused Guy to bump his head on the underside of the bed and Paul to cower even more.

"Well, what's it gonna be?" Bill asked.

A fist slowly emerged from under the bed and emptied a few nickels, dimes, and pennies onto the wood floor at Bill's feet.

"All of it," Bill growled.

With a groan, the still hidden Guy pulled his hand back under the bed and produced a few more pennies.

"What about the other money?"

"What other money?" Guy asked from under the bed.

"The money in the kitchen, in the cigar box."

There was a long pause, then Guy muttered, "That? That wasn't real money."

Bill's brow tightened, as did his hold on Paul. "Yes, it was. Where is it?"

"The paper money?" Paul asked, looking up at Bill in confusion.

"That's right," Bill nodded. "Where is it?"

"That's just play money," Paul replied.

"Yeah, play money," Guy repeated from under the bed.

Bill's pulse quickened. "No, that *wasn't* play money. That was close to twenty dollars of *real* money!"

"Twenty dollars?" Paul gasped.

"We don't have it," Guy insisted.

"We'll see what your pa has to say about that," Bill steamed.

"We thought it was play money," Guy pleaded from under the bed.

"Well, where is it?"

"We…" Paul gulped. "We buried it in the backyard. We was playin' banks and robbers."

"Buried it? Show me!" Bill growled, his jaw tight. "You too, Guy. Get your thieving fanny out from under there, or I'll tell the sheriff *and* your pa! Banks and Robbers," Bill fumed as Guy climbed out from under the bed. "You're gonna be playing 'Let's Go to Jail' if you keep that up!"

"Here it is," Bill announced, triumphantly entering the kitchen and placing the crinkled bills on the counter before Mildred.

"You got it back?" Mildred gasped with a hand to her mouth.

"Every last penny," Bill said proudly. "I told you I would."

"Yes, but what will Mr. Whitney have to say when he hears you went into his house?" Mildred fretted.

"I don't think we have to worry about that," Bill chuckled. "Those boys got the fear of God and Bill Kane in 'em now." He glanced at Alma and Alva seated at the table, their eyes wide and hopeful. "I got your coins back too," he said, emptying his pockets onto the table.

"Thanks, Pa," sighed Alma.

"Yeah, thanks, Pa," echoed Alva.

"Let this be a lesson to you two," Bill said with a stern finger. "You don't tell people where you hide your money! And don't spend your time with boys like that. They're trouble and won't amount to anything!"

"Is that so?" Mildred asked, eyeing her husband knowingly.

Bill turned to his wife's questioning gaze. In an instant, he knew she was referring to him, and it reminded Bill he was that same kind of trouble as a boy…

October 1907

BILL AND HARRY scampered through the shadows along the leaf-littered walk, shoving and jostling each other in a feeble game of tag as the biting Chicago wind caused bright colored leaves to swirl and dance at their feet. As they approached a flickering gaslight, Harry kicked it and watched its flame flicker and go out.

"There it is, old Whitebeard's wagon," Bill said, pointing to a withered wagon parked in the shadows.

Harry scratched his head as he eyed his mischievous friend. "I don't know, Bill. I'm still in trouble for what we did to Mr. O'Leary."

"Oh, that was the best ever!" Bill roared. "When he came out that night and saw that bag of fresh manure on fire and stomped it out, I thought I'd die laughing!"

Harry couldn't hold back the grin. "That was pretty funny, but when my old man found out, boy was he ever sore. How'd you get out of that one?" he asked, eyeing Bill.

"What makes you think I didn't get in trouble?"

"'Cause you get out of all the stuff that I get whipped for!"

"If you don't get caught, you don't get in trouble; that's what I always say."

Harry shook his head and sighed. "I don't know."

"What's not to know?" Bill persisted. "It's a perfect plan! We take old Whitebeard's wagon to the church and set it on fire. Just think how funny that'll be with everyone comin' outta church tonight! Besides, tomorrow's Halloween. It's perfect!"

Harry admired his friend's exuberance and fearlessness, but he wasn't sure about it being a joke. "If we burn the wagon, what's old Whitebeard going to peddle with?"

"Oh, he's an old Jew," Bill said dismissively. "I'm sure he's got plenty of wagons."

With Harry being Jewish himself, he wasn't entirely sure what his friend meant by the comment, but he finally relented and said, "Well, maybe we can burn it a little."

"Now you're thinking!" beamed Bill.

While the old wagon was not particularly large, it was cumbersome for the two nine-year-olds to push along the cobbled street, and they twice had to hide in the shadows as passersby approached. With the church only two blocks away, their scheme was close to being realized. A match and some stolen kerosene tucked inside the wagon were all the two young vandals needed to light up the front court as the faithful exited the evening Mass, making their Halloween prank complete. That the church stood atop a hill and was well visible by all on the busy boulevard below made their prank even more appealing.

On either side of the cobbled street were old masonry dwellings that either touched or left barely a man's width between. Steps led up to the front doors of the two-story homes from the walk, which was lined with overgrown shrubs. With the gas streetlights few and far between, it was the glow of the windows that gave light to the little pranksters.

As Bill pushed from behind the old moaning wagon, Harry pulled and guided it from its dry and weathered whiffletree, careful to keep in the darker shadows of the night.

"Hold up a minute," Harry whispered breathlessly.

Overheating in his wool coat, Bill willingly paused and wedged his shoulder against the cart to keep it from rolling back as he undid his buttons. Having just passed an intersecting street, he looked down the hill at Washington Boulevard, which ran parallel. Bill spotted a passing street-car, horses and buggies, and people on foot and thought it was perfect for their tomfoolery. Bill chuckled as he visualized men and women falling over themselves to put out the fire. The trick, as Bill said, was not to be caught. Their plan was a simple one: place the wagon in front of the church, set it ablaze, and then hide and watch the show.

The two little hellions had scarcely resumed pushing the wagon up the hill when an approaching clip-clop raised the hairs on the back of Bill's neck. His ear had become well attuned to the sound of mounted police, and he breathed a warning to Harry, who hastily placed a rock under one of the wagon's front wheels before slipping into a nearby bush with him. They could hear the muffled goings-on from inside the home through the glowing kitchen window above them as a family cleaned up from an evening meal. Hunkered within the prickly bush, the naughty boys listened hard as the clattering hoofs approached.

"It's a cop," Harry whispered, looking from the horse to their stolen wagon parked across the lane.

Bill hushed his friend as the clip-clop grew louder and then slowed before their parked wagon. His eyes widened when he spotted the police-man's shiny black boot in the stirrup, just feet away.

Holding his breath, Bill glanced at the wide-eyed Harry hidden beside him and gulped when the officer swung his leg off the horse and his boot dropped just two feet away. While Bill couldn't see the officer's face, he could tell from his careful steps around the wagon an investigation was underway.

When Bill turned to Harry, he noticed his friend's shoe sticking out from under the bush. He knew any warning to Harry might give them away, but so would his shoe, should the policeman spot it. After making several contorted faces to get Harry's attention, Bill turned back to the policeman re-situating the rock holding the wagon in place.

With the policeman on the far side of the wagon, fifteen feet away, Bill considered making a break for it but knew even if he could free himself from the entangling bush in time, he would have trouble outrunning the policeman on his mount. Upon seeing Harry was even more stuck, Bill decided it was best for them to stay.

Convinced the wagon was secure, the officer moved back around his horse, brushing by the shallow-breathing Bill. He placed his foot in the stirrup and pulled himself back up into the saddle. As he did, his nightstick slipped from its ring and fell onto the cobbles just inches from Harry's exposed shoe.

Harry's eyes widened as the policeman lowered back off his mount, causing the horse to snort impatiently and look directly at Bill. As the officer bent over to gather up his club, his shoulder brushing into the shrub just inches from Harry, the window above them opened, and a woman nervously yelled, "Who's out there? Who's making a rumpus?"

"Oh, it's only me, ma'am," the officer replied, straightening up and tipping his hat. "Sorry for the disturbance."

With eyes bulging, Harry pulled his foot into the bush.

"Oh, it's you, constable," sighed the woman, who had wild, unkempt hair. "I thought there was mischief about."

"No, ma'am, just checking out this wagon, you see. Is it yours now?" the officer asked, with a hint of an Irish brogue.

"No, sir," the woman said. "But it might be those people next door. They're new and have been bringing all manner of rubbish." Turning a pot out the window, she dumped its contents into the bush onto the crouching Bill. The surprise of the dishwater running down his neck and back gave him a shudder, but to his amazement, he didn't let out a peep.

"Very well then," the officer said, taking a step back.

"Good night, constable," the woman said, closing the window.

"And good night to you, ma'am," the officer replied.

Bill exhaled as softly as possible as the policeman re-mounted his horse, holding his nightstick in place. With a snort and the clatter of hooves, the horse turned from Bill and clip-clopped down the avenue into the shadows.

"Whew, that was close," Harry sighed as he climbed out of the bush and brushed the dead leaves from his coat.

"Did you see what that hag did to me?" Bill gasped, shaking off his wet cap. "She dumped water down me!"

Harry fought back a laugh as Bill looked into the kitchen to see if she had spotted them. "You deserve a medal for that one!" Harry whispered, exhilarated by their narrow escape. "What do we do now?"

"We finish our job," Bill replied with a devilish gleam.

"All right," Harry nodded with renewed conviction.

They had just resumed pushing the wagon when the woman opened the window and yelled, "Hey, what you little brats doing out there?"

Bill ducked to the side of the wagon, but without him pushing, the wagon rolled backward with Harry still behind the whiffletree.

"Harry! Get outta there!" Bill cried, forgetting the stern-eyed woman.

Nearly falling backward, Harry ducked below the crossbar as the wagon rolled down the hill.

The two boys watched with gleeful dismay as the wagon gained momentum. As it reached the steep cross street, which intersected both theirs and the much busier boulevard below, the wagon hit an upturned stone, took an abrupt turn to the right, and started down the hill. Bill and Harry ran to the corner and watched with hanging jaws as the wagon sped down the hill, going faster and faster. As it angled toward the side of the road, it struck a pair of trashcans, launching them into the air with a thunderous *ker-bash*. Flinging their contents wildly about, the dented cans crashed to the street and rattled their way down the hill after the wagon, making a racket that could be heard for blocks.

The boys watched in amazement as the wagon rolled on, leaving a trail of debris and destruction with the two clattering trashcans chasing behind. The thought of the ruckus continuing for blocks caused Bill to cackle with glee, and the sight of the very policeman they had evaded galloping down the hill after the wagon caused their stomachs to ache with laughter.

The appearance of a streetcar loaded with passengers on the boulevard caused Bill's laughter to wane and then stop altogether. Suddenly, the humor was gone; their wagon was racing towards the stopped streetcar.

Harry's devilish grin and gleeful laugh had likewise stopped, replaced by a look of horror and a pointing arm as he followed the runaway wagon to the streetcar.

With the officer charging after the wagon, the boys watched in astonishment as it inexplicably veered to one side, crashed into the curb, and toppled on its side before stopping only yards from the streetcar.

Bill had no sooner turned to Harry with a did-you-see-that? look, then he felt a jerk on his ear. "OUCH!" Bill cried as the wild-haired woman from the window grabbed hold of his and Harry's ears.

"I saw what you two rascals did! What do you have to say for yourselves?" she demanded, her glare harsh and unforgiving.

Harry, grimacing in pain with his head askew, was speechless as he looked from the woman to Bill.

"You could have hurt a lot of people, you know," she scolded.

Harry's face was pale, his voice absent as he tried to speak, but Bill raised a reassuring hand and said, "No, we tried to stop it. It was an accident," he lied. "We're choirboys, and we were taking the wagon up to the church as a favor for the priest. We wanted to surprise him. He's having a Halloween bazaar for the needy tomorrow."

The woman scowled at Bill and said, "I never heard nothin' about no bazaar."

"Ahh! It's a secret bazaar," Bill winced as she twisted his ear.

"I'm turning you into the constable, just the same."

Harry gasped, but Bill remained calm. "That's fine," Bill nodded. "We were going down there to clean up the mess ourselves. We feel terrible about it, don't we, Walter?"

"Huh?" Harry asked, then going along said, "Oh, that's right...uh...B-Bob."

"You were now, were you?" The woman asked with a scrutinizing scowl.

"Yes, ma'am," Bill said with his well-practiced innocent smile.

"Well, all right," she said, releasing her grip on their red and twisted ears. "I just thought you were up to no good. You go on down there and tell that constable your story."

"Yes, ma'am," Bill said, holding his ear, as he and a wide-eyed Harry turned and started down the hill.

"What are we gonna do?" Harry muttered as he nervously eyed the chaos ahead of them.

Bill said nothing for a few steps. Then, seeing the woman had turned her back, he grabbed Harry by the arm and pulled him into the shadows, where the sounds of their hooting and hollering faded into the night.

· · ·

"WHAT?" Bill asked, realizing Mildred had addressed him.

Mildred shook her head and repeated, "I'm sure you can tell them to avoid troublesome friends, as you were such an angel yourself at that age."

Bill looked from his wife to the twins, who were still distraught over the stolen money. Then, after a moment's consideration, said, "Well, maybe the Whitney boys aren't so bad, just a little misdirected."

"Misdirected," Mildred repeated with a wry grin.

"I guess you boys are pretty good, aren't you?" Bill asked, eyeing the twins.

"Yes, they are," Mildred replied, but she thought, *No thanks to you.*

"Well," Bill started, somewhat deflated at having lost any moral authority, "just be careful who you run with."

"Yes, sir," Alma nodded.

"Yes, sir," Alva echoed.

Bill glanced at the smirking Mildred, then gave an acknowledging nod and left the room.

∾

PRAYERS AND BEER

*B*ill smiled proudly at the decorated Christmas tree in the window as he approached his front door. Unlike the previous year, he took no chances letting John Young or anyone else beat him to the punch and presented the family with a tree in early December. Being Christmas Eve, Bill looked forward to sipping hot cocoa and reading Christmas stories to the children by the fire. But when he opened the door, the sound of two-year-old Patty crying was the first thing to greet him.

Bill's eyes narrowed as he hung up his coat and hat. When he entered the kitchen, he saw Mildred attending to Patty, whose face was pale and glistening with sweat. Her cry was tired and raspy and interrupted by coughs. "Oh no. What happened?" he asked as he passed Bobby and Helen sitting at the table.

An exhausted Mildred pulled the washcloth from Patty's face. "She took ill this morning after you left. She's been running a fever all day."

"Is it the croup?" Bill asked, standing back.

"I think so. They have something too," Mildred sighed.

Bill's brow tightened as he turned to Bobby and Helen and saw the red spots scattered on their face and neck. "What's happened to you two? It's Christmas Eve. You can't all be sick!"

"I don't wanna be sick," groaned Helen.

"Will Santa still come?" Bobby asked with concern.

"Yes, he will," Mildred assured him.

"They have the measles," Bill sighed after looking closer. "So does Bart's kids."

"Oh dear," groaned Mildred, holding the crying Patty.

"Where are the twins?" Bill asked.

"I sent them upstairs. They seem okay, for now," Mildred said, her face creased with worry.

"Did you send for Doc Boeck?" Bill asked, hands on his hips.

"I rang him up from the neighbors. He said to keep them warm and hold tight until he can get here."

"When's that?"

"Maybe tomorrow," Mildred said, looking as though she might cry.

Bill gave a cranky sigh. It wasn't how he expected to spend Christmas Eve. He considered making an excuse and going to Pengilly's for a drink, but pushed that thought aside. Bill turned from the spotted Helen and Bobby to the damp and miserable Patty and shook his head.

DOCTOR ALBERT BOECK, a middle-aged man who wore a bowtie and chin beard and smelled of liniment, pulled up from the sleeping Patty with his stethoscope and shook his head.

"Is it just the croup?" Mildred asked hopefully.

"I'm afraid not," Boeck frowned.

"What is it then?" Bill asked.

"She has pneumonia. Quite a bad case, I might add," Boeck said, pushing his thick round-rimmed glasses up his nose, "Pneumonia is never good at this tender age."

"What-what do you mean?" Mildred asked, wide-eyed.

"It puts a strain on the lungs. When did she first show signs?"

"Day before last. Christmas Eve," said a worried Mildred.

"Hmm, two days," the doctor said, scratching his beard.

"Will it spread to the others?" Bill asked, glancing at the speckle-faced Bobby and Helen.

"Too soon to tell," Boeck said. "I would be more worried about the measles spreading to this little one," he added, running his fingers along Patty's arm. "Or you," he said, glancing at Mildred.

Mildred put a hand to her belly. She wasn't due until the summer, but knew such things could be dangerous for babies not yet born.

"What do we do?" Bill asked glumly.

The doctor gave a slight shrug, then said, "There's not much you can do. Rest, don't overwork yourself," he said to Mildred. "What about the older boys? How are they?"

"I think they might be getting it too," Mildred groaned.

"Don't be hard on yourself," said the doctor. "It's to be expected in a house like this—with family. I'll bring by some liniment, which will help with the itching when the spots stain, but you'll want to keep a close eye on this little one."

"We will," Bill said, eyeing the still resting Patty.

Mildred glanced at Bill. She was grateful for the gesture, but she knew "we" meant her.

FOUR DAYS HAD PASSED. While Mildred had not yet succumbed to the measles, Bill had a nasty rash of sores inside his mouth. Running a fever and unable to work, he stayed home, adding to Mildred's already busy load. Bobby, who had come down with the rash first, was improving, but now complained of itching as the red spots turned brown. The twins were now also feverish and developing neck rashes, which told Mildred it was only a matter of time before it spread to her. The bright part of the day was Patty waking and playing with her doll as if nothing had been wrong. Still, Mildred watched her closely as her fever had only slightly broken, and her eyes were still red.

Bill had just shuffled down the stairs, bundled in a sweater and blanket, when he saw Patty lying on the floor, her tiny body twisting in convulsions. "Patty! Patty! Mildred, come quick!" he yelled, rushing to Patty's side.

"What is it?" Mildred cried, bursting into the front room with a look of fright.

"She's having a seizure!" Bill exclaimed. "Quick! Get a spoon before she swallows her tongue!"

Horrified, Mildred rushed back into the kitchen as Bill pried open her mouth, her limbs twitching, her eyes rolling. "Hurry!"

Mildred stumbled across the rug, nearly falling as she rushed back into the room with a spoon. Bill quickly placed it in Patty's mouth and pressed down on her tongue. "Run to the neighbors and call for the doctor!"

. . .

Bill and Mildred watched closely as Dr. Boeck examined their daughter. Two hours had passed since Patty's first seizure, which was followed by another.

"What's wrong?" Mildred fretted, her face worn and tired.

"She must have had an epileptic seizure—from the sustained fever, no doubt," the doctor said as he pulled his stethoscope from his bag.

"Oh, Patty, my baby," Mildred whispered.

"Is-is that normal? To have a fit like that?" Bill asked, his brow gathered with worry.

"It's not normal to have a fever for so long. It does things to the brain," the doctor said, placing the stethoscope on Patty's gently swelling chest. After a moment, he pulled away from Patty, folded up his stethoscope, and returned it to his black bag.

"What do we do?" Bill asked.

Doctor Boeck considered his words, then said, "It's been a week now, and the pneumonia is only getting worse."

"But she was playing with her doll just an hour ago. She was better!" Mildred insisted.

"Maybe so, but the seizures didn't help."

"What can we do to stop them?" Bill asked.

The doctor shook his head. "I don't know. The pneumonia is the problem. When it goes to the lungs like this, it makes it very hard to breathe, you understand? There's fluid inside." He looked from Mildred to Bill and, seeing they weren't grasping his explanation, said, "The seizures are simply a sign of what is happening to her body. She could literally drown, I'm afraid. Keeping her propped up will help, but I'm sorry to say there is nothing else that can be done. We can only wait."

"Wait for her to get better?" Bill asked, uncertain of his meaning.

The doctor glanced down as he formed his words, then turned back to Bill and said, "There is a strong possibility she won't get better."

"What?" Mildred gasped. Her eyes filled with tears as she kneeled beside the sleeping Patty and tenderly rubbed her feverish face.

"What about the hospital?" Bill asked. "Can they help?"

Dr. Boeck shook his head.

Bill drew in a ragged breath, and his eyes welled with tears at the thought of his child, his precious little Patty, dying. He didn't feel the hand of the doctor on his arm or hear him go out the front door; all Bill felt was the painful thought of another loved one leaving him.

As Bill gazed across the darkened front room to the stairs, he saw in his mind the dark paneled walls of the stairway in his childhood home.

22 September 1900

AS THE FOUR-YEAR-OLD Bill stood at the foot of the stairway and looked up, he saw a strange beam of light filtering through the window atop the stairs illuminating particles of dust sifting and swirling through it like tiny flakes of snow in a gentle breeze. The sound of crying in the sitting room to his left caused his large blue eyes to swell. *Why are they crying?* he wondered as he looked up at the strange woman standing beside him.

"William, hold my hand," came the sweet voice of his sister Iliene who was just two years older than he. "I'll take care of you."

Bill saw his sister's red, weepy eyes. He didn't understand her fear and sadness as he took her hand.

"Children, your mother is gone now," said the woman in a black dress and a white nun's habit. "It's time for you to go upstairs."

Bill looked up the empty stairs to the shimmering shower of dust and watched as the beam of filtering light disappeared in a passing cloud. He saw his sister wiping at her tears. Bill watched as the corners of her mouth fought to stay up. *Something's not right*, he thought.

Holding Iliene's hand, they started up the stairs. Each step was an effort for the young boy, and as he climbed, Bill considered the words he had heard—words painfully uttered by people he didn't know: *She was a dear woman. She was too young to pass. How will the children get along?* He didn't understand why everyone was so sad, but the sadness and the words and the tears weighed each step down.

Pausing halfway up the stairs, Bill looked down into the sitting room, where people quietly sobbed and comforted each other. *Mama's gone? Where did she go?* he wondered.

Upon reaching the top of the stairs and the window, young Bill looked to Iliene bathed in the sun's light. He watched as her uncertain gaze moved to the open doorway. It was their mother's bedroom. With the drapes drawn, the dark bedroom flickered in candlelight.

Iliene led Bill into the glowing room to their mother's bed. Their father and his brother, along with others, were in the room, but Bill's uncertain gaze was fixed on the body lying on the bed. *Mother is still here, sleeping. She hasn't left yet*, he reassured himself.

The sound of his father sobbing caused Bill's eyes to widen. Bill had never seen him cry and watched with increasing distress as his father buried his face in his hands.

"Mama?" the young Bill called, his voice frail and fearful. He watched as Iliene climbed upon the bed and lay beside their still mother. Bill heard her sob and stretched to see. He didn't feel the hands lifting him to the bed where he kneeled by his mother's side and touched and then softly stroked her wrist and hand laid across her stomach. With his mother's eyes still closed, he pressed a little harder, shaking her hand to stir her, and felt the coldness of her skin. "Mama?"

"BILLY, is it all right if I have the elders come and administer to Patty?" Mildred asked, her face filled with worry.

Bill's distant gaze returned to the present. He looked from his wheezing daughter to Mildred. "What? What was that?"

"Can I send for the elders to administer to her? A blessing saved my life years ago. We must do all we can."

Bill was thinking of how to reject her suggestion when, to his surprise, he said, "Yes. Call for them."

Mildred embraced Bill, then got to her feet and left the room, leaving Bill at the side of the faint little Patty.

"HELLO, BILL," said George Robertson, a lean, bony-faced man in a blue suit. George paid no attention to the red spots spreading from Bill's mouth as he shook his hand. "I'm sorry about your little girl. Is it all right if Walter and I ask God to bless her?"

Bill gave a helpless nod to the four-inch-taller George, who spoke in a somewhat shrill voice and reminded him of a captain he hated in the Army. Bill pushed the memory aside, hoping this "Brother Robertson" and his friend might be able to help his dying daughter.

"You know Walter Weaver?" George asked.

"I don't think so," Bill said, glancing at the shorter, balding man who reverently stood by with hat in hand.

"Hello, Brother Kane," Walter said.

"Pleased to meet you," Bill muttered, shaking his hand. "Maybe Mildred didn't tell you; I'm-I'm not a Mormon. I'm Catholic."

Walter Weaver smiled and said, "We're all God's children."

Bill's brow furrowed in thought, and he followed Mildred as she guided the two men to the listless Patty's bed. He watched as Walter tipped a small bottle of oil onto her head, then placed his hands on her and gave a brief prayer. George Robertson then added his hands to Patty's head, and in a calm yet direct voice, pronounced a blessing. Bill had seen Mormon blessings before and hoped this one would help his daughter, but all he could think about was how sad it would be at Patty's passing.

When they finished, Bill offered polite thanks as the two men quietly left their home. Turning to Mildred, he saw a face not sad and dreary, but one filled with hope and faith.

"Thank you," Mildred whispered as she embraced Bill. "That blessing will help her. I know it will."

Bill gently stroked Mildred's back and thought, *How sad it will be when little Patty dies.*

≈

BILL SHOOK his head and blew a smoke ring across the table away from Sylvester Schmig, who had just set his empty glass down and called for another.

"Come on, Bill, it's New Year's Eve," Sylvester whined. "You can't go home yet. We got another hour 'til the new year!" he said over the plinky piano music that filled the stale, smoke-filled Pengilly's.

A part of Bill wanted to stay and finish drinking down his troubles, but all he could think about was Patty.

"You said she's doing better," Sylvester reminded Bill, winking at the waitress walking by.

Bill nodded and sipped his beer. "She's awake now and jabbering like she used to."

"See, doctors don't know much," Sylvester huffed. "In fact, I say they're more wrong than they're right!"

Bill heard Sylvester's comment, but his gaze was still fixed across the bar. "The elders came and gave her a blessing," Bill mumbled before glancing at Sylvester.

Sylvester sighed and shook his head disapprovingly. "You could have told them no! You're the man of the house! Or have you forgotten?"

"No, I *haven't* forgotten," Bill glared. He sighed, gazed into his beer, then shrugged. "Maybe...maybe it helped."

73

"Ahhh, that's all nonsense. Just hocus-pocus, you know," Sylvester scoffed with a dismissive wave.

"Maybe the doctor was right," Bill said, still staring at his drink. "Maybe she would've died, but their blessing saved her?"

Sylvester shook his head and jabbed Bill in the shoulder with a finger. "Listen, fella, I ain't gonna drink with you no more if you're gonna get all holy on me. Got it?"

The jab stirred Bill from his trance, and he looked at his friend, embarrassed. He didn't tell Sylvester that the ladies from the church had been at his house most of the day helping Mildred with chores or that they had brought enough food to feed them for a week. Instead, Bill took a drink and tried to forget.

$\sim$

STOWAWAYS

Outside the Kane's front room window, long fingers of ice reached down from the eves toward the fresh blanket of snow. The sound of Mildred's hands dancing across the piano keys filled the warm and toasty air inside as the children played on the floor. Little Patty gently cradled her faded rag doll while Helen flipped through the worn pages of a Sears and Roebuck catalog, longingly eyeing the toys they could not afford. Bobby, who still had a few brown spots on his face from the measles, watched with great interest as the twins put the last of a second-hand electric train set together with their watchful father lying on the floor beside them.

"Careful. That's it," Bill directed, having already done most of the work.

"When can I play with the train?" whined Bobby.

"When you're older, like us," Alva said, his eyes never leaving the coal car he was coupling to the engine.

"Yeah, when you're older," Alma echoed, setting a passenger car in place.

Bobby sat back on his knees and sighed.

"Watching is the best part anyway," Bill said with a wink as he placed a passenger car on the track.

"Well, how come you're not watching, then?" frowned Bobby.

"Because they need my help," grinned Bill.

The two freckled twins gave each other a look but said nothing.

"Besides, I have lots of experience on trains."

"Did you work on trains too?" asked Bobby.

"No, I just rode 'em a lot. But I did work with track-layers one summer." Bill's brow gathered as he remembered the terrible day the man died under the train. He sighed and pushed the memory back to where he kept all of his unpleasant memories.

"Is that when you went to the fair?" asked Alma.

"Yep," grinned Bill.

"I don't remember that story. Is it a train story?" asked Bobby.

"Yep," nodded Bill.

"Will you tell me?" Bobby asked, sitting up.

"All right, let me think. That was a long time ago," Bill said, scratching his chin. "I must've been twelve. My friend Harry and I had saved up quite a lot from working on the steamer and decided to go to the state fair in Detroit. We made friends with a freight conductor, who told us we could ride in one of the empty boxcars…"

Summer 1908

YOUNG BILL'S eyes shot open at the sound of the boxcar's sliding door. "What? We're stopped?" he muttered as he sat up and ran a hand through his thick brown hair. It was dark inside the boxcar, and when a beam of light cut through the blackness, Bill wondered if he was still dreaming. His weary eyes followed the light until it met him squarely in the face. Winching and shielding his eyes, Bill turned to Harry, still asleep on the hard floor that smelled of motor oil and molasses.

"What 'cha boys doin' in here?" barked the voice behind the light. "Stowaways go to jail in my town, ya know. So, get your stuff and come on out. Let's go."

"We ain't stowaways, mister," Bill groaned, wincing as the light again blinded him. "The conductor said we could ride in here."

"You don't say. Come on! Hurry up, you two! I don't got all night. Get on out here!"

Bill gathered up his shoes and knapsack and pulled himself to his feet. "Honest, mister, the conductor said it was okay." As the beam moved to the stirring Harry, spilled light from the bicycle lantern glinted off the badge on the man's chest. *A deputy*, Bill sighed.

"You boys don't expect me to bite on that line, do ya? How old are ya anyhow?"

"Twelve," Bill answered, seeing no advantage in lying.

"Your folks know where you're at?" the deputy asked as the boys climbed out of the boxcar. "Or are ya runnin' away from home?"

"No, sir. We've been on the road all summer," Bill said proudly. "We're workin' men!"

"Is that so, now?" the deputy chuckled, the whites of his eyes just visible in the lantern light.

The brisk night air helped Bill come more to his senses, and the stumbling, half-awake Harry made him laugh.

"Get your shoes on. We got some walkin' to do," grunted the deputy as he pushed the boxcar door closed.

"Yes, sir," Bill said, stooping to tie his shoes. He noticed the deputy's potbelly and knew they could outrun him if Harry weren't still half asleep.

"You don't got nothin' in them bags you stole, now, do ya?" the deputy asked, eyeing their knapsacks.

"No, sir. They're all ours," Bill said, standing back up.

"You boys ain't from around these parts, are ya, now?" the deputy asked, tucking his thumb between his belly and pistol belt.

"No, sir. We're from Chicago," Bill answered, glimpsing the deputy's drooping eyes and saggy chin.

"Chicago! How in blazes did ya get here?"

"We were working on a steamer and got off in Petoskey," replied Bill.

"We're heading to the state fair," Harry explained, a little more awake now.

The pot-bellied deputy pushed up his hat and said, "You boys sure took the long way if you're comin' all the way down from Petoskey. Your parents know where you're at?"

"Yes, sir," Bill lied.

"We sent them a letter," Harry added.

"Well, at least you're closer to home. You sure you wanna go to Detroit now? That's a big city, ya know."

"Ain't no bigger than Chicago," Bill shrugged.

"There are a couple of escaped convicts on the loose. That's how I found you two, you know. But I don't suppose you're convicts, now, are ya?"

Bill had to think about the question as he had seen the inside of more than one jailhouse.

The deputy noticed Bill struggling with the question and, with a wry grin, asked, "It wasn't you that escaped from the Lansing State lockup, was it now?"

"No, sir," Harry answered as soberly as possible.

"Well, I didn't think as much. Still, you two need to be careful. Let's get you back to the station. I'll see if I can't round up a few tickets in the morning to get you back home. How does that sound?"

Bill glanced at Harry and said, "Well, mister, we really wanted to go to the fair."

"I can see that, and the fair's plenty fun, but it's just too far for you boys. I'm sure your folks are worried sick about 'cha. And I wouldn't be doin' my sworn duty if I let you go off now, would I? Not with those outlaws roaming about. So, come with me, and you'll be okay."

Bill sighed. "Well, I guess we are getting a little homesick."

Harry eyed Bill.

"I thought as much," replied the deputy as he turned and shuffled off with the lantern, lighting the way before them.

Bill's wink set Harry at ease, and the two followed behind.

"Now, let me see," started the deputy, his lantern swinging as he walked. "With it being early Sunday morning—about two, I s'pose—there won't be another train 'til Monday. But there's plenty you can do around the jailhouse, you know. You can get some shuteye, and well, the missus will probably have you go to church."

The deputy, who was expounding on the virtues of obeying the law, hadn't gone twenty yards when he paused and asked, "Say, boys. What are your names anyhow? You never told me."

After a few more steps, his heavy feet crunching on the gravel, the potbellied deputy turned back and asked again, "Boys, what are—" With hands on hips, the deputy shook his head when he saw he was alone.

"Do you think he'll follow us?" Harry whispered, looking back over his shoulder at the train tracks disappearing into the blackness.

"Are you kidding? With a belly like that, a fella don't walk any further than he has to," Bill replied as he looked up at the moon cresting above the trees and glistening off the leaves in the gentle breeze.

"What about the escaped convicts? What do we do if we run into them?"

"Aw, there ain't no escaped convicts," Bill sneered. "He was just sayin' that to scare us into followin' him."

"But...what if there are?" Harry asked with concern.

Bill thought for a moment, then said, "Well, I suppose we just talk to 'em and see what kind of trouble they're in."

"Convicts... Doesn't that scare you? I mean, just a little?"

"No. Not really," Bill answered with a casual shake of his head.

"What if they're wanted for robbin' a bank?"

"Then I suppose they'll want to give us some hush-up money. Fifty dollars, I figure. Each. That would keep us from tellin' the marshal."

"Hush-up money. Ya think?" Harry asked, looking at his friend sideways.

"Sure."

"What if they're murderers?" Harry asked, nervously eyeing the shadowy bushes and trees bordering the tracks.

"Murderers... Well, that would be a different story, I guess," Bill said, still considering the question. He turned to Harry and asked, "What would they want with us? We're just a couple of wanderin' kids."

Harry gulped. "Maybe they're wanted for killing wanderin' kids. Stowaways and the like."

"Now you're being silly," Bill huffed.

"You won't think I'm silly if they come up on us and hit us over the head!"

Bill gave Harry a sideways glance.

The two boys hadn't gone twenty feet when Bill lurched to a stop, his shoulders hunched and head cocked to the side. He pointed to the darkened underbrush to their left. "Did you hear that?" Bill whispered, the whites of his eyes glistening in the moonlight.

"What?" Harry gasped, eyeing rustling bushes across the tracks.

"Someone's over there," Bill whispered.

"Wh-wh-where?" Harry stammered.

"Right there. Right there in that shadow," Bill pointed as he backed away.

Harry stared breathlessly into the bushes, searching every shadow for an escaped convict.

"AHHH!" yelled Bill as he goosed Harry.

"AGGHHH!" cried Harry as he jumped in the air.

Bill doubled over with laughter as Harry, white as a ghost, his chest heaving and heart pounding, eyed Bill in disbelief. "Why'd you do that?" Harry shrieked. "You could've stopped my heart right there!"

"Sorry," Bill laughed, wiping away his tears.

"What if that marshal heard you?"

"Are you kidding? He's miles back there."

"What about the escaped convicts? What if they heard?"

"You don't really believe that, do you?" Bill sneered. "That was just a story to scare us. There ain't no convicts out here."

"You don't think?" Harry asked, his eyes still wide.

"Naw."

Harry eyed the dark bushes on either side then said, "You know, you didn't have to scare me like that."

"Sorry," Bill chuckled. "But it was pretty funny."

"You'll think it's funny when I get you back."

Not much was said the next half mile as the two boys walked along the railroad tracks, the wind gently rustling the trees and the moon gliding in and out from behind clouds.

After coming to a bend, Bill's eyes followed the outline of the tracks until they disappeared into the darkness. He was about to tell Harry how hungry he was, eating nothing but apples since leaving Lansing, when he noticed an orange glow in the shadows forty yards ahead. Bill first thought it was a firefly, but the glow dimmed and lowered before fading away.

As the two boys continued along the tracks, Bill searched the darkness for the strange orange glow. He was about to dismiss his concerns when he spotted the glow again, thirty feet ahead. This time, Bill knew what it was: the glow of a cigarette. "Did you see that?" he whispered, grabbing Harry's sleeve as he stopped.

"Oh, nuh-uh. Fool me once, shame on you; fool me twice—"

"No, I mean it," Bill breathed, his eyes wide and fixed.

"You must think I'm a real stooge, don't ya?" Harry huffed.

Bill's hold on Harry tightened at the sound of a shoe sliding across rock ten feet closer than the glowing cigarette. "Ain't it a little late for you boys to be out?"

Harry's head spun to the voice as a man stepped partly out of the shadows, twenty feet ahead. "Marshall?" Harry breathed.

"I told you," Bill whispered.

"What-what do we do?" Harry gulped.

"I don't know. Keep going, I guess," Bill muttered.

While Harry sometimes questioned Bill's instincts, he followed when Bill resumed walking along the track. The two boys were nearly parallel with the shadowed man when Bill saw the fiery glow of the cigarette in the hand of another man, six feet away.

"There's two of them!" Harry gasped.

A lump formed in Bill's throat when a large man holding a glowing cigarette stepped out of the blackness. "Where you boys from?" he asked in a raspy voice before taking another drag from his cigarette.

Bill saw the dark, recessed eyes of the man still in the shadows and mouthed the word "*Run*," but no sound came out. When the glow of the burning tobacco illuminated the scars on the man's craggy face and the stripes on his prison uniform, Bill cried, "RUN!"

While Harry was a fast runner, Bill pulled away from his friend with his feet barely touching the ground.

"Hey, come back here, you kids!" barked the convict as he threw his cigarette down and chased after the boys, with the second man following behind.

Running as fast as he could, Bill glanced back at Harry, ten feet back, with the two men quickly closing. "Run, Harry! Cross the tracks!" Bill gasped, his feet flying from one tie to the next as he angled across the tracks. Harry was right behind him.

The two convicts were quickly gaining on the boys, but when the leader tried to cross the tracks, he tripped and flew headfirst into a thick wooden tie. The second man, running right behind, attempted to hurdle the first but was upended by a flinging leg and cartwheeled across the gravel.

Bill heard the tumble behind them and looked back to see the convicts rolling in pain. "Ha-ha!" Bill cried, stopping to point in ridicule, but when the second man angrily climbed to his feet, ran a few steps toward them yelling and cursing, then collapsed again, Bill yelled, "MARSHAL, WE FOUND 'EM!" as he and Harry disappeared into the night.

"Wow! Did the marshal catch 'em?" Alva asked; the work on the train set stopped.

"We didn't stick around. We went on to the fair," grinned Bill.

"Can we go to the fair?" Helen asked, still in front of her catalog.

"Sure, we will. This summer," nodded Mildred. She watched the boys play with the train for a moment, then got up from the piano. She paused when she noticed their landlady walking up their snow-packed walk. "Billy, Mrs. Echles is coming to the door."

Bill's brow gathered. "The landlady? You paid the rent, didn't you?"

"Of course," Mildred answered as the knock came. With some concern, she stepped around the train set to the front door and pulled it open. A rush of cold air flooded the room as the thin, wrinkle-faced woman wearing a fur hat and coat and too much makeup stepped inside.

"Hello, Mrs. Echles," Bill said, getting to his feet. "What can we do for you this fine Saturday morning?"

"You received our rent money?" Mildred asked, with the children lined up behind her.

"Yes, I received it," the stern-faced landlady nodded. Ignoring the children, she turned to Bill and said, "I'm afraid I have some bad news."

"Bad news?" Bill asked, his brow gathered.

"Yes. I have sold this house. I'm sorry, but the new owners will be moving in the first of February."

"The first of the month?" Bill repeated, aghast.

"Yes, that's right," the wrinkle-faced woman firmly nodded. "I'll need you out the week before."

"That only gives us two weeks to find a new place and move," Bill protested.

"I'm sorry. There wasn't any other way."

"But we're paid through the end of the month!" Mildred exclaimed.

"And you'll get that back, assuming everything is in order," the old woman said, glancing at the children.

"Mother, do we have to move?" asked Bobby.

Bill raised a quieting hand, then turned to the landlady and asked, "Was it something we did?"

The landlady paused, looked at the five children, and said, "No, the house simply sold. That's all."

"I didn't know it was for sale," Bill grunted.

"You have two weeks. Good day." The landlady turned and went back out through the door, again flooding the room with a chill.

Bill watched the door close, then turned to Mildred, who looked as though she might cry. Filled with frustration, he walked to the coat rack and donned his heavy coat and hat.

"Where are you going, Billy?" Mildred asked, her voice filled with emotion. "Not to Pengilly's for a drink, I hope! We need to talk about this!"

Bill looked sadly at the children, then turned to Mildred and, with a shrug, said, "What is there to talk about? I'm going to find a new place to live."

~

DOWN BY THE RIVER

*M*ildred and the children were finishing their dinner when Bill finally came home. Getting up from her seat, she saw it was half-past-seven as she served up her husband's bowl of potato and ham soup. Mildred glanced at Bill as he entered the kitchen, his hair matted from his hat, his brow tight, and eyes tired. Helen pointed at her father's hair and laughed, but Alma and Alva recognized his mood and kept their eyes in their bowls.

"We waited for nearly an hour, but I went ahead and fed—"

"That's fine," Bill grunted. He took his place at the head of the table, and Mildred placed the bowl of soup and a half sleeve of saltines before him.

"How was work?" Mildred asked out of habit as she sat beside him.

"Long and cold," Bill muttered as he crushed crackers into his soup.

Mildred wanted to ask how Pengilly's was but knew that would only make matters worse. Instead, she turned to Patty, noisily playing with an uneaten potato chunk, took away her bowl, and helped her down. Bill was quietly eating with his head hanging when Mildred said, "Children, run along and play or finish your studies."

Helen had picked up on their father's sour mood and quietly followed the other children out of the kitchen.

With the warm food taking the edge off, a still frustrated Bill sighed, then turned to Mildred and said, "It's been three days now, and I haven't found a thing we can afford."

Mildred's brow raised. *Maybe he didn't go to Pengilly's.* "You've been looking for a house?"

"Of course, I have."

"What have you found?"

Bill gave an irritable sigh. "I just said they're all too expensive or too small." He glanced at Mildred's just-showing belly and swallowed some of his anger.

"We can make do with a smaller house," said Mildred.

"Smaller than this?" Bill scoffed. "I don't think so."

Mildred placed a loving hand on his and said, "Thank you for looking. You'll find something. I know you will."

Bill sighed. "I don't know what. There's nowhere else to look."

"Have you looked down by the river? In that new area?"

Bill's brow furrowed. "You mean down by the slaughterhouse?"

"Yes. There are homes there, aren't there?"

"Well, yes, but they're by the slaughterhouse. The stench from the cattle in the summer must be horrible."

"It's worth a try. Will you look there tomorrow?"

Bill shrugged. "I doubt there will be anything there."

"Please? Will you check anyway, just for me? We don't have much more time."

Bill sighed. "Fine. I'll check."

MILDRED and the children had just sat down for another late dinner waiting for Bill when they heard the front door open and the excited yap of a dog.

"What on earth!" Mildred exclaimed as she got up from her seat and was greeted by an eager pup who rushed from one child to the next.

"A dog!" Bobby exclaimed as Patty watched with giant eyes.

"Can we keep him?" Helen pleaded as the twins' faces lit up.

"Where did you come from?" Mildred asked as the short-haired pup jumped up to her knees.

"Can we keep him? *Please?*" the kids pleaded in unison.

"It's a *she!*" Bill beamed as he entered the kitchen. "And yes, you can!"

"What?" Mildred asked in dismay as she picked up the squirming pup, its tongue licking at her frantically.

"Well, we're gonna need a dog in our new house," Bill shrugged.

"You found a house?" Mildred gasped, the pup still licking her.

"Yes, it's perfect! It has seven rooms and a cellar, a large garden spot, a place for our chickens, and even a spot for a milk cow! There's a barn in the back and even some fruit trees! You gotta have a dog with a home like that!" exclaimed Bill, giving Mildred a wink.

"Yay!" the children cried.

"But best of all, the rent is only fifteen dollars a month!" Bill said proudly.

"Where is it?" Mildred asked, setting the bouncing pup down before the excited children.

Bill turned to Mildred, sighed, and then said, "It's down by the river on Madison Avenue. Right where you said."

"You went and looked!"

"Yup."

A beaming Mildred embraced Bill.

"Yay! We have a dog!" cried Helen. "Can I name her?"

"I don't see why not," Bill replied as he smiled at Mildred.

"I'm gonna call her Trixie and teach her lots of tricks!" cried Helen.

"That's a dumb name!" Alma said, waiting for Alva to follow, but he said nothing.

"Trixie, it is," Bill said, still grinning at Mildred.

SHE'S NOT CRAZY

It was a snowy February morning. Wispy snowflakes floated down through the gray sky to the white-blanketed earth as the bundled-up milkman made his daily rounds.

Inside the Kane's new warm and toasty home by the river, six-year-old Helen plinked out a melody on the old upright piano as Mildred swept the floor.

Their new home was everything Mildred had hoped for. Its roomy kitchen, sturdy cabinets, cast iron sink, and Majestic wood-burning range made Mildred's countless hours of food preparation easier. And with two stories, a cellar, and a large yard, it gave their growing family plenty of room. To top it all off, its low rent was ideal for their tight financial situation, which was a constant worry to Mildred. But the house wasn't perfect. Though less than ten years old, it was already in disrepair, and its shake-shingles needed a fresh coat of paint. Its low-rent location meant a twenty-minute walk into town, which was an inconvenience, especially on a cold winter day. On the upside, the butcher shop and a string of sausages or a rump roast were only a block away.

With school canceled and all five children at home, Mildred's burden was no lighter. Not yet eleven o'clock, Mildred had already been working five hours. After getting herself ready, cooking breakfast, getting Bill off to work, baking six loaves of bread, and now cleaning, she hoped there might be time for a nap after lunch, but with it being a wash day, she doubted she would get any rest.

Mildred was sweeping out from under the front room table when she heard the milkman making his daily delivery. After emptying her dustpan and returning the broom to its closet, Mildred pulled open the front door and pushed open the screen to retrieve the fresh quarts of milk. To her surprise, she saw only one bottle where there were usually two. *That won't get us through dinner, let alone tomorrow's breakfast!* Mildred thought as a cold gust cut through her housedress and apron and brought on a shiver. She was about to gather up the lone bottle when she noticed the depression in the fresh snow where the second quart had been. *What the dickens?* Mildred's eyes shot up at the sound of laughing children walking up the street. No stranger to mischief, she strained her nearsighted eyes until she spotted one carrying her missing quart of milk. "Oh! Those little rascals! Stealing my milk! They're not going to get away with that!"

After hastily pulling the front door closed, Mildred made her way down the slippery steps and chased after the children, shouting, "Stop, you kids! Put that bottle of milk down this instant, do you hear?"

Forty yards up the street, the three bundled children paused at the echoing command. A boy in a red hat and scarf looked back to see the coat-less woman chasing after them through the snowstorm, her feet slipping and arms flailing like a drunken pelican trying to take flight. Startled by the sight, the boy's legs flew out from under him, landing him hard on the snowy street. The two other boys, one short with fogged glasses and the other taller with earmuffs, laughed and pointed at their fallen friend before seeing the arm-waving and shrieking Mildred charging at them. Startled by the sight, the boy with the glasses stooped to help his fallen friend while the tall one turned and ran. The red-scarfed boy's eyes darted from the approaching crazy woman to his foggy-eyed friend. He was scarcely back on his feet when the other boy slipped and fell, yanking him back down to the icy street with him.

Mildred was just twenty feet away when the two slipping and falling children finally got to their feet and scampered off. "Wait! You bring that milk back this instant!" Mildred cried as her feet slipped out from under her. Her frightful shriek abruptly ended as she landed hard on her back. Gasping for air, Mildred found herself looking up into the gray sky at the swirling snow. "Ohhhh," she groaned. When Mildred remembered her milk, she rolled to her side in the snow, raised her arm, and called out, "You bring that milk back this instant!"

Upon seeing the little thieves would not be caught, Mildred painfully climbed to her feet, slipping twice before gaining her balance. She dejectedly wiped the snow from off her dress and started back to her house, her breath puffing in the wintry morning air.

By the time the beaten Mildred gathered up her lone quart of milk and went inside, she was cold, wet, and shivering.

"Mommy, why were you chasing after them kids?" Six-year-old Helen asked as Mildred angrily placed the quart in the refrigerator.

With snow still in her hair, Mildred turned and was about to expound on the evils of thievery when she noticed a mostly full quart of milk on the table beside Alma. "Where did you get that milk?" she gasped.

"On the front porch," Alma shrugged.

Mildred eyed the milk bottle blankly, trying to understand. "When?"

"Right before you went chasin' after them kids."

"Oh no," Mildred groaned, realizing what she had done.

Mildred was rubbing her sore back when Bobby rushed into the kitchen, yelling, "Mommy! Mommy!"

"What now?"

"Here comes a boy with a big stick!" Bobby exclaimed. "And he looks plenty mad!"

"What?" Hearing a loud rap at the door, Mildred pushed past Bobby into the front room. Uneasily approaching the door, she was startled when the twins rushed to her side. After glancing down at Alva's frightened face, Mildred opened the door to a boy, older than the ones she had chased, glaring at her from the front porch with a large stick in hand. "May I help you?" she asked, warily eyeing the fuming eleven-year-old.

"Don't scare my little brothers!" he yelled, his stick twitching.

Mildred felt the twins clutching at her skirt and laughed nervously. "Oh, I'm afraid there's been a misunderstanding," she blushed. "You see, I thought they made off with one of my bottles of milk, and... I'm sorry," she sighed, "I hope I didn't frighten them too much."

The boy's glare softened, and he lowered his stick. "They said a crazy woman in a nightdress was chasin' em for their meat."

"*Oh*, that's what I saw. They had just come from the butcher," she said, shaking her head. "Please tell them I'm sorry," she added, the twins still buried in her skirt.

"Well, I guess it's okay," the boy said, backing off the porch. "You don't seem too crazy."

"Oh, thank you," Mildred said, before closing the door. She tiredly sighed, then turned to a wide-eyed Bobby and a grinning Helen. After guiding Alma and Alva out from her skirt, she shook her head, laughed, and then resumed her labors.

$\sim$

BY THE TIME Bill returned from work, Mildred had finished her cleaning, baking, and washing, walked to and from town with groceries, and made chicken and dumplings.

With Patty crying in her highchair and Bobby banging his spoon on the table, Mildred was dishing up soup from a large pot when Bill entered the kitchen. "Billy, how was your day?" she asked, forcing a smile.

"Long and cold. The storm took out a lot of lines," Bill grumbled as he pulled out his chair. "You don't know how good you got it working in a nice, warm house."

Mildred clenched the ladle over the pot as she drew a haggard breath. After filling Bill's bowl, she dutifully placed it before him and went back for more.

"And to top it all off," Bill continued, shaking his head, "that damn—" he glanced at the children, "that darn car wouldn't start!"

"Let me guess, you had to walk to Pengilly's after work," Mildred said, trying to hold her tongue.

"No," Bill said with a dismissive wave, "I'm late 'cause that darn car wouldn't start! I think it's a problem with the coil. It's about as reliable as a...as a...well, it's just not reliable!"

"Maybe you should buy a new one, Daddy," Helen said as Mildred set a bowl before her.

"You know, sweetheart, I think you just might have something there," grinned Bill.

Mildred turned to Bill in dismay. "No, Billy! We don't have the money!" she blurted, before bursting into tears.

All eyes were on Mildred as she buried her face in her apron and rushed out of the kitchen.

"What's wrong with Mommy?" Helen asked, looking as though she might cry herself.

Bill turned to the still crying Patty, then to the twins, and asked, "Okay, what did you two do?"

"We didn't do anything," Alma and Alva said in unison.

"Well, why's your mother so upset?"

"Today a boy came to the door with a big stick," Bobby said, waving his spoon in the air. "He was mad but left 'cause Mama's not crazy."

"What?" Bill frowned in confusion.

"She's not crazy," Helen shrugged.

Bill shook his head and got up from the table. Starting after Mildred, he paused in the doorway and said, "Boys, one of you finish dishing up the food, and the other take care of Patty."

"What about the blessing?" Alma asked.

"You say it," Bill said as he turned and left.

On his way to their bedroom, Bill wondered what to say. Mildred was, at times, emotional, but mostly as stable and dependable as the rising sun, and her breakdown came as a complete surprise to him. Gently pushing open the bedroom door, he saw Mildred lying on their bed, sobbing. Bill scratched his head, pushed the door closed behind him, and moved beside her. He watched helplessly as her shoulders trembled in her sobbing. Uncertain of what to do or say, Bill sat at the foot of the bed and searchingly asked, "Is everything okay?"

Mildred offered a weak nod, which Bill took as an excuse to leave, but then her sobbing resumed, and she shook her head.

"Well, what does that mean?" Bill asked, confused.

Red-faced and tear-streaked, Mildred sat up and looked at him directly. "Do you know how hard my days are?"

"Watching the kids?" Bill asked innocently.

Mildred gave a tearful laugh. "*Watching the kids?* That's not all I do! Besides, it takes at least three people to watch *these kids!* I don't tell you what happens when you're at work because I don't want to add to your burden!"

"What do you mean?" Bill asked, his brow gathered.

"What do I mean?" gasped Mildred, beside herself. "The other day, when I came back from town, do you know what I found? A house full of chickens! The children decided it was too cold for the chickens outside in the henhouse, so they brought them all in! Do you know how much mess ten chickens and a rooster can make in an hour?"

"No," Bill muttered, his brow raised.

"A lot!" Mildred exclaimed, both angry and relieved by her venting. "Last week, the metropolitan nurse came to visit. She sat on the nice couch and asked me all kinds of questions to make sure our kids were eating right and that I was a fit mother. Right in the middle of that, the children trooped into the front room with their faces all painted black, like some minstrel show! The nurse left thinking we run a circus here, I'm sure of it! I've never been so embarrassed! And just today," Mildred continued, laughing away the tears, "I chased three boys down the street for stealing a bottle of milk off our porch, only they didn't steal it! Alma brought it in when I wasn't looking. I chased them down the street in the middle of a snowstorm and fell right on my backside! Twice! If that wasn't enough, their older brother came to the door with a stick, ready to whip the crazy lady who scared his little brother. I'm just glad they didn't call the sheriff!"

Bill helplessly watched as Mildred fought away the tears. He had no idea her days were so hard. Swallowing, Bill slid closer and gently stroked her arm. "Is everything okay with the baby?" he asked.

Mildred nodded.

"Is it too much walking to town? I told you, I'd teach you how to drive."

Mildred tearfully scoffed at the notion and said, "Can't you just see me driving down the icy street in a car? I can't even walk down it. I'm far too irresponsible for such a thing!"

Bill swallowed, then asked, "What do you want me to do?"

Mildred at first shrugged but then said softly, "You can help me."

"Help you?" Bill asked, pulling back at the words.

"Billy, I try to pay the bills every month, but…sometimes there's just not enough to go around. We're scraping the bottom every month, and when you talk about going into more debt, it's just too much."

"Oh, it's about money," Bill groaned. "When old man McCracken promised me a raise, how was I to know it would only be ten cents?"

"Billy, I know you're working hard," Mildred said tenderly.

Bill sighed. "Yeah, I know, but it's not enough," he said, not in a hurt sort of way, but more in realization. He gently wiped away one of Mildred's tears, then, looking past her in thought, muttered, "I suppose I can get another job."

"Billy, I realize you haven't always gotten along with John, but he's a good man," Mildred said, studying Bill. "He has some Saturday work. He's already offered."

Bill sighed. While he had had his differences with his brother-in-law, he thought John Young was a good, honest man. After a moment's consideration, Bill turned to Mildred and, with pride stinging, said, "Ok. I'll talk to him and see what he has."

Mildred smiled warmly and embraced Bill. "I know it's a sacrifice, but it will be worth it. We'll still have Sundays and the evenings together."

"Except when you and the kids go to church," Bill muttered.

"You can come with us, you know," Mildred whispered. "Then we'll be together still."

Bill's eyes met Mildred's, but he said nothing.

I'LL TAKE YOU HOME AGAIN

*I*t was late April in Boise. The snow was gone except on the mountains, and the last of the cherry blossoms were clinging to their branches. While the early mornings were still cold, Bill thought the days were perfect for working outdoors on the power lines during the week and on John Young's construction projects on Saturdays.

While not part of his brother-in-law's regular crew, Bill was determined not to let any of the full-time employees outwork him. Bill had pushed himself hard the eight weeks he had been on the job, and his skills as a laborer had grown—so had his regard for John.

While Bill carried some resentment toward his brother-in-law when he first started working, John had no such feelings for Bill, who he found to be a hard and dependable worker quick to solve problems.

It didn't take long for Bill's attitude toward his part-time employer to change. Bill quickly learned he had misjudged John, whose honest and principled behavior stood in stark contrast to some of his coworkers at the power company, such as his cynical friend, Sylvester Schmig. The rivalry Bill once felt was now replaced by gratitude and respect.

"Well, that should do it," John said as he slid his hammer back into his belt. While John spoke softly, he wasn't afraid to let his workers know if they were in the wrong.

"Is it already five?" Bill asked, about to hammer a nail.

"No, not quite, but it's a good place to stop. Go spend time with your family. You fellas too," John nodded to the two other workers.

Bill hammered in the last two nails, then climbed off his ladder.

"I appreciate your help, Bill," John said as he gathered his tools.

"Well, I appreciate the work," Bill nodded. "It's a good change of pace. Sometimes the guys at work…" he paused, searching for the right word. "Sometimes they're kind of harsh, if you know what I mean?"

John nodded.

"Thanks, boss," called out a thick-shouldered man in bib overalls.

"You're welcome, Al. See you Monday," John waved as the other two workers walked off.

Bill was sweeping up a pile of sawdust when John slid a trashcan before him and said, "Can I ask you a question?"

"Sure," Bill shrugged.

"You've been working Saturdays for a couple of months now and know all about Al and Ben. All about their past and their families, but you never talk about yours."

Bill paused, then said, "I guess there's not much to talk about. Plus, they don't leave much room."

"That's true," John nodded. Then his dark brows gathered, and he said, "Only, I'm your brother-in-law, and I don't know that much about you, other than you grew up in Chicago, spent time in the Philippines in the Army, and are good at baseball."

"I don't think you want to get me started on baseball; we'll be here all night," chuckled Bill.

John grinned, then grew serious again and asked, "What about growing up? What about your family? Do you have brothers and sisters?"

Bill straightened up and shrugged. "I did, but lost touch after I joined the Army. They were gone when I went back after the war."

"Oh. Sorry to hear that." John pulled off his hat and ran a hand through his thick hair. "What are their names?"

Bill sighed. "I had two brothers. Hubert was the oldest, then Thomas. We called him Doc 'cause he was smart. I had a sister, Iliene. There were two others that died as babies. I was the youngest. I never wrote home after I joined up. See, I was underage and lied about my name."

"Oh. Sounds like you were ready to get out on your own."

"I don't know if I'd call the Army 'on my own.'"

"No," said John.

Bill shook his head. "I don't know. Part of me was glad to be gone and didn't want to look back. But I think I was also afraid the Army would find out and kick me out."

"I see. You went by another name. 'Pete,' wasn't it?"

"That's right," Bill said with an embarrassed laugh. "Pete Carberry,"

"So, you haven't talked to your family since? When was that?"

Bill sighed. "I joined up in 1914."

"Fourteen years," John said, eyeing Bill. "What about your folks?"

Bill sighed. "My mother died when I was four. I don't remember much about her. Little things here and there."

"What about your pa?"

Bill looked down and shook his head. "He died too."

"I'm sorry," John said, sensing Bill's discomfort with the subject. "It musta been hard growing up without a ma."

Bill shrugged. He didn't enjoy discussing such things, but somehow John's interest made him feel better. "It was hard," Bill finally nodded. "My friends all had mothers. I watched them and knew I was missing something —something that would have made me better."

John nodded, then said, "You turned out okay," patting Bill's back.

"I wonder," Bill muttered, his mind still pondering the void in his life. He thought of his friends' mothers, of the love they showed and the direction they provided, and wondered how different his life would have been had his mother lived—had God not taken her from him at such a young age. There were substitutes, he recalled—women who tried to fill in, such as the nuns at his school, but they were not the same.

"You know, it's funny," Bill said, shaking his head. "The first time I really felt a mother's love—that I remember, anyway—was when I was in the Philippines."

"You don't say. Who was that?"

"Her name was Marga. She was a little Filipino grandmother, but I'd never met anyone like her. She fed us lots, and we talked about all sorts of things," Bill said distantly. "She was special."

"Sounds like she was a good mother."

Bill nodded as he placed his tools in the back of John's truck.

"All right. Next week then?"

"Yes. Thank you," Bill said, shaking hands with John.

Bill's mind was still in the past as he got in his car. He thought back to the day he and his friend Joe Slaton met Marga while patrolling the barrios not far from their post. Bill remembered the warm, musty smell of the jungle, her worn chairs, and how good her English was, having once worked as a housekeeper for an English family. He remembered the savory pork she fed them that first night as she spoke of her beloved land and gave thanks for the Americans liberating her country from the oppressive Spaniards. She talked of the Filipino rebels, who had been a problem since the Americans had arrived, and explained their desire for total freedom. Bill recalled marveling as she spoke of her people's customs and how their culture had changed under Spanish rule.

The memory seemed like another life to him now—Peter Carberry's life...

April 1915

WITH DARKNESS FALLEN, Bill knew it was time for them to return to Fort McKinley, but he didn't want to leave the little Filipino grandmother.

After pouring them each a cup of tea, the kind old woman went back to her seat and said, "I have talked far too much. I want to hear more about each of you. Peter, tell me about your family."

"There's not much to tell," Bill shrugged.

"Tell me what Chicago is like," the old woman warmly insisted.

"Well..." Bill started, eyeing the ground. "Chicago is a big city... I don't know what to tell."

"What things did you like to do there?"

"Play ball," Bill said with certainty.

"Baseball?"

"Yes."

"Do you play for your army team here?"

"Yes, I do," Bill replied, perking up even more.

"I should like to come and watch you play, then. Do you also play, Joe?" Marga asked.

"No, ma'am. Not as good as Pete, anyhow."

Marga turned back to Bill. "Peter, tell me about your family."

The coziness Bill had felt slipped away. "My family?"

"Yes. What of your father? What does he do?"

Bill glanced at Joe in uncertainty. "Well," Bill gulped and stared into the fire. "My father...he worked at a department store in downtown Chicago. It was a big store. We used to visit him there. He managed their carpet department."

"Carpet," Marga said with a reminiscent gleam. "That is one thing I *do* miss. I have rugs, but carpet, filling an entire room. *That* is a luxury. What does he do now?"

Bill sighed. "He's passed on. He died a few years back."

"Oh, I'm terribly sorry," Marga groaned, moving her hand across her chest in a cross. "And your mother?" she asked searchingly.

"She died when I was four," Bill whispered.

"Oh, Peter. I am so sorry." Marga moved to Bill and embraced him.

Bill's eyes filled with tears. He bit his lip and looked away as he blinked them gone.

Marga sat on a chair beside Bill and, with a loving gaze, looked into his desolate eyes and said, "Peter, we all feel pain in our lives. It's okay to feel that pain—to feel that loss for your mother and father. God works in mysterious ways. Sometimes he takes people from us, and we must learn to go on without them. If we let it, we can grow from it." She stroked his cheek, then said, "I know it has been hard for you, but someday you will see this all had a purpose."

SITTING IN HIS FORD, Bill half saw John Young motor off. His mind was still on Marga. He wondered if she was still alive. Bill didn't know how many times he and Joe visited the loving Filipino grandmother, but each time he experienced a little of what God had deprived him of.

At thirty-two, Bill had seen and done more than most twice his age, but he still felt an inner smoldering rage, and didn't know why. He guessed it had to do with his mother dying, but didn't like to dwell on it too much. Bill sometimes wondered how different his life would be had she lived—had God not taken her. They were thoughts he had worked hard to push aside, but sitting inside his old Ford, Bill allowed the thoughts to grow. As they did, so did a sense of despair and the plaguing notion his life had been forever altered and broken at the hands of death.

Bill pushed the questions away. He knew people who spent their lives feeling sorry for themselves. *They're pathetic. Thinking about what might have been will do me no better,* he told himself as he lit a cigarette and put the car into gear. But his thoughts returned to his mother.

As Bill drove, his mind stretched back to his farthest memories. He could just see the outline of his mother's features, her dark hair and eyes that seemed sad even when smiling. It was a memory tied to his lone photograph of her. Bill could hear his mother's sweet, comforting voice in his mind. It was an amalgam of all the kind women he had ever known. As a boy, Bill once asked his father about her, and he longingly told him of her beauty and kindness. He then sang Bill a song, choking on the words. It was a song Bill had never forgotten. As Bill drove, he first hummed and then sang the song aloud:

> I'll take you home again, Kathleen
> Across the ocean wild and wide
> To where your heart has ever been
> Since you were first my bonnie bride.
> The roses all have left your cheek,
> I've watched them fade away and die
> Your voice is sad when e'er you speak.
> And tears bedim your loving eyes.
> Oh! I will take you back, Kathleen
> To where your heart will feel no pain
> And when the fields are fresh and green
> I'll take you to your home again
> There all your grief will be forgotten.

OBSERVE THE TIME

*B*ill felt all eyes on him as he pulled up to the Boise Tabernacle in his old black Ford with his wife and five children packed inside. If the car's sputtering engine and billowing gray exhaust were not enough to draw attention, there was a fourteen-inch white question mark Bill had painted on the back window, as if to shame the unreliable clunker.

After climbing out of the car, Bill closed the door and gave a feeble wave and nod to the passing church-goers. On the other side, Mildred and the children, also dressed in their Sunday best, piled out of the dusty old car. As the children gathered around a very pregnant Mildred for a final look-over, Bill glanced down at his tired gray suit. It was the same suit he wore the day he met Mildred, nine years before, and had grown tight around the waist.

While Bill attended church with his family on Christmas and Easter and sometimes in-between, he still felt uncomfortable and something of a spectacle when there. "Here comes the Catholic married to the nice Mormon woman with all the kids," Bill imagined them saying. The truth of the matter was, the members there were always friendly to him, sometimes too friendly, and it made Bill wonder what they said about him on the weeks he didn't attend. He once attended two Sundays in a row just to see if they could keep it up, and they did.

Following Mildred and the children toward the red-bricked church, Bill paid no attention to the sour-faced jostling of the seven-year-old twins, dressed, as always, in matching suits and ties.

"I don't want to hear another thing about it," said Mildred with a scolding glance.

"But we don't want to look the same anymore!" Alva whined.

"You're twins, and that's that!" Mildred snapped. "You'll always look the same!"

"But do we have to always *dress* the same?" groaned Alma.

"Hush up now. We don't want to be late for church," glared Mildred, taking Patty by the hand.

As Bill started up the front steps, his gaze remained fixed on the tabernacle's stately white pediment and columns rising into the blue June sky. While he had been to this church before, it somehow appeared different to him now. It reminded him of another church. It wasn't the grand cathedral in Chicago—that building was far more spectacular, or even the humbler, but still impressive St. Edmund's near his home in Oak Park. It was another church—its bell tower, actually. Suddenly it came to him: it was St. Mary's in San Francisco. He remembered passing the red brick church as a young Army private before leaving for the Philippines, but it was the placard below the bell tower clock that teased his memory. *What did it say?*

"Billy, are you coming?" Mildred asked, her eyes already tired from her day's work.

"Yes," muttered Bill, still trying to remember.

As the Kane family walked up the steps and entered the foyer with Bill at the rear, the smiling face of Brother Beaumont, a counselor to the bishop, greeted them. "Good afternoon, Sister Kane," he said with an outstretched hand.

"Good afternoon," Mildred replied as Brother Beaumont stooped and shook Patty's hand, causing her to blush. One by one, the rest of the family trooped by, first the twins, then Bobby and Helen. "Hello there, Brother Kane," Brother Beaumont said, giving Bill a firm handshake. "Wonderful to have you here."

"Thank you," was all Bill said, wondering how many other eyes were on him.

As Bill followed his family down the aisle with a reverent hymn filling the air, another shadowed memory came to light. In Bill's mind, he saw people standing and watching him walk down an aisle. He was wearing a blue coat and knickers. It was twenty-four years earlier at St. Edmund's in Oak Park. It was Bill's first communion. He knew these people watching him. In his mind, he saw his Uncle John and Aunt Rosanna. Beside them stood his father. Bill remembered his father's proud eyes that day. It was something the mischievous Bill rarely saw. He wanted to look at his father more, but his memory traveled forward instead. He saw the priest in all of his robes beckoning him with a welcoming smile, the resurrection crucifix and altar behind him. Bill took a step closer, and then the memory was gone.

Bill looked up the aisle to the front of the chapel. There was a painting of a living Jesus Christ on the wall behind the podium, but there was no altar and no cross. While a part of him missed the ornateness of the Catholic churches he had occasioned, the church he was in now felt simple and focused.

After slipping into the pew with his family, Bill looked around the congregation and pretended not to notice the nod of Bishop Gilmore from the stand. He listened as the organ music stopped and the bishop, wearing only a humble suit, stood and spoke to the congregation.

Bill half-listened as his mind traveled back to the cathedral in San Francisco. *What was it the sign said?*

Bill remembered that day. He was waiting for their troopship to depart and had walked back to the church in search of answers...

September 1914

BILL PUSHED up his broad-brimmed campaign hat and eyed the red-bricked St. Mary's Cathedral. Standing across the street in his mustard green uniform, Bill looked uneasily at the church's open front door. The cathedral had been on his mind since his company had marched past the day before, and Bill recognized this was his last chance to have his questions answered and his spirit calmed before leaving for the Philippines.

Bill noted the time on the giant belfry clock. He had less than an hour. His anxious gaze lowered to the large bronze placard below the clock and the inscribed words: SON, OBSERVE THE TIME AND FLY FROM EVIL. He wondered if the words had some deeper meaning for him. *Why am I even here?*

Bill stared at the open door for a long while before finally crossing the street. After ascending the steps, he removed his hat and paused as he tried to see into the darkened sanctuary. Gulping, Bill stepped inside, moved to one of the vacant pews, and sat down. His gaze shifted to the altar, then rose to the towering mural of Mary surrounded by cherubs. He thought of his mother, who shared the same name. After a moment, he turned to the corner shrine, where the glow of candles danced and flickered off the dark paneled wall. It reminded him of the day his mother died and left him with a sinking feeling in his chest. He looked back at the painting of Mary and wondered if angels now surrounded his mother.

Pained by thoughts of his past and questions unanswered, Bill stood and turned back toward the entrance. Part of him wanted to leave. Religion had done nothing for him in his short life, and he wondered why he was wasting his time in a church while his buddies were exploring the town. But another part of Bill told him to stay.

Bill shielded his eyes from the harsh light of the outside world as a cloaked figure opened a confessional door and disappeared inside. *Maybe he can answer my questions.* A shudder of doubt ran through Bill as he slowly stepped toward the confessional. He hesitated as he looked at the screen through which he would address the priest. Bill didn't hear his anxious breathing or feel his chest swelling as he considered what he should do. In just a few hours, he would be leaving all that he knew. Talking to the priest would do him no harm, he told himself.

Bill glanced back at the harsh light of the outside world and then kneeled before the screen. After making a cross, his hand slow and uncertain, he said, "Bless me, Father, for I have sinned. It's been…a long time since my last confession." Bill was not sure what to say next.

"Yes, what are your sins, my son?" came a velvety voice through the screen.

Bill hesitated. "I don't know…"

"Why don't you start with the most recent," the priest said, his voice smooth and calm.

"I-I don't have that much time."

"Why are you here?" asked the priest.

"I'm in the Army. We're waiting for our ship to leave for the Philippines."

"No, my son. Why are you here speaking to me? Is it to clear your conscious before you leave?"

Bill shook his head. "No, not really."

"There must be a reason."

Bill sighed.

"Are you frightened of where you are going?"

"No, not really. I haven't been to Mass for a long time. When we passed by here yesterday…"

"You felt compelled to return."

"Yeah," muttered Bill.

"Perhaps it is time to find God again in your life."

Bill hesitated. "It's just that… I-I want to know."

"What is it you want to know, my son?"

"I-I don't know if… I don't know if I believe anymore," Bill said, looking down in shame.

"What made you stop?"

Bill thought of his mother's death. Why she was taken from him was the overlying question of his life, but he didn't know how to say it. Feeling the pressure of the time, he finally blurted, "If God is real, why does he take people we love from us?"

The priest sighed, then said, "My son, we do not always understand the will of God, but we must trust in his will—and his ways."

BILL'S MIND returned to the present as those around him sang a joyous hymn.

Fourteen years, and Bill had yet to receive a satisfactory answer to his question. He wondered if there was an answer.

As Bill's mind drifted, he wondered how his life would be different had his mother lived. *Would I be sitting here right now with my family, or would I be somewhere else? I probably wouldn't have left home for the Army had she lived. I would have stayed in Chicago. I would have still been drafted—probably sent straight to France. Who knows if I would have come back?* Bill looked down the pew at his children, and Mildred smiled warmly at him. *Maybe…maybe those things happened for a reason.*

Bill turned to the speaker at the pulpit. It wasn't a priest or even the bishop, but a teenage girl with a distractingly large bow to the side of her head. Bill's attention waned as his thoughts and memories collided.

It was the next speaker, a large man with a string tie and thick, combed-back hair, that caught Bill's attention. He listened as the man spoke of faith and repentance, of the trials in his life and the choices he had made to come back to God—choices that had brought him peace and happiness.

Soon the speaker was finished, and the congregation was singing. Bill heard sniffles and noticed people wiping their eyes. He wasn't sure why. Bill looked at the people around him as the large man sat. Those in the congregation weren't the judging hypocrites he imagined, but openly fallible people who wanted to become better, and he thought that was a good thing.

BILL WAS only half listening as Sylvester Schmig droned on about the unfairness of their boss, Mr. McCracken, and how he had cheated them both out of raises. Bill stared into his half-empty glass of beer, his mind not on the happenings at work or the fairness of their boss, but the large man with the combed-back hair who had spoken at church the day before.

Sylvester stopped mid-sentence and asked Bill, "Are you even listening?"

"What? Oh, yeah. It was hot today," Bill said, looking up at his friend.

"That's not what I said. I was talking about—you haven't even been listening, have ya?" glared Sylvester.

Bill looked at his friend blankly.

"What's the matter? Is your girl sick again?"

"Patty? No, she's okay," Bill nodded. He sighed as he considered what he wanted to say. He wanted to tell his friend about church and what he had felt, but he knew how Sylvester would respond.

"Well, what is it? Spit it out."

Bill looked from his drink to Sylvester. "Do you ever go to church?"

Sylvester laughed. "Not unless I have to. Just in cases of death: funerals and marriages," he smirked. Then his brow raised in realization. "They drug you to church yesterday, didn't they?"

"They didn't *drag* me," Bill frowned. "I drove."

Sylvester shook his head like a disappointed mother.

"They're very nice," Bill replied, surprising himself at defending them.

Sylvester blew a smoke ring up toward the ceiling and said, "Just what has religion ever done for you, Bill? What has God done for you? Has he made your life easier? Has he given you everything you asked for? Or has he turned a blind eye to your troubles?"

Bill's brow gathered. He remembered the mean nuns in Chicago and the well-intended priests whose words had rung hollow in his ears. A part of Bill wanted to believe in God and heaven and angels. He wanted to believe his mother was up there watching him, and someday he would be there too. But there was another part of Bill that felt believing in such things made him weak and out of control of his life. He wanted to believe he was in control, but he knew it was all an illusion. Bill was just as much a victim of circumstance now, at thirty-two, as he was as a mischievous schoolboy or as a private in the Philippines or as a sergeant waiting to go to war. *What does it all mean?*

Bill sighed and took another drink.

~

TWIN FALLS OR BUST

The delicious aroma of baked cakes and chocolate filled the kitchen as Mildred frosted the last of the cupcakes while Helen, Bobby, and Patty looked up at her like baby birds awaiting a juicy worm.

"Are you done yet?" asked Helen as three-year-old Patty stood on her toes beside her.

"I want to lick the spoon!" Bobby whined, shoving Helen aside.

"Don't push!" cried Helen, careful not to do anything that might jeopardize her chance to lick the bowl.

Mildred was aware of the jostling, but like a prized baker, remained focused as she put the finishing touches on her decadent chocolate cupcakes. Satisfied her work was complete, she looked down at the hungry birds and said, "Billy, Billy Beekser, who speaks first?"

"I DO, I DO!" cried Bobby and Helen with outstretched arms, Patty joining in after.

"Hmm," Mildred frowned as she weighed her decision. "Helen gets the bowl."

"Yippee!" cried Helen.

"And Bobby gets the big spoon."

"Yay!" Bobby exclaimed, jumping up and down.

"What about me?" whined Patty.

Mildred was about to offer her a smaller spoon when Bobby turned and said, "Ha, ha! You lose," as he walked away.

"I'm sure your brother wouldn't mind giving you *his* spoon," said Mildred, eyeing Bobby, who was looking back in dismay.

"But I…"

"Don't taunt the misfortunate," chided Mildred as she took the chocolate-covered spoon from Bobby and handed it to Patty. "Someday, you could be the one in need."

"Thank you, Mommy," Patty said in a small voice. Then, seeing her devastated brother, she held the spoon out to him and said, "You can have some."

Mildred grinned warmly and was about to return to her dinner preparations when the twins and her nephew, J.O. Young, who was holding his shoes in hand, came in from the front room.

"We didn't get any frosting!" protested Alva.

"That's because you weren't here, but you may have a cupcake after dinner," Mildred replied as Alva licked his lips.

"Do you want to see my pollywogs, Aunt Mildred?" asked six-year-old J.O., who had dark, wavy hair and large eyes. "I caught 'em in the ditch," he added, holding his shoes up for her to see.

Mildred warily bent down and looked into his wet shoes, where she saw a tangled mass of lifeless pollywogs. When the sour and stagnant smell reached her, she pulled back and gasped, "Oh! What happened to them? They look dead."

"I was walkin' in 'em," J.O. explained. "They were gushy."

"Oh," Mildred grimaced, wringing her hands in disgust. "Why don't you take your shoes out back and wash them out? I think your mother would appreciate that."

J.O. and the twins had just started for the back door when it flew open, and Bill stormed in shouting, "THAT'S IT! I'M FINISHED!"

"Goodness gracious, Billy!" Mildred gasped with one hand to her heart and the other holding her pregnant belly. "You nearly started me!"

Bill paid no attention to the scattering children as he stood irate before Mildred, pulled off his hat, and ran a hand through his hair with a smoldering cigarette wedged between his fingers.

"Whatever do you mean, finished?" Mildred calmly asked as a chocolate-faced Helen and Bobby peeked around the corner.

"I've had it with McCracken! I put in for the Twin Falls transfer. Maybe I can earn a decent living there!" he exclaimed before taking a nervous drag from his cigarette.

"Billy, please don't smoke in the house," Mildred chided. "You agreed—"

"I know, I know!" Bill grunted, mashing the cigarette in the sink.

"Now, Twin Falls, what are you talking about?" Mildred asked, feeling the emotion building within her.

"It's a rural service and sales job," Bill huffed. "I have all the experience. It'll be better for us."

Mildred's eyes widened. "Better for us?"

"Yes! I'm tired of scrimping and saving! They promised me two raises, and the money's half what they said it would be!" fumed Bill.

"But what about your Saturday job with John? That's helping quite a lot," Mildred said, thinking of not only the money but also the positive influence John Young was having on him.

"I don't want to work for your brother-in-law the rest of my life—or Saturdays! I want to spend time with you and the kids!"

"With me and the kids, or with your buddies playing baseball?" Mildred asked, the calmness in her voice now gone.

"Baseball?" Bill grunted. "What does baseball have to do with anything? I won't even be here. I'll be in Twin Falls!"

"Maybe you haven't noticed, but I'm eight months pregnant! We can't just pick up and move!" protested Mildred. "And what about this house? It's perfect for us! It's what I've always dreamed of, and we have it here and now!"

"There are plenty of other houses like this one," Bill said with a dismissive wave.

"Billy, please. We can't move! Not now!" Mildred pleaded.

Bill drew in a deep breath. "I already took the position. I start in a week."

"Billy!" Mildred cried, both hurt and angry. "We're supposed to talk about these things first! That's what married people do!"

Bill shook his head and said, "I'm sorry. I've made up my mind."

"But what about—" Mildred dropped her shoulders and turned to the stove in defeat.

Bill saw Mildred was upset and sighed. "It's the best thing for us."

Still turned away, Mildred wiped at her tears.

"I'll leave you and the kids here and find a place for us in Twin Falls," Bill said, trying to make amends. Seeing he was making no progress, he added, "I won't move you and the kids until after you've had the baby. That will make it easier."

Mildred turned to Bill, her eyes red and weepy. She wanted to tell him how selfish he was being. She wanted to remind him of the hopes and dreams they had once shared. Mildred wanted to tell him of the dream man she had once believed him to be, but merely nodded in agreement and went on preparing their dinner.

~

THE OLD BLACK Ford was covered in dust, and its painted-on question mark was barely visible when it sputtered into Twin Falls on a hot July evening. The trip had started well enough, but what should have been a three-and-a-half-hour jaunt had turned into a ten-hour odyssey.

It all started on a desolate road a half-hour out of Boise. Bill was driving along, thinking of the fortune he would make in sales, when a spring broke, bringing the car's radiator down on the front axle. Unable to move, and with no help in sight, Bill shimmied up a power pole where he found metal strips to fashion a bracket that would hold the radiator in place.

After getting the Ford going again, the road soon turned rough. Bill was halfway to Mountain Home when a tire blew out. Rolling up his sleeves again, he pulled off the wheel and repaired the flat; but in his haste, Bill drove off, leaving the jack behind. Unable to go over ten miles per hour, it took Bill another two hours to reach Mountain Home. Once there, the town's mechanic told him it would be hours before he could get to the broken-down Ford. Tired, frustrated, and impatient, Bill purchased a new spring and jack and did the repairs himself.

While the stubborn Bill never once considered his car troubles a sign, he should have, as he had five more flats in the remaining ninety miles.

Exhausted and hungry, the dusty and grimy Bill pushed open the door to the motor lodge, stepped up to the counter, and rang the bell. He looked about the floral wallpapered room, which was bathed in a golden hue from the thin yellow drapes that sagged in front of the window, and breathed in the stale air of a burned cigar.

"Evening," a short, balding man said as he came around the corner, wiping his mouth with a napkin.

"Do you have a room?" Bill asked, rubbing his throbbing head.

"Sorry," the clerk said, pointing to a sign in the window. "Full up."

"I'll take anything. I've been on the road all day," Bill pleaded.

"Where you from?" the short clerk asked, picking his teeth.

"Boise," Bill replied, hoping he was making a friend.

"Boise," the clerk frowned, "that's only a four-hour drive. Have car trouble?" he asked, looking out the window at the Ford.

"Yeah," Bill steamed.

"What's that you got on the back of your rig?" the clerk asked, seeing the barely visible question mark through the dust.

Bill sighed. "It's a question mark."

"A question mark? Not too reliable, huh?" the clerk laughed.

"No," Bill muttered, losing patience. "So, about a place to stay."

"Sorry," the clerk said, pointing to the sign. "Full up."

"Is there another place close by?"

The short clerk was sucking his teeth when he shook his head and said, "Just Barker's place up the street. Just talked to him. He's full too."

Bill sighed and looked out the window.

"There's a campground back behind. You can try that."

Bill hung his head in defeat and turned back to his car.

By his second week in Twin Falls, Bill had still not gotten used to the mildewy smell in the boarding house, which reminded him of the Read's barn in Oreana. While the other guests and the owner were pleasant enough, Bill was ready to get a place of his own that would accommodate his growing family.

After making his way down the narrow, creaky stairs, Bill nodded as he slid by the blind Mr. Morris, wondering after why he hadn't spoken instead. Bill passed the dining room, where the two Baxter brothers and another fellow were playing cards, then walked to the end of the hall near the back door and coatrack, where the house telephone hung. With no phone in their Boise home, Bill could only reach Mildred through their neighbors, the Eytchisons. After pulling off the earpiece and ringing the operator, Bill gave the necessary information, then waited for the operator to make the connection.

"Hello? Hello? Ollie?" Bill asked.

"Yes, this is Ollie Eytchison. Is that you, Bill?"

"Yes, it is," Bill answered, speaking louder than normal. "Did Mildred get my message?"

"Yes, she's right here."

"Yes, hello Billy," said Mildred, her voice small and distant in Bill's ear. "How are you?"

"I'm fine, thanks," Bill grinned. It had been a long day, and it was good to hear his wife's voice. "How are you? Are you feeling well?"

"I'm as good as can be expected," replied Mildred, with the muffled sound of children playing in the background. "This baby has been kicking quite a bit. I think he wants out."

"Tell him to hold his horses. When he sees what's out here, he may want back in," Bill laughed.

"You may be right," Mildred said, a little less amused. "You're sure it's a boy. What if it's a girl?"

"I guess we'll find out soon enough."

"How is your job?" Mildred asked.

"Just dandy!" Bill said, stretching the truth. He hadn't told Mildred the job paid on commission, and he was already fighting to make what he was back in Boise. "I had a real full day today."

"That's good."

"Did you get the money I wired?" Bill asked.

"Yes, and I paid what bills I could with it."

"There'll be more next week," Bill said, wishing he could see her face to gauge her reaction.

"Good," Mildred sighed.

"Oh, and I found a place for us," Bill said as if he had just remembered. "It's a little smaller, but it will work. It will be a stepping-up house," he said, trying to sound optimistic.

"What's the rent?"

Bill paused. "Well, it's a little more than what we're paying there."

"How much more?" Mildred asked.

"Thirty," Bill winced.

"Thirty dollars a month!" Mildred gasped, "That's double what we're paying now!"

Bill looked down at the floor and shook his head. "No, it's thirty dollars a month more."

There was a long silence, then Mildred said, "Forty-five dollars a month? Billy, we can't afford that!"

"Yeah, I know, but it's the only place in town for rent."

"Only place or not, it must be a mansion!" Mildred said in dismay. "We can't afford that!"

Bill sighed. "All right. I'll-I'll keep looking."

"Good," was all Mildred could say.

"Are the kids well?"

"Yes." There was a pause, then Mildred said, "Billy, when will you come home?"

Bill could hear the loneliness in her voice, and it pleased him. "You mean to move you? Whenever you're ready."

"I don't think I'll be much good until after this baby kicks its way out, and Doc Boeck says that could be another month."

Bill looked down the hall as a burst of laughter came from the dining room. It had only been a few weeks, but he was already tired of being away from his family. "I guess we'll just have to make do," he finally said, shaking his head in disappointment.

"Like we always have," Mildred whispered.

"Yeah," Bill muttered.

"So, did you get on that baseball team?" Mildred asked, trying to sound more upbeat.

"Yes, we've had two games already. They have me at first base," Bill replied, still deflated.

"That's good. I wish I were there to watch you."

Bill sighed. "You'll be before you know it." After more talk of the house he had found, and how much she and the children would like it, they said their goodbyes, and Bill hung up the earpiece. He stared at the phone as he thought about his family and how he missed them, then tiredly returned to his room.

~

MILDRED HAD JUST LAIN down on her bed and closed her eyes for an afternoon nap when the knock came at the door. With a tired sigh, she climbed out of her bed as scurrying feet rushed past her bedroom door. "Patty, you should be napping," she called as she opened the door.

Standing in the doorway of her bedroom, which was just off the front room, Mildred lazily watched as Patty pulled open the door and squealed, "Grammy, Grammy!" as she bounced up and down.

"Mother?" Mildred asked as she waddled into the front room.

The fifty-two-year-old Irene Read, although graying, was still an attractive woman with a beaked nose and sparkling eyes. While Mrs. Read was considered a rather elegant young woman, years of raising children and making do in the small town of Oreana had made her practical. To Mildred, her mother was someone who never steered away from work and always had the right answer.

Entering the house with the beaming Patty in her arms, Mrs. Read's gaze turned first to Mildred's tired face and then her protruding belly. "My stars and garters!" she gasped. "You're about to pop, aren't you?"

"I wish so," sighed Mildred. "I don't know if I can take much more of this heat."

"Get off your feet this instant, dear. I'm here to help," said Mrs. Read as she set Patty down with a kiss.

Mildred managed a tired smile, then asked, "Did Daddy come?"

"No, it's just me. No need to add to the burden," Mrs. Read winked. "Now, what are you up to today?" she asked, looking around. "I can smell the bread."

Mildred sighed. "I was going to start on the laundry after a nap."

Pointing to Mildred's bedroom, Mrs. Read said, "You'll go take that nap now, thank you very much, and we'll get started on the laundry. Won't we, Patty?"

Patty nodded excitedly, and Mildred obediently turned to her room.

MILDRED AWOKE three hours later to the smell of cooking dinner and the sound of giggling children. "Oh, my!" she gasped, realizing she had over-slept. After rolling off her bed, Mildred straightened her dress and adjusted her pulled-back hair. Leaving the bedroom, she waddled into the front room and saw her mother reading the children an Aesop's Fable.

"Well, I should say, you were exhausted," Mrs. Read said, looking up from the book.

Mildred groggily nodded.

"The children are home from school, and we hung the laundry. Are you ready for supper?"

"Oh yes, it smells delicious," Mildred smiled, her hands resting on her protruding belly.

"I whipped up some potatoes and chicken; you didn't have a lot," Mrs. Read said in a way that didn't offend.

"No, we don't," Mildred sighed.

WITH MRS. READ overseeing the older children's cleanup and dishwashing, and Patty quietly flipping through a book at the table, Mildred sat uncom-fortably on the couch with her feet up. Feeling somewhat invigorated by her long nap, Mildred found it at first hard to sit still while the others did the work, but the longer she relaxed, the more comfortable she became.

Mildred grinned at the sound of her mother giving directions in the kitchen. She had long marveled at how her mother could accomplish so much in a day, but then Mildred remembered how everyone would chip in, given tasks by their mother with the efficiency of an Army general. The realization she was not as capable as a mother caused Mildred's grin to fade and left her flat.

Mildred was feeling sorry for herself when her mother came out from the kitchen, pulled off her apron, and sat in the rocker beside her.

"How are you feeling, dear?"

"Oh, very rested now, thanks to you," said Mildred, forcing a smile. "I wish I could do that."

"Do what, dear?"

"Whip them into shape like that. It would be better for them and me if I gave them more duties," sighed Mildred.

"We all have our own style," nodded Mrs. Read, "But it would help. I learned years ago that many hands make light work."

Mildred nodded blankly.

"I also learned small hands make *more* work," Mrs. Read winked.

Mildred laughed.

Mrs. Read's face grew serious. "In your letter, you said Bill took a job in Twin Falls, and he intends to move you there."

Mildred nodded.

"And when do you intend to move?"

Mildred sighed. "I guess after this baby is born."

"What happened to his job here in Boise?"

Mildred could feel her emotions building. She looked across the room, shrugged, and said, "He wasn't happy with it. He got raises, but they weren't as much as he thought. He's been working nights and Saturdays for John, you know. I think he just got fed up with it all."

"Do you think he'll be happier in Twin Falls?" Mrs. Read asked, her brow gathered.

"*He* thinks so," muttered Mildred, fighting back the emotion.

The twins came out from the kitchen, and Alva proudly announced, "The dishes are dried and put away."

"Wonderful," Mrs. Read smiled. "Do you have studies?"

The twins nodded.

"Then why don't you go off and do them? After, I want you to tell me all about what you learned."

"Me too?" asked Helen, moving behind the twins with Bobby.

113

"Yes, dear."

With respectful nods, the children disappeared into the kitchen.

Upon seeing Mildred was fighting back tears, Mrs. Read slipped onto the couch beside her and asked, "Dear, whatever is the matter?"

"Oh, Mother," Mildred whispered, "I don't know. I just get so sad sometimes. I think it's the weight of the baby, and the children, and the money and…" She wiped at her tears. "Some days it's all just too much! Sometimes I just want to be a little girl again, frolicking around Oreana without a worry, watching Daddy with the sheep and talking to old Uncle Rube."

Mrs. Read pulled her daughter tight. "Now, now, dear. You know this is what life is all about. We are meant to have these trials. How would we ever grow if we were left to frolic without a care? You have a wonderful family with beautiful children and a hard-working husband. You've had to make do, and that's a blessing, of sorts. You know your father and I have had our share of money troubles. After all of these years, it's still a constant worry, but it makes us stay focused and prioritize. You'll get through it all just fine."

"I guess," Mildred sighed. "Am I being terribly selfish if I don't want to move to Twin Falls? I love our home here and, well, Billy was making such progress working with John. He was going to church with me. Now I'm afraid that's all going to go down the drain."

"Only if you let it," Mrs. Read whispered.

There was a long silence then, with tears filling her eyes, Mildred asked, "Mother, do you think I made a mistake marrying Billy?"

Mrs. Read's brow creased. "Do you remember what I told you before you married Bill?"

"That I was making a terrible mistake and shouldn't rush into marriage?"

"After that."

Mildred thought for a moment, then said, "That it's not fair to try to change a man?"

"That's right. You fell in love with him through all of your letters. When you finally met him, you knew it was right. Do you remember?"

Mildred nodded and wiped at her tears.

"Well, if it was right then, why wouldn't it be right now?"

Mildred's shrug caused more tears to streak down her cheeks.

"You need to think about that," Mrs. Read said, her eyes soft and loving.

After some consideration, Mildred swallowed and said, "I guess I supposed things would be different by now."

"You thought you could change him."

Mildred nodded.

"Dear, people *do* change, sometimes for the better, sometimes for the worse, but for it to be a *genuine* change, it has to come from them. You can't force it. They have to *want* to change. It's all about agency. Now, Bill may change for the better, but he may not. When you married him, you made a promise to love and support him, and so did he to you."

"Yes, I know all of that," Mildred groaned as she fought to sit up. "But what do I do? What can I do to help him?"

"That part is simple. Just love Bill," Mrs. Read said, her eyes sparkling.

Mildred's gaze trailed away. After some consideration, she looked back at her mother and asked, "Is that what you did for daddy?"

"Of course," Mrs. Read beamed.

~

SAINT OLLIE

$\mathcal{B}$ ill eyed the kitchen chair hanging over the side of the old black Ford, its legs intertwined with another. He shook it to make sure it wasn't going anywhere, then pulled the rope through the tangled maze of furniture and belongings and tied a seaman's knot. Standing back, he wiped away the sweat and surveyed the car loaded high and wide.

"It looks like a giant spider," Helen said, holding up a lamp.

Bill scratched his head as he searched for a spot, then took the lamp and set it into a crevice between the chairs.

"Is there any room for you to drive it?" Mildred asked as she waddled past him.

Bill shook his head. "I think there's just enough if it doesn't all come crashing down on me. You'd think I'd be used to this trip, three weekends in a row now, but it gets longer every time." He turned to Mildred, eyed her protruding belly, then asked, "Still nothing?"

"No," Mildred sighed. "I'm beginning to think the baby is taking up permanent residence in there."

"It's the end of August. If I had known he would take this long, we would have moved already, and you could have had the baby in Twin Falls," Bill said with hands on hips.

"I'm sorry," Mildred shrugged, "There's not much I can do."

"I know," Bill nodded.

"Maybe we should come with you on this trip. The baby may not come for another week. I've sold the cow and the chickens. There's not much left in the house. Another trip would do it. Mother said she and father could even bring it when they come to visit."

"That fine by me," Bill said, perking up.

"Ollie Eytchison said he could drive us," she added, almost pleading her case.

"What if you get halfway there and the baby comes?" Bill frowned.

"Then we'll do the same thing the pioneer women did; pull off the road and have the baby."

Bill sighed. "All right. I'll ask Ollie if he'll drive you."

With a happy clap, Mildred waddled back toward the house.

Bill liked that she and the kids would finally be with him, but as his gaze turned to the house and settled on its colorful flowerbeds beside the front porch, his face emptied. Mildred had lovingly tended to the snapdragons and petunias, and he wondered if the new occupants would be so careful with them. Bill eyed the whitewashed shake shingles. He snickered as he thought of Bobby spilling a half-empty can of whitewash onto his head. It had taken him and the boys a week of evenings to paint the exterior, but it had transformed the weathered house. He knew Mildred was sad leaving their house by the river, but he would miss it too. It wasn't long after they had moved in that Bill had told Mildred they would put down deep roots there. But now they were leaving, and it made Bill wonder if he was doing right. He shook off the sentiment. His work was in Twin Falls now. They would find another home and like it just as well, he told himself as he started for Ollie's house.

Mildred was going up the steps to the front door when she doubled over in pain. "Oh, my!" she exclaimed, looking back at Bill.

"What happened?" Bill asked, looking back. "Is it starting?"

Mildred saw the puddle of water on the step below her and gasped, "I think so! Maybe this little one doesn't want to be born on the side of the road after all!"

THE SHRILL CRY of the newborn baby caused the sweat-drenched Mildred to gasp, "Is it a boy?" as she caught her breath.

"Yes. It's a fine plump boy, Mrs. Kane," Dr. Boeck said, his eyes small through his thick glasses.

"He's beautiful, Mildred," Mrs. Read said, blotting at her daughter's face with a damp rag.

"He's a nine-pounder, I venture," Dr. Boeck added, dangling the baby by the legs like a trophy fish.

"Oh, my," Mrs. Read gasped. "No wonder he didn't want to come out. He was fit as a fiddle in there!"

"Billy? Is Billy still awake?" Mildred panted, turning back towards the closed door.

"He was asleep with the children on the back porch last I looked," replied Mrs. Read as she handed the doctor a towel for the baby.

"Oh, will you go tell him, Mother? I'm sure he would want to know he has another son."

"Now, that's my job," said the doctor as he finished cleaning up the still crying baby. After tying up the umbilical and wrapping the baby in a towel, he laid the quieting infant on Mildred's chest and pulled off his apron. "I'll be right back," he said with a wink.

Mildred nodded as she held the plump little boy, whose cry had faded to a whimper.

"So, this is Baby Glen," Mrs. Read beamed as she leaned closer. "So nice to meet you."

"Yes, it is," Mildred said with an exhausted smile. "Glen Arnold. Billy will be so happy for another boy." She looked up as Dr. Boeck returned, shaking his head. "What's the matter? Where's Billy?"

"Mrs. Kane, I tried to wake him—I even shook him—but that man is dead asleep. What did you do to him?"

"He's been working very hard lately," Mildred said, caressing little Glen.

"He's been having babies, has he?" Mrs. Read scoffed. "Oh, my stars. I'll handle this." Straightening up and wiping her hands, she marched past Dr. Boeck out of the bedroom, through the kitchen, and out to the back porch, where she saw Bill laid out on a blanket with the children sprawled beside him. Kneeling, she nudged the snoring Bill, but to no effect. Mrs. Read shook him harder, but still, Bill slept. She considered speaking loudly, but didn't want to wake the children. With a sigh, Mrs. Read got back to her feet, and with hands on hips, kicked the bottom of Bill's shoe, springing him up like a mousetrap.

"No, that's not where the baby goes!" Bill exclaimed, still half-asleep.

"Bill," Mrs. Read whispered with stern eyes.

"What? What happened?" Bill asked as he looked around the darkened porch. Upon seeing his mother-in-law, Bill ran a hand through his hair and said, "Mother?"

"Bill, you have a son," Mrs. Read beamed.

"Another boy," Bill grinned. "How's Mildred?"

"She's doing splendidly."

Bill gave a contented nod, then lowered back down to the blanket, closed his eyes, and went back to sleep.

~

WITH MOST OF their belongings either moved or sold and Bill back at work in Twin Falls, Mildred and the children made do the best they could for the twelve days before Dr. Boeck gave her the go-ahead to travel. It was a breezy September morning that Mildred, with her bundled up newborn and five other children, piled into Ollie Eytchison's Oldsmobile.

Ollie, a tall, solidly built Swede with golden hair and mustache, scratched his head as he watched the five children climb into the back of the automobile, rocking the car back and forth as they fought for a seat. "No fighting back there," Mildred warned from her comfortable front seat, holding the newborn baby in arm.

"But there's no place to sit!" protested Helen.

Ollie walked around to the back of the car and checked the knot that secured Mildred's two worn suitcases to the bumper as the car swayed. After moving back to the side window, he watched as the children pushed and shoved for a place to sit. But no matter how they tried to fit, one or two of them were left standing.

"Alma and Alva, Bobby and Patty need to sit on your laps, and that's all there is to it," Mildred called back, losing patience.

"But I don't want to sit on his lap," protested Bobby. "What about that seat?" he asked, pointing to the empty driver's seat.

"Oh, that is where I sit," Ollie said in his thick accent, wondering just what he had gotten himself into.

"Bobby, unless you want to walk alongside, you must sit on Alma's lap," Mildred ordered.

"But he's got bony knees," whined Bobby.

"Do not," cried Alma.

"Do so!" Bobby insisted.

Ollie ran an unsettled hand through his hair. Then, in his thick Swedish accent, said, "Please, just find a seat, and we'll get started. It's quite a long journey, you know."

"I'm terribly sorry," Mildred apologized as baby Glen cried. "Bobby, get on your brother's lap this instant!"

With folded arms and a cross look, the six-year-old Bobby got out of the car and fumed as Patty dutifully climbed onto Alma's lap.

"Bobby," Mildred warned, rocking the crying baby, "Don't make me come out there!"

"But I don't want to go!" Bobby said, stomping his foot.

"I don't want to go either!" Helen joined in, standing up in the back. "I like it here!"

"We're going, and that's that!" insisted Mildred. When she saw Bobby had not moved, she started for her door handle with a scolding look.

Finally relenting with a noisy huff, Bobby climbed back into the car and flopped on Alva's lap with arms folded in protest.

"Now, I'll have no more of that," Mildred said, glaring back.

"We're off then," Ollie announced with some relief as he climbed into his seat and started up the engine.

"Ouch!" cried Helen, "Alma pinched me!"

"No, I didn't!"

"Get off me!" snapped Alva.

"Where am I supposed to sit?" cried Bobby

With eyes wide, Ollie snugged his cap down, placed the car into gear, and motored up Madison Avenue, taking with him the sounds of a crying baby, a scolding mother, and bickering children. Left behind, the house by the river sat alone and empty.

≈

BALLS AND STRIKES

The crack of the bat brought the spectators to their feet, where they watched the ball sail deep into the outfield. Mildred Kane, who was holding baby Glen, was among those standing as the ball dropped into the glove of the Ogden left fielder. A collective groan ran through the Twin Falls bleachers as the dejected onlookers sank back in their seats.

"What happened?" Alva asked, looking around at the boisterous home crowd.

"The other team caught the ball," said a tense Mildred rocking her baby. The family had joined Bill in Twin Falls just the week before, and the ballgame was the perfect diversion from the drudgery of setting up a new house.

"Oh," Alva said, wondering why everyone was so upset.

"I thought that was over the fence," cried Bobby.

"Nearly," Mildred replied, shaking her head. She saw Bill standing on deck and gave a worrisome sigh.

With the Twin Falls Bruins down two runs in the bottom of the ninth, one out, and a man on first and second, all eyes were on Bill Kane.

"Daddy's up," Mildred said as Bill moved to the plate in his white and black pinstriped uniform, which had a large merged letter T and F on the left breast.

"Daddy?" Patty asked, standing on her seat.

121

"Dad, let 'em have it!" Bobby cried as he pulled up the strap of his baggy overalls. "Knock it over the fence!"

"Oh, I don't like this Ogden team," Mildred fretted. "They look so angry and mean all the time."

"These Gunners always make it interesting, they do," said a stout man beside Mildred.

"Come on, Daddy!" shouted Helen, "Hit it hard!"

"Is this your husband?" the stout man asked as Bill took a practice swing and stepped into the batter's box.

"Yes," Mildred nervously replied.

"He's the new first baseman, isn't he?"

"Yes," she nodded as the pitcher stared down her husband. "Oooh, he just looks so mean. I can see why they're called Gunners," Mildred said as the children stretched to see better.

"Hogwallup that ball, Kane!" yelled the stout man as the tension in the stands grew.

Mildred was unblinking as the first pitch popped into the catcher's mitt.

"STRIKE!" called the umpire as he pumped his arm.

The Twin Falls' side groaned while the visiting crowd cheered.

"Come on, Dad!" hollered Bobby as others cheered around him.

Mildred clutched the baby as the pitcher wound up and released his next throw. The crack of the bat brought the crowd to its feet as the ball flew toward right field and went foul.

"Oh, no," groaned the stout man.

"You can do it!" cried Mildred.

"You can do it, Daddy!" shouted Helen, stretching on her toes.

"You can do it," echoed Patty, uncertain of what was happening.

With the crowd cheering, Mildred glared at the pitcher, hoping she might disrupt his throw.

"Look!" Bobby gasped as the runner on second base charged for third. The pitcher spun and fired the ball to third, but the throw was high and went over the outstretched arm of the baseman as the runner slid into the bag. The home crowd and dugout exploded, urging him home. The runner jumped to his feet and was nearly home when the left fielder grabbed the errant ball and threw it in. Mildred gasped as the ball sailed toward home plate. "GET DOWN!" was the cry from the dugout as the runner slid into home between the catcher's legs a split second before the ball arrived.

"SAFE!" cried the umpire.

The home crowd roared their approval.

"Haha!" cried the stout man, "That oughta rattle Sparks!"

"Who's Sparks?" Mildred asked, eyeing the tying runner on third.

"He's their pitcher," the stout man said, his jowls dancing.

Mildred held her breath as the next throw went wide, and the crowd sighed. With one ball and two strikes, she watched unblinkingly as the pitcher paced around the mound, looked Bill down, and then released the throw. Bill swung. The snap of the bat caused Mildred to jump. She watched wide-eyed as the ball sailed up, up, and over the center-field fence and dropped into a pasture beside an unsuspecting cow.

The Twin Falls bleachers exploded as Bill proudly ran the bases. Rounding third, he tipped his hat to the dejected opponents.

"Yay! Dad did it!" Bobby and Helen exclaimed, jumping.

"Hooray!" Alva and Alma joined in.

"That was a heck of a hit!" beamed the stout man.

"Yes, it was!" Mildred cried as she bounced baby Glen, who had burst into tears from the cries, hoots, and hollers around them.

"Did Father win the game?" Alva asked with wide eyes.

"Yes, he did!" Mildred beamed as she looked down on home plate where Bill's teammates were piling on top of him.

It was a lazy Sunday afternoon, the day after the big game. Bill was asleep in his chair with the newspaper straddling his lap when Alma warily nudged him.

Bill opened his eyes and asked, "What?" in a way that made Alma take a step back beside his brother.

"Will you teach us how to hit the ball like that?" Alva asked.

Bill eyed the twins. He had tried for years to interest them in baseball. "You want to hit some balls?" he asked, sitting up.

Alva nodded.

"Maybe play catch?"

Alma shrugged and then nodded.

"Okay," Bill said, tossing off the paper. "What about church?"

"We have time," Alva replied.

"All right," Bill said, perking up even more. "Get the gloves and bat. I'll get a ball!"

Mildred happened by an open window when she heard her husband giving directions. It surprised her when she looked out to see eight-year-old Alma holding a bat and Bill squatting behind him as the catcher. She moved closer to the window, and her eyes widened when she spotted Alva pitching. Mildred cringed when Alva's pitch missed the batter and catcher by four feet. With her hand covering a snicker, she watched Bill scramble to the ball. Mildred knew how Bill loved baseball and how he had tried for years to get the twins interested, and it did her heart good to see them on the dandelion lawn together.

She grinned as Bill threw the ball back to Alva, who watched it sail past. "Go get the ball," Bill directed in as gentle a way as she had ever heard him.

After another failed throw, with Bill giving as much patient direction as he was capable, he took the bat from Alma and handed him the catcher's mitt. Mildred watched Bill lead Alva to the home plate, fashioned from a newspaper, then show him how to hold the bat. Bill then moved Alma a safe distance behind and showed him where to hold the glove. Mildred was grinning as Bill walked out twenty feet from the boys and held up the baseball. "Just keep your eyes on the ball," Bill instructed.

The twins nodded in unison.

The first pitch arched gently before dropping a foot behind home plate. Bill sighed. "Son, you're supposed to swing at the ball when it comes by."

Alva anxiously nodded.

Bill was encouraged when Alma picked up the ball and made the throw back. "Nice throw. Now, Alva, swing the bat when the ball gets to you."

The next pitch, moving faster, passed the late-swinging Alva and struck Alma in the face. "OW!" Alma wailed, dropping the mitt and grabbing his nose.

"You're supposed to catch it!" Bill hollered with hands on hips as Mildred rushed out the front door to comfort the crying Alma.

"You broke my face!" wailed Alma as blood streamed from between his fingers.

Horrified by the scene, Alva dropped his bat and darted for the house as Mildred looked at Bill for help.

"He's okay," Bill sighed, moving to the howling Alma. "It's just a bloody nose."

"What if it's broken?" worried Mildred.

"I didn't throw it that hard," Bill said, remembering another time…

Summer 1906

FOR A TEN-YEAR-OLD CHICAGO BOY, there was no better place to be than the West Side Grounds watching the Cubs play baseball. Already well on their way to clinching the National League Pennant for the first time in the twentieth century, the Chicago Cubs were the hottest ticket in town. The sly Bill and Harry had snuck into nearly every game where they oohed and aahed over the pitching of Mordecai "Three-Finger" Brown, the catching of Johnny Kling, or the lethal Tinker to Evers to Chance triple play connections.

To Bill and Harry, the next best thing to watching the Cubs play baseball was watching them practice, and thanks to their relentless prodding and persistence, the two boys, were allowed to gather up bats, chase foul balls, and sweep up piles of spent chewing tobacco.

"Wow. You see that pitch?" Harry gasped as a ball zipped past the batter and snapped into Kling's glove. Three Fingers Brown, who had lost a forefinger and mangled his middle in a farming accident as a child, had a deadly spin every batter in the league feared.

"Hey, kid, gather up those balls, will ya?" called out the smooth Frank Chase, leaning over the side of the dugout. Chase, who split his time as the Cubs' manager and first baseman, was who finally gave in to the pesky boys.

"Yes, sir," hollered Bill as he jumped to his feet, leaving Harry on the wooden bench outside of the dugout contentedly watching his heroes at work. Scurrying behind a still squatting Johnny Kling and a practice-swinging Jimmy Slagle, Bill began scooping up balls and dropping them into an apple basket.

Bill's ball gathering was slow, and he sometimes reached for balls that weren't there as he followed the fastballs, curves, and sliders Brown was putting past Slagle. Amazed at the form and velocity of Three Finger's pitches, Bill watched as he slowly gathered up the balls, a few of them missing the basket and dropping back to the ground.

After a remarkably smooth curveball, which Bill watched goose-necked, Fred Beebe, who was warming up with a handful of bats, yelled, "Hey kid, let's get these balls gathered up. What do ya say? You don't get paid for gawking."

"Actually, I don't get paid at all," Bill grinned.

"Well, pick 'em up anyway," Beebe huffed as he walked away.

With Bill's back turned to home plate, he didn't see the next pitch, which came hard off the side of Kling's glove and slammed in-between his shoulder blades. The ball's impact caused Bill's eyes to roll up into his head and dropped him first to his knees and then flat on his face beside the bushel basket.

Finished warming up, Beebe dropped all but one of his bats and casually walked over to the facedown boy before spitting to the side. Kling soon joined him and smirked, "Geez, Brown. I think you killed the kid." Shaking his head, Three Fingers came off the mound.

"Kid! Kid! You okay?" Beebe asked, nudging the boy with his bat.

"Aw, he's okay," Three Fingers muttered, casting a shadow over the motionless Bill sprawled on the ground.

After coming over from the dugout, Frank Chase shook his head and said, "Mordecai, you pickin' on little kids again?"

"For cryin' out loud, Frank, Johnny was the one that missed it. Don't make me the bad guy," Three Fingers grumbled as Harry slipped in beside him, more interested in seeing his heroes close up than his unconscious friend.

"Yeah, well, my arm's not five feet long," Kling sneered.

"Hey kid, you okay?" Chase asked, first stooping over to nudge Bill, then kneeling to give him a closer examination.

With it being a practice, there were only a few people in the stands, including several of the player's girlfriends, all of whom were standing with hands to mouth or chest and fretful looks of concern.

Bill's first movement was a twitch of his hand. Then came a flutter of his eyelids as he raised his head with a moan.

"See, he's okay," shrugged Three Fingers. He had just started back to the mound when he caught the scolding glare of his girlfriend. With a sigh, the pitcher turned back to the moaning Bill.

"Bill, are ya okay?" Harry asked, relieved to see his friend moving.

"Wha-what happened?" groaned Bill as his eyes joined together.

"Yeah, he's fine," Three Fingers grunted, but his girlfriend's stern look kept him at the dazed Bill's side. After pulling off his mitt, Three Fingers sighed, then stooped over and pulled Bill to his feet.

"What happened?" Bill asked, surprised by all the attention.

"You took a fastball in the back, kid," explained Frank Chase. "Knocked you cold. You okay?"

"I think so," Bill said, rubbing his back.

"Well, why don't you take it easy, kid," Kling said, his catcher's mask up on his head, his cheek bulging with a wad of tobacco.

"Yeah," Chase agreed. "Come over here to the dugout and have a good sit down. Hey!" he called up to the stands, "Will one of you gals get this kid a lemonade? You like lemonade, kid? Or would you rather have a soda?"

Bill's wide eyes moved from Frank Chase to Three Fingers. "A soda would be swell."

"A soda it is," Chase nodded. "What kind?"

"Sassafras?"

"He wants a Sassafras soda!" Chase yelled.

A gorgeous blonde holding a dainty parasol called back, "You got it, Frankie."

"Come on, kid, let's get you over to the dugout, where you can rest for a spell."

"Yes, sir," Bill said, grinning at Harry, who was beside himself with envy.

"Hey, kid. What's your name?" Kling asked Harry.

"Harry Mandel," he beamed.

"Oh yeah," Kling nodded. "Harvey, we need to get going here. Gather up the rest of the balls."

"What?" Harry asked, his smile fading.

"The balls. Get 'em picked up! We got a practice to run here."

"Oh, sure thing, Johnny—I mean, Mister Kling," Harry replied as two of the girlfriends lavished attention on Bill in the dugout.

Thinking he had died and gone to heaven, Bill's eyes widened as the most beautiful woman he had ever seen bent forward and presented him with a soda.

"Are you okay, little boy?" she asked.

In a stupor from her fragrant perfume and ample cleavage, Bill couldn't respond.

Harry shook his head in disgust. Then, having an idea, he glanced over his shoulder at the pitcher and backed up to the catcher with the apple basket, hoping for another missed pitch.

"Hey, kid!" yelled Three Fingers, "Get out of there before you get hit!"

BILL GRINNED as the sweet memory faded. He looked down at Alma, still holding his nose, then helped him to his feet. "He's okay." Bill patted his son's arm and smiled. "What you need is a root beer."

"A root beer?" asked Alma, still holding his nose.

"Sure," nodded Bill.

"We don't have any root beer," Mildred quietly reminded Bill.

Bill's brow gathered. "Well, a hug from your mother should do just as well."

Mildred lovingly squeezed Alma, who then said, "I don't want to play catch anymore."

~

DAYS GONE BY

It was early October. Flag-waving breezes and red and gold rustling leaves had replaced the warm days of summer. With the league championship looming and just one game behind the Boise Senators, the Twin Falls Bruins had been practicing hard.

In the months since joining the team, Bill had made a name for himself, both playing first base and at bat. While Mildred was proud of her husband's success, his time at practice and away from sales meant less pay and had put them even further behind on bills. The financial stress, along with being shoehorned into a small, overpriced two-bedroom home with six children underfoot, left Mildred wishing they had never left Boise.

Mildred was preparing dinner when she heard the front door open and brawny men's voices. Wiping her hands, she stepped into the front room around a stack of boxes yet to be unpacked and saw Bill, still in his uniform, being helped into the house by two teammates. "Oh, no. What happened?" Mildred fretted, seeing the pain in her husband's face.

"I'm all right. It's nothing really," Bill winced as they set him on the couch beside a wide-eyed Helen.

"You are obviously *not* all right," Mildred replied, eyeing his heavily wrapped right knee. "What happened?"

"I'll be okay now, fellas. Thanks," Bill winced. The two ballplayers offered words of encouragement, then tipped their caps to Mildred before going back out the front door.

"Do I need to call for the doctor?" Mildred asked, still unsure of what had happened.

"I just came from the doctor," Bill grumbled, glaring at Helen, who had not moved from the couch.

"What happened?" Alma asked, coming in from the kitchen.

Bill sighed. "It's nothing. I'm sure it will be fine by morning."

"I think not!" Mildred exclaimed. "You needed two men to carry you into the house! What happened?"

"I twisted my knee, is all," Bill shrugged. "Baker was having me throw some pitches. I must have caught my foot on the rubber. The doctor said I tore some ligaments, but I don't think he knows what he's talking about." Bill shook his head then added, "I was throwing good too."

With all the children gathered around, Mildred threw up her hands and said, "So, now what do we do?"

Bill sighed. "I don't know. I may not be able to play Saturday."

"Play? I'm more worried about you being able to walk!" Mildred cried.

Bill threw off his cap, then mumbled something.

"What?" Mildred asked, fighting back her frustration.

"Do they have to all be here?" Bill snapped.

Mildred turned to the children and said, "Helen, boys, will you go into the kitchen and see how supper is coming? Bobby, will you take Patty into our room and read her a story? But don't wake Glen."

With looks of concern and confusion, the children left the front room. After drawing in a breath, Mildred sat next to the dejected Bill and asked, "What did the doctor say?"

"He said to stay off it for a month," grumbled Bill. "He's a quack!"

"*A month?*" gasped Mildred.

"I know!" Bill said, beside himself. "I'll miss the playoffs!"

"Never mind baseball. What about your job? How will we pay the bills? We're already behind!"

"Don't worry about it!" snapped Bill. "I'll take care of it. I always do. Besides, doctors don't know what they're talking about half the time. A little liniment and a good night's sleep, and it'll be fine. I'll be back to work tomorrow. It's already feeling better," he lied.

Mildred looked from her stubborn husband to his knee. She carefully unwrapped the bandage until she saw a knee red and swollen to twice its size. "Oh, Billy!" she gasped. "That doesn't look good at all! We must get that leg up. In fact, let's get you into bed. I'll bring supper into you."

Bill saw his knee was more swollen than before and groaned.

～

THE NEXT MORNING, Bill's knee was no better. After easing out of bed, he tried to stand with one hand on the dresser and the other on Mildred's shoulder, but he could put no weight on it. Determined not to let a bad knee incapacitate him, Bill hopped around the room on the other leg before an unimpressed Mildred ordered him back into bed. With the next day being Saturday, Bill stayed in bed. But when it was no better on Sunday morning, he became angry to the point of swearing.

"Just what is going on in here?" Mildred demanded as she pushed open the bedroom door with a nervous Alva standing behind her.

"It's no better! I can't work like this?" Bill shouted, throwing his pillow.

"It's only been two days," Mildred calmly reminded him. "The doctor said to stay off it a month."

"How do you know? You weren't there!" snapped Bill.

Quietly seething, Mildred turned to Alva and Bobby and calmly said, "Run along now. Your father isn't feeling well."

"I feel fine!" hollered Bill. "It's just my damn knee!"

Mildred entered the room and closed the door. With arms folded and brow bent, she exclaimed, "Listen, you stubborn Irishman! You're going to have to be patient!"

"How am I supposed to work like this? How am I supposed to support us?" bellowed Bill.

Mildred glared at Bill as she considered their predicament. They were already behind on their bills, and a month without pay would only make matters worse. She wanted to tell him how selfish he had been, quitting his job and moving them to Twin Falls. Mildred wanted to tell him playing baseball had put his family in a situation where they could be kicked out on the street, but she held her tongue and quietly seethed.

Bill saw her brewing frustration and asked, "Why are you upset? I'm the one with the lame knee."

Mildred could hold back no longer. "BILLY, I FEAR THIS HAS ALL BEEN A TERRIBLE MISTAKE!"

Bill stared blankly at Mildred. She rarely had such outbursts, and he was about to dismiss it when he remembered a coworker telling of how his wife had become fed up and left with his kids. Bill looked at the seething Mildred and wondered what the terrible mistake she was referring to was. *Is she talking about me? About marrying me? She wouldn't leave me, would she?*

Bill wondered what he would do without her. The idea was paralyzing. Bill swallowed his pride and asked, "What?"

Still upset, Mildred spoke with folded arms and a tight jaw. "I think it was a terrible mistake for us to leave Boise. Nothing has been good here. Our financial state is worse, and this house is too small for us to live in! I can't imagine how it will be in the winter months when the boys can't sleep outside!"

Relieved her complaint was not with him, Bill sighed, then said, "I'll find us a bigger house. We'll be okay."

"But you can't work like this! The doctor said—"

"I don't care what he said! They're wrong more than they're right! Just like Patty, remember? Doc Boeck said she was going to die, and she's fine!"

Mildred's frustration turned to sadness as she realized her husband was no closer to recognizing the workings of God than the day she had met him. "Patty was sick. She might have died without that blessing."

Bill's gaze moved across the room as he remembered just how sick Patty was. He had even given up on her, accepting that she would die. *But she didn't die. Was it the blessing that saved her?* he wondered.

Surprised her words had calmed Bill, Mildred stepped closer and, with a loving touch, asked, "Billy, can I call the elders? They can give you a blessing. They can heal you like they did Patty."

Bill sighed. "Those men are in Boise."

"There are elders here too. It's the power of God, not the man," Mildred whispered.

Bill's gaze faded across the room.

"They can bless you, if you'll have them," Mildred said tenderly. "You just need to have faith God can heal your knee."

Bill looked down at his knee and muttered, "What if I don't have faith?"

Mildred shrugged. "It's still worth a try."

Bill reached down to his unwrapped knee and gingerly felt it. He sat in thought for a time, then drew in a ragged breath. After a pride-emptying sigh, Bill turned to Mildred and muttered, "Okay, have them come."

THE FOLLOWING DAY AFTER CHURCH, Bill Kane's bedroom was filled with his children and a hopeful Mildred as Bishop Campbell and his counselor anointed Bill's head and blessed his knee that it would quickly heal. Bill listened to the words, at one point wondering if he was feeling something different with his knee, then offered thanks as they left with their hats in hand. While Mildred saw them to the door, Bill moved his knee to see if it was any better but wasn't surprised when it felt the same.

"Daddy, are you sad about your knee?" little Patty asked with large, dark eyes as she leaned against the bed.

"It'll get better," Bill replied, hoisting her onto the bed beside him.

Helen climbed up on the bed and said, "Mother said the blessing will make it better, just like it did Patty."

"I'm sure it will," Bill said as Alva and Bobby drew closer.

Bill looked at his children somewhat regretfully. They always seemed willing to look past his orneriness and loved him despite his flaws. He felt undeserving of them. With a tightness in his throat, Bill pulled Patty close with one arm and opened his other to Helen, who willingly snuggled up next to him. When Bill felt his eyes welling with tears, he quickly blinked them away, but not before Bobby noticed and asked, "Are you sad because you can't play baseball?"

Bill sighed. He wasn't sure. A part of him was sad for missing out on the end of the season, but as he looked at his forgiving children, he felt sorrow for being no better a father than his own.

"You'll be able to play again next year, won't you?" Alva asked.

"I suppose so," said Bill, still melancholy.

"Tell us about how you played baseball as a boy," Helen said with adoring eyes.

"Yeah!" Bobby joined in, leaning forward.

"Back in Chicago, you mean?"

"Yes," Helen smiled.

Bill sank back into his pillow and relaxed a little more. He told how his father, who had played for the Troy Haymakers in New York, had taught him how to play baseball. Helen grimaced as he spoke of his father's hands, which didn't have a straight finger on them from playing in the days before gloves. Bill grinned as he spoke of his boyhood in Chicago. He told of how he started as a catcher and got knocked out with a broken nose after being hit by a thrown bat when just nine. The boys laughed, and Helen covered her eyes when he told of how his teammates pushed spider webs up his nose to stop the bleeding.

Bill closed his eyes as he spoke of the Cubs and the grand games he had witnessed at West Side Park, of his chasing balls for Frank Chase and wishing he could throw like Three Fingers Brown.

Bill said his neighborhood team was called the Pirates and told of the countless Saturdays spent playing baseball in a vacant lot near his house. He shook his head and grinned as he spoke of his old friends and teammates James Murrin, Leo McDonald, Max Mandel, Frankie Rio, Tony Leon, and the Healy brothers. Bill chuckled as he reminisced about nearly being run over by a horse while covering home plate. And the twins' eyes widened when Bill spoke of the hated Guardian Angels team who were "cheating, good-for-nothing, wops." Bill grew serious when he spoke of their epic ball games, often settled by game-ending brawls.

Bill's eyes grew distant as he spoke of the uniform his father had surprised him with. While the entire team had received them, the gift had even more meaning coming from his father, who always seemed otherwise occupied. His voice cracked as he spoke of the large letter "P" cut from lamb's wick and sewn on by his sister.

Upon seeing the tender side of their father, the children pressed closer and were unaware of their mother listening from outside the room.

"Will you teach me how to pitch?" asked Bobby.

"Sure, I will," Bill said, studying his son, "but you know, a good infielder draws more money than the best pitcher in the world, and with a great deal less effort. That's what you should become."

"Okay," nodded Bobby.

"Daddy, didn't you play ball in the Philip-Philip-Philippines?" asked Helen.

"Yes, I did," beamed Bill, "but that's a whole other story."

"Tell us about the Philippines," Alma asked eagerly.

Bill looked down at his knee and sighed. "I guess I'm not going anywhere."

"Good," Helen smiled.

Bill cleared his throat as his mind shifted to another place and time, to a lush green and wet land with small brown people. While his time in the Philippines was more recent than his boyhood adventures in Chicago, it somehow seemed more distant to him. His children's eyes widened as he told of the month-long voyage to the Philippines and the terrible seas they had to cross to get there. He remembered their ship stopping at Hawaii and their relief at being on dry land. He chuckled to himself as he recalled him and his buddies waking the next morning in a field of sheep with half of their uniforms gone. Whether they had lost their things trading for liquor or playing cards, he still didn't know. He wanted to tell how he and his buddies got back on board the ship by stealing other soldiers' uniforms, but thought it wiser not to.

The twins' eyes widened as Bill spoke of the giant snakes and wary-eyed natives who watched from the shore as they made the long, rainy boat ride up the Pasig River to Fort McKinley. Bill remembered how hungry he was after hours on the river and a mile and a half march through the rain. And how good the food tasted when he and the others finally ate that night.

Bill thought of how homesick he was those first weeks in the Philippines, and how baseball gave him a purpose and an identity.

Bill smiled as he spoke of the Army baseball league and how his team won the title.

"So, did you play in China, Daddy?" Helen asked with wide eyes.

"You better believe it!" he beamed. "We were the Champions of the Orient! After winning it all in the Philippines, we spent a month playing games in China. The things we saw…" he said, his gaze fading once again. "Do you know they have a wall that is as wide and tall as the church but runs for ten thousand miles?"

"WOW!" the children exclaimed.

"They have temples all over," Bill continued, his eyes wide. "We saw the Temple of Heaven, the Temple of Hell—they say they're two thousand years old! We even went to the Forbidden City—that's where their ruler lives." Seeing his children were spellbound, Bill continued. "They have wagons there—little ones that people ride in—called rickshas. Only they're not pulled by horses, but by little Chinamen."

"Wow," Alma and Alva said in unison.

"Did you ride on one?" Helen asked.

"Yes, I did," grinned Bill. "China is a wonderful and mysterious place with its music, temples, and dragons."

"Dragons?" Bobby lit up. "They have dragons there?"

"Yes," Bill laughed, "but they're wood and stone. Say, Alva, go over to that top drawer and look inside. There's a cigar box."

Alva moved to the tall dresser and, standing on his toes, pulled open the drawer and lifted out a brown wooden cigar box. "This?"

"Yes," Bill nodded.

Alva placed the cigar box on his father's lap, then took a step back as if something might spring out at any moment.

Bill studied the box. It had been years since he had last opened it. When he lifted its lid, Bill's face lit up at the memories sealed inside. Bill gulped down his emotion as he removed a stack of letters bound by twine.

"What are those?" Helen asked.

"These are letters from your mother," Bill grinned.

"When did she send those to you?"

"A long time ago. Before you kids were born." Bill removed a handful of strange coins and set them on the bed beside him.

"Wow, is that their money?" Alva asked.

"Yep," Bill nodded as he removed a long black wooden spoon with a dragon carved in its handle. "There it is, my dragon."

A breathless "Wow," came from the children who were crowding closer now and watching with wondering eyes for the next relic to be pulled from the box. It was a black-and-white photograph of a baseball team.

"Is that your team?" Bobby asked.

"Yep," Bill breathed. "See? That's me," he pointed.

The children drew closer to view the photograph, careful to avoid their father's injured knee.

"You really like baseball, don't you?" asked Helen.

Bill nodded as he eyed his old teammates fondly.

"Do you wish you were still playing baseball in China?" asked Bobby.

Mildred, who had been standing just outside the bedroom door the entire time, listened carefully for his response.

Bill's eyes narrowed as he considered the question. He looked from the photograph to the uncertain twins, then to the doting Helen and curious Bobby before pulling Patty in tight next to him. Bill gulped as a rush of sentiment overcame him. It was at that moment he knew there was no place in the world he would rather be than stuck in his bed with his children gathered around. Bill shook his head and, with a grin spanning his face, whispered, "No. I would rather be here."

Bill didn't see his smiling wife standing just beyond the bedroom door or the happy tear she wiped from her cheek, but he saw the looks of admiring love from his children, and it made him forget about his knee.

PICKUP STICKS

*T*hat night, Bill dreamed of an elegant room with beautifully ornate carpets and draperies, elaborate woodwork, and glistening golden chandeliers. As he moved through the archway, his eyes lowered to his fine slacks and polished shoes. Bill smiled as he remembered the place, but he didn't know where he remembered it from. Upon entering the magnificent dining room, he stood before a grand table laid out with a feast. As Bill moved toward the feast and the people gathered, he remembered his knee, which no longer hurt. Glad to be healed, Bill looked back up to the feast, but to his disappointment, the table was bare, and the welcoming guests were gone.

Bill sat up in his bed and looked around the darkened room in confusion as his dream faded and reality filled its wake. Mildred was still asleep beside him when Bill reached for his knee. It was still sore to the touch, but not as painful. He carefully swung his legs over the side of the bed and then pushed himself to his feet, gingerly testing his injured knee. To his surprise, while still stiff, he could place his weight on it. Bill took a hobbled step, and then another, amazed at his quick recovery. *I knew it! All it needed was a good night's sleep.*

Careful not to awaken Mildred, who was usually up before him, Bill dressed and then left for work.

~

THE RAIN HAD STOPPED, and gaps in the clouds revealed a blue sky overhead as Bill and his delivery partner, Walter Chesterfield, drove their truck along the back road. With his knee still tender, Bill let the younger Walter drive the truck, which pulled a trailer loaded with thirty-foot log power poles.

With his window halfway down and a cigarette in hand, Bill was enjoying the fresh morning air and speculating aloud that he might only miss one more game when a jolt ran through the truck.

"What was that?" frowned Walter, looking around the cab.

"You run over something?" Bill asked, looking out his window down the steep embankment to a field on their right.

"I don't think so," replied Walter.

Bill's eyes widened when he glanced out the back window. A rope had come loose and the top row of poles had shifted forty-five degrees and were sticking out into the oncoming lane. "Oh, no! We're losing the poles!" he yelled.

"What should I do?" asked the inexperienced Walter.

"Pull to the side and stop before we lose the whole load!" Bill replied. "But watch this side!" he added, reaching a hand to the wheel to keep the truck from going off the steep embankment.

"I got it," Walter said, putting his foot on the brake.

"Easy," Bill warned, eyeing the steep drop off to the right as they neared the crest of a hill. But when a log slid off and struck the road, it yanked the steering wheel from Walter's hand, and the truck swerved into the other lane. Walter regained control of the truck, but not before the top row of poles swung out and off the trailer onto the rain-slick road. Still attached to the trailer, the poles' ends dragged across the opposite lane as the truck slowed, creating a moving roadblock.

The delivery truck was all but stopped when a black Oldsmobile crested the hill, doing forty miles an hour. "WATCH OUT!" Bill yelled, but there was nothing Walter could do. The sound of tires skidding on the wet road lasted only seconds before the Oldsmobile struck the dangling poles and half-turned trailer with a mighty crash. The force of the impact sent the Oldsmobile spinning off the road into a nearby ditch and knocked the poles and trailer back across the road toward the steep embankment. Bill's wide eyes were on the spinning Oldsmobile when their truck lifted off the ground.

Walter cried out as the road before them turned sideways.

"Hang on!" Bill exclaimed as the delivery truck and trailer rolled down the hill.

The crashing and banging were over in seconds, leaving the two electricians staring out their broken windshield, wondering what had happened. While the trailer had twisted loose and was lying on its side with the load of power poles strung down the hill, the truck, with its caved-in cab, had stopped right-side-up and was resting on its bent wheels. It took a moment before Bill realized they were in the field twenty feet below the road. Bill turned to the stunned Walter, who had a trickle of blood running down his head, and breathlessly asked, "You okay?"

"I think so," was Walter's dazed response.

Bill tried to push open his door, but it wouldn't budge. After giving it another shove with no better results, he saw Walter's door was wide open. Smelling gasoline, Bill searched for the cigarette he had lost rolling down the hill. Not finding it, he gave Walter a shove and said, "Smell that gas? Get out before there's a fire!"

Forgetting about his knee, Bill followed Walter out the driver's side door. The still-dazed Walter staggered across the muddy field before regaining his balance. Bill looked at the wrecked truck, shaking his head in dismay. Upon remembering the crashed Oldsmobile, he started up the embankment to the road.

"Where are you going?" asked Walter.

"To see if they're okay," Bill breathlessly replied.

"What about us?" cried Walter, sitting down in the field.

Oblivious to the pain in his knee, shoulder, and back, Bill climbed to the top of the hill where the mangled Oldsmobile sat, a plume of steam rising from its crumpled hood. He looked up the road to the blind crest, then yelled down the hill to Walter, "Get up here and wave down the cars! They can't see over that rise! Hurry!"

"Okay," Walter said, pulling himself up from the muddy field.

Bill had to step over three of the strewn poles to cross the wet road. Upon reaching the crashed car, Bill groaned at the slumped forward driver. "Hey! You okay?" Bill yelled, knocking on the window. He opened the door as the driver sat up with a large gash on his forehead.

"What happened?" moaned the driver as blood streamed onto his blue suit.

"You hit those poles," Bill said, suddenly realizing he was trembling. "You okay?"

The driver put a hand to his head and slowly nodded.

~

"YOU'RE HOME EARLY. How's your knee?" Mildred asked as she went about preparing dinner in the cramped kitchen with a plump, drooling Glen hanging from her arm. She didn't notice Bill's bruised face as he hobbled past her, set his cap on the rack, and then eased onto a dining chair.

"I was half-surprised to see you gone to work this morning," Mildred continued, handing Glen to Bill and then resuming her cooking. "I know just how stubborn you are about letting things like broken legs slow you down, so I wasn't too surprised. Just how is your knee feeling?" she asked as she emptied cut carrots into a pot of stew.

A visibly drained Bill looked at his baby son and muttered, "All right, I suppose. It could be worse."

"Yes, it could be," she replied, still not looking.

"Daddy, what happened to your face?" Helen winced, coming into the kitchen.

"Oh, it was an accident at work," Bill sighed.

Mildred turned at the words and gasped at Bill's bruised face. "My stars, Billy! Whatever happened to you? Did you get into a fight?"

"With an Oldsmobile. I think it was a draw," he painfully smirked.

"Are you okay? What happened?" she asked, leaving the stove.

"We had a load of power poles come loose on the road and got hit by a traveling salesman from California."

"He hit you?" Mildred gasped.

"No, he hit the poles and the trailer, and they rolled us down a hill."

"Is everyone all right?" Mildred asked, her hand still to her mouth.

"Yeah, the salesman fella got a pretty good gash on his head, but we all walked away. The truck and his car, not so good."

"Billy," Mildred breathed, shaking her head. "You should have stayed in bed. None of this would have happened."

"I'm okay," Bill nodded, but he had been considering the same thing since the accident. It wasn't the first time he had pondered the significance of events and wondered if they had any meaning or were just random acts. A part of him thought the wreck was a warning from God for refusing to believe, even after He had made his knee better. But he pushed aside that notion, believing instead it was his own dumb luck, and his knee would have gotten better on its own. Strangely, Bill had been thinking of his old friend Sylvester Schmig since the accident, and what he would have said about it and the blessing. While Bill recognized Sylvester's negativity, he thought his friend had a way of keeping his feet planted in reality and had saved him from being swept away by religious hocus-pocus. But Bill knew the wreck could have killed him, and the thought left him sober-minded.

"What did your boss say?" Mildred asked, still looking him over.

Bill shrugged. "He said accidents happen. He was glad we're okay."

"So am I," Mildred tearfully whispered as she leaned close and gently embraced him.

"Oh, it takes more than a roll down a hill and a busted knee to keep a good man down," Bill grinned, burying his sentiment.

Mildred stepped back and said, "Well, if you're sure you're all right, I have some good news."

"What is it?" Bill asked with some hesitancy.

"Sister Whipple came by and told me of a house to rent. It's over on Kimberly Road. She said it's twice this size and half the rent! Isn't that wonderful?"

Bill, who was still weighed down by the events of the day and the thoughts in his head, smiled at Mildred and said, "Yes, let's take it."

PERSERVES

There was a reason the Kane's new home was less rent; it was old and drafty and difficult to heat. It also stood forty feet from the train tracks. At first, the passing trains were exciting for the children as they shook the house and rattled things off their shelves. But after the tenth train on the first day, Mildred wondered how anyone could live with such a thunderous racket. However, by month's end, they had all grown accustomed to the earth-shaking locomotives.

With the New Year came fresh snow and brutal cold. Even with the fireplace roaring and the kitchen stove lit, Mildred found the house chilly and wore a sweater over her housedress to stay comfortable.

Mildred had just pulled four pans of baked bread from the oven when she heard the front door close and the excited voice of Patty saying, "You're home already?"

Mildred set the hot bread pans aside, then went into the front room, wiping her hands on her apron. Surprised to see all four of her school children standing at the door holding their books and about to remove their coats, she raised a halting hand and said, "Wait just a minute. Why are you home? It's not even noon!" While Mildred's days were filled with cooking, mending, and cleaning, the hours her children were at school gave her some peace, and she wasn't prepared to have them home yet.

"They sent us home," eight-year-old Alva shrugged as he pulled off his coat.

"Why? What did you do?"

"We didn't do nothin'," Bobby shrugged. "They just said go home."

"Bobby, go out and stomp that snow off your feet," Mildred directed, with a twirl of her finger.

Bobby looked down at the puddle forming below him, then turned back to the door.

"Now, *why* are you home?" Mildred asked like an inspector solving a case.

"It's the corn-teen," Helen said, her dark eyebrows gathered.

"Corn-teen? What the dickens?" Mildred asked, with hands on hips. "And why all the books?"

"So we can do our studies," Alma timidly replied.

"Yeah, we gotta stay home for three weeks," added Alva.

"What?" Mildred gasped. "School just started back up again."

The rattle of Bill's Ford coming to a stop caused her to go to the window and push aside the drapes. "Your father's home too? How am I to get anything done?"

The children stepped aside as Bill pushed open the front door and eyed his gathered family. "Well, it looks like you all got the news," he huffed, closing the door.

"And what news is that?" Mildred asked, trying not to be cross.

"The county's under quarantine," Bill sighed, pulling off his coat.

"Quarantine? Whatever for? What does it mean?" asked a wide-eyed Mildred.

"There's a meningitis outbreak," shrugged Bill. "They've closed all the schools and theaters for three weeks. Churches too."

"Meningitis," Mildred gasped, her mind racing back to the Spanish flu epidemic, which took hundreds of thousands of lives and nearly her own, ten years before. "For three weeks?"

"Yep," Bill nodded as he moved past the still standing children and dropped on the couch.

"But what about work?"

"All non-essential personnel are to stay home. I guess I know where I stand," frowned Bill.

AFTER A WEEK, the family had still not settled into the changes brought on by the quarantine. Even though Mildred did her best to occupy the children in the afternoons by reading to them, the near-zero temperatures meant the children ventured out to play for only short periods before coming back inside to whine, quarrel, or otherwise get on Bill's nerves.

While Bill and the children became increasingly stir-crazy for being confined in the house with little to do, Mildred had no such problem. Her workload was unchanged and only hindered by whining children and husband.

Bill was sitting at the kitchen table finishing his breakfast and grumbling about the quarantine when Bobby, who was helping clean up, dropped a jar of preserves on the floor.

"Bobby! See what you've done!" Bill scolded, seeing the mess of broken glass and sugared strawberries. "Why are you so clumsy?"

"Oh, it's all right," Mildred said as she turned from the sink where she was doing the dishes.

"It's not all right!" snapped Bill. "That's a waste of money! Money we don't have when I'm not working and forced to stay in here!"

Mildred kneeled beside Bobby, looking down at the broken jam with his lower lip sagging, and placed her arm around him. "Get the dustpan, and we'll clean it up."

Bill shook his head. "Coddling them won't help, you know."

"It was an accident, and he's only five," Mildred frowned. "Why don't you shovel the front walk? The fresh air will do you good."

Bill huffed, "I think I will." After putting on his hat, coat, and gloves, he stomped out onto the front porch, where four inches of fresh snow covered the walk. Still frustrated and angry about his captivity, he thrust the shovel into the snow and tossed it aside. Feeling some relief from the exertion, Bill rammed his shovel into the snow even more forcefully, but this time, his legs slipped out from under him, and he found himself lying on his back, wincing in pain. After rolling to his side, Bill felt his left elbow, which had taken the brunt of the impact. With a few choice words, he rubbed away the pain as his mind faded in memory…

Spring 1905

EIGHT-YEAR-OLD BILL KANE barely noticed the beauty of the day as he pranced down the street. Having been restricted to his room for that week's mischief, which included skipping two days of school, breaking a neighbor's window with a baseball, lighting a cat's tail on fire, and a few other misdeeds, Bill was as free as a man on parole.

Never one to follow directions too closely, Bill stopped by Harry Mandel's house to include him in the errand. Harry was in trouble himself over the flaming cat incident, but the curly-haired boy managed his escape, climbing out of his upstairs window and down the rain gutter after Bill tossed a few pebbles against his window.

After teasing three girls playing jump rope on the corner and throwing rocks through the broken window of old man Thornton's carriage house, the two cut through an alley on their way to the market.

Inside the market, the white-aproned shopkeeper, all too familiar with the little hooligans, closely watched as they gathered and then brought their supplies to the counter. The shopkeeper eyed the boys sternly as he tallied the cost of the wedge of cheese, jar of preserves, and loaf of bread.

Used to the scrutiny, Bill looked up at the shopkeeper from under his Irish cap with innocent blue eyes. Harry fought to keep a straight face as Bill meekly set four coins on the counter, then loaded his groceries into his empty flour sack. Not fooled by Bill's choirboy act, the shopkeeper shook his head, gave Bill his change, then raised a stiff finger toward the door. Bill and Harry acknowledged the grocer with placid smiles and polite nods before exiting the store with folded arms.

After rounding the corner, Bill burst into laughter and slung the bag over his shoulder. "Did you see the look on old Mr. Grayson?"

"Sure did," Harry laughed as he stooped to pull his socks up to his knickers. "What a sap!"

"What we gonna do next?" Harry asked, repositioning his flat cap.

Bill looked up and down the street, then sighed. "I don't know. I s'pose I gotta get this back, or I'll get in more hot water."

"Ahhh," Harry groaned. "You're no fun."

As they walked down the street, the two watched a steam-powered car sputter past. Bill's jaw slackened as he met eyes with the driver wearing a long coat, hat, and goggles. Once passed, Bill saw the park down the street and said, "We could race to the fountain."

"Naw, I don't feel like it," Harry replied. "Besides, you cheated last time."

"I didn't cheat!" Bill scoffed. "I beat you fair and square."

"Ah, scram! You cheated!" Harry cried.

"No, I didn't!"

"*Yes, you did!*"

"*No, I didn't!* How'd I cheat?" Bill asked, holding his cloth grocery sack over his shoulder.

"You got a head start. You called it after you already started running."

"Well, I can't help it if you're slow," Bill said dismissively.

"Oh yeah? Slow, huh? Well…BEAT YA TO THE FOUNTAIN!" Harry yelled as he knocked the sack off Bill's shoulder and dashed toward the park.

"Hey!" Bill cried, snatching the sack before it hit the ground. "I'll still beat you!"

After tucking the sack under his arm, Bill charged down Adams Street after his friend. With a ten-yard advantage, Harry glanced back with the grin of an expectant winner. But as the gap between the two boys narrowed, so did Harry's grin. Knowing he couldn't outrun Bill, Harry cut in front of a pair of horse-drawn wagons. Not to be outfoxed, Bill slipped between the wagons, causing a horse to rear up.

With the Columbus Park fountain in view, Bill knew he could beat his friend, but it would be close. As Bill veered to miss a sleeping wino, the grocery sack slipped from under his arm and fell between his churning legs, tripping him up. Stumbling forward, Bill winced as he braced for his collision with the walkway. He slammed elbow-first into the curbstone with the jolt of a hundred funny bones and slid along the pavers before rolling on his side in agony.

"You okay there, little fella?" a passing man in a suit and bowler hat asked as he looked down at the sprawled and writhing boy.

Bill looked up at the silhouetted man, but could only manage a tearful nod as he cradled his arm.

"What's this? Are you bleeding?" the man asked.

Bill fought back tears as he looked down at his wounded arm. He expected to see blood gushing from it, but there was only the white cloth flour sack stained red from the preserves.

ROBERT KANE WAS BUSILY PREPARING dinner, his eyes intent, his dark hair neatly combed to the side and his mustache long and curled at its ends. Raising four children without a mother and working full-time to support them was no simple task for Robert. His days managing the Carberry carpet store in the city were often long, which meant the children were unsupervised. When he returned in the evenings, he would sit down to the remains of a meal prepared by the older children and learn of the day's happenings—including Bill's antics. With Saturdays just as busy, Sunday was the only day he could be with his children. While there had been single women eager to step in, including some who went to great lengths pursuing him, Robert found the idea of replacing his cherished Mary unpalatable.

On this Saturday, Mr. Kane was home in time to help Hubert and Iliene with the meal. After all were seated, Mr. Kane bowed his head and, with his handlebar mustache dancing, said, "Bless us, oh Lord, and these thy gifts which we are about to receive from thy bounty, through Christ our Lord. Amen." When Mr. Kane gave the nod, the children eagerly passed around the fried catfish, mashed potatoes, fresh corn sliced straight from the cob, and cornbread biscuits. Mr. Kane didn't see Iliene dishing up young Bill's plate. He purposely looked away from the boy, who was drawn to mischief like a fly to a trash can, to avoid any conflict and enjoy the meal.

The sound of clattering utensils, clinking glasses, and smacking lips soon filled the room as Hubert, Thomas, and Iliene ate. But Bill stared at his food.

Of the Kane children, sixteen-year-old Hubert was the quietest and as different from Bill as could be. For nary a word to leave his lips at dinnertime was the norm, and he often required prodding to speak. It wasn't that Hubert was bashful; he simply found little to say and spent much of his time with his head in a book. But Hubert's subdued nature was rooted in sadness, and he was perhaps affected the most by their mother's death four years before.

Twelve-year-old Thomas was the responsible one and frequently acted as Bill's misplaced conscience, reining him in when necessary and providing discipline in an older brother sort of way.

Adorable ten-year-old Iliene, though the second to the youngest of the children, was the woman of the house. Mature beyond her years, she filled a vital role in bringing a sense of femininity to the family. Musically talented, her singing and piano playing often soothed their father's tattered soul. And she often acted as a buffer between the mischievous Bill and their short-tempered father.

Like any good Irish Catholic, Robert Kane encouraged regular attendance at Mass and emphasized the importance of being a good Catholic. That meant being good citizens and, by extension, obtaining an education. Unfortunately, his efforts lacked the finishing touches of a mother and often fell short. This was especially apparent in Bill, who stretched every truth, bent every rule, and broke as many laws as his small frame would allow. Frequently exasperated by his youngest boy's antics, Mr. Kane often muttered, "That boy will be my undoing."

Upon learning public schools were no match for Bill, Mr. Kane sent him to The Hull House, where child expert Miss Jane Addams tried to break Bill. When she failed, the Benevolent Nuns at the Holy Family Catholic School took their turn. But they too proved to be no match for the difficult and wily young Bill.

Mr. Kane was enjoying his meal and the unusual quiet when he realized something was amiss. His tired eyes moved to Hubert, quietly eating at the far end of the table before turning to his lovely Iliene. Her dark hair pulled up in a bun reminded him of his dearly beloved wife. Iliene was unusually quiet, and he caught her more than once looking across the table at Bill with motherly concern.

Mr. Kane's brow gathered as he eyed Bill, who could have been a ghost for all the noise he was making. He noticed Bill had barely touched his food and was fumbling with his fork. Not wanting to ruin the peaceful silence, Mr. Kane returned to his plate and last bites of catfish.

Upon finishing, Mr. Kane wiped his mouth and mustache with a napkin and said, "Thomas, this catfish is delightful. Where did you go to catch it?"

"Just down at the river," Thomas said, trying not to look at Bill.

Knowing something was wrong, Mr. Kane cleared his throat. He was about to speak when he realized Bill was fumbling with his fork in his left hand and that his right hadn't moved from his lap the entire meal. "William?" he asked, his voice resonating in the quiet.

"Yes, Father?" Bill muttered, turning to him sheepishly.

"Don't you care for the catfish?"

"Yes, Father. It's good," Bill answered, his face pale.

"That's odd," frowned Mr. Kane. "I don't recall you ever eating with your left hand. When did you start?"

"Oh, sometime back," shrugged Bill, wincing as he did.

Mr. Kane's brow tightened. "And why so?" He glanced at Iliene, looking down at her plate, and then at Thomas, fighting a grin.

"Well, I just got to thinking," Bill started, "if anything ever happened to my right hand, I should probably know how to eat with my other. Don't you think? Otherwise, a fella could starve."

"Makes perfect sense," snickered Thomas.

"Well, it does!" exclaimed Bill, on the verge of tears.

Mr. Kane laid his napkin on the plate, leaned forward, and asked, "William, what have you done to your arm?"

"My arm?" Bill asked, his face even paler.

"Yes, your arm, that appendage dangling from your shoulder. Were you in a fight?"

"What arm?"

"Your *right* arm, boy. What did you do to it?" Mr. Kane asked, losing patience.

"Nothing," shrugged Bill, forgetting the pain it brought.

"Hmm. Very well then. Let's see you eat with your right hand."

"Well," Bill delayed, "I think I should practice with my left one some more. Sister Penelope says practice makes perfect."

"With your right hand, William. Now."

"Yes, sir." Bill gingerly pulled his right hand up from his lap, moved his fork over to it with his left, and gave a painful sigh.

Mr. Kane saw Bill's swollen wrist and said, "William, what happened to your arm? Pull up your sleeve."

Grimacing, Bill pulled his sleeve up over his swollen and bruised arm.

Iliene gasped. "Oh no, William! You didn't say it was that bad!"

"You all knew about this?" glared Mr. Kane.

Both Thomas and Iliene nodded reluctantly. It wasn't the first time they had hid Bill's antics from their father, both to protect him and their brother.

"I didn't know about it, Father," frowned Hubert.

Thomas rolled his eyes.

"Come here, lad," directed a stern-eyed Mr. Kane.

Bill pushed back his chair and walked to his father's side.

After examining Bill's bruised and swollen arm more closely, Mr. Kane groaned, "Oh, William. What happened?"

Tears filled Bill's eyes as he wincingly replied, "I fell."

"You fell? Tell me the truth," glared Mr. Kane.

"It is."

"You fell? Fell off what? Our house? The Madison Bank? The water tower? What?" Mr. Kane barked.

"Well, I was racing Harry…and I tripped and fell. I hit the curbstone by the park and broke the…"

"Broke the what?"

"The preserves from the market," Bill said, looking down.

Turning to his daughter, Mr. Kane said, "Iliene, you told me you dropped the bag and broke the jam."

"Sorry, Father," Iliene said with eyes that thawed him. "It's just that

William is always getting into trouble, and, well, I didn't want you to get mad at him. It had been such a good day and…well. I'm sorry."

With a heavy sigh, Mr. Kane turned to Bill and said, "William, I don't care about the preserves, but I do care about your arm."

Bill was still rubbing his elbow when his mind returned to the present. He looked down the snow-covered walk, then back at his house. He thought of his father as he picked up the snow shovel. It was easy for Bill to remember the man's sternness, a hardness brought on in part by Bill's childhood mischievousness, but his father had a soft side as well that showed through from time to time. *Why is it so hard to remember that side of him?*

While Bill had long blamed his father for their failed relationship, deep inside, Bill feared it was mostly his own doing. As Bill reflected on his father now, he realized he was a man in pain. Losing his mother, while hard on Bill and the other children, was something his father had never recovered from. Bill paused his shoveling and looked back at the warm glow of his home. A shudder ran through him as he considered what he would do if something happened to his dear Mildred.

Bill shook off the sad thought and resumed his shoveling. Suddenly, more than anything, Bill wished he had been given the chance to reconcile with his father. Bill knew his father was a good man at heart, merely trying to do his best under difficult circumstances. Bill wondered what he would have said to his father had he been given a chance—or if he would have said anything at all.

Bill sighed as he tossed a shovel full of snow aside. He thought about his children and the father he had been to them. He wondered what issues they would deal with as they looked back on him as adults. Bill shook the thought from his head and thrust the shovel back into the snow. He had work to do.

∾

PECANS AND PUNCHES

*B*y early spring, the Kanes had moved from the drafty house beside the tracks to another home. It was peaceful in comparison, with a yard full of nut and fruit trees, sweet-smelling lilacs, and colorful petunias. After a long, cold winter and weeks of quarantine, they found it to be the perfect home to enjoy the lovely spring. But this home had its drawbacks too, namely their demanding and ill-tempered landlady.

"Hello, Mrs. Cross," Mildred said as she answered the door. "Won't you come in?"

"No, thank you," snapped Gertrude Cross as she peered through her dark-rimmed spectacles. While not unattractive, Mrs. Cross had a perpetual scowl that drew her wrinkles in toward her upturned nose and scrutinizing eyes. Even though she had never married, she insisted on the title "Missus."

"What can I do for you?" Mildred asked uneasily.

"Do you see this?" Mrs. Cross asked, holding up a severed rope swing.

Mildred glanced out the side window to the pecan tree that had held the swing but saw only cut ropes remaining. "That's the children's swing. Is there a—"

"Problem?" Mrs. Cross finished for her. "Yes, there is. I thought we had an understanding about my trees."

Mildred gulped. "Yes, we are—"

"To care for my trees," Mrs. Cross again interrupted.

"Yes, ma'am," Mildred nodded, uncertain of what misdeed she had committed.

"This, *this swing*, is NOT caring for the tree. The rope will strangle the poor branch or break it!" a red-faced Mrs. Cross barked. "The pecans for my award-winning pecan pie come from that tree, and I will not have you harming it!"

"I'm sorry, the children do love to swing and—"

"I don't care what your little brats love. It is my tree and my house," she glared, looking around Mildred to see inside.

"I'm sorry," Mildred shrugged. "I had no idea the swing was harming the tree. We won't put it back up."

"No, you surely won't," Mrs. Cross snapped. Turning, she started for her car with the rope swing in hand.

"But—"

"But what?" Mrs. Cross asked, turning back.

Mildred wanted her to leave the swing for their next house, but felt it better to say no more.

"And I'll remind you," Mrs. Cross scowled, "that the fruit from my trees —and especially my pecans—are not for your consumption. They are strictly my property. Is that clear?"

"Yes, ma'am," nodded Mildred.

"Oh, and one last thing," Mrs. Cross said pointedly, "Your rent is going up."

"Again?"

Mrs. Cross surveyed the front of the house and nodded decisively. "Yes. Five dollars."

"Five dollars! My gracious!" gasped Mildred.

"You can move if it's too much."

Mildred's brow gathered in defeat. The rent had gone up twice in as many months, but it was still less than their first house in Twin Falls. "All right, we'll pay it next month," she muttered as she pushed the door closed.

JUNE WAS on pace to be Bill's best month at work since moving to Twin Falls. That said, he was making little more than when they left Boise, and finances were as tight as ever. With the coming school year only a few months away, he had hoped to surprise Mildred with enough money for the children to have one new outfit each, but the news of their ever-increasing rent made such a plan doubtful.

"What does she think? We're made of money?" grumbled Bill.

Mildred, who was sitting on the couch and stroking Patty's back, shrugged and said, "I don't know what to think. She certainly isn't very nice, though."

"She's a mean lady?" asked Patty, raising her head.

Mildred's eyes flashed from Bill to their five-year-old. "Why don't you run outside and see what the other children are doing?"

Patty got up from Mildred's lap and obediently pushed open the front screen door. Bill watched the door close, then sighed and said, "I'm beginning to think it was a mistake to leave Boise."

Mildred's eyes met his, but she didn't say what she was thinking. She didn't remind him she never wanted to leave, or that they had gone from one bad situation to another since being in Twin Falls. Instead, she nodded in agreement. "Are you thinking of moving back to Boise?"

Bill shrugged. "Maybe."

"What about your baseball? You've become something of a star here in Twin Falls."

"Naw," Bill sighed with a dismissive wave as he flipped through the paper. "Besides, with the change in the league, it hasn't been the same this year." He watched Glen crawl along the floor to Mildred and asked, "Do you think she's trying to make us leave?"

"Mrs. Cross?" Mildred asked, picking up the baby.

Bill nodded.

"Well, she's made it clear she doesn't like our children—or us."

"Does she like anyone?" huffed Bill.

Mildred shrugged. She thought about their situation and how much she missed Boise. She especially missed their old house by the river and wished they had never left it. After a tired sigh, she turned to Bill and asked, "Will you see what the children are up to?"

Bill glanced out the window, then returned to his newspaper and casually said, "The twins are building a house in the pecan tree, and Bobby is chopping down the peach tree."

"What!" Mildred gasped, rocketing from her seat with the baby. But when she saw the boys playing army in the orchard and Helen pulling Pattie in a wagon, her frantic look faded, and she kicked Bill.

Bill laughed and went back to his paper.

~

WITH THE SUMMER over and the four older children back in school, Mildred was looking forward to a less hectic schedule. But with no one to help watch the toddling Glen and the ever-curious Patty, she found her days were even busier. To make matters worse, Bobby was suddenly unwilling to go to school, forcing the twins to carry him, kicking and screaming. After a week of such protests, Mildred knew it was time to get her husband involved.

"Bobby, your mother tells me you don't want to go to school," Bill said, looking down with folded arms at the sandy-haired first-grader.

Bobby shook his head, his lower lip down, his hands tucked into his hand-me-down bib overalls.

"Why not? School's fun," Bill said, almost choking on the words.

Bobby shook his head.

Bill's eyes narrowed. "What's the matter?"

Bobby shrugged, and his gaze lowered to the rug.

Bill thought back to the things he hated about school, but didn't know where to start. With brow gathered, he asked, "Is someone picking on you? Is someone teasing you?"

Bobby shrugged again, but more slowly this time. Then, looking up with his large blue eyes, he said, "Maybe."

Bill sighed. Being smaller as a child, he was all too familiar with bullies and had learned young how to deal with them. "You know, it's okay to stand up for yourself," he said, kneeling beside his son. "This is what you do. If someone tries to bully you, you sock him in the nose! Like this," Bill said, making a punching motion. "Try it," he said, holding out his open hand.

Bobby gulped, then weakly punched Bill's palm.

"No, that was like a butterfly landing," scowled Bill. "Make a fist like this, then punch hard, like you mean it! And don't stop. Punch him like his nose is on the other side of his head."

Bobby nodded. Then, with steely eyes, slugged Bill's palm.

"That's it! Do that to any bully, and they'll leave you alone."

With renewed confidence, Bobby gathered up his books and headed out the door to the waiting twins and Helen.

More than a little pleased with himself, Bill went back into the kitchen, where Mildred was cleaning up breakfast. "Well, I better get to work," he said, pulling on his cap.

"What about Bobby?" asked Mildred.

"I took care of things," Bill said proudly. "He's off to school."

Mildred eyed her husband rather suspiciously then, realizing one of her problems was resolved, she kissed him goodbye and resumed her labors.

HAVING FORGOTTEN ALL about his conversation with Bobby that morning, Bill was happy to see him and Mildred standing on the front stoop when he pulled up in his old, unreliable Ford.

"This is a fine welcome home," Bill smiled as he pushed the car door closed and stepped on his cigarette. But his smile faded when he noticed Mildred's serious face and a downcast Bobby. "What's the matter?"

"And just what was it you told your son this morning?" asked Mildred, with one hand on Bobby's shoulder and the other on her hip.

Oh-oh. Bill stopped, pulled off his cap, and scratched his head. "I told him to stand up to any bullies. To sock them in the nose."

Bobby raised his head somewhat ashamedly, revealing a blackened eye and swollen lip.

Bill's brow gathered as he considered what he had said that morning. Boyhood brawls and street scuffles were a way of life in Chicago, and he couldn't imagine his advice being wrong.

"To sock them in the nose?" Mildred asked with wide eyes. "Your son did that very thing and was sent home for fighting!"

"Hmm," Bill said as he considered the situation.

"That's all you have to say?" Mildred asked, shaking her head.

"How did the other kid fair?" asked Bill.

"Ugh!" Mildred gasped before turning back into the house.

Bill waited for the screen door to slam close, then took a step closer to the ashamed Bobby. "Son, there's nothing wrong with defending yourself," Bill said, lifting Bobby's chin to see the bruising better.

Bobby nodded, though not convinced.

Bill sat on the stoop, and his son sat beside him. "What about the other kid?"

"He got a bloody nose," Bobby said, uncertain of how he would be judged.

Bill nodded approvingly then, after a moment's thought, said, "The teacher sent you home for sticking up for yourself?"

Bobby nodded.

"Hmm. Times have changed."

"Did you ever get into fights when you were a boy?" Bobby asked, looking up at his father.

Bill laughed as his mind returned to his boyhood in Chicago…

June 1909

A TWO-FOOT RIBBON of sunlight ran the length of the dingy alley. Stacks of empty wooden crates lined one side, and a row of smelly trashcans with mangy cats milling about stood against the other. Through the center of the alley were murky puddles of rainwater with wet, pasted-down newspapers and shattered fragments of crates smashed by passing carriages or mischievous boys.

At one end of the alley, between the wooden crates and smelly trashcans, stood Bill and two of his twelve-year-old friends.

"Here they come," gulped the frizzy-haired Harry Mandel as he peered down the shadowed alley.

"Right on time," Bill nodded, glancing at Harry and the stout Leo McDonald, whose hair was always neatly parted down the middle.

"Sorry we're late," huffed Dan Healy as he and his buck-toothed and crooked-eyed brother Jerry ran up from behind.

"Oh! You scared the crap outta me!" Harry gasped as he spun around.

"Sorry. We didn't miss it, did we?" asked Jerry, pushing his shaggy bangs out of his eyes as he caught his breath.

"Do you think we'd be standin' here like this if we already fought 'em?" asked Leo, exposing a gap between his front teeth.

"Here they come," announced Bill as four dark-haired boys emerged from the shadows.

"There's only four of 'em," Harry whispered, somewhat relieved. "You fellas don't even need me. I'm going to get back and—"

"We need you, Harry," insisted Bill. "Dan or Jerry can sit this one out."

"Oh, all right," sighed Harry.

The four tough-faced Italian boys continued down the alley, stopping ten feet from Bill and his friends. "We hear you clowns wanna fight," Marzio Mancini grunted, his single thick brow gathered and his nose curled in disdain.

"We know you've been stealing from the rabbi," glared Bill. "Isn't that right, Harry?"

Harry, who was the slightest of the group, had on his most threatening scowl when he nodded and said, "Yeah."

"I never figured you Irish bums for Jew-lovers," sneered Marzio as he stared down Harry. "You and your fancy Jew-boy."

"Who you callin' a Jew-boy?" Leo asked, taking a step closer.

"Your fuzzy-haired freak here," said Marzio, pointing to Harry.

"Yeah, your fuzzy-haired freak," echoed Marzio's brother Orazio, who hadn't yet lost his baby fat.

Leo made a scoffing face and said, "It's too bad you two have to share the same brain."

"It's too bad I'm gonna mess up your face and your nice hair your fat mother combed for you," snarled Marzio.

Leo clenched his fists as his chubby cheeks turned red. "Don't talk about my mother like that," he growled, shaking his head.

"You mean your fat, ugly mother?" glared Marzio.

The other Italians, and especially Orazio, laughed.

Bill glanced at Leo, the largest of the group, and grinned. Leo McDonald was a tenderhearted boy until he got mad, and then he was a wrecking machine. "You've been stealin' from the rabbi," Bill growled as he pulled up a sleeve, "and you're going to take it all back."

"Yeah? Or what?" Marzio asked, his head tilted, his hand to his ear. "What's your cross-eyed freak over there gonna do when I knock his other eye crooked?"

Jerry Healy, who had been quietly listening to the exchange, made an angry face at the comment.

Orazio was about to repeat his brother's words when Jerry Healy jumped forward and put him in a headlock, yelling, "Take it back! Take it back!" Caught off guard by Jerry's move, Bill looked forward in time to see Marzio's fist flying toward him. He moved, but not in time to miss the blow. Marzio struck the side of Bill's head, knocking him backward. By the time Bill responded with a punch of his own, Leo had leaped into the fray, knocking Fiorentini Palmiro and Steven Barese down single-handedly and leaving Harry Mandel and Dan Healy looking on.

The brawl widened as Palmiro and Barese retaliated against the larger Leo, causing Harry and Dan to jump in. Soon all were rolling around the alley, grunting, cursing, and throwing weak blows. Bill had Marzio's coat over his head and was landing punches to his midsection when the shrill sounds of police whistles echoed down the alley.

The whistles caused all but Bill and Marzio, whom Bill was getting the better of, to back away. Orazio tried to run off when a hulking, blue-uniformed policeman, with a row of brass buttons running down his tunic and a six-pointed star on his left breast, emerged from the shadows and grabbed him. When a third and fourth officer arrived, the boys knew the fight was over.

Bill was still landing blows when officer McGuire pulled him off Marzio, who still had his coat over his head.

"All right, you little rats!" shouted McGuire, a large man whom Bill had run from on more than one occasion. "What have we told you about fighting?" McGuire, who had a dark, bushy mustache and a hard, unforgiving face, spoke with an Irish accent.

"These wops here were stealing from the rabbi, and we're just makin' it right!" Bill exclaimed.

"We weren't stealing!" grumbled Marzio, finally getting his coat situated, his thick black hair standing every which way, his lip swollen and mouth bloody.

The others on both sides joined in the banter, resuming fighting postures.

"Shut up!" McGuire barked as he jumped between the boys with separating arms, his tall, bowler-like precinct hat nearly falling off. Instantly, the group quieted. After repositioning his hat, McGuire pointed his nightstick at Bill and growled, "I've had enough of you!"

Bill couldn't help the grin that formed as he recalled, perhaps his greatest feat, knocking Officer McGuire's hat off with a snowball from forty feet away. Suddenly Bill remembered their cause and blurted, "But they were stealin' from the—"

"I said, shut up!" McGuire bellowed. "You can tell it all to Judge Pickney!"

Bill's grin vanished.

JUDGE PICKNEY WAS A TIRED, middle-aged man with a beard that was full and bushy below his chin but shorter on his cheeks. His hair was all but gone on the top of his head, except for a lone, clinging tuft above his forehead, which he colored with shoe polish and spread about to cover his otherwise naked scalp.

The judge's chambers were simple with dark wood paneling, a desk that stood on a raised platform below a hanging electric light, and a glazed window badly in need of cleaning. Before the judge, opposite his gavel, were an overturned pipe and an old inkwell for his relic dip pen he refused to part with.

Sifting through papers on his desk with his spectacles resting on the end of his nose, the judge let out a tired groan at the sound of arguing boys. He pulled off his spectacles and looked with dread at the door as Officer McGuire herded nine dirty-faced, dusty, and tattered boys inside. The weary-eyed judge hastily scanned the rowdy hellions, most of whom he knew by name, then shook his head in disapproval.

"I said, shut up!" Officer McGuire bellowed as he dragged Bill and Marzio to the front of the group by their collars.

The squabbling of who was to blame for what continued until Judge Pickney lowered his gavel. The loud crack resonated through the chamber and brought the two bickering boys to attention.

"That's enough, that's enough!" Judge Pickney exclaimed, tired of dealing with such things.

Bill, whose coat collar was pulled up to his ears, tried to pull away from Officer McGuire, but the large Irishman held firm.

The irritated judge drew in a tired breath, looked squarely at Officer McGuire, and said, "What do we have today, Jim?"

"These rascals here were fighting in an alley," McGuire explained.

"And why were you fighting?" Pickney asked as he tiredly rubbed his forehead.

"They were stealing!" Bill cried.

"No, we wasn't!" Marzio shouted.

"From the rabbi! We saw ya!" yelled Harry.

In an instant, the room was re-engulfed in pre-pubescent accusation and defamation.

"That's enough!" Pickney yelled, bringing his gavel down hard once again and running an exasperated hand down his face. Once the boys quieted, he looked over their sour faces then said, "I've warned you, I won't stand for your gang fights. We won't have it here. We are civil people. You don't want to grow up picking a fight just because you don't like someone."

Bill shook his head, certain the judge hadn't heard him correctly. "But they—"

"QUIET!" the judge barked, stopping Bill mid-sentence. "You. You're Robert Kane's boy," he said with a pointing finger. "I remember you all too well. I don't know how many times I've had you in here with your father. You haven't given him a bit of peace. Should I send for him now?"

Bill's righteous indignation promptly faded, and after lowering his head, he quietly answered, "No, sir."

"I think I might, just the same," grumbled the judge. "Here it is, only just June. School hasn't been out two weeks, and you're already causing trouble. I think you all need something to do—something besides these damnable gang fights every day." Pausing, he looked over the boys, whose heads were now hanging low. "I have just the thing for you," he smirked. "Something that will keep you boys out of trouble and out of my hair. Something that will give you some proper military discipline and set you straight!"

Bill looked up, his eyes wide with dreadful expectation. *Is he sending us to jail? Or the chain gang?* he wondered. He remembered seeing the black-and-white striped prisoners knocking down an old factory wall and separating bricks and thinking it looked like fun.

"I'm sending all of you to the Chicago Parental School for the summer."

"What? No!" Bill gasped. "Not more school!"

"It's a home for delinquent boys, and you fit that to a tee," Pickney sneered as he eyed Bill. "They'll teach you how to act properly—since your parents seem to lack that capability." He then added under his breath, "And then maybe I'll be able to enjoy my summer."

"Well, did you, Dad?" Bobby asked, still waiting for an answer.

Bill turned to his son sitting on the stoop beside him and tried to remember the question.

"Did you ever get into fights?" Bobby asked again.

Bill gave a little shrug and said, "A few. But your mother would tell you it's better not to," he quickly added.

~

CROSS TIMES

October 1929

*B*ill rubbed his eyes as he sat at the kitchen table across from seven-year-old Helen. She had before her a slice of toast and a cup of hot water mixed with sugar and a touch of milk. "Morning," Bill mumbled as he picked up the morning paper and breathed in the smell of cooking bacon, eggs, and coffee.

"Good morning, dear," Mildred said as she turned from the stove and poured him a cup of coffee. "How did you sleep?"

"Fine," grumbled Bill, sipping his coffee, not quite awake.

"Morning," Alma said as he entered the room with his hair slicked back and blue flannel shirt buttoned to the collar.

"Morning," Alva echoed, looking much the same but for a green flannel shirt.

"Good morning, boys," Mildred smiled warmly. "Helen already blessed the food."

"Good morning," Bill nodded as he set his coffee down.

Helen watched Bill for a moment, then asked, "Daddy, why do you drink that?"

"Drink what?" Bill asked, knowing full well what she meant.

"That," Helen said, pointing to the steaming black cup.

"Because I like it," frowned Bill. "Why do you drink that?" he asked, nodding to her hot sugar water.

"Because that's what mommy gives us," answered Helen.

"Well, this is what Mother gives me, and it wakes me up in the morning," Bill said, as Mildred set a plate of eggs and bacon before him.

"Mommy doesn't drink it, and she wakes up before you," shrugged Helen.

The twins, waiting for their hot water and toast, looked from Helen to their father, anticipating an angry reply.

"Hmph," More annoyed than angry, Bill gave Mildred a did-you-put-them-up-to-this glance, then said, "I like it, and it's my business."

"Oh," Helen said, thinking about the answer as she finished her toast.

Mildred held back a smirk as she eyed her moody husband. "Billy, Helen said she would like to be a princess for Halloween. What do you think about that?"

He looked from his inquisitive daughter to Mildred and nodded. "Sounds fine."

"Yipee!" Helen said, bouncing in her seat.

Bill had just finished his breakfast and opened the newspaper when his eyes were drawn to the bold headline: STOCK MARKET CRASH! Billions Lost. "Hmm." Bill read the article with a gathered brow. Then, looking over the paper at Mildred, said, "Says here, the rich folks in New York lost all their money."

"How so?" Mildred asked, wiping her hands.

"The stock market crashed," Bill said, still reading.

"What did it crash into?" asked Bobby, his mouth full.

"No, it's a place where rich people put their money," replied Bill.

"Like a bank?" Alma asked.

"Something like that," nodded Bill.

"And they lost it all?" Helen asked, uncertain how to respond. "Isn't that sad?"

"No, they're rich," Bill shrugged. "They probably had it coming."

"What does that mean for us?" asked Mildred, finally sitting down with her toast.

"Nothing," Bill shrugged, turning the page. "We don't have any money there."

"Do you have money in a real bank?" Alma asked.

"That's none of your concern," Bill said pointedly.

"Yes, sir," said Alma, returning to his hot water and toast.

~

WITH THE FIRST days of November came an icy wind and rain, which stripped the trees of the last of their leaves, including the fruit and nut trees outside the Kane home.

Mildred had sent all but baby Glen and Patty off to school three hours earlier and was sitting down for the first time since waking when a rapid knock came at the front door. With a groan, Mildred tossed off a shawl, pushed herself up out of the chair, and scooped up the crawling Glen before opening the door. Her eyes widened as she saw their landlady, Mrs. Cross, standing under a dripping umbrella with a perturbed scowl.

"Good morning, Mrs. Cross," Mildred said tiredly.

"Is it?" Mrs. Cross asked with a perfunctory glance at the gray, drizzling sky.

"What can I do for you?" Mildred asked, doing her best to muster a polite smile.

"You can move," Mrs. Cross said sharply.

"Pardon me?" Mildred asked, taken aback.

"You heard me," snapped Mrs. Cross.

"Do-do you want to come in?" Mildred asked.

"I do not." Mrs. Cross replied, wrinkling her nose at the delicious aroma of baking bread.

Mildred gulped as she grasped the full meaning of Mrs. Cross' words. "Have we done something wrong?"

"Yes. Do you see those leaves that have fallen?"

Mildred turned to the side window and saw the bare fruit and nut trees surrounded by a bed of fallen, wet leaves. "Yes."

"You were to care for those trees and the yard!"

"And we have," Mildred protested as baby Glen started fussing.

"You have NOT! If you had, I wouldn't see that carpet of leaves out there! They will suffocate the lawn, you know!"

Suffocate the lawn? Mildred wanted to argue the point, but knew it would be to no end. "But it's been raining," she explained. "We haven't had time—"

"I don't want to hear your excuses!" exclaimed Mrs. Cross, glaring at Patty hiding behind Mildred's skirt. "I want you out by the end of the month, and that's that!"

"What?" Mildred gasped. "Where will we go?"

"I imagine to some indiscriminate homeowner who is not bothered by your delinquent children. It's not my concern!"

Staggered by the venomous words, Mildred grabbed the door. She wanted to slam it in Mrs. Cross' face but resisted. "Can-can we have until the first of the year?" she asked, holding back her anger.

"You may not. Do I need the sheriff to give you notice? Are you that type of people?"

Mildred could take no more. "No, we are not *that type of people!* We are law-abiding and pay our debts and rent on time! Even when it continues to raise unfairly!"

Mrs. Cross huffed.

"And I'll have you know; my children are not *delinquents!* They are very well-behaved children, and you would know that had you been kind enough to marry and warm enough to conceive children of your own!"

Mrs. Cross staggered back, speechless.

"We will be out of your house with your precious trees by the end of the month, and you can care for them yourself!" Mildred exclaimed, slamming the door.

BILL SCRATCHED his head as he looked down at the table in thought. "That's it then. We move."

"I'm sorry, Billy," Mildred said with a sad shake of her head. "I should have been more patient and Christ-like, I know, but I couldn't help myself. She's a cruel and evil woman."

Alma entered the kitchen, but his father's stern look stopped him in his tracks and turned him back into the front room without a word.

"I'm sorry, Billy."

"Don't be," sighed Bill. "It was just a matter of time. And better you than me."

"What do you mean?"

"If I'd been there, you'd be visiting me in jail," he smirked.

Mildred smiled and reached a hand across the table to Bill. "What do we do now?" she whispered.

Bill drew a deep breath, then said, "I've been thinking. Ever since we've been here, we've had nothing but trouble. It's been one problem after another—starting with the drive here. I'm beginning to wonder if Twin Falls is cursed for us."

Mildred pulled her hand back and, with a look of concern, asked, "You're not still considering moving the family to Chicago, are you?"

Their eyes met, and Bill said, "No. I think we should go back."

"Back to Boise?" Mildred gasped. "Do you mean it?"

"Yes. Sylvester told me there's an apprentice lineman spot open. I'm going to put in for it. Twin Falls has been nothing but a mistake. We should have never come here."

"We're going back to Boise?" Alma excitedly asked, sticking his head around the corner.

"Get out!" Bill yelled, half-smiling.

"What if they don't hire you back?" Mildred fretted.

"Sylvester says I'm a shoo-in," Bill replied.

As bad as Mildred wanted to return to Boise, Bill's assurance did not entirely comfort her. With the recent news of the stock market crash and job losses back East, she feared Bill quitting his job in Twin Falls might be a mistake. Her other concern was Bill returning to the influence of the unprincipled Sylvester Schmig, who never had a good thing to say about anyone or anything. Still, there were more positives than negatives, she decided. They would be closer to family, including John Young, who had offset Sylvester's influence. Mildred remembered the house by the river they had left. It had been perfect for their family, and it saddened her they would have to find somewhere else to live.

It was the day before Thanksgiving. The first snow of the season had fallen, and with it, the temperature. While the news Bill had the lineman job in Boise was a great relief to Mildred, it meant they would once again be moving their family and belongings, only this time without the help of friends. As the deadline for them to be out of the house loomed, Mildred's stress climbed. Along with her usual chores, she now had packing to do. She was managing the pressure well, but when the furnace went out for the third time in as many weeks, she threw up her arms and stomped out of the house. If not for Helen looking out of the window, no one would have seen her kicking and shaking the leafless pecan tree.

Three days had passed since Bill left for Boise in his rickety old Ford to find them a new home. Mildred tried not to dwell on all the things that could happen to him along the way, with the roads being slick, and hoped he was safe. With no phone in the neighborhood, the only message she might have gotten from him would be via telegram or through someone in the ward. While Mildred would have liked to have heard from Bill regarding his progress, she knew it was unlikely, as he was an independent and stubborn man who only grew more so in times of trouble.

With the house cold from the broken furnace, the children spent their time in the kitchen, warmed by Mildred's cooking.

Mildred had just shed her sweater and re-donned her apron when a nervous-looking Alma entered the kitchen and said, "Mother, I think the sheriff is here."

"The sheriff?" gasped Mildred as she turned from the stove. "My stars, whatever for? We still have nearly a week left!" Pulling off her apron, she moved past Alma into the front room, put on her sweater, and looked out the window. The sight of a shiny black Oldsmobile parked outside their house brought a dark and disturbing thought. *What if the deputy is not here about the house? What if something happened to Bill? I haven't heard from him in days. What if there was a wreck? What if...* Mildred cautiously approached the front door expecting the loud knock of a deputy and braced for the worst kind of news.

Reaching for the door, Mildred pulled her hand away when the knob turned and the door opened. "Oh, my," she gasped, taking a step back as a man in a coat and hat, whose face she could not see, started into their home. "Hello? Can I help you?" Mildred asked in surprise.

"Yes, you can," grinned Bill, pulling off his hat.

"Oh, Billy!" Mildred exclaimed, wilting in relief. "Alma said it was the sheriff. I thought he was coming to kick us out into the cold or to give me terrible news!"

"I'm just fine," chuckled Bill, giving Mildred a comforting embrace.

"Daddy!" Helen yelled, rushing in from the kitchen with Patty close behind. "Did you find us a house?"

"Yes," Bill smiled as the twins and Bobby, with Glen in his arms, gathered around.

"We missed you," Alma said quietly.

"And I missed you," Bill nodded as he pulled off his coat. His brow gathered, and he asked, "Why is it so cold in here?"

"The furnace went out again," shrugged Mildred, still somewhat emotional.

"Why didn't you have Mrs. Cross fix it?"

"Oh, I couldn't bear dealing with that woman again," sighed Mildred.

"She kicked the tree instead," explained Helen.

"What?" Bill asked, confused.

166

"Oh, nothing," Mildred blushed. "How did it go? And what's that car you're driving? What happened to old Question Mark?"

"That old wreck was on its last leg, so they gave me a company car to come back and get you."

"Oh, my," Mildred said with wide eyes, "We're moving up in the world!"

"Yes, we are!" Bill grinned, holding back the best news of all.

"What about a house? What have you found?"

"I found a house," said Bill with a casual shrug.

"Good, where is it?" Mildred asked, her curiosity piqued.

"It's on Madison Avenue," Bill said, fighting back a grin.

"Madison Avenue?" Mildred repeated, somewhat confused. "We used to live on that street. Is it near our old house?" she asked, wounded by the thought of being so near to the home she loved.

"It *is* our old house," beamed Bill.

"What?" gasped Mildred, her hand to her chest.

"It's true," Bill emphatically nodded. "I visited the house, and it was empty and for sale. I rang up Mr. Garrison, and he agreed to sell it to us!"

"What?" The excitement on Mildred's face faded as she considered the burden of a mortgage on their finances.

Bill's brow gathered as he saw Mildred's concern. "You have your old house by the river back. Isn't that what you wanted?"

"Well…yes," Mildred replied, but the worry in her face was plain to see. "Can we afford it?"

"Yes! He's willing to work with us. With this new job, I'll be making even more money!"

Mildred shook her head in disbelief, her eyes wide, her jaw hanging. "We're getting our old house back?" she finally managed, her eyes welling with tears.

"Yes," smiled Bill.

∼

THE CLOUDS OF SPRING

March 1931

More than a year had passed since Bill and his family had returned to Boise and the house by the river. With the closure of their disastrous Twin Falls chapter, the family was doing better than ever. The twins, now in their eleventh year, had grown out of their newest pants and some of their shyness. Nine-year-old Helen and the ever-teasing eight-year-old Bobby were as noisy as ever and spent much of their time playing by the river and chasing pollywogs in the ditch by the butcher shop. Six-year-old Patty and two-year-old Glen, who was starting to speak, kept Mildred busier than ever.

Even though their finances were still tight and they had little left after paying their bills, Mildred was happy, and so was Bill. He seemed content with his work and, for the first time in their married lives, Mildred felt a sense of stability and hoped they could finally set down roots.

But a dark cloud was looming.

It had been sixteen months since the 1929 stock market crash, and despite the ongoing money trouble back East, with billions of dollars lost and millions of people out of work, Boise had been mostly unaffected. Early on after the crash, many thought the economic hardships would be short-lived and only affect New York and the larger cities, but like the spreading shadows of dusk, the financial strain spread wider and darker.

168

It was a lovely spring day, the type that pulled people out of doors. The warm breezes had brought cherry blossoms and birdsong to the Kane's Boise home. Patty and Glen watched from the front porch, laughing and pointing as two squirrels scampered through the lawn and up the tree. Mildred, six months pregnant, was on the front stoop talking to Mrs. Marsh, their kind old neighbor from across the road, when Bill pulled up in his rattly old Ford. With a wave and a smile, Mrs. Marsh, who looked to be from another time with her sunbonnet and long calico dress, turned and started back across the road.

Mildred waited for her husband to emerge from his car, but after several minutes, she sat on the stoop beside Patty. Holding Glen on her shrinking lap, Mildred pointed to a brown squirrel looking back at them from the side of the tree as Bill sat quietly in the car with occasional puffs of smoke rising from its open window.

"Why won't Daddy come out?" asked Patty.

"I don't know," frowned Mildred as she looked from the squirrel to the car.

"Hi, Daddy!" Patty shouted as Bill finally got out of the car.

Bill pushed the door closed and stepped on his cigarette before coming around the car with his head down and shoulders slumped.

"Daddy, do you see the squirrel?" Patty asked, pointing to the tree.

Bill barely heard her and didn't notice her disappointment when the squirrel disappeared up the tree.

"Hello, dear," Mildred said as she set Glen down and pushed herself up with one hand under her protruding belly. Her eyes narrowed when she noticed Bill's expression. It was a defeated look she had seen before. Her heart sank. "Is something the matter?" she asked, already knowing there was.

"What?" Bill asked, looking up with defeated eyes.

Mildred could tell he had been drinking. She smiled nervously and asked again, "Is something the matter?"

Bill sighed and muttered, "They laid me off."

"What?" Mildred gasped, her nervous smile wiped away.

"They laid me off," shrugged Bill. "Me and a dozen other guys."

"What? Why?" Mildred asked, her eyes wide.

"Last hired, first fired," mumbled Bill.

"But…how? Was it something you did or said?"

Bill looked at her, not in anger, but helplessness. "No. I didn't do anything. The rich bums in New York did all this. We have them to thank." Bill shuffled past Mildred, pulled open the screen door, and went inside.

"But I thought they said the money troubles wouldn't come this far, that we would be safe here," Mildred said, waddling behind. "Besides, people need electricity to run their homes, don't they?"

"That's just it," Bill shrugged as he pulled off his hat and jacket. "People aren't paying their power bills. That's all we've done the last week is shut off people's power."

"Well, what will we do about food?" Mildred asked, following Bill inside the house. "How will we make the house payment? We can't lose this house!"

Bill stopped and turned back to Mildred, his face bleak but determined. "I'll find some work. I'll take care of things. I always do. Don't you worry about it."

"Don't worry about it?" Mildred gasped. "Billy, we only have fifty dollars to our name! That will only last us a month!"

"Just be glad it's not in the bank," Bill said, running a hand through his hair. "Those poor saps are getting fifty cents on the dollar—or nothing at all!"

Mildred's face was pale now. "What are people going to do? Surely this can't go on much longer. President Hoover will fix things."

"Ha! Hoover's a laughingstock," Bill said, shaking his head. "All I know is, I'm outta work."

"What will we do when our money's gone? What about the children?" Mildred asked, her face racked with concern.

Bill looked across the front room to where the twins and Helen were standing. He saw their young faces filled with uncertainty and said, "Don't worry. I'll take care of things."

BILL SAT at the lunch counter and watched the milky cloud dissolve in his coffee as he slowly stirred in the cream. A week had passed since the power company had laid him off, and he had earned only two dollars in two days of work cleaning out a warehouse. Bill had spent that morning walking the streets of Boise looking for more work, but had found nothing. He glanced across the counter and caught the eye of the sandwich shop's thick-spectacled owner, Charley Baskins, and gave a faint nod.

"Get you something besides the coffee, Bill?"

"No, thanks," Bill said with a subtle shake of his head. He looked around the shop, which had fewer people than usual for midday, then pulled from his coat pocket a sandwich Mildred had made for him that morning. Bill was unwrapping the wax paper when Charley said, "Ah, come on, Bill. You're going to eat that here?"

"I bought a coffee!" Bill protested.

"A coffee? That's gonna keep my doors open?" Charley said with a dismissive wave.

"Hey, I don't have a job," insisted Bill.

"Well, if this keeps up, I won't either," Charley said with a shake of his head. Then, with a helpless shrug, he added, "Forget I said any of that. You're welcome to eat your wife's sandwich here. Just don't let me catch you selling any."

Bill nodded.

"Well, look what the cat drug in," Sylvester Schmig said, sitting beside Bill.

Bill turned to his thin-faced friend and offered a feeble nod.

"You gonna buy a sandwich or just use my stool too?" smirked Charley Baskins.

"Yeah, give me a coffee and a Reuben, but put some meat on it this time," frowned Sylvester.

"You got it," replied Charley.

"So, how's work?" muttered Bill, his head down, his mouth half full.

"It's work. I'm glad to have it," said Sylvester, rubbing it in.

Bill's brow gathered. "You should be."

"Six more got laid off yesterday," sighed Sylvester.

"I heard," Bill said, eyeing his sandwich.

"You know, if you wouldn't have left for Twin Falls, you would probably still be on," Sylvester said, eyeing Bill.

"Yeah, but for how long?"

"I don't know," Sylvester sighed. He drummed his fingers on the counter as he watched Charley Baskins make his sandwich, then asked, "How's your family? Kids okay?"

"Yeah, they're still eating, if that's what you mean."

"How's that little girl of yours? The one with the seizures?"

"Patty? She's okay. She hasn't had one for a while."

"That's good." Sylvester nodded as Charley placed a coffee before him. He added cream and sugar, then asked, "Your wife still trying to get you to join her church?"

Bill sipped his coffee, then nodded.

"You'd think they'd figure it out by now," sneered Sylvester.

"Figure what out?" Bill asked, taking a bite of his sandwich.

"That this God they talk about doesn't exist. Either that or he doesn't care."

"You know, they're not the only ones who believe in God," frowned Bill. "I know the Catholics do, and I'm pretty sure the others do too."

"You're defending them now?" Sylvester smirked, staring into Bill's ear.

"I'm just speaking the truth."

"I see," Sylvester nodded. "Look around you. Do you know we shut down the power to three more businesses this morning? And I don't know how many houses we've turned off this week. Half the town is out of work. Little kids, like yours, won't have a place to lay their heads at night or food to eat—all 'cause of greedy businessmen in New York. I heard people there have it real bad. Some are jumpin' outta windows, for cryin' out loud. They'd rather die than go on like us. The ones that haven't killed themselves live in tents in the park—they call it Hooverville. That's what we have to look forward to. People are going to starve—little kids like yours. If there was a God, would he let this happen? I don't think so."

Bill finished his coffee and then crumpled up the wax paper from his sandwich and muttered, "Nice seeing ya."

"Where you going? You don't have nowhere to be," Sylvester said, giving Bill a sideways glance.

"I gotta go. You're draining what life I got left right out of me," Bill said as he turned and walked away.

Sylvester looked back at his sandwich, pulled off the top slice of bread, and said, "Oh, look, Charley, I can actually see some corned beef today."

BILL PUSHED the last bite of fried potatoes onto his fork with the piece of bread and looked at Helen, who was quietly stabbing her few remaining peas. Two weeks had passed, and their cupboards were now bare.

"I'm still hungry," Bobby whined, looking up from his wiped clean plate.

"Have another piece of bread," Bill said.

Bobby was getting up for more when Mildred said, "We won't have enough for breakfast."

Bobby slumped back in his chair.

Bill's brow gathered. He handed Bobby his fork with the last bite of potatoes. "Here, have this. I'm full," Bill said, forcing a smile.

"I'll make more bread tomorrow after breakfast, and for a special treat, you can have grease and sugar on top!" Mildred said brightly.

The children nodded happily.

"I found a fish today," Helen announced.

"Found?" Bill asked with a raised brow.

"Floating in the ditch," Bobby muttered.

"Oh. Well, we don't wanna eat that, but you boys could go fishing down by the river after school," Bill said.

"What about me?" Helen asked.

"You bet," Bill nodded.

"If you can bait a hook," sneered Alma.

"Can I try too?" asked Patty.

"Yes, dear," Mildred nodded.

There was a rap at the front door. "You expecting anyone?" Bill asked as he got up from his chair.

Mildred shook her head.

Bill went into the front room and opened the door to a young man in wrinkled clothes standing with a hat in hand. A downcast young woman wearing a tattered coat stood behind him.

"Evening, sir," the young man said, pushing his thick bangs aside, his eyes barely visible in the fading light.

"Evening," Bill replied, feeling the briskness of the spring night air.

"We're not beggars, sir, but my wife and I are in dire need of any help you could offer us."

Bill looked from the humble young man to his wife and noticed her dress protruding from a pregnant belly. "I'm afraid I can't offer anything," Bill said with a sad shake of his head. "I'm out of work myself."

"I see. Well, thank you," the humble young man nodded as he stepped back from the door.

Bill sighed and watched as the young man put an arm around his expectant wife. She wiped away a tear as they turned to the street.

Bill was about to close the door when he stopped and called out, "Wait."

The young couple stopped and turned.

"I don't have anything to give you, but I've got an empty room out back above the pump house. You can sleep there," Bill said, surprising himself with his words.

"Oh, thank you, sir!" the young man replied with a happy nod. "It's awful cold at night. If it was just me…"

"No, it's okay." Bill saw the young mother was crying harder now, and it made his heart ache. "There's no bed there, but we have blankets."

"Oh, thank you, sir," the young man beamed. "God bless you. You're a good Christian man, I can tell. I can't pay you, but I'll work it off. Anything you need me to do. I'm a hard worker."

"Me too," the pregnant wife added, wiping away her tears as a grateful smile appeared.

"I'll get some blankets and take you back there," Bill said, amazed at the satisfaction his simple offer gave him. Turning back into the front room, Bill was surprised to find Mildred standing behind him, holding two blankets and looking at him as though he had just risen from the dead. "Oh, thank you," Bill said, taking the blankets.

Mildred could only nod as she stared at Bill in astonishment.

"What's the matter?" Bill asked, uncertain of her look.

"Nothing," Mildred whispered. She proudly watched as Bill led the young couple around the house.

IT WAS JUST after five when an exhausted Bill, having spent three more fruitless days looking for work, arrived home. After climbing out of his old Ford, Bill stepped on his cigarette and eyed the blue Dodge truck parked beside him. He knew it was his brother-in-law's when he spotted "Morrison Knudson Co." painted on its door in white letters.

"Daddy!" Patty exclaimed, her dark, bobbed hair bouncing as she rushed out the front door to greet him. "Did you find any jobs?"

Bill forced a smile and patted her on the head.

"Uncle John's here."

"I saw that," Bill replied as he glanced enviously back at the new truck. After pushing open the front door, Bill looked into the darkened front room as his brother-in-law got up from the couch. Mildred stood beside him nervously wringing her hands.

"Hello, Bill," said the tall, gentle-mannered John Young as he moved toward Bill with an outstretched hand. "Good to see you."

"Good to see you, John," Bill said, any hint of his previous resentment now gone. It had been nearly three years since the Kanes had moved to Twin Falls, and Bill had left John's part-time employ. He knew John's construction business had done better than ever during that time, but he wondered if it was still the case now. "How are things?"

"Pretty good," John nodded. "Mildred tells me you've been quite the Good Samaritan lately, putting up a young couple in your pump house and letting another family camp in your backyard."

"Times are tough," Bill shrugged. He glanced at the fidgeting Mildred, wondering what else she had told him.

"That they are," nodded John. "I just heard the power company let you go. I'm sorry."

"Just laid off, actually," Bill corrected.

"Well, that's good. Have they said when they'd bring you back on?"

"I guess when things get better," shrugged Bill.

John nodded.

There was a long silence. Then, with open palms, John said, "Bill, I don't know if you need work, but I'm right in the middle of the Capitol Bridge project and could use another man."

Bill felt emotion growing in his throat and forced it down with a swallow. His gaze lowered to Patty. She was wrapped around his leg and looking up at him with wide, questioning eyes.

"It pays twenty dollars a week. I could use you tomorrow—if you can start."

Bill gulped again, unable to speak. Three weeks had passed since he had been laid off, and he had only three dollars to show for it. Even worse, the family was down to half a bag of flour and two cans of vegetables. That John was offering him steady work was more than Bill could have asked for.

"If you have a better offer, I understand," John said with a gathered brow. "You should know the project will end in June, and I don't know what I'll have after that, but I could sure use you now."

Bill turned to Mildred, who nodded encouragingly, then forced a smile and said, "Thank you, John. I…we would be in your debt."

"Good," nodded John. "But you're not in my debt. You're a great worker. I'm glad to have you back."

Bill was bursting inside, but he tried to not let it show.

"I'll see you in the morning. Seven o'clock."

"I'll be there," Bill nodded. Standing a little taller, he shook hands with John, then watched as he walked back to his truck.

"That was an answer to prayer," Mildred sighed, moving to Bill.

Bill turned to his wife, gave a stress emptying sigh, and wrapped his arms around her. "Yes, it was," he breathed.

❧

SOUNDS OF LIFE

The wet, moonless night was alive with dancing shadows as the wind swayed the bushes and branches. Bill's eyes were alert and searching as he and the rest of his company spread out through the darkness along the edge of the road. Bill slipped the bayonet from his belt as the warm rain dripped from his wide-brimmed hat. He felt a slight tremble from his wet and dripping hand as he slid the long knife onto the end of his rifle, where it fastened with a click. Up and down the line, dozens of similar clicks were lost in the sound of raindrops striking the broad-leafed shrubs around them.

"Advance through the thicket to the edge of the field and then down on your bellies," came the order from man to man.

Bill passed the word on and waited. His anxious eyes narrowed as he scanned the rice paddy to the hedgerow thicket that lined its opposite side, fifty yards away. The paddy was flat and empty but for a lush carpet of rice shoots pushing up from the soggy earth. His eyes moved to a sprawling Acacia tree across the field to his left. Bill thought he noticed movement in its branches, but when he looked again, he saw only the dark outline of its foliage shifting in the inky night.

When the signal to advance came, Bill drew an anxious breath and tightened the grip on his rifle. Along with the rest of the men, he stepped through the clump of overgrown grass, shrubs, and tangled vines to the edge of the rice paddy. The line of men, stretching into the night to his left and right, then sank to their knees before lying flat in the spongy bed of rice sprouts. In an instant, any part of Bill's uniform that was before dry was soaking wet.

Lying prone, with his rifle trained on the uncertain shadows across the field, his finger ready at the trigger, Bill didn't feel his elbows and knees sink into the organic ooze. Slowly, carefully, his chest raised and lowered as it filled with air, his breathing controlled to not interfere with his rifle's aim, should he need to fire.

As Bill lay in the paddy, soaking up the island rain, the seconds stretched to minutes. With his senses heightened, he heard not only the sound of his breathing but also the *pit-pat* of rain battering the earth around him. The sound could have been mistaken for a hundred tiny footsteps had he not been so used to it.

Bill was staring across the dark and lonely field when the rain stopped, revealing another layer of sounds. The distinct whistling of the toads soon accompanied the deep croaking of frogs. Not wanting to be left out, the lizards and water monitors soon joined in the jungle chorus, making *poot, poot*, and *love-you, love-you* sounds. Last to enter the ensemble were the crickets, whose harmonic legs added to the music, like a string section to a midnight orchestra. As Bill listened to the sounds that filled the night, he found his attention slipping from the dark shadows across the paddy. He tried to block the symphony of insects, reptiles, and amphibians, but their song remained.

A sudden commotion from far across the field brought Bill's attention back to his rifle. The sound of men's voices and feet trampling through the thicket at the end of the paddy caused Bill's grip to tighten and his breath to shorten. The Filipino guerrillas were there. It excited Bill to be on the hunt for the animals who had beheaded two of his fellow soldiers.

"Be ready. No one fires until I give the order," came from somewhere behind. The words only half registered.

There was a flash of light across the field, followed an instant later by the crack of a rifle and the zing of a bullet passing just feet overhead. A dozen more followed before Bill heard the command, "FIRE!"

The night exploded with a torrent of lead that raced over the rice sprouts into the crouched shadows of the thicket.

The ferocious noise echoed in Bill's ears as he cycled his rifle's bolt, ejecting the spent cartridge, which tumbled through the air before landing a foot away in a puddle with a sizzle. In an instant, a fresh round was in his rifle's chamber. Bill's front sight followed a dark form of a man rushing through the blackness, twisting in the night, confused or wounded by a bullet's sting.

"FIRE!" came again, illuminating the night like a lightning bolt shot along the edge of the field.

In no time, Bill's right hand had pulled his rifle bolt back and then forward, ejecting and reloading. Again, the order came, and again he fired—three more times. Then there was silence.

Bill's eyes strained through the smoke and night to the shadows of the distant thicket. What had been moving before was still. What had been making noise before was silent. There was no *pit-pat* from the rain. No groaning or croaking of frogs. No whistle from the toads or loving sounds from the lizards. There was only the distant echo of a hundred rifles ringing through his head.

It seemed an hour had passed since his last shot, but it had only been a minute. Bill watched, his eyes unblinking. His mouth was dry as he forced a swallow, which seemed to crack his throat.

We got 'em, Bill told himself as he watched for any sign of life. *How many did I hit?* he wondered with at first a sense of awe and then a rush of exhilaration.

"Move forward!" came the order, followed by, "Be ready!"

With his eyes on the dark thicket and his chest pounding, Bill pushed himself up from the spongy ground, muddy water seeping through his fingers as his hand broke away with a sucking pop. With his rifle raised to his shoulder, he and the others started forward in a skirmish line. Bill's feet were cold and wet as he sloshed through the paddy. His eyes were tireless as they followed the front sight of his rifle.

Bill jumped at a flash and bang from the thicket to his right. By the time he turned his rifle to fire, fifty others had, leaving another cloud of spent gunpowder and the sounds of shots fired echoing through the blackness. Like statues with rifles aimed, the advancing Americans waited tensely to see if there would be another flash and bang.

All was still.

Again, Bill and the others moved toward the thicket, their legs and arms trembling under the weight of their outstretched rifles and sustained adrenaline. A crack in the blackened sky let down moonlight and brought the shadows to life. Bill held his breath at the changed surroundings. He searched for the shape of a pointing rifle or threatening face—any reason to fire his weapon again.

The sudden volley of rifle fire from the field to their right caused Bill and others to drop to their knees. The blasts lit up the trees lining the paddy as if filled with fireflies. But then there was silence and darkness.

With a shuddering sigh, Bill studied the trees and bushes that lined the far side of his paddy, only twenty yards away. It was so very close now. As the ringing in Bill's ear faded, he heard the frogs again—only they were different this time. They were low, guttural sounds coming from the shadows just ahead. Bill realized it wasn't the groaning of frogs he was hearing, but the agonizing moans of wounded men.

Bill gulped. His rifle was tight against his shoulder as he rose to his feet and stepped forward. The formation of men, before straight and even, was now bowed and gaping, not from injury but strained nerves.

Bill heard a man crying ahead of him in the thicket. His eyes were wide and searching as the crack in the sky closed, plunging the rice paddy and thicket into darkness.

"Watch for tricks," came from behind Bill's left shoulder.

"Check the dead and wounded with your bayonet," came from his right.

Bill tried to choke saliva down his parched throat as he took another step closer to the thicket. He turned his rifle when a wiry Filipino sprang to his feet and dashed across the thicket. His and five other rifles barked in the night. Bill lowered his rifle as the thin silhouette fell into the shadows.

"Hold your fire!" came from somewhere behind Bill, followed by, "Prisoners! Take prisoners!"

Bill's anxious eyes searched the shadows of the thicket as his heart pounded in his chest. He saw nothing and everything. He saw a hundred muzzles pointed at him. *No, they're just branches. What do I do if one jumps up and tries to run? Do I shoot him or tell him to surrender?* Bill wanted to turn and ask, but kept his eyes forward. He already knew the answer.

Now less than fifteen feet from the edge of the thicket, Bill's eyes shifted from left to right. Other soldiers were entering the thicket on either side of him. Closing the distance, he carefully raised his dripping boot over a tangle of vines and stepped up out of the spongy paddy onto ground that seemed firm and unforgiving. He heard a man moaning ahead of him.

Creeping through the thicket, Bill's rifle pointed the way, his finger on its trigger, its bayonet catching on the branches and vines.

"I got a dead one over here!" came an anxious voice to Bill's right.

"Make sure!"

"I got one too!"

"I want prisoners!" yelled the captain.

Bill edged closer to the sound of the moaning, his eyes wide, the tip of his bayonet ready. The crunch of boots on branches ten feet to his right caused Bill's head to turn. He saw the distinct outline of another soldier's campaign hat. As the soldier looked up, Bill noticed the faint glistening of his searching eyes.

After allowing himself to exhale, Bill turned back to the moaning sound and took another step forward. He froze as the sky opened and bathed the killing field in moonlight. He spotted a naked foot through a fern. The panting and moaning were just beyond the fern.

With his bayonet pointed, Bill stepped forward. The naked foot grew to a white-panted leg, stained by mud and grass. Bill moved the fern with his bayonet and saw a Filipino man in agony, his mud-stained chest and belly pulsing with the dark ooze. It was then Bill realized it was not mud he was looking at, but blood—dark and rich like chocolate syrup in the moonlight. He spotted a round hole where a bullet had entered right below the man's heart and knew the moaning would soon stop. Bill took another step and saw the pained, frightened face of a young man, his eyes closed and teeth clenched. Saliva and blood bubbled from the corners of the young man's mouth as he fought for air.

Bill watched the dying rebel, horrified and yet intrigued. They had bagged their prey. He was one of a thousand Filipino guerrillas they had been told to hate—a filthy goo-goos, lower than scum. But what Bill saw was a frightened boy, not much younger than him, gasping and clinging to the last bits of life. And then he was gone.

Bill studied the little brown man. The blood had stopped oozing. His chest had stopped heaving. Bill raised his bayonet and pushed it into the goo-goos chest to be sure, just as he had been taught. The dead Filipino's eyes and mouth shot open with a gasp, and his arms reached up to Bill.

Bill catapulted up in his bed, his arms extended, but the rifle was years gone. Drenched in sweat, his heart racing, he looked around the darkened room. The dead Filipino and the muddy thicket were gone. Bill's chest was still heaving when he turned to Mildred lying peacefully beside him. He reached a tentative hand to her protruding belly. Bill was not in the Philippines. He was home.

Bill looked around the darkened room, breathed out his angst, then laid back down, his eyes wide open.

It was not the first time Bill had dreamed of that wet and dreary night in the Philippines so many years before. He had relived that night skirmish many times over. It always ended with the twisted bodies and anguished faces of those he may have killed. To Bill, the emptiness and despair of that night had become synonymous with death itself, and he feared its tormenting images might be his punishment for a life not well lived.

SITTING ON A GRASSY HILL, Bill was looking over the partially completed Capitol Boulevard Bridge and admiring his work on the concrete railing when he spotted John Young walking toward him. Bill carefully mashed his cigarette into the grass to save for later. While he still smoked, he did it less so as it was a luxury he could no longer afford.

"Nice day for bridge building," John said as he sat beside Bill and opened his gray metal lunchbox.

"Nice day to have a job," replied Bill.

"Yes, it is," said John, removing a sandwich wrapped in wax paper.

Bill nodded to the bridge and asked, "How we doing?"

"Right on schedule," John replied, his mouth half full. "In fact, we're ahead of schedule."

"We need to work slower," Bill said half-teasingly, as he wondered what he would do for money after the job was done. He watched as a line of ducklings followed their mother through some reeds into the gently flowing river and started across the water near the bridge.

"How are the rails coming?" John asked.

"Good. We should have the next span in today."

John nodded and took another bite of his sandwich.

Bill had been working for his brother-in-law for six weeks and had come to esteem him like never before. Bill was grateful to John for the steady work and admired his gentle and honest way. But John was not only a good boss, he had also become a friend, and Bill wondered how he could have ever despised him.

Bill had been pondering his dream most of the day about. It had been sixteen years since that Christmas Eve battle in the Philippines, but he could still feel the dampness in his bones from that dark and rainy night. Bill remembered the smell of spent gunpowder, the sound of the moaning wounded, and the ghastly faces of the dead and dying. He had often wondered if any of his bullets had killed that night. There was a time Bill had hoped they had. There was a time he wished he could have gone to France and killed the Hun, but those wishes seemed distant and futile to him now. He thought again of the dark and troubling dream and wondered why it had invaded his sleep now.

Bill had asked John for advice before. While John was a man of few words, what he said was always encouraging and often contemplative. Still considering his dream, Bill turned to John and said, "You were in the war."

John's brow gathered. "Sort of. I built barracks."

Bill heard a hint of dishonor in John's reply and knew exactly how he felt. Bill and his battalion had returned to the States from the Philippines to prepare to go to France, but instead, he spent the war training others to fight and die in his place. The feeling he had somehow failed his country had remained with him. "So, you stayed stateside?" Bill asked searchingly.

"Yeah," John nodded, looking down the hill at the river. "I was only in for nine months, then it ended. How 'bout you?"

"I was in the whole time, and before that too."

"Right. The Philippines, I remember. But you never got to France?"

"No," Bill mumbled, his eyes miles away. "In fact, we were loading up on the ship when the armistice was signed."

"Good timing," chuckled John.

"Yeah," Bill said, not convinced.

There was a long pause, then Bill asked, "Do you ever wish you would have gone over? To fight in France?"

"No," John replied without hesitation. "From everything I heard about the war, I thank the good Lord I was spared from it. Those it didn't kill were changed just the same." He turned to Bill and asked, "What about you?"

Bill sighed. "I don't know. Back then, I thought part of me died staying at home and not being able to fight. But I think about it now and wonder how different things would be if I'd gone."

"You mean whether you would've come home?"

"Yeah…that, and if I would have ever met Mildred. Probably not."

"Did you see much action in the Philippines?"

"Some," Bill nodded as he pictured the young Filipino dying in the wet grass before him. He wondered what the young rebel's life would be like had he lived. Bill sighed, then asked, "Do you ever wonder what the difference is between killing another man in a war and killing someone in cold blood?"

John considered the question. Then, in his deep yet gentle voice, said, "I don't know there's ever a reason cold-blooded murder would be all right, but killing someone in war, that's self-defense. That's defeating evil."

Bill's brow gathered. "But what if in the war the other person thinks the same thing? That they're fighting evil?"

John stared down the hill and shook his head. "I don't have a good answer for that one."

Bill sighed, then took the last bite of his sandwich.

After a while, John turned to Bill and asked, "Did you kill someone back in the Philippines?"

Bill looked down. "I don't know. It was at night. They were rebels who had killed some of our soldiers. I shot five or six times—but so did a hundred other men. I watched one of them die. I think I shot him."

"Huh. I never had nothing like that," John said with a grave shake of his head. "But you were following orders, and them Filipino rebels were in the wrong. There's nothing to feel remorseful about there. The good Lord won't judge you harshly for that."

Bill considered John's words, then asked, "What do you think happens after we die—if we've done wrong, I mean."

John scratched his head. "Well, I'm not rightly sure. Ask me after I'm dead."

Bill laughed. "What do you think about what our wives believe? About heaven and being judged and so on?"

John drew a deep breath. "Well now, I've given what them Mormons preach a lot of thought, and I can't find any wrong in it. You know somethin' else? All the ones I know—the good practicing ones, at least—are all good people. Good, honest citizens, just like the Reads. They don't come any more honest than our father-in-law, Alva."

Bill gave the comment some consideration. Then, turning to John, he asked, "If you think so highly of them, why haven't you joined them? You act just like one of 'em."

John's brow raised.

"Doesn't LaVerda pester you about it?"

"No, no, she doesn't," John said, wiping his mouth. "I know she wants me to. I guess she figures when I'm ready I'll come along, and I s'pose I will... one of these days."

"What's holding you back?" Bill asked, surprised at his words.

John looked at Bill and shrugged. "Stubbornness. But I wanna do it for the right reason. Not just to fit in."

Bill nodded.

"The way I see it, there are a whole lot of churches out there. They all do the same thing, really—bring you closer to God. I figure we're all a little lost, and if one of 'em can show you the way home, well, that's good. If one gives you the good feeling inside and makes you a better man, then I s'pose that's the one for you."

Bill turned back to the bridge and stared across the river in thought.

~

CHICAGO STARS

$\mathcal{M}$ildred looked up from her nursing baby as the screen door opened. A smile grew on her tired face as her sister, LaVerda, entered the front room with a basket of peaches.

"And how is my dear sister today?" asked LaVerda.

"Good, but tired," replied Mildred, visibly drained from a miserable night's sleep.

LaVerda placed the basket on the coffee table and winked at Patty and Glen as they gathered near the large juicy peaches with hungry eyes. "I brought some peaches to celebrate your new little sister. Do you want some?"

They both nodded, their eyes never leaving the peaches.

"Good morning, LaVerda," said Mrs. Read, coming out from the kitchen in an apron.

"Good morning, Mother," smiled LaVerda.

"Oh, those look lovely," said Mrs. Read, eyeing the peaches.

"They're scrumptious," LaVerda said as Bobby entered with his arm in a sling. "Oh my, Bobby, what happened to your arm? Let me guess; you fell out of a tree—no, you crashed on your bicycle."

Unamused by her conjecture, Bobby shook his head.

"He got it caught in the wringer," said Mrs. Read with a don't-ask-me-how look.

"Ouch!" LaVerda winced. "I'm sorry."

"It's okay," Bobby shrugged. "Dr. Boeck says it ain't broke, just squashed."

"*Isn't* broken," Mrs. Read corrected.

"Isn't," Bobby repeated before leaving the room.

"How about some fresh peaches and cream?" Mrs. Read asked, clasping her hands together.

"Oh, that would be delicious," Mildred nodded, perking up.

LaVerda stepped closer to Mildred, kissed her on the forehead, and said, "Violet Virginia looks as though she's doubled in size."

"She is a plump little darling," Mrs. Read said as she gathered up the peaches and disappeared into the kitchen.

"How are you feeling?" LaVerda asked, sitting beside Mildred.

"Oh, I'm fine. I didn't get much sleep, is all. I don't know what I would do without Mother's help."

"She is the best, isn't she?" LaVerda nodded, her eyes still on baby Violet, whose tufts of blonde hair were neatly pasted to the side.

"Yes, she is."

"I'm sorry Bill had to go clear to Bend for work," said LaVerda.

"Oh, don't be. You and John have done so much. I don't know what we would have done without you."

"John says Bill's a good, hard worker and is sorry he doesn't have any work closer to home."

"He was here for Violet's birth, so that worked out nicely."

LaVerda nodded and then, with a thoughtful look, asked, "Myndig, how is he doing?"

"Oh, he's doing all right. I got a letter yesterday, and he said his foreman is a slave driver—not like John. He has those poor men working from dawn to dusk, and it's back-breaking work too!"

LaVerda nodded, but that wasn't what she was really asking. "How is he with everything else? John said they had some wonderful talks when they were together on the bridge job, but he wouldn't say what about."

Mildred sighed. "Billy's a good man. He's a good husband and a good father. But I don't know if he'll ever change."

"Join the Church, you mean?" asked LaVerda as she reached for the swaddled baby Violet.

"That and other things. He's a very stubborn man, if you haven't noticed."

"No, I haven't," LaVerda smirked. "He's a lot like John."

"Bill's come a long way. He still smokes, but does it more privately. At least he did before he left. I'm not sure what to expect when he gets back. Some of those cement men are heathens."

"Oh, you don't have to tell me," laughed LaVerda. "John has told me plenty of stories."

Mildred pulled two-year-old Glen up onto her lap and squeezed him. "I just have a calm feeling about things. I have since before I ever met him in person," she said, holding back her emotion. "We'll never be rich, but that's okay; we're happy. I know Bill may never be religious, but he takes care of us, and I love him."

LaVerda put a comforting hand on Mildred's knee and smiled.

"Besides," Mildred added, returning the smile, "it's your fault we ever met!"

"I know," LaVerda beamed, "and I'm quite proud of it."

LAYING ON HIS BEDROLL, Bill pulled the cigarette from his lips and exhaled as he gazed up at the Oregon stars. Exhausted from the day's labors, he was surprised sleep hadn't already overcome him. After taking the last drag from his cigarette, Bill mashed it into the dirt beside him and slowly released the smoke, which caused the starry night to fade into a temporary haze. He could hear the subdued voices of other workers, along with their occasional laughs, but paid no attention to what they were saying. Instead, Bill considered his childhood in Chicago and how he used to lie on the roof of his house with his friend Harry and gaze endlessly into the night sky.

The nuns had told Bill his mother was looking down on him from heaven—one of many failed attempts to reform the mischievous boy. While their ploy caused Bill to behave no better, it gave him an interest in the stars, and he spent hours studying the night sky, trying to discern just which twinkle in the sky was his mother. He wondered if she was looking down on him. Maybe his father was too? *Mildred would say they were,* he told himself.

Bill thought of Harry. He was dead now, killed in the war. Bill wondered why he was lucky enough to be alive when so many others he had known were not. Bill considered his life and what little he had to show for himself. He was poor before the hard times hit. Now he was even worse off.

Bill thought of Mildred. She had seen something in him before they had ever met. He wondered what it was. *Have I disappointed her? Was there something more I could have done with my life? What could I have done differently, a poor orphan with barely an education?* For an instant, Bill felt worthless, trapped in a life of mediocrity, and then he remembered that night in San Francisco. It was years before when he was in the Army waiting to go to war. Bill remembered having those same feelings as he looked up at a giant moon. His brow gathered as he recalled the voice that told him he wasn't worthless. Bill had nearly forgotten about that. He wondered if that memory was even real or just something his pathetic mind had dreamed up. *It was real*, he told himself. *It happened. But was it true? Would my mother or father be proud of me now?*

Bill sighed as he considered what little he had to show for himself. *A house, that's something—if I can keep it—and an old broken-down car.* But then the thought hit him, just like the voice back in San Francisco, so many years before. *You have a wife who loves you and seven beautiful children. What have you done for them?*

The question caused Bill's face to fill with concern. He thought of his father, but not with the anger and resentment he had for so long carried. Bill felt a sadness as he considered the stern and imperfect Robert Kane. He sighed. Bill had promised himself he would be a better father than his own. He stared up into the starry night and wondered if he was.

∽

RADIO DAYS

*B*ill sat down in the chair across the desk from the droopy-eyed Mr. McCracken and offered a respectful nod as sunlight streaked through a nearby window. He waited as his old boss, who had a curly beard and bushy brows, shuffled through papers. When Bill looked down, he noticed wrinkles on his shirt and smoothed them out.

"Just what kind of work are you looking for, Kane?" McCracken asked, looking at Bill over his reading glasses. "We don't have any lineman jobs open," he said, his voice gravelly and brusque.

"I understand that, sir," Bill replied. "I'm applying for the maintenance job."

"Maintenance job?" McCracken huffed.

"Yes, sir."

"You mean the night maintenance job?" frowned McCracken.

"Yes, sir," Bill nodded uneasily.

"That was Tom O'Neil's job. Right to the end."

Old Tom O'Neil had been with the company longer than anyone could recall. He was a hardworking, quiet man who never missed a day. Bill remembered seeing him leave in the mornings just as he would come to work. "It says something about a man that will work right to the grave," Bill said, wondering after if he should have said anything.

McCracken's droopy eyes raised over his glasses as he accessed Bill's sincerity. Then, with a nod, he said, "Yes, it does. He was a dedicated man. Dedicated to the end. Do you see yourself that way?"

"Yes, sir," Bill nodded confidently.

"You left and took that Twin Falls job," McCracken said with narrowed eyes.

Bill gulped. "Yes, sir. I thought I was doing the best thing for my family. And I was still with Idaho Power," he quickly added.

McCracken drew a deep breath as he studied Bill. "I've got fifty people wanting this job—maybe more. What kind of maintenance experience do you have?"

"A lot. You name it, I can fix it," Bill nodded with forced confidence.

"Is that right?" McCracken asked, his eyes narrowing.

"Yes, sir."

McCracken turned in his chair to the mantle clock on the shelf behind him and scratched his beard. He reached for the black rectangular clock, which had bronze claw feet and bezel around its cream face, and placed it on his desk before Bill. "This clock stopped working a month ago. You fix it, and you have the night maintenance position."

Bill looked from the clock to McCracken. "I'm not a clockmaker, sir."

"You said you can fix anything. This is anything."

"Okay," Bill nodded, his mind spinning. "I'll take it home and give it a shot."

"No. Do it here on my desk. I'm going to lunch. You've got one hour."

Bill stared at the black mantle clock. He pulled open the dusty glass cover to better see the creamy face with black Roman numerals and stalled hour and minute hands. He put a finger to the minute hand stuck at two and gave it a little push. The hand dropped to the six o'clock position. *Oh no. What have I gotten myself into?* he wondered as McCracken got up from behind his desk and pulled on his coat.

"You up for the task, Kane?"

"Yes, sir," Bill nodded, his eyes still on the clock. "But, sir, what about tools?"

"Any maintenance man worth his salt has his own tools," McCracken grunted.

"It's a clock, sir," Bill said, looking up.

Mr. McCracken put on his hat, then pointed to a cabinet to his left and said, "That bottom drawer should have what you need."

"Thank you, sir." Bill didn't see McCracken leave the office shaking his head.

He was all too aware of the stakes should he fail, and was already focused on his challenge. After retrieving a coffee can with an assortment of screwdrivers and pliers, Bill removed the clock's wooden top and his intent eyes peered down into the clock's dusty and cobwebbed innards to its dull brass mechanism. As Bill studied the various gears and springs, he thought of a similar clock from his childhood. He remembered his father winding the clock, which rested on their fireplace mantle. He remembered its rhythmic tick-tock and melodic chime. Shaking the memories from his mind, Bill took a deep breath and went to work.

A little less than an hour had passed when the curly bearded Mr. McCracken pushed open his office door. When he saw Bill sitting before his desk, just where he had left him, McCracken barked, "Kane, you're still here. You haven't given up yet?"

"No, sir," Bill said, sitting calmly with folded hands.

"You get no 'A' for effort here, Kane," McCracken said, moving around his desk. He was hanging up his coat when the clock released a deep euphonic chime, marking the hour. "What-what was that?" McCracken asked, looking down at the clock. "You fixed it? You fixed the chime too? It hasn't rung in years!"

Bill said nothing, but sat quietly with a pleased grin.

Mr. McCracken walked around the desk and looked down at the clock. Then, with a disbelieving shake of his head, put his ear to it and listened to its steady tick-tock, tick-tock. "Well, I'll be damned," he muttered. McCracken scratched his beard, then turned to the still-seated Bill, stretched out his hand, and said, "All right then. I'm a man of my word. You got the job. It pays eighteen dollars a week. Congratulations."

Bill stood from the chair, accepted McCracken's hand, and with a smile that lit his face, said, "Thank you, sir. I can start tonight."

McCracken looked into Bill's blue eyes and, with an amused grin, said, "I'm sure you can."

MILDRED HAD JUST PUT Glen and Violet down for their afternoon naps, a daily ritual that required a stern hand and a quiet house, when Bill pushed open the front door with a clatter. "Hush," Mildred said as she entered from the kitchen and saw Bill carrying a large shawl-covered object and a proud smile.

"Whatever do you have there?" Mildred asked as she closed the front door to shut out the chilly November air. "And why is it wrapped in my shawl?"

"Something you've always wanted," Bill grinned as he held the large and mysterious object, which had a black cord dangling from under the obscuring shawl. "But you have to close your eyes."

"It's too large for a breadbox," said a curious Mildred.

"Close your eyes," Bill insisted.

"Oh, all right," Mildred said playfully.

After making sure Mildred's eyes were closed, Bill cleared a spot on top of the small bookshelf by the corner window and set the rounded object onto it. He then gathered its black power cord and plugged it into the wall.

"What is it?" Mildred asked, her hands still over her eyes.

"Okay, you can look." Bill pulled off the shawl, revealing a wooden box with an arching top. It had a fan-shaped cloth grill that covered its upper half, a small glass window in the middle, and three round knobs along the bottom.

Uncovering her eyes, Mildred's playful smile faded, and she cocked her head. "What is it?"

"Guess," Bill smiled as he turned a knob, causing the box to come to life with a pop and a hiss.

"A radio?"

"You got it!" Bill beamed, his ear bent as he carefully turned the dial.

"Billy, we can't afford a radio!" gasped Mildred, her eyes round.

"We can now!" exclaimed Bill as a voice boomed from the box's speaker.

"Shh! You'll wake the children!" warned Mildred.

Bill turned down the volume as Mildred stared at the walnut-veneered radio. "Billy, we can't afford it!"

"Don't worry. I got a good deal. It's secondhand," Bill smiled.

"But we *still* can't afford it," insisted Mildred.

Bill grinned and said, "I got a job at the power company!"

"You did?" gasped Mildred, her hand to her breast.

"Yes," nodded Bill with open arms.

Mildred embraced her husband and said, "Oh, I'm so happy for you, Billy! It's an answer to prayer!"

Bill held Mildred tightly and nodded.

"You'll be working as a lineman again!"

"Not exactly," Bill said, his grin fading. "They don't have any lineman jobs open right now."

"Well, what is it then?" Mildred asked, pulling back.

"It's a maintenance job."

Mildred's brow gathered. "Oh. Well, you're good at fixing things."

"And custodial," Bill added, his grin fading.

"Oh." Mildred considered the idea of Bill working as a janitor, then shrugged and said, "Well, there's no shame in working, that's for sure."

"I start tonight."

"Tonight?"

"It's a night job. That's why I got you the radio, so you can have some company after you put the kids down."

Mildred looked at him blankly.

"You can listen to all the radio programs you've heard about, 'Amos and Andy,' 'Myrt and Marge,' 'Thompkins' Corners,' all of them! You won't be lonely in the least," Bill said, forcing an uncertain smile.

Mildred's brow gathered. "They don't have a daytime job?"

"Not now, but I'm sure they will. Believe me, I was lucky to get this one. McCracken said there were fifty others after it. It pays eighteen a week."

"That's pretty good," nodded Mildred, her gaze distant.

"I've got my foot in the door," smiled Bill. "It's a stepping-up job, for sure. And with so many fellas outta work, I'm lucky to have it!"

"Yes, we are lucky to have it, and I'm grateful," Mildred smiled as she squeezed and kissed Bill.

"You like your radio?" Bill asked, nodding to the walnut box.

"Why, yes I do," beamed Mildred. "But I'm delighted with you and all of your hard work."

The smile on Bill's face grew wider as he turned to the radio and fidgeted with the dial. It hissed and popped and squawked until there was suddenly music. Then, taking Mildred by the hand, he led her to the small open space between the coffee table and the piano and asked, "May I have this dance?"

"Why, yes, you may," Mildred said with a slight blush.

He pulled Mildred in tight against him with his right hand and led her as they danced.

"I hope my mother doesn't see us dancing this close," whispered Mildred.

Bill chuckled, and they kept dancing.

~

193

MISSING QUESTION

With only a week until Christmas, there was still much to do in the Kane home. Even though the tree had been up for two weeks, decorating it was an ongoing process for Mildred because she had so many other things to tend to. Their Christmases had been meager in years past, and this one would be no different with a few of the gifts purchased and most of them made. While the older children understood their modest circumstances, having made do all of their lives, they still had Christmas wishes, and it broke Mildred's heart that even their most basic gift requests were not affordable. Even though their financial situation had improved with Bill's new night job, Mildred knew how hard times were and that the blessing of employment might not last.

While the evenings that Bill worked were at first lonely, Mildred found company through her secondhand RCA radio. With the children in bed, sewing patches on pants or darning holes in socks by the glow of the corner lamp were much more enjoyable thanks to the antics of Amos, Andy, and the Kingfish. Even her daywork passed faster with the lovely music and lively talk that filled the front room.

With the older children off to school, Mildred was cleaning up the kitchen and watching the pot of oatmeal that awaited Bill's morning return when she heard a squawk and a pop from the radio. "Glen, what are you doing with that radio?" she hollered, setting her washcloth aside and scooping up Violet, who was crawling toward the back door.

"Jus' lookin' for the station," the three-year-old Glen said, standing on the seat of the rocker and reaching for the radio as he looked back over his shoulder at Mildred.

Mildred shook her head as she drew closer with their white-haired terrier, Tuffy, happily following. "And just what station are looking for?" she asked as a string of drool stretched down from Violet's mouth to the eagerly lapping Tuffy.

"The gas station," Glen answered matter-of-factly as he turned back to the radio's dial.

Mildred laughed and pointed to the floor. "Why don't you hop down from there before you break your crown?"

"Oh, all right," Glen sighed, climbing down.

"Where is your father?" Mildred wondered aloud with some concern as it was half-past nine, and he was an hour late. She moved to the window by the door and looked down the empty street. Mildred was about to turn back to the kitchen when she saw a man in a coat approaching a hundred yards away. "Is that...your father?" Mildred asked, straining through her new glasses.

After hurrying back into the kitchen, she stirred some water into the oatmeal, then returned to the front room in time to see Bill stomp through the door. "Good morning, Billy," she said with some uncertainty, seeing the frustration on his face. "Why did you walk home? And where's Question Mark?"

"It's gone!" Bill snapped as he pulled off his coat.

"Gone? Whatever do you mean?" Mildred asked, with Violet still hanging from her arm.

"Gone!" Bill barked as he hung his hat. "Someone stole it!"

"Stole it?" gasped Mildred. "Here in Boise?"

"Yes, here in Boise! It might as well be Chicago with all the common street crooks we got here!"

"Are you...are you sure it's stolen?" Mildred cringed, not one to question her husband openly.

"Sure as sure can be! It's gone! Unless you drove it off and are playing a trick on me, someone stole it!" huffed Bill.

"Well, I have an alibi," Mildred said with an uneasy grin.

"I know! You don't drive!"

"Well, what do we do now?" Mildred asked, realizing the implications of their loss.

"We find it! And when I get my hands on that crook..." Bill growled, shaking his knuckles for emphasis.

"Have you gone to the police?" Mildred asked, setting Violet down.

"That's where I came from, and they were no help! No help at all! And I don't feel any safer having talked to those numbskulls either!" Bill fumed.

"Well, I have some breakfast ready for you," Mildred said delicately. "You'll feel better once you get something in your tummy."

"I doubt that!" Bill snapped as he stomped into the kitchen.

Mildred had hoped to talk to Bill about Christmas gifts for three of their children. In particular, the rubber-headed doll Patty had pleaded for the past few weeks, but she knew now was not the time. Upon entering the kitchen, she glanced at Bill, who had planted himself at the table and was waiting to be served. Turning off the stove, Mildred spooned up a sizable helping of oatmeal, added a tablespoon of brown sugar, and poured in some cream. Then, with as happy a smile as she could muster, she placed the steaming bowl before him. "Here you go."

"Coffee?" Bill grunted.

Mildred straightened up and said, "You want coffee? Will you be able to sleep?"

"That's the point," Bill growled as he jabbed his spoon into the mush. "I won't be sleeping. I have to find that car!"

Mildred sighed, then turned to fetch the coffeepot.

AFTER THREE DAYS, Bill had still not found the old black Ford, and each trip walking back and forth to work made him angrier. The loss affected Mildred too. While she didn't know how to drive, nor desired to learn, Bill took her to and from the market each week. Without a car, she had to make the precarious walk along the slick roads with grocery bags in hand.

Finished with his supper and waiting to go to work, Bill was flipping through the evening paper when Mildred turned to him from the sink, where she and Helen were doing the dishes. "Have you heard anything from the police lately?" she asked, knowing there was a good chance he would snap at her.

"No," Bill huffed, turning the page.

Mildred took a deep breath and turned to her husband with soap suds covering her hands. "Shouldn't you check with the police?"

Bill sighed and then glared over the paper at Mildred. "They said they'd notify me."

Mildred gave the look right back to him. "What harm will it do for you to check with the police station one more time? We need that car, and I think they might have it."

"And why do you think that?" Bill asked, returning to the paper.

"Because I've been praying about it and…I just have a strong feeling."

With his eyes still on the newspaper, Bill let out an even louder sigh. He considered the other times Mildred had given him advice and how often her counsel was right. Bill wondered if there wasn't something to her prayers. A crack formed in his stubbornness, and he glanced at the clock. *I have to leave for work in a half-hour. Maybe I should go now and stop by the police station. It wouldn't hurt,* he told himself. Bill folded up the paper, then set it down and announced. "I think I might start off to work a little early tonight."

"Oh? And why's that?" Mildred asked, pretending not to know.

Bill shrugged. "I think I'll swing by the police station and see if they've found anything."

"Oh, that's a fine idea," said Mildred, with as straight a face as possible.

"All right. Wish me luck," Bill said as he got up from his seat.

"Good luck," Mildred said, before giving him a peck on the cheek. "Have a good night at work."

"Bye, Daddy," Helen waved as she looked back from the sink.

"Good night." Bill took a step, then stopped. Standing just outside the kitchen, he turned back to Mildred and said, "I don't suppose it would hurt if you said a prayer for me."

Mildred looked back in surprise, then smiled and said, "I always do."

Bill looked at her for a moment, then said, "To find that miserable car, I mean."

"Oh. I will," Mildred nodded, fighting back a laugh.

Bill eyed her a moment longer to be sure he wasn't missing anything, then turned and started for the front door.

EVEN WITH BILL'S thick coat, the cold December night air cut to the bone, causing him to rethink walking all the way to City Hall. While moving more briskly warmed his core, it did little for his face and feet, which were now numb. As Bill walked down Idaho Street, he considered turning and going directly to work, but his stubbornness kept him on the course, and soon City Hall was in sight.

Bill looked up into the frosty night sky with his breath billowing before him. He saw stars twinkling brightly and thought about the warm summer nights in Bend. Bill realized he was lucky to have a job, while so many didn't. He knew he was lucky to keep his home while so many others had lost theirs. Bill thought he was lucky to have a lot of things. "Blessed" was the word Mildred would have used, and he knew she was right.

As Bill walked, he thought of how having old Question Mark stolen had affected him. *I've been angry and impossible these past days,* he conceded. *And for what? A piece of junk car that isn't worth its weight in scrap. The crook got what he deserved for taking it,* Bill laughed to himself. *Truth be known, he would have done me a favor had I had insurance on it.*

Bill looked back up into the night sky, but the stars were less visible now, lost in the glare of the city light. After making his way to the corner across from the four-story City Hall, he watched a police car roll past. Bill was walking toward the station's main door when he noticed an old black Ford parked across the street. It looked exactly like his. His eyes narrowed as he studied the dark and dusty car. *There's gotta be a fifty just like it,* he told himself as he continued down the walk. He was in front of the station door when he glanced back at the Ford and saw the faded question mark he had painted on its back. "What the! Well, I'll be!" he exclaimed, shaking his head. "The cops came through for once and found it!" Clapping his stiff hands together, an energized Bill pushed open the station door.

After entering the warm station, Bill stepped cheerfully to the police counter. He smelled old coffee and heard a typewriter and muttering voices. Rubbing the feeling back into his hands, he thought of the policemen in Chicago he had given so much grief. *They'd be happy to know I've grown up to be a law-abiding citizen,* he told himself proudly. *Good thing the cops here don't know what a menace I was back then; they never would've found my car!* he chuckled.

"May I help you?" asked an old man in a police uniform from behind the counter, his voice high and whiny.

"Yes," Bill nodded happily. "I see you found my car."

"Your car?" asked the old officer, who had a thick gray mustache and baggy eyes.

"Yes. Oh, Bill Kane here. I reported my Ford stolen from the Idaho Power building three days ago."

"Just a moment," the baggy-eyed officer said with a halting hand before disappearing into a back room.

Bill leaned against the counter, humming *My Wild Irish Rose*. Besides having his car found, he enjoyed being in a police station and not being in trouble. "Evening," Bill cheerfully nodded as another officer walked by.

"Did you say Kane?" called out the old officer from the backroom.

"Yes. That's Kane with a Kay A-N-E," Bill clarified, unbuttoning his coat.

After a few minutes, the baggy-eyed officer returned with an open file. He shook his head and said, "I see your report here, but we haven't found your car yet."

Bill's humming stopped. He leaned forward and asked, "What do you mean?"

The old officer shrugged. "They haven't found your car yet. It's still missing."

"No. It's parked right out in front, just across the street," Bill said, his arm pointing.

The old officer looked back down at the file and shook his head. "Our detective didn't find it."

Bill scratched the back of his neck, looked out the front door where he could see Question Mark's front fender, then turned back and said, "Did your *detective* bother looking across the street for it? 'Cause it's right there, plain as day!"

The old policeman squinted as he followed Bill's pointed arm to the car. "Well, why'd you report it stolen if you know where it's at?"

"Because I didn't park it there!" Bill exclaimed. "I parked it at my work three nights ago, and someone stole it!"

The old officer looked at Bill with impatient eyes and said, "You're sure that's your car?"

"Yes, I'm sure."

With a nod, the baggy-eyed officer slapped the file shut and said, "Case closed. Congratulations, we found your car."

Bill eyed the old man. "Well, thank you," he laughed. "I feel better knowing my tax dollars are at work." Bill then turned and started out the door for his old unreliable Ford.

It was a dark and cold Christmas morning. With the front room's coal furnace stoked, Bill finally allowed the children out of their bedrooms to gather around the Christmas tree and its half-dozen carefully wrapped gifts. He and Mildred grinned as an excited Glen and Patty dropped to their knees to survey the presents under the tree.

"I hope I get my dolly," Patty whispered with round, hopeful eyes.

Mildred did her best to maintain an air of excitement as the children opened their simple gifts, treating the twins' new denim pants, Helen's hand-sewn pink and white dress, and Bobby's new shoes like precious riches. The older children pretended to be happy with their gifts, but Bill could see the disappointment in their eyes as they looked around the room for their unrealized dreams.

"Patty, it's your turn," Mildred said, handing the six-year-old her only present.

Bill watched as the wide-eyed Patty carefully opened the wrapping, revealing the rubber head of a baby doll.

"It is! It is!" Patty exclaimed, tearing off the rest of the wrapper and holding the doll tight to her chest. "Oh, thank you, Mommy! Thank you, Daddy!" she cried as she rushed to each of them with grateful hugs.

"You're welcome," Mildred smiled, wishing she could have given each child a cherished gift.

"You take good care of that baby," Bill nodded. "It wasn't cheap."

Mildred hushed Bill as she handed two-year-old Glen his gift.

The excited Glen made quick work of the wrapping, revealing a carved wooden airplane that had once been Alva's.

"Hey," Alva protested.

Mildred winked at Alva and mouthed, "You're too big for it."

Alva sighed and looked down at his new pants.

"Merry Christmas," Mildred smiled as Patty cuddled her new baby.

"Merry Christmas," the twins halfheartedly repeated.

"Thank you for the dress," Helen said, holding it up.

"Thanks for the shoes," Bobby smirked, causing the twins to laugh.

Bill cleared his throat, and the laughing stopped.

"What about baby Violet Virginia?" Patty asked with concern.

"What do you mean?" asked Mildred.

"Doesn't she get a present?"

Mildred glanced at Bill and said, "Next year, she'll get something."

The happiness emptied from Patty's face. She looked down at the doll cradled in her arms and then, holding it out to her baby sister, she said, "She can have my baby."

Mildred put a hand to her mouth. "No, she's your baby, sweetheart," whispered Mildred.

Patty looked from Mildred to Violet, then back before cradling her doll once again.

"What are you going to name your baby?" Bill asked, surprised by the tightness in his throat.

Patty considered the question, then turned to her baby sister and said, "Virginia."

"That's a fine name," Mildred said, fighting back the tears.

"Let's see if they have some Christmas music on," Bill said, getting up from his rocker and moving to the radio. With the turn of a knob, *Oh Little Town of Bethlehem* filled the room.

Bill looked at his family with a mixed sense of happiness and regret. He wished he could provide better for them, but reminded himself times were tough, and they were lucky to have what they did. He sat back in his rocker, looked from Mildred to the children, and listened to the music.

Bill thought back to his Christmases in the Army, the steamy jungle Christmases in the Philippines, and the cold and lonely Christmases in San Francisco waiting to go to war. Bill remembered hoping to one day have a family, to have a wife and children, and a chance to be the kind of father he felt he never had. The realization he was now living that life caused Bill's brow to gather. He wondered if that long-ago self would be happy seeing him now. Bill wondered why he wasn't happier with all he had. He wondered if something was missing or if it was simply the hardness of the times that weighed him down.

Steeped in thought, Bill didn't notice Patty standing before him with her doll cradled in her arms until she pushed against his knee. Hoisting her onto his lap, Bill looked down at his beautiful little girl as she snuggled up to him. His gaze turned to his other children. Helen was trying on her new dress. Bobby was showing Glen how to play with his hand-me-down airplane. And the twins were lying on the floor listening to Christmas music. For an instant, all of Bill's gruffness and frustration were gone. He saw parts of himself in each of his children and, for perhaps the first time, recognized them for the miracles they were.

Bill's enlightened eyes turned to Mildred, who was humming as she contentedly rocked. A smile filled his face. It was a smile he couldn't hold back. Bill thought again of his old self and knew the answer to his question. He would be proud.

THE TROUBLE WITH DANDELIONS

July 1932

The warm, lazy days of summer had arrived. For the children, it was a magical, carefree time. Unhindered by thoughts of school, the twins, Bobby, and Helen played down by the river for hours before returning famished, sunburned, and exhausted. For Mildred, the summer mornings, like any other day, were filled with chores. But the afternoons were calm and peaceful, with the sweet fragrance of lilac and playful sounds of children filling the air. Sitting on the back porch, Mildred watched Patty and Glen play in the yard or swing from the tree while Violet napped in the shadows or played with the dropped plums in the shady grass. The occasional breeze ruffled the clothes drying on the line and rustled the corn leaves in the garden as it brought temporary relief from the sweltering heat. Now and then, the sound of Bill's snoring resonated through the open window, like a bear hibernating in a cave, and caused Mildred to smile or laugh. Even though they had little, it was a happy time.

While Mildred loved Bill, he was not the easiest to live with. She thought him a good man troubled by his past and believed him getting closer to God would heal him. While Mildred still had hopes of Bill joining the Church, she understood he might never do so. She had learned early in their marriage that her pushing and prodding did little good against his stubbornness, and knew any change would have to be on his terms. Since returning to Boise, Mildred had prayed that Bill might be surrounded by good influences. Ironically, it was her brother-in-law, John Young, who wasn't a Mormon, who had done Bill the most good. But now, with Bill's night job at the power company, John's influence had lessened, and Mildred feared Bill's daytime sleeping would give him another excuse to stay home from church.

Mildred looked at the dark blue Oldsmobile as the afternoon sun pooled on its dusty surface. Gone was old Question Mark, which had proven its unreliability one too many times. She smiled as she remembered her excited husband coming home with the five-year-old Oldsmobile, which, along with the traded Ford, set them back nearly a hundred dollars. So far, it had proven to be much more reliable than the old Ford and had enough room for the entire family with the children stacked two-deep in the back seat. Even their little white terrier Tuffy approved of the upgrade as he could sit behind Bill and bark out the window at every passing dog and car.

Mildred smiled as Tuffy chased Glen around the plum tree, stopping to lick Violet ferociously as she tried to stand. Mildred fanned herself for a time, then turned to Patty. She was lying in the grass examining a ready-to-seed dandelion with wide, curious eyes.

"What happened to this flower, Mommy?" Patty asked, propped up on her elbows with her baby doll beside her.

"What do you mean?" asked Mildred.

"It used to be yellow. They all did, now just some of them are."

"That's what happens to flowers," Mildred said.

"What happens?" asked Patty.

"They get old and die," Mildred explained.

"But it's not old," Patty frowned. "It wasn't even here when summer started."

"That's just what happens," shrugged Mildred.

Patty looked from her white and fluffy dandelion head to another, just a foot away, that was still yellow. "Why is that one still pretty and this one... like this?" she asked, pointing.

"Some die sooner than others, I guess," was Mildred's reply.

Patty turned from her mother and continued examining the intricate snowflake-like head.

"Pick that dandelion very carefully and bring it here. I want to show you something," Mildred directed.

Patty leaned forward, put her tiny fingers around its stem, and gently pulled, separating the thin green stalk from its base.

"Now bring it here," Mildred said, with welcoming arms.

Patty carefully got to her feet and tucked her doll under her arm. With the delicate dandelion held out before her, she moved to the shaded porch and her mother. Patty had no sooner stepped up on the porch than a gentle breeze came up, freeing some of the seed spores from the flower's head. "Oh! What happened?" Patty asked.

"That's what I wanted to show you." Mildred moved the flower closer to Patty's face and said, "Now blow."

Patty's curious eyes turned from her mother to the flower. She filled her lungs with air and blew out. Patty's eyes swelled as the fluffy head of the dandelion burst before her and floated through the air, leaving a bare green stem. "What happened?" Patty asked, watching the fluffy white seeds settle on the porch, only to be whisked away by the gentle breeze.

"It's gone now," Mildred shrugged.

"It's dead?" Patty asked.

Mildred nodded.

Patty looked down at the empty green stem and asked, "Mommy, do flowers go to Heavenly Father when they die too?"

Mildred thought for a moment, then said, "Why yes, I'm sure they do. I don't think heaven would be such a lovely place without them."

Patty nodded in agreement, then scampered off the porch with her baby in her arm, searching for another dandelion.

GONE WERE THE HOT, relaxing days of summer. No more were the dandelions, or the flowers planted near the front stoop with care. The brisk fall winds caused the crisp painted leaves to fall and crackle underfoot before being whisked away in a thousand pieces, giving the shorter days a sense of demise. Bill was sitting on the front porch, savoring a cigarette and watching a busy squirrel scurry about, when he spotted Patty and her friend Mary Jordan walking toward the house. With the same dark hair and eyes, it was difficult to tell them apart until they drew closer. Bill saw them talking intently and wondered what could be so consuming for two seven-year-olds.

"Hello girls," Bill said, mashing his cigarette on the step as they approached.

Patty paused her recitation and looked up, noticing her father for the first time. "Hello, Daddy," she said with a distracted smile.

"Hello, Mr. Kane," Mary Jordan nodded, her pigtails bobbing.

"What are you two doing this afternoon? You're not just coming from school now, are you?"

"No, we were at the minister's house," Patty replied.

"Minister?" Bill asked, his brow gathered.

"Yes," Mary said excitedly, "Reverend Sprague, at the end of the street, started a Bible class."

Bill nodded, remembering Mildred speaking of the Methodist minister who had moved in, and wondered why a Mormon and a Catholic girl would spend time with him.

"He's teaching us the twenty-third song," Patty nodded proudly.

"The twenty-third song?" Bill wondered aloud.

"He's going to pay us a dime when we memorize it," added Mary.

Bill whistled. "A dime? Teach it to me! I could use a dime!"

"Okay," Patty said with a serious nod. "It goes like this, 'The Lord is my shepherd; I shall not want. He maketh me to lie down in green pastures: he leadeth me—'"

"Wait, I know that," Bill said, with narrowing eyes. "That's the Lord's Prayer."

"No, it's the twenty-third song," Patty corrected.

"Psalm," smiled Bill. "The twenty-third *psalm*."

"That's what I said," Patty replied.

"Well, it's good you girls are learning that. Good for you."

"Do you already know it?" Patty asked, a little surprised.

Bill considered the question, then shook his head and said, "No, not really. I forgot it, I suppose."

"I'll teach it to you then," Patty said with a serious look.

"You do that," Bill smiled. He slid over on the step, allowing Patty and her friend to go inside, then watched a half-dozen leaves float to the ground. Bill thought back to his youth in Chicago and to the nuns, who had forced scripture memorization down him daily, and wondered why the thought of learning such things now no longer rankled him. He remembered his father reading from the Bible. His father was not a perfect man, but Bill remembered someone calling him a "God-fearing man" and wondered what that meant. Bill wondered why his father's reading of the Bible didn't make him a better man. He wondered if his not reading it would have made him worse of a man. Bill wondered when he had last opened his Bible. He wondered where it was. Bill knew Mildred read her scriptures regularly and spent a lot of time in the Book of Mormon. He wondered if it was any different from the bible. He doubted it could help him put food on the table and pay the bills.

Bill listened to the rustling of the leaves for a time, then reached into his pocket for another cigarette.

MORRIS HILL

December 11, 1932

With two weeks until Christmas, the mood in the Kane home was increasingly electric. Mildred was arranging decorations on their Christmas tree when Patty and her friend Mary Jordan entered through the front door. "Wipe your feet," Mildred reminded them as a blast of cold air washed into the front room, rattling the paper snowflakes she had just hung.

"Mommy, my head still hurts," whined Patty as she wiped her feet, one hand held to her head, the other grasping her doll, Virginia.

"Come here, let me feel you," Mildred said, adjusting an ornament.

Grimacing, Patty held her head as she approached her mother.

After wiping her hands on her apron, her pregnant tummy now show-ing, Mildred felt Patty's head, then said, "You're a little warm but not bad. Is this the same headache from this morning?"

"Yes," groaned Patty.

"You've probably just been playing too hard. Especially after not eating your breakfast or lunch."

"Food doesn't sound good," shrugged Patty, still wincing.

"Well, you need to eat. You've just overexerted yourself, that's all. Take off your coat and lay down for a while. You'll feel better."

"But we were playing jump rope!" whined Patty.

"I can think of better things to do when you have a headache. You can do that later," Mildred said, surveying the tree.

"Not if it snows! It's not fun to jump rope in the snow!"

Mildred was about to usher Patty off when Alva burst through the front door covered in eggshells. Alma and another wave of cold air followed. "Hell's bells!" protested Mildred as they hurried past. "Wipe your feet! And just where are you going in such a rush?"

The boys disappeared into the kitchen without a word, but when an angry Bill came through the door with a slingshot and two eggs in hand, Mildred knew the boys had been up to no good. "Are those my eggs?" she asked as yet another gust of cold air blew off paper snowflakes.

"There'll be no supper for you two!" hollered Bill as he stormed past Mildred, shaking his head.

"Oh, phooey!" cried Alma from the kitchen.

"Is that where my eggs went?" Mildred gasped. "Ooh, I'd just like to knock their heads together!"

"I think I'll go home now," said a wide-eyed Mary Jordan, unsettled by all the commotion.

"I don't blame you, dear," groaned Mildred. "Can I come with you?"

Mary Jordan looked up at Mildred with her large brown eyes and, with a sympathetic nod, said, "Yes."

"Mommy," Patty moaned as she tugged on Mildred's housedress.

"I know, dear. You have a headache," Mildred sighed, turning back. "I think I'm getting one too. Get a cool cloth and lie down. Go into my bedroom; you might get some peace there."

"Bye," waved Mary as she looked back at Patty with concern.

"Bye," Patty answered weakly.

Mildred watched the door close, then looked down at Patty. "Go lie down, and I'll bring you a cool cloth and some soup."

Patty nodded listlessly, then shuffled into the bedroom.

After serving the family supper and learning a half-dozen of her eggs had gone to war against the West brothers, Mildred entered her bedroom with a bowl of soup and a damp cloth. "How are you feeling?" she asked as she sat on the bed beside a pasty-faced Patty.

"My head hurts," Patty whimpered as a tear escaped the corner of her eye and rolled into her ear.

"Oh, dear. I'm sorry," Mildred sighed. She felt Patty's head for a fever, then placed the damp cloth across her forehead. "Here, sit up like this, and

I'll feed you some chicken noodle soup," Mildred directed as she placed another pillow behind Patty.

"I'm not hungry," groaned Patty.

"You need to eat something, anyway. You'll feel better," said Mildred, raising the spoon to her mouth.

Patty accepted the spoonful of soup and closed her eyes.

"There, isn't that better?"

Patty nodded weakly. After a second spoonful, Patty opened her eyes and asked, "How many days until Christmas?"

"It's two weeks from yesterday," Mildred smiled. "Have you decided what you want to ask for?"

Patty closed her eyes for a moment, then opened them and said, "A doll dre—" She winced in pain.

"Sweetheart, you can't get another doll this Christmas, remember?"

"I know," Patty nodded as the pain passed. "I just want a new dress for Virginia."

Mildred saw Patty's doll tucked lovingly beside her and smiled. "I don't think that's too much to ask for. What color of dress do you think Virginia would like?"

"A pink one," Patty breathed, her eyes closed.

"All right, I'll see what I can do." Mildred was raising the soupspoon when Patty began to twitch and tremble. "What's wrong, dear? Do you have a shiver?" she asked as Patty's eyes rolled up. "Oh, no! Oh no! Patty! Patty!" Mildred exclaimed as Patty arched her back in spasm. Mildred set the soup on the dresser as Patty twisted to her side and convulsed more violently. "Bill! BILL!" Mildred yelled, frantically trying to remember what to do. It had been years since Patty's last seizure, and Mildred had hoped they were forever gone.

"What is it?" a wide-eyed Bill asked as he crashed into the bedroom.

"Patty!" Mildred gasped, pointing. "I forgot what to do!"

"Hold down her tongue so she doesn't choke on it!" Bill said, moving to Patty's side. "Quick, get a spoon, then go call Doc Boeck!"

"What—what should I do first?" cried Mildred, halfway to the door.

"Get a spoon so she doesn't choke!"

Forgetting the nearby soupspoon, Mildred rushed from the bedroom past Helen and Bobby, standing in the doorway.

Bill shook Patty's shoulders and yelled, "Patty! Patty!" but her convulsions continued.

"Here's a spoon," Mildred cried, pushing past the children into the bedroom. "Oh, no! She's turning blue!"

Bill took the spoon and carefully placed it between Patty's blue-gray lips to hold down her tongue. "Run to the Chapman's and call Doc Boeck!" Bill yelled, but Mildred was already on her way.

"Breathe, Patty!" Bill urged as she spat and fought against the spoon. "Breathe!"

"What's wrong with Patty?" a round-eyed Bobby asked as a whimpering Helen watched.

Bill frantically studied Patty, uncertain of what to do. The agonizing minutes slowly passed as he waited for the seizure to stop, but it didn't.

"Dr. Boeck's on his way!" Mildred gasped as she burst through the front door.

"Good," Bill muttered as he looked up helplessly from the convulsing Patty, now covered in sweat.

"Is this the same fit?" Mildred asked, knowing she had been gone at least ten minutes.

Bill nodded.

"Why doesn't it stop?" Mildred fretted. "It's never gone this long before!"

"I don't know," said Bill. "Patty! Wake up!" he yelled, slapping her cheek.

"No! Don't hit her!" Mildred cried as she pressed closer.

"I'm trying to snap her out of it!" Bill frantically insisted.

"What's wrong with Patty?" Bobby blubbered with the twins and Glen watching from the door.

Mildred turned to the children and, composing herself as much as possible, said, "Alma, will you go outside and play Fox and Geese with the children? Alva, will you watch for Dr. Boeck?"

Slowly, the children pulled away from the bedroom door, fearful and uncertain of what may come.

Bill wiped the sweat-matted hair from Patty's face and tried to remember how they had comforted her when she had her seizures years earlier, but he could only remember the doctor telling them she would die. *But she didn't die! What did we do?* he wondered. Then it came to him. *The elders gave her a blessing! How could I forget?* Turning to Mildred, his face desperate, Bill said, "You should call someone for a blessing."

"I already have," nodded Mildred, her face racked with worry.

"Who? When are they coming?" Bill asked, the thought of a blessing now as much comfort to him as the doctor's presence.

"I called Brother Williams. He's bringing Charley Borup," Mildred replied, holding Patty's trembling arm.

"Good," Bill muttered as he wondered if God was punishing him through Patty.

"It's stopping!" Mildred cried as Patty's twitching lessened. "She's getting her color back!"

As Patty calmed, Bill removed the spoon from her mouth and released a stress-emptying sigh. "Patty, sweetheart, are you all right?"

"It's stopping," Mildred breathed. "I'll freshen up the cloth."

Bill's heart was still pounding as he gently stroked Patty's sweaty cheek.

When Mildred returned to the bedroom with the damp washcloth, she placed it on Patty's head and wiped away the sweat. "Patty. Patty, darling, wake up," she urged, but Patty's eyes remained disjointed, and a slight tremble persisted.

"She's not coming out of it," frowned Bill.

"Alva! Is the doctor here yet?" Mildred called out.

"No!" Alva replied, his voice pitched with worry.

"Oh, please hurry!" muttered Mildred.

After another few minutes of gentle twitching, with Patty nearing consciousness, the convulsions worsened. "Oh, no!" cried Mildred.

Bill replaced the spoon in Patty's mouth when she shook more violently than before.

"The doctor's here!" cried Alva.

"Good!" gasped Mildred as she backed away from the bed and looked into the front room.

The thick-nosed and round-spectacled doctor pushed through the front door with his black bag in hand and hurried with Mildred into the bedroom. "What's happened?" he huffed, having run from his car.

Bill glanced up and said, "She started to come out of her fit, but another just came on. It's been at least a half-hour now! Will she be okay?"

The doctor pulled off his hat and coat and rubbed his chin beard as he studied Patty. "Thirty minutes is a long time for a seizure. It's a grand mal. A bad one," he muttered to himself.

"What does that mean?" Mildred asked with wide, fretful eyes.

"How was she acting before?" Dr. Boeck asked, removing the damp cloth and feeling her shaking head for a fever.

"She's had a headache all day. And she hasn't eaten much the past two days," replied Mildred as she wrung her hands.

"I see." The doctor adjusted Bill's hold on the spoon. "You want to keep her throat open so she can breathe, but don't push too hard." He then turned and pulled a stethoscope from his bag.

"I didn't know what else to do," Bill shrugged.

"You did fine," Dr. Boeck said as he held the stethoscope to Patty's damp and pasty chest. After a few seconds, he pulled it away and shook his head.

"What is it?" Bill asked. "What's wrong?"

The old doctor scratched his beard, pushed up his glasses, and then said, "Her heart. It's beating too fast."

"Why?" Mildred gasped. "What can we do?"

"It's the seizure. The brain controls everything, and hers is all haywire right now. As for what we can do…" Dr. Boeck paused and scratched his head. "It looks like meningitis. It's been going around. I'm going to give her something to calm her. It should help the seizure pass; then we can take her to the hospital."

"The hospital?" Mildred gasped, the idea ominous to her.

"Yes. If it's meningitis, she stands the best chance there." Turning to his bag, the doctor pulled out a small dark medicine bottle and a spoon. Unscrewing its lid, he filled the spoon. "I'm going to put this in her mouth," he said to Bill, moving closer.

"Okay," Bill nodded, watching closely as the doctor approached with the medicine.

"Now. Sit her up and take away your spoon."

Bill gently lifted Patty and watched as the doctor placed the spoon between her blue-gray lips. She coughed and spat most of it out as she gagged and gasped for air.

"PATTY!" Mildred cried, her face panicked.

"Now lay her back down," the doctor calmly directed as he felt for a fever.

Bill did so, then watched as the brown-tinted medicine drooled and spattered onto the pillow.

"The home teachers are here!" Alva announced, peeking into the bedroom.

"Good," Bill sighed. He was sometimes annoyed at the persistence of the two men who insisted on visiting their home monthly with a Church message, but he couldn't have been happier to have them now.

The sound of the front door opening and then closing, along with two men's hushed voices, caused Mildred to move to the doorway. "Thank you for coming so quickly," she said as she shook hands with the tall, thin, and serious Milton Williams. Beside him stood the jovial and bespectacled

Charley Borup, who had a perpetual smile and wavy hair that stood high on his head.

"We came as fast as we could," Milton said, his face drawn and sober.

"Thank you," Mildred anxiously nodded, guiding them into the bedroom.

"You want to give her a blessing," the doctor concluded, looking back at the men.

"If that's okay," Bill said with pleading eyes.

Doctor Boeck considered himself a man of science, but even he had no explanation for the miracles he sometimes witnessed. "I don't think it can hurt," he muttered, shaking his head. He knew not much more could be done, even at the hospital.

Bill looked from the doctor, who was backing away, to Milton and Charley Borup, holding a vial of oil.

"I'll be out here," Dr. Boeck said, gathering his coat and hat.

"No, please stay," Mildred said with a strained smile.

The doctor hesitated, then continued out of the room. Bill nodded to Milton, and Charley Borup opened the small glass vial of olive oil. After putting a drop of oil on Patty's trembling head, he placed his large, gentle hands on her wet and matted hair. Still holding Patty and the spoon, Bill closed his eyes as Charley gave the anointing prayer.

Milton then joined Charley, adding his hands to Patty's head. As Milton spoke, his words concise and powerful, Patty's convulsions lessened. Bill opened his eyes and carefully removed the spoon from her mouth. He placed a comforting hand on Patty's arm and listened to the blessing.

"It stopped," Mildred breathed as the two elders backed away. She gulped when she saw Patty's chest rising and falling. "Thank you. Thank you so much."

Bill looked from Milton, who seemed worried and uncertain, to the doctor, watching Patty from the doorway. "Thank you for coming," Bill said, shaking the men's hands.

Milton nodded somberly, then turned to Mildred and forced a smile.

"Yes, thank you," sighed an exhausted Mildred. "I think Patty will be better now."

Bill was watching Milton and saw his eyes lower at her hopeful comment. He wondered if Milton knew something different. A heavy sense of dread filled Bill as the two men left, and Dr. Boeck checked Patty.

"Is she all right now?" Mildred asked, hoisting Violet, who had toddled into their room.

Dr. Boeck listened closely with this stethoscope, then shook his head and said, "Her heart is still beating too fast. We should take her to the hospital now."

"Whatever you think," Bill said nervously.

"Oh, no!" Mildred gasped as another seizure began, just as violent as the last.

It was long past midnight when Bill made his way up the stairs, his footsteps heavy and plodding. Uncertain of where to go or what to do, his head hanging, his shadowed gaze vacant, Bill hesitated outside the bedroom Helen and Patty shared. After wiping away tears and straightening up as best he could, Bill pushed open the door, stepped into the small room, and sat on the foot of Helen's bed.

"Daddy?" Helen asked, sitting up in the shadows, the moonlight glowing through the nearby window.

Bill at first said nothing. He didn't know how to tell Helen their sweet Patty was forever gone. After breathing in strength, Bill turned to Helen and finally choked out the words, "Your sister died at the hospital."

"What?" Helen gasped, staring at her father's sad, shadowed face in disbelief.

Bill could say no more. He pulled himself to his feet and quietly left the room. He paused again at the twin's door before going inside and repeating the same tragic news.

After going back down the creaky stairs, Bill went into the front room and stood over the furnace for a moment before inserting a few more pieces of coal. He could hear Mildred's quiet sobbing from inside their bedroom, but knew of nothing to do or say. He sank to the floor beside his bedroom door and stared at the furnace's flickering light as it danced on the wall across the room. Numb and heartbroken, Bill didn't hear Helen come down the stairs. He didn't see her look of lost hope as she entered his bedroom and climbed into bed with the still-sobbing Mildred. He didn't hear his wife's tearful whisper, "Oh, Helen Irene, our dear little Patty is gone," or their combined sobbing as they tried to comfort each other.

The morning light caused the bedroom window to glow, but did little to brighten the oppressive darkness that filled the Kane home. The bed on which Patty had twisted and seized was messy and empty. Bill was still sitting on the floor by his bedroom door with his head in his hands. On the couch across from him sat Mildred, her eyes red, her hair tousled, with Helen clinging to her for comfort.

Why did this happen? Bill wondered. *Why did she die? She did nothing wrong. Is God punishing me? Why else would God let this happen?*

Bill ran his hands through his hair in painful frustration as he stared at the rug before him. He felt a sickening emptiness welling deep inside him and felt as though his insides were rotting away. His chest ached, and he wondered if his heart was breaking. As the pain and misery overcame him, Bill remembered seeing his dead mother lying on her bed. He tried to remember the pain, but he was only four years old, and the memories were faded fragments plucked out of time.

After raising his head, his mind weary from fatigue and tragic loss, Bill turned toward the kitchen, where the twins and Bobby looked on helplessly. He watched as three-year-old Glen came from his bedroom rubbing his eyes, unaware of their family's loss, and thought about the still sleeping baby Violet who would not remember her sweet older sister.

Bill half-heard the knock at the front door. When he saw the thick-spectacled Dr. Boeck enter, he wondered if it was all a terrible mistake. Perhaps the miserable night was just an awful dream, and he was here to say Patty was fine? Bill hoped that was the case, all the while knowing it was not. He saw Mildred staring at the coffee table as the doctor spoke words that seemed hollow and foreign; her face drawn and empty of emotion, her last tear long spent.

"I'm sorry to tell you, but there can be no funeral," a drained Dr. Boeck said, his hat in his hands.

"No funeral?" mumbled Mildred as she emerged from her wretched trance.

The doctor shook his head and said, "No, not with meningitis. There's too great of a risk of it spreading. It will have to be a graveside service only, and we'll have to do it tomorrow. It will have to be without your children."

"What?" Mildred gasped, unable to put up a fight.

"I'm sorry. It's just too contagious," sighed Dr. Boeck.

Bill said nothing.

Mildred squeezed Helen and cried.

❧

IT HAD SNOWED during the night, leaving the trees and grass and tombstones of Morris Hill frosted in six inches of white. Flakes floated through the cold, damp air, the midday sun hidden behind the gray sky. The cemetery was still and silent but for a few people huddled around an open grave and two cars parked nearby. Bill stared bravely into the darkened pit and the lowered pine casket that held his Patty as snowflakes fell on his dark coat and hat. Leaning against him was a devastated yet stoic Mildred. Standing sixty feet away, huddled under a tree, were Mildred's parents, Alva and Irene Read, and beside them, Milton Williams and Charley Borup. Their caring and loving faces, though dampened by heartbreak, reached out to Mildred and Bill through the twenty yards of winter.

Bill stood numbly as their bishop spoke, his breath billowing from under his dark hat. Bill didn't hear the comforting words of godly love and salvation through Christ's atonement; he was lost in overpowering pain and grief. *Why did Patty die?* he wondered. *Why did God take her from me? Why did he take her from us?* Bill considered Patty's blessing and wondered why it had worked years before, but not this time? He wondered if it was all coincidence and would have happened the same, regardless. He wondered where his Patty had gone. Bill had no answers.

CHRISTMAS ANGELS

The days following Patty's death were long and painful. Christmas, just ten days away, was all but forgotten, even by the children. While the ward sisters lightened Mildred's load with their meals, it gave her too much time to dwell on the loss of their sweet little Patty, and she looked for things to do. Bill was no better. Told to take a few days off work, he spent his time staring out the window at the snow-covered yard or quietly rocking Glen and Violet. Lost in their misery, neither parent noticed the pain and uncertainty in the older children. At just twelve years, Alma and Alva, along with Helen and Bobby, who were ten and nine respectively, struggled with what to do and say as the residue of death, this cruel and mysterious visitor, refused to leave.

The days passed, but the pain lingered, and few words were uttered. In their place were frequent painful glances and too few tender embraces. On the fourth day, Mildred and Helen were washing dishes when Bill approached and took the drying towel from his daughter. With his nod, she quietly stepped aside. Mildred looked at Bill in uncertainty as he dried a plate, a task he usually left to the others. Their eyes briefly met.

"Are you all right?" Bill asked with loving concern Mildred had not often seen.

"The baby's fine," Mildred nodded, feeling her belly.

Bill's brow tightened. "No. Are *you* all right?"

Mildred sighed and turned to Helen, standing by watching. "Helen, will you check on Violet?"

"Yes, Mother," Helen said, leaving the kitchen.

Mildred started to speak, then returned to washing her pot. "I see her face everywhere I look," she finally managed, her eyes welling with tears. "I miss her *so* much."

Bill shook his head. He felt sadness and anger and misery all balled up inside.

"All I can think about at night when I lay in bed is her cold body lying in that wooden box under the dirt and snow at Morris Hill," breathed Mildred, her voice cracking with emotion.

Bill wiped away a tear and shook his head as if to jar the heartache loose. "I miss her too," he said, fighting back the tears.

"Yesterday, I found her doll, Virginia, tucked under a blanket, just like Patty used to do when she put her down for a nap. For a moment, I thought Patty had done it, but she couldn't have. It must have been Helen," whimpered Mildred. "All I could think about was her wanting a new dress for her baby for Christmas. That was the last thing she said to me." Mildred turned to Bill with tears streaking down her cheeks and reached out to him. Bill set the dishtowel aside and held his wife.

"Why did she have to die?" Mildred sobbed.

"I don't know," whispered Bill.

Mildred wept on his shoulder.

Bill choked down his emotion and said, "I keep thinking about her and Mary Jordan reciting the twenty-third psalm. She called it the twenty-third *song*." They laughed, forcing more tears down their cheeks. For an instant, they forgot the pain.

"I keep thinking of that too," Mildred said, wiping away her tears. "'The Lord is my shepherd, I shall not want. He maketh me to lie down in green pastures: he leadeth me beside the still waters. He restoreth my soul: he leadeth me in the paths of righteousness for his name's sake. Yea, though I walk through the valley of the shadow of death.'" Mildred paused, her chin quivering with emotion. "'I will fear no evil: for thou art with me; thy rod and thy staff they comfort me. Thou preparest a table before me in the presence of mine enemies: thou anointest my head with oil; my cup runneth over. Surely goodness and mercy shall follow me all the days of my life: and I will dwell in the house of the Lord forever.'"

Bill's brow gathered. "It's almost like…" He couldn't finish the sentence. *She knew she was going to die.*

"What are we going to do without her?" Mildred sobbed, moving closer to Bill. "You've had loved ones die. What do you do? How do you get through it?"

Bill's mind stretched back through time. For days, he had been trying to remember the feelings he had when his mother died, but he was only four then, too young to feel such grief. But then he had another memory. It was a memory he had locked away for so many years he had nearly forgotten it altogether...

February 1913

THE FROST WAS thick on the windows of the George S. Searing Company, an electrical parts and supply business in downtown Chicago, where the sixteen-year-old Bill worked as a clerk.

Bill was seated at a desk, carefully writing in a shipping ledger, when he noticed someone standing over him. Bill looked up at his brother, Thomas, who had many of their father's features. It had been two days since Bill's clash with his father over his mother's broken plate, and he had not seen him since. "Did our old man send you?" Bill fumed as he returned to his ledger. He didn't notice his brother's red eyes and sad face.

"William," Thomas said, reaching out a hesitant hand. While often serious, Thomas was especially grim as he searched for the words.

"It was an accident," huffed Bill. "I didn't mean to break the plate. I know, it was one of Mother's favorites. It just fell, and I'm still mad at what he said to me." Bill looked up from his ledger at Thomas, who was holding back tears. "What is it?" Bill asked, realizing something was wrong.

Thomas gulped. "Father's dead."

Bill sat back in his chair. He released the grip on his pen and the tightness in his jaw. "What?" he asked, staring at his brother blankly.

"He died this morning. We had Doc Hall come, but it was too late."

"What...what happened?" Bill asked, his voice faltering as he remembered his father's terrible cough and the blood on his handkerchief.

Thomas shook his head. "Doc Hall thinks it was pneumonia. He was pretty sick. Iliene said he worked himself to death."

Bill stared past his brother. His father was dead. The words were hard to comprehend, and he didn't want to believe them. Bill wanted to cry. He wanted to embrace his brother, to have someone to hold. To have someone to comfort and to comfort him, but he couldn't. Bill felt empty. Empty and alone.

Bill gulped as Mildred stood by. After nineteen years, Bill could still taste the grief and heartache of that day. It wasn't just the realization his father was dead, but also the pain of knowing their last words were in anger. Bill's chest tightened. He remembered his loneliness, realizing he was alone in the world. He felt that same loneliness now, only worse. Bill considered Mildred's question. Then, slowly shaking his head, his gaze distant, he whispered, "This is different."

"What do you mean?" Mildred asked, seeing the pain of his recollection.

"I've watched people die. I lost my parents, but this…this is different." Bill's eyes welled with tears. "This was my little girl."

Mildred wept and painfully nodded.

Bill began to cry before suddenly catching himself and pulling back. *What am I doing?* He wondered. *I'm acting like a woman! People die. It's part of life!* He looked at his heartbroken wife and gave a bewildered shake of his head. Then, with a huff, he turned away from Mildred and left the kitchen.

It was a Saturday night, a week before Christmas, and Bill had hardly spoken to Mildred or the children in two days. His return to work on Thursday and Friday had proved to be a diversion, but he still didn't know how to deal with the pain and feelings he was experiencing. Bill numbly sat in his rocker while Mildred and the children listened to the Christmas program on the radio. It was filled with singing and talk of joy and giving, but he felt none of it. Instead, Bill wanted the world to go away and the pain to stop.

When cute, little blonde-haired Violet pressed up against his leg and reached up to be held, Bill ignored her. After a moment, she moved to the couch, where Helen hoisted her onto her lap.

Soon the festive Christmas carols and words, which should have been uplifting and joyful but instead were flavorless and hollow, were over, and the radio was silent. "It's late," Mildred said, nudging the dozing Glen as she got to her feet. "Tomorrow is the Christmas program, and the children are in it." She turned to Bill and asked, "Father, will you drive us to church tomorrow?"

Bill heard her words but pretended otherwise. He stared at the front door, where he could still see Patty and Mary Jordan standing.

"He's asleep," Bobby joked, wondering after if he should have.

"Billy?" Mildred gently prodded, trying to break him from his trance. She had seen him this way before and knew pressing him would do no good.

Bill said nothing as he got up from his rocker, went into their bedroom, and closed the door.

"Is Daddy going to take us to church tomorrow?" Glen asked, looking up at his mother.

Mildred sighed, then turned to the twins and said, "We should plan on walking."

BILL HAD NOT BEEN ASLEEP LONG when he dreamed of a grand and elegant room with beautifully ornate carpets and draperies, elaborate woodwork, and glistening, golden chandeliers. Luxurious, velvety fabric covered the finely crafted furniture, and a massive stone fireplace in the corner glowed with a beckoning flame. Bill smiled as he remembered the lovely surroundings. He knew just where to go. Bill turned toward the ornate archway and started toward the sounds of conversation. He could hear children's voices, and the idea that Patty would be there caused him to walk even faster. But no matter how quickly he walked, he seemed to go nowhere.

After much effort, Bill found himself at the entry of the fabulous dining room, where a dozen or more sat, preparing to feast. Bill felt he knew them all, but he could visualize none of them when his eyes moved to their faces. Frustrated, Bill rubbed his eyes to clear his vision, but their obscured features remained. *Why can't I see them?* He took a step into the dining room, but moved no closer. After a second and then a third step, he was in the same place. Frustrated, Bill was about to turn away when a small girl got down from the table and started towards him. Bill strained his eyes as the girl approached until he saw his darling daughter's brown bobbed hair and dark eyes. *Patty!* he beamed. *I knew you would be here! I've missed you so much!*

Patty smiled and reached for his hand. "Come and eat with us, Daddy."

Bill had just taken a step toward the beckoning Patty when a clock chimed. Its sound resonated throughout the lovely dining room. Bill at first ignored the sound, but when it chimed again, he turned to it. It came from a mantle clock on the fireplace behind him. Turning back to the dining room, Bill saw all eyes were on him. He reached down for Patty's hand when a third chime rang. She was gone. Gone also were the splendid table and the lovely white dining room. In its place were his darkened bedroom and the cold emptiness of a winter night.

Bill turned to Mildred lying in bed beside him, her sleepless gaze fixed on the ceiling. He stared into the darkness as he considered the fading images of his dream and wondered what it meant.

IT WAS an hour later when Bill quietly dressed and went into the chilly front room. After stoking the coal furnace, he looked around the room, bathed in a strange light. For a moment, Bill thought he was in his dream, but then realized it was the light of the moon shining off the freshly fallen snow. He sighed as he looked out the window across the white stillness.

Bill wondered what the dream meant, or if it meant anything at all. There were parts of the dream that stood out in his mind, such as the large dining table and the people seated around it, but he couldn't help thinking of Patty and her psalm. *What did it say about a table?* he tried to remember.

Bill moved to the credenza by the kitchen where Mildred kept her Bible, careful to avoid the creaky spots on the floor. He turned on the lamp. After opening the cupboard door, Bill found the Bible and reached for it. He was about to open its cover when he realized he held Mildred's Book of Mormon. Bill swallowed as he studied its golden typeface. Mildred had long been after him to read it, but he had never bothered—partly out of laziness, mostly out of stubbornness. For years, Bill felt like an outsider in the Read family, who were descendants of Mormon pioneers. Even though he felt loved and accepted by them, he had clung to his Catholic roots. Bill wasn't sure whether it was the religion, the traditions, or merely the last tie to his fading past.

Bill studied the book for a moment longer. Then, with a tired sigh, set it aside and reached for the Bible. After opening its cover, he flipped through Genesis, then skipped ahead to I Kings, then to Zechariah, a book he had forgotten existed. Bill turned a few more pages and found himself in Luke. *Where is Psalms?* he wondered, glad none of his old teacher nuns were watching.

Bill soon found the book and the verse Patty had memorized. After reading it through, he found the reference he was searching for:

4 Yeah, though I walk through the valley of the shadow of
   death, I will fear no evil: for thou art with me; thy rod and
   thy staff they comfort me.
5 Thou preparest a table before me in the presence of mine
   enemies…

'Thou preparest a table before me,' what does that mean? he wondered. *Is God preparing a table for me? For all of us?* He read on:

…Thou anointest my head with oil; my cup runneth over.
6 Surely goodness and mercy shall follow me all the days of
   my life: and I will dwell in the house of the Lord forever.

Anointest my head… Bill remembered the elders' blessings and how they anointed the heads of the sick. *Just like it says here. What does it all mean?* he wondered. Bill pondered the question for a time. Then, thinking there was no clear answer, he closed the Bible and set it back on the shelf. Bill reached for The Book of Mormon and studied its cover. It was dark blue with golden text and had embossed motifs at each corner. After drawing in an emboldening breath, Bill opened its cover and thumbed through the introductory pages. He stopped at what appeared to be the start of the book and read:

I Nephi, having been born of goodly parents, therefore I was
   taught somewhat in all the learning of my father…

Bill pondered the words. While he considered his dead mother a saint, he never really knew her. Bill's brow gathered, and his throat tightened as he remembered his father. Bill had long blamed him for his mother's death and for every other painful thing in his life. Looking back now, Bill wasn't sure where all the anger came from.

He re-read the verse and tried to remember what his father had taught him. *Nothing,* frowned Bill. But then he remembered his father had tried. *I wasn't willing to listen.* Bill shook his head and wondered why he always made life so difficult for his father. He wondered why he had for so long hated him. Bill sighed. He was only sixteen when his father died. He wished now he had known him better. Bill's brow gathered when he considered himself as a father. *Will my children call me a good father? Or will they remember me with fear and loathing?* Bill didn't like the answer.

When Bill heard Mildred dressing in the bedroom, he quickly closed the book and returned it to the credenza.

Bill was leaning against the cupboard, looking as inconspicuous as possible, when Mildred exited their bedroom. She paused when she saw him.

"Good morning," Bill nodded. Mildred's face was tired and drawn from too much heartache and not enough sleep.

"Good morning," Mildred said, straightening up with renewed composure. "How did you sleep?"

"Okay, I guess," shrugged Bill.

Mildred approached him with a look of profound seriousness. It wasn't an expression of despair or irreparable loss—looks they had both shared in the preceding days—but more of a look of introspection and discovery. She moved to within whispering distance and glanced at the bedroom door to her left where Helen, Glen, and Violet were still sleeping. "I had a dream," she whispered, the words spoken with such meaning Bill knew it was no ordinary dream.

"Oh," he said, his brow gathering.

"I saw Patty," Mildred whispered, her eyes welling with tears.

"You did?" Bill asked, uncertain of what to think after his dream.

"Yes." Mildred took Bill's hand and led him into the kitchen. Sitting at the table, her face straining to remember the details, she said, "I was climbing a hill. It was dark and rocky. I remember nearly falling. I was nearly at the top when I saw Patty. She was standing there with a smile, and she had a lovely whiteness about her."

Bill leaned closer, his gaze transfixed.

"I was so happy to see her again," Mildred whispered, her eyes overflowing with tears. "I spoke to her...I called out to her. She was at the top of the hill, where it was bright and the ground was smooth. I tried to get her to come down the hill to me, but she wouldn't. I wanted to stay and talk to her, but she told me to go back. She was happy and didn't want to leave," Mildred said with a tearful shake of her head. She reached out to Bill's hands and said, "I woke up after that with the most peaceful feeling. I still miss her. I'll always miss her, but our Patty is back in her heavenly home. She is safe, and she is happy. I can go on now. I know she is where God wants her to be."

Bill squeezed Mildred's hands and nodded in understanding. He wanted to tell her about his reoccurring dream, the dream he first had before they ever met. He wanted to tell Mildred he had seen Patty too; that she had called for him to join them at the beautiful table, but he couldn't.

With a sigh, which seemed more liberating than sorrowful, Mildred got up from the table and began preparing breakfast.

Bill pondered Mildred's dream for a long time. He wondered where Patty was. He knew her body was lying deep in the cold ground of Morris Hill, but where was she? Was she in heaven on a cloud with a harp and other angels, as the nuns had taught him? Was she in a happy place with others he knew? With his mother and his father? Or was she nowhere? Lost to the cold emptiness of oblivion? Bill didn't know the answer.

The sound of Helen and Violet leaving the bedroom beside the credenza caused Bill to look back. With Patty being her upstairs bed partner, Helen didn't want to sleep alone and had crowded into the bed with the other two.

"Good morning," Helen said as she eyed her mother and father, still uncertain of how to react to her sister's loss.

Bill only half-heard Helen's greeting; his gaze was still on the credenza which concealed the curious book of scripture.

"Mother, we're going to go to the Christmas program today, aren't we?" Helen asked, somewhat distressed. "I'm supposed to be an angel."

Bill gulped.

"Yes, dear," Mildred said, turning to her daughter with a smile that had been gone for too many days.

"Do we have to walk in the snow?" Helen asked, glancing nervously at her father, still steeped in thought.

"No," said Bill, coming out of his trance. "We're all going to the program together."

Mildred turned to Bill and smiled warmly.

~

THE QUESTIONS OF SPRING

*W*ith spring came warming breezes, beautiful flowers, birds singing, and the newest member of the Kane family, a dark-haired nine-pound baby girl. The busyness of caring for a newborn did much to distract Mildred and the children from their sorely missed Patty. Ever busy with his night maintenance job, Bill was likewise thrilled with the sweet little Donna May, even though her shrill cry made it sometimes difficult for him to get his daytime sleep.

It was the last Sunday in May, and the family was gathered in their ever-shrinking front room, listening to their ward teachers give their monthly message. Dressed in a suit and bowtie, the ever-serious Milton Williams had a long, thin nose and deep-set eyes. Seated beside him was the jolly and bespectacled Charley Borup, whose dark wavy hair stood high on his scalp, giving him a somewhat zany appearance. Bill sat with folded arms, eyeing his older children, hoping they would take to heart the message of obedience, not realizing they were likewise directing it at him.

"And so," Charley concluded, "it is important that we follow Jesus's example and be baptized." The ever-grinning home teacher turned to Mildred, who was nodding in agreement as she watched Bill through the corner of her eye.

"Bill, do you have anything to add?" the pointy-nosed Milton asked, his gaze intent and earnest.

Bill, who was sitting with folded arms, nodded and said, "I agree whole-heartedly. You children need to obey your mother—and me, of course."

Charley's smile broadened. "And what about following the Savior's example of being baptized?"

"Of course," Bill said, "that's why these kids have been baptized. Glen will be next," he added, nodding to the five-year-old crammed on the couch between the twins.

Milton sighed, realizing the point was lost on Bill. "What about you, Bill?" he asked, with piercing eyes.

"Me?" Bill asked, a little taken aback. "I've been baptized."

"Bill was baptized Catholic as a baby," Mildred reminded them.

Milton thought for a moment, then said, "Bill, I know you've played a lot of baseball—heck, you're the star of the ward team—I s'pose you've won your share of championships too, haven't you?"

"Why, yes," Bill nodded proudly. "In fact, when I was in the Army, back in nineteen sixteen, we were crowned the Champions of the Orient."

Charley fought back a smirk when Alva and Alma rolled their eyes in unison.

"So, in baseball," Milton continued, "is it necessary to have an umpire?"

"Sure," Bill nodded, wishing they had asked him to recount his tale.

"Why?" asked Milton.

"Why?" Bill said reflectively. "Well, without an ump, you don't have anyone to rule on the game, whether a pitch was a ball or a strike, fair or foul, and to tell if a runner's safe."

"So, the umpire makes sure the game is played correctly?"

"You could say that," Bill nodded.

"We read in the Bible how John took Jesus down in the water. What do you think about that?" asked Charley.

"I s'pose that was how they did it back then," said Bill.

"Do you think it matters how one's baptized?"

Bill's brow gathered. "I suppose so." He sat back and quietly listened as they continued their message. Bill understood the Mormon faith meant a lot to Mildred and the Reads; it was not only a system of beliefs, but a way of life. While Mildred had never pressured him to join, Bill knew she yearned for their family to have that religious like-mindedness. But Bill had never seen the need. He was a Catholic, and that was that. Even so, Bill's mind often went back to his conversation with John Young on the banks of the river while building the bridge. John had concluded that the purpose of all the churches was to bring one closer to God. "We're all a little lost," he said, "and if one of 'em can show you the way home, well, that's good. If one gives you the good feeling inside and makes you a better man, then I s'pose that's the one for you." Bill's brow gathered as he considered what John called "that good feeling." Bill had experienced it more than once in his years with Mildred. He considered his Catholic upbringing. He thought it was a fine church, but it had answered none of his questions. Bill didn't know if the Mormons knew any better, but they certainly tried to answer those questions, and the answers he had heard over the years had mostly made sense and felt right to him.

Charley Borup had given a closing prayer, and the children were dispersing when Milton turned to Bill and said, "I would like to hear more about your baseball days. I played a little myself."

"Sure," Bill beamed.

They spoke of baseball for another twenty minutes. Some of it involved current players in the big league, but mostly they asked about Bill's experiences, to which he happily answered. He told of his years in the Philippines before the Great War and how his Thirteenth Infantry team won the championship and spent a month traveling and playing in China.

After following them out onto the front porch, the conversation continued until Bill paused. He looked back to be sure no one from the family was listening, then asked, "Say, what does it take for someone to get baptized in your church? Someone was asking at work, and I wasn't sure what to tell him," Bill quickly added.

Charley watched with his pleasant smile as Milton said, "Well, I guess it all depends."

"On what?" Bill asked with a gathered brow.

"Well," Milton continued, "there are some lessons they would have to take. Lessons that would teach them more about the Church."

"Who would teach those lessons?" Bill asked.

"Missionaries or someone like us," smiled Charley.

"Hmm," Bill nodded.

"Does your friend read the Bible?" asked Charley.

Bill's brow gathered. "Some—I think. I'll have to ask."

Charley nodded.

"You—that person at your work—would also need to read The Book of Mormon," Milton added. "It goes along with the Bible and tells about the resurrected Jesus's teachings on this continent."

Bill rubbed his chin in thought. "I'm sure he's got a Bible. Do you know where I can find the other one? For him?"

"I'll bring one by," grinned Charley.

"Thank you. Is there anything else—he should know?"

Milton gave a slight shrug and said, "Does this person smoke or drink?"

"You know, the Word of Wisdom," Charley prodded. "God wants us to care for our bodies."

Bill shook his head and said, "Drink? No, not much anymore, but he smokes."

Milton nodded and said, "He would need to stop."

"Hmm," Bill said, even further in thought. "Is that it?"

"Pretty much," Charley smiled.

"It would be good if your friend would pray about all of these things too. God would help him know he's doing the right thing and give him the strength to make these changes."

Bill nodded slowly, drew in a deep breath, then said, "All right, I'll let him know. Thank you."

"Our pleasure," Milton said with a serious nod.

"Call us if you have any more questions," Charley grinned, and the two turned to leave.

"I will. Thank you."

"Our pleasure," Milton said. After shaking hands, the two men turned and left Bill on the step, pondering their words.

～

LUCKY STRIKE

July 1935

Seated at his workbench in a recessed corner of the power company's shop, Bill crossed off the last item on his repair list and tiredly rubbed his head. With nearly an hour left before his night shift was over, he looked around the empty shop for something to do. With a tired sigh, Bill turned back to the workbench and looked over the rows of hanging mason jars that held every size nut, bolt, washer, and electrical connector he needed for his repairs. Bill reached for the pack of cigarettes in his shirt pocket, then remembered it wasn't there. With a jittery groan, he rapped his fingers on the dented and grooved workbench and tried to put his mind on something else. It had been two days since Bill's last smoke, and he was feeling the effects of nicotine withdrawal.

After shaking his head to free the nagging cravings, Bill pulled open the heavy drawer to his right. He reached deep inside and pulled out a Bible Milton Williams had given him and opened it to where he had left off. Cradling the book in his callused hands under the workbench's dusty light fixture, he resumed his reading.

Bill was steeped in thought as he considered the passage and didn't notice the man walking up behind him.

"What's that you reading, Kane?" sneered the thin-faced and full-mustached Sylvester Schmig.

Bill closed the book in surprise and turned to Sylvester.

"I thought more of you than that, Kane. They got you sucked into their mindless balderdash, don't they?" scoffed Sylvester.

"I'm just reading, that's all," glared Bill.

Sylvester nodded, and with a smirk, asked, "Does McCracken know?"

"Know what?"

"That he's paying you to read the Bible all night?"

"I'm finished with my work," Bill replied as he pulled open the heavy drawer and replaced the book.

"Is that so?" Sylvester sneered. "I wonder what he would say if he knew? It would be a shame for you to lose your job over a *church*."

Bill gulped. He knew of Sylvester's disdain for religion and feared such a report to his boss might not bode well for him.

Sylvester spat in the corner. "They probably already got you baptized."

Bill bristled at the thought of anyone forcing him against his will. "No. I was just reading."

"No? Not baptized? Then there's still time," laughed Sylvester.

Bill eyed his old, cunning friend as he considered what to do next.

"How 'bout we go out for a drink tonight before you come on to work? It will do you some good to get all that fluff out of your head." Sylvester said, studying Bill.

Bill's brow gathered. "No thanks. Tonight's not good."

"Tomorrow then?"

Bill shook his head. "I don't think so."

"Come on," Sylvester coaxed, pulling a pack of Lucky Strikes from his pocket and offering one to Bill.

Bill eyed the cigarette. A part of him yearned for it and the comfort it would bring. After breathing in determination, Bill shook his head and said, "No thanks, I quit."

Sylvester pulled back the cigarettes and looked at Bill like a disapproving father. "You might be right about that."

Bill gulped as Sylvester walked away.

DRIVING down the alley behind his house, with the morning sun cresting over the trees to the east, Bill was not expecting to see Bobby and Glen chasing Tuffy into the gravel alleyway and had to slam on his brakes to keep from hitting them. The dusty Oldsmobile slid sideways on the loose rock and stopped just inches from the fence in a cloud of dust.

"What the!" Bill angrily exclaimed as the boys stood wide-eyed, looking back at him from just feet away. "What are you two doing out here, running around like that?" he shouted, waving his arm out of the car's open window.

Fourteen-year-old Bobby, who had just captured the rambunctious terrier and was looking through his stringy bangs, didn't dare move, but the younger Glen turned and ran.

"Well, get out of the road!" Bill yelled as he slammed the car into reverse and backed away from the fence.

Bobby stepped aside and watched as his ill-tempered father ground the car's gear into first before kicking up a storm of gravel and lurching into the backyard.

Mildred had just come out to the back porch humming a cheery tune and casting feed to the scampering chickens when Bill pulled up and got out of the car. "Good morning, dear. How was work?" she asked cheerfully.

"Did you see that? It's like we got a tribe of wild Comanches living here!" Bill grumbled as he stomped past her into the house.

After sixteen years of marriage, it took Mildred no time to pick up on one of her husband's sour moods. While she now knew how to defuse Bill's grumpiness, she often endured his occasional fits. Resuming her cheerful tune, Mildred followed him into the kitchen and the delicious aroma of cooking bacon and eggs. Tending to the breakfast, she considered how to best approach Bill's blowup. "Good morning, dear," she said again, watching him from the corner of her eye.

"I don't know what's so good about it," Bill muttered. "I nearly crashed into the fence trying not to run over two of your sons!"

Oh dear, Mildred thought. "How was work?" she asked, not bothering to look back at her fuming husband.

"Work was fine," Bill snapped as he hung up his hat and sank into his kitchen chair.

Helen was about to enter the kitchen holding the newest Kane arrival, one-month-old Shirley Joan, but when she heard her father's grumpy voice, she made an about-face into the front room.

"Where are the twins?" Bill asked.

"They've already gone to work," Mildred said, setting a plate of bacon and eggs and a bowl of oatmeal with honey and cream, just like he liked it, before him.

"Work, huh? Well, it's good someone else in this house is working," he huffed.

"Yes, it's surely a good thing," Mildred sighed, wiping the sweat from her forehead. Turning back to the table, she saw Bill looking down restlessly at his breakfast with a nervous Violet sitting across from him. "Is something the matter, dear?" Mildred asked. "Did I forget something?"

"Well, who's going to bless it?" Bill grumbled, still eyeing his food.

"Oh," Mildred said, taken aback. "Violet, why don't you do it?"

Violet gulped, then blessed the meal in her sweet, innocent voice.

"Amen," Bill huffed as he picked up his spoon and began eating.

Mildred was wondering what had happened to cause such a sour mood when she saw his shirt pocket was empty. *He's stopped smoking again*, she tiredly concluded. She envisioned herself bravely sitting down beside him and saying something like, *Mr. Kane, I think it's very noble that you are trying to stop smoking, but I think we would prefer you happy with a cigarette than not*, but she chose instead to say, "Did something happen at work?"

"Nothing you would care about," Bill sharply replied.

Annoyed, Mildred forced a smile and said, "Are you cranky because you stopped smoking?" as she poured him a glass of juice.

Bill paused with his fork halfway to his mouth and then looked at Mildred, clearly irritated. "It's not that," he growled.

"Oh? How long has it been?" she asked as calmly as possible.

"Two days, and I'm doing fine," Bill said, tearing off a bite of bacon.

"I can see that," Mildred muttered as she returned to the stove.

Bill looked down, gave an irritated sigh, then said, "It's something else."

"Oh? Whatever is it?" Mildred asked, giving Bill her full attention.

Bill eyed his bowl of mush. He thought for a moment, then mumbled, "Nothing."

"Oh. That's good to know. Then you should be right as rain."

Bill said nothing more as he finished his breakfast.

DESPITE EVERY WINDOW being open and fan purring in the Idaho Power building, the afternoon heat hung heavy as Bill nervously paced outside Mr. McCracken's office. He wiped the sweat from his forehead as he wondered why his boss had called him in. It had been two days since Sylvester Schmig had caught him reading the Book of Mormon, and while Bill knew he had done nothing wrong, he worried about what Sylvester could have told their boss that got him into trouble. While once a friend, Bill knew Sylvester all too well and wondered why he was so antagonistic towards religion in general and Mormons in particular.

Bill paused his pacing and looked up and down the hallway. After seeing he was alone, he closed his eyes, bowed his head, and whispered, "God, I don't think I did anything wrong here. I was just reading one of your books and trying to get an answer. Please let me keep my job."

He had just resumed his pacing when Mr. McCracken's secretary, a middle-aged woman with red pulled-up hair, came out of his office with a notepad in hand. "Mister Kane, Mister McCracken will see you now."

Bill gulped and started into the office, which had two fans stirring the weighted-down documents on McCracken's desk.

"Kane, come on in and have a seat," said the droopy-eyed McCracken, who had traded his curly beard for a trim mustache.

"Yes, sir," Bill said. Still uncertain of what awaited him. His eyes moved to the still-ticking mantle clock he had repaired years earlier, then watched nervously as his employer flipped through a file that had *Kane* typed on its side.

"You've been back with the company a little over four years now," said McCracken, giving no hint as to his disposition.

"Yes, sir," Bill nodded.

"And how are you liking your night maintenance job?" McCracken asked, looking over his glasses.

"Very much, sir," Bill said with a jittery nod.

"I've heard reports…" McCracken closed the file and met eyes with Bill, his expression all business.

"Yes, sir," Bill said, bracing himself for the worst and wondering how he would tell Mildred he had lost his job.

"Reports you're doing an excellent job," nodded McCracken.

"Oh. Thank you, sir," Bill said, surprised. His eyes flashed from his personnel file to his boss, and he said, "I'm not in trouble?"

"Trouble?" McCracken scowled. "Why would you be in trouble? I called you here to talk about a promotion to the day shift and head of maintenance."

Bill melted in his chair. "Days?"

"Yes. You would be over maintenance and custodial. I know you have a growing family, and it would give you some normal hours. Oh, and your pay would go up five dollars a week. Are you interested?"

"Yes. Yes, sir!" Bill said with an enthusiastic nod.

"Fine," said McCracken, leaning back in his chair. "Fredrickson will take over for you on nights. Will you show him the ropes?"

"Yes, sir," Bill said with a mystified nod.

"All right, then." McCracken clasped his hands together and got up from behind his desk. "We'll have you start days next Monday."

"Thank you, sir," Bill said, getting up from his chair. He started to turn, then paused and said, "Sir, I just have a question."

"Yes, what is it?" McCracken asked, already moving on to his next task.

"Is it all right if I read at the end of my shift—after all of my work is done, I mean?" Bill asked, wondering if he should have done so.

"Read?" McCracken pulled off his glasses.

"Well, I was told to stay 'til the end of my shift, and sometimes I have spare time after all the repairs and maintenance is finished. I just wanted to make sure."

"Yes, that's fine," McCracken said with a dismissive wave. "If your work's done, I see no problem. Call it a break."

"Yes, sir," Bill smiled, turned, and left the office.

THE DOUBLEHEADER

*I*t was a warm August afternoon, but the chapel was comfortable with the side windows open, allowing a gentle breeze to flow across the congregation. Following the closing hymn and prayer, Bill, Mildred, and their eight children got up from the hard wooden pew and started for the foyer.

Bill was following Mildred and the younger children when Bishop Harris, a soft-spoken man with a gentle smile and a cleft chin, approached and said, "Brother Kane, it's nice to see you."

"Nice to see you," Bill nodded.

"You're getting to be quite a regular. I'm going to have to give you a job someday," the bishop winked.

Bill chuckled.

"And you, young man," the bishop said, looking down at Glen, who had a band of freckles across his nose and dark combed-back hair, "you had a birthday this past week. Are you looking forward to getting baptized?"

Glen, who had a reputation for being a quiet mischief, simply nodded.

"Say, 'yes, sir,'" Bill nudged his suddenly bashful son.

Glen gulped. "Yes, sir."

"So, next week then?" the bishop asked, looking from Glen to Bill.

Bill nodded.

"I'm glad to hear about your decision, Brother Kane," Bishop Harris said with a loving hand on Bill's shoulder. "It will be quite a day for you and your family."

Bill's anxious gaze shifted to Mildred, who was preoccupied with Donna and Shirley. She knew nothing of his decision to be baptized. It was to be a surprise, and he wanted to keep it that way.

"Don't worry, I won't spill the beans," winked the bishop.

Bill nodded as Glen looked up, wondering what they were talking about.

While Bill had considered becoming a member of The Church of Jesus Christ of Latter-Day Saints before, it had only been the last year that he knew his joining would be for himself and not just to appease Mildred and the kids. After months of studying the Church's teachings and years of observing practicing Mormons, Bill had concluded that such a lifestyle could only help him become a better man.

As Bill entered the congested foyer, he stopped behind a visiting Mildred, who was holding Shirley in one arm and playing tug-of-war with a ready-to-leave Donna with the other. Bill grinned as Charley Borup and Milton Williams approached. The two had spent four patient years working with Bill, most of it right under Mildred's nose, and were overjoyed their efforts were finally paying off.

"How are you doing, Bill?" Charley asked, his grin as wide as ever. "Are you excited?"

"Yes," Bill smiled.

"Saturday, then?" Milton asked.

Bill was about to reply when Mildred turned and asked, "What's Saturday?"

Not seeing Mildred standing there, both Milton's and Charley's faces went blank, uncertain of how to respond.

"Baseball," Bill said, thinking quickly, "We were just talking about a base-ball game Saturday."

"My stars, don't you three ever tire of talking about baseball?"

Milton looked from Mildred to Bill, uncertain of what to say, but Charley shook his head and said, "No, ma'am, we love talking about base-ball, especially with your husband."

"Yeah, that should be quite a game Saturday," Bill nodded.

"Yes, it should be," Milton said rather awkwardly.

"A doubleheader," smirked Bill.

"A doubleheader," grinned Charley, looking down at Glen.

Mildred's brow gathered. "Wait a minute, Billy. Saturday Glen's getting baptized."

"Oh, that's right," frowned Bill.

Milton was as stiff as a board, but Charley shrugged and said, "Well, I know what I'll be doing next Saturday."

Mildred looked strangely at the two men as they walked off, then turned to Bill, who shrugged.

September 6, 1936

Dressed in her nicest Sunday dress, Mildred sat before the tiled baptismal font holding Shirley on her lap while Violet and Bobby sat on one side and Helen, Donna, and the twins on the other. Beside Alva was an empty chair saved for Bill. As reverent piano music filled the room, Mildred glanced back at the door, looking for her husband. *Where is he?* Turning forward, she saw Glen dressed in a baggy white jumpsuit sitting beside Bishop Harris. She smiled proudly at Glen before continuing her search for Bill, whom she had not seen for half an hour. *Oh, I hope he's not off listening to some ball game!*

When Mildred glanced back, she saw a grinning Charley Borup seated two rows behind. When the serious Milton Williams entered dressed in white slacks and shirt and sat on the front row beside Brother Loveland, who was to baptize Glen, Mildred thought nothing of it but was glad to have such good friends.

Mildred was trying to occupy a fussing Shirley when the hushed socializing in the room suddenly stopped.

"Mother, look!" gasped Helen, pointing to the front of the room.

Looking forward, Mildred saw Glen seated beside the bishop, but her eyes swelled when she saw another man dressed in white sitting beside him. *My stars, he's the spitting image of my husband!* Mildred blinked slowly as her mind tried to understand what she was seeing. "Bill?" she muttered, "What's he doing?"

"Why is Father up there?" asked Alma, just as confused.

"Mother, is Daddy getting baptized too?" asked a wide-eyed Violet.

Mildred stared at the grinning Bill in stunned silence as the meeting began. She could scarcely sing the opening hymn as the realization that her husband was getting baptized sunk in.

Nearly forgetting about Glen, who was just as confused as the rest of the family, Mildred watched Bill put his arm around his son and whisper something into his ear. Glen's smile and happy nod caused Mildred to shake her head and wonder, *Who is this man?*

Mildred only half heard the bishop's talk about baptism and the Holy Ghost; her eyes were on Bill, who never looked more handsome to her.

When the time came, Mildred watched as Brother Loveland led Glen into the cool water of the font and baptized him. When the dripping Glen came up out of the water and gave an audible shudder, everyone laughed. Holding back tears, Mildred caught Glen's eye with a smiling nod of approval only a mother can provide.

Mildred's chest heaved with emotion when Bill stepped down into the baptismal waters with the lanky Milton Williams. With right arm raised and prayer given, Milton lowered Bill into the water. When the dripping Bill came up out of the water, he shook hands with Milton, whose smile exposed a never-before-seen gap in his teeth.

After stepping out of the font, Bill met eyes with Mildred, shaking her head in dismay. He winked and smiled.

After changing into dry clothes, Bill guided Glen back into the baptismal room, where they were met by a roomful of loving faces.

"Congratulations, Bill," said an overjoyed Charley Borup, the first to reach him. "You too, Glen." Charley then turned to a beaming Mildred, patiently waiting with open arms. "I think you have someone who would like to congratulate you," he said, stepping back.

"How did you do this without me knowing?" Mildred asked in wonderment.

"It wasn't easy. I wanted to surprise you," grinned Bill.

"And that you did!" exclaimed Mildred. "I'm so proud of you! Both of you!" she said, stooping to hug and kiss Glen.

Bill looked at his children and smiled.

THAT EVENING, it took some time for the excitement in the house to calm down. While Mildred went out of her way to recognize Glen's achievement, the bulk of the attention went to Bill, who had surprised the entire family. Even eight-year-old Glen realized the significance of his father being baptized.

With the ice cream and cake long gone, and the children in bed, Mildred sat on the couch beside Bill, marveling at him as he read the evening paper.

"Billy Kane, you are a little more of a surprise to me every day," grinned Mildred.

Bill turned to his wife and smiled.

"How long ago did you hatch this plan?"

Bill shrugged. "I don't know. I've been thinking of doing it for a couple of years, but it was really just a month ago."

Mildred gave a loving sigh. "I'm so happy you did." A hint of concern filled her face. "Billy, I hope you didn't do it just for me and the children."

Bill set the paper down and turned to Mildred. "You know I love you and the kids, even though I don't always act like it."

"Of course, I do."

Bill's gaze lowered, and he shook his head. "Truth be known, I've felt like a man with a chip on his shoulder for as long as I can remember. It's like I'm always trying to measure up, but am never enough."

"That's not true," breathed Mildred, stroking his arm.

Bill's cheeks quivered with emotion. "But Mildred, what I did today wasn't about fitting in or being accepted by your family and the Church. I did it for me. I want to be a better man." Bill gulped. "I want to be a better husband and father."

"Oh, Billy, you are a good husband. Look at you. When I married you, I wasn't sure what I was getting. I knew you were handsome from your pictures and kind from your letters, but I felt there was something else about you that—even with your grumpiness and vices—made you special. I never expected you to get any better, but you have. And for that, I'm so delighted."

Bill nodded faintly, then said. "You know, I've made more than my share of mistakes in my life. So I just figured, if God can give me a clean slate and accept me for the…" Bill shook his head as he fought the emotion filling his throat. "If God can see my willingness and accept me for the broken man I am, then I had better do it."

"We're all a little broken, Billy." With tears streaming down her cheeks, Mildred leaned into Bill and kissed him.

~

TURNING THE OTHER CHEEK

The changing of the seasons was in the air, and a cool fall breeze met Bill as he stepped out of the Seventeenth Street substation. Breathing in the fresh air, Bill started down the gravel walk, but slowed when he spotted Sylvester Schmig leaning against the brick building, having a smoke. While Bill once considered Sylvester a friend, their paths now seldom crossed, which Bill thought good for all the trouble Sylvester had caused him.

"Hey there, Bill, how are you?" Sylvester asked with a feigned smile.

"Sylvester," Bill nodded, coming to a stop. "Haven't seen you for a few weeks."

"Smoke?" Sylvester asked, presenting Bill a pack of Lucky Strikes.

Bill eyed the cigarettes, which he still craved from time to time, and shook his head. "No thanks, I quit."

"You don't say," smirked Sylvester. "How 'bout a drink? We haven't been to Pengilly's for ages. I'll buy."

"No thanks," sighed Bill. "I don't drink anymore."

"I heard you joined up with 'em," smirked Sylvester.

Bill stopped and turned.

"What about it?"

Sylvester shook his head in scorn and said, "I thought you were smarter than that, Kane."

Bill's jaw tightened. He took a step back toward his old friend. "And what's that supposed to mean?"

"Just what I said," Sylvester shrugged as he put the cigarette to his lips.

"They're good people," Bill frowned. "I don't want you talking bad about them anymore. Not around me, at least."

Sylvester removed the cigarette and blew smoke into Bill's face. "Whatever you say, *Brother Kane*."

Bill shook his head. He'd had enough of Sylvester and wanted to teach him a lesson—something he would have done without hesitation a few years earlier—but there seemed to be no point to it now. He turned and started back down the gravel walk.

"That's right, turn the other cheek."

Bill shook his head and kept walking.

"I don't blame you, really," Sylvester sneered. "I'd do it too for an extra wife."

Bill stopped, his fists clenched.

"Especially since you used yours all up, popping out all those kids like a rabbit," Sylvester smirked.

Bill spun on his heels, walked back to Sylvester, pulled back his arm, and hammered his fist into Sylvester's jaw. The blow knocked Sylvester against the wall and onto the gravel. "Don't you ever talk about my wife like that!" Bill warned as he glared down at the stunned and wincing Sylvester.

After spitting out blood, Sylvester looked up at Bill and asked, "What about turning the other cheek?"

"I just did. Yours," Bill growled. He then turned and walked away.

BILL WAS STILL FUMING when he pulled his dusty Oldsmobile into his backyard. While he cared little about what Sylvester thought, he wondered how his other coworkers viewed him. Once a popular baseball-playing lineman who regularly drank with "the boys," Bill was now a lowly custodian, happy to have a job supporting his wife and eight children. He was wondering how he had gotten himself into such a situation when he noticed his youngest daughter toddling toward him with six-year-old Violet close behind. Bill's heart melted when he saw their looks of adoration. He knew he was a failed man, but seeing they loved him anyway caused Bill's throat to tighten.

"Well, hello there, little miss Shirley Joan," Bill managed as he pushed the car door closed. He hoisted Shirley into his arms, kissed her on the cheek, and pulled Violet in tight. Bill half-listened as the chatty Violet went on about her day; his thoughts were on another time.

It was the day he left San Francisco for the Philippines. Bill and the other men were waiting to board the ship when he spotted the happy young family in the park. He could still visualize the man in the fine suit and bowler hat, his mustache curled at its ends, and the woman wearing an elegant dress and hat with a sash that tied under her chin. She held a baby as a small boy dressed in knickers danced around them holding cotton candy. Bill remembered their smiles and laughter, and the husband putting a loving arm around the wife and holding her close. To Bill, that image embodied a perfect family and a successful life. Bill had imagined himself someday having those same things: a loving wife, adoring children, and money to lavish on them. Bill wondered where his dream had gone wrong.

With Violet still chattering and Shirley's arm around his neck, Bill started toward the back porch when Glen came around the house kicking a can across the gravel. "Hi, Daddy," Glen waved before pulling back his leg and sending the can onto the lawn. It was then, with the same force as Glen's shoe striking the can, that the profound realization hit Bill. His smile faded, and his jaw slackened as Bill looked down at Violet and Shirley. His dream *had* come true.

Bill set Shirley down and looked into her loving face. His gaze moved to the jabbering Violet before turning to Glen, who was being chased around the plum tree by Bobby. A melancholy came over Bill as he realized he didn't deserve them.

When Bill entered the kitchen, Mildred was standing at the stove. It was the place she had toiled for all of their married life, and he wondered if he had ever once thanked her.

"Hello dear," Mildred said with a loving smile, her tousled hair up on her head, her apron stained from a decade of use. "How was your day?"

Bill nodded vaguely and choked out the words, "Good," but all he could think of was how bad a husband and father he had been. He saw forgiveness and love in his wife's eyes and wondered how he was deserving of it.

Bill saw Alma sitting at the kitchen table. *He and his brother are nearly men now. What have I taught them about being a loving father and husband?* Bill wondered, but he knew the answer. *Precious little more than my father taught me.* The notion caused his gut to tighten. A wave of remorse swept over Bill as his shortcomings piled on top of him.

Full of emotion, Bill left the kitchen and walked through the front room where Helen was playing the piano. His feelings of inadequacy and remorse were overpowering as he entered his bedroom. He closed the door and sank onto the bed. Feelings of doubt and self-loathing continued to gather around him, like a suffocating quicksand rising from the floor. Bill knew he was not worthy of his family's love. He knew he was a flawed and broken man and deserved none of it. *I'm trying to change, but is that enough?*

When Bill thought of his father, he sobbed. Bill knew how hard it had been on him losing Patty. He tried to fathom his father's pain after losing his wife. For the first time, Bill realized his father's overwhelming task, raising four children without a mother. Bill's heart ached with regret.

After choking down his emotions, Bill reminded himself how far he had come. He knew he still had far to go to prove himself, but he was no stranger to work. Hard work and stubbornness had gotten him this far. Bill hoped it could carry him the rest of the way.

FIVE DAYS PASSED. While no one in the family knew of Bill's resolution to be a better man, the signs of his changing were all around them. He had made every effort to compliment Mildred on her meals. Even the overcooked Sunday roast received his approval. When Shirley and Donna danced and played loudly behind his rocker while he read the paper, he ignored them rather than chase them off to another room. Even Bobby denting the Oldsmobile with a rock proved relatively uneventful, with only a minor reprimand and a warning against throwing rocks. Aware of these episodes and seeing the visible strain on her husband's face as he peaceably dealt with each, Mildred watched Bill with increasing interest, wondering how long his transformation would last.

IT WAS twenty after five on a Tuesday evening when a tired and grumpy Bill came in through the back door, hung up his coat and hat, and entered the kitchen. Mildred could feel Bill's glare as he looked over the unset table and still-cooking chicken. He liked dinner ready by 5:30, and the events of the day had Mildred a half-hour behind.

"Hello dear," Mildred said, busily at work.

"When will dinner be ready?" Bill huffed.

Mildred half turned to Bill, afraid to see her new man gone, and said, "It should be ready by six. I'm sorry, dear."

"Six," Bill muttered disapprovingly. *She's had all day to fix dinner.* Bill tried to remind himself Mildred had other things to do besides fix his meals, but his hunger-fueled cantankerousness remained.

Deciding it best to sit at the table and watch his wife in the hopes his quiet fuming would speed her cooking along, Bill's brow bunched up when Bobby ran through the kitchen holding Helen's diary. Bill looked as though he might burst when a yelling Helen chased behind Bobby, demanding it back. Bill's instincts were to go after the boy, tear the stolen diary from his hands, and scold him for such tomfoolery, reminding him thievery would land him in jail, but he held it all in.

Surprised by Bill's restraint, Mildred turned back to see him glaring at the floor with his lips moving as he talked himself out of a blowup. She turned back to the stove, fighting a snicker. "How was work today, dear?" she asked, hoping her husband would not spontaneously combust.

"What?" Bill asked, distracted by his efforts.

"How was work?"

"Oh. It was fine," grunted Bill.

"I'm sorry dinner is late. I had to discipline Glen."

"Oh?" Bill asked, "What'd he do this time?"

"He put the West's old tomcat into the Chapman's henhouse and created quite a commotion," she said, watching Bill out of the corner of her eye.

That was all Bill could take. He jumped to his feet and cried, "What's wrong with your kids? They act like a band of wild Comanches! Where is he? I'll teach him a thing or two!"

"Dear, it's all right. I already took care of it," Mildred said with a calming hand.

Bill was halfway to the front room when he lurched to a stop. Fighting against his pent-up anger, he turned back to Mildred, who was trying not to laugh. "What's so funny?"

"Dear, they're *your* children too," Mildred reminded him. "From your stories, would you expect them to be any different than you were?"

Mildred's words struck Bill hard. He knew she was right, but he also knew that their antics were a far cry from his, even on their most rambunctious days. Returning to the table, Bill wondered what good traits he could pass on to them. He had long blamed his father for his bad temper. Bill wondered what bad qualities his children would blame on him. Bill sank into his chair and wished he were a better man.

"Bill," Mildred said, turning from the stove, "I know what you're trying to do, and I love you for it. Change is not easy. It takes time. I can do better too. Together, we can be better."

Bill nodded, but he wasn't convinced. He stared at the table, questioning everything he knew about being a father. He thought of his father, whom he had for years hated. But Bill's feelings of anger and hostility toward his father had softened the last few years, and now all he wanted to do was go back and be a son all over again.

KANE'S KINGDOM

December 13, 1937

*W*ith the tree up and decorated and a few presents already in place, excitement was building in the Kane home. The anticipation was not only for Christmas but also the imminent birth of a new baby.

Mildred, who was now forty-one years old, had relied on her mother to help deliver her other children as Dr. Boeck was notoriously late and usually arrived after the babies were born. But with Mrs. Read being ill at her home in Nampa, Bill had encouraged Mildred to go to the hospital for the delivery. Having an aversion to such places since her near-death bout with the Spanish Flu, twenty years earlier, Mildred had her doubts about such a birth. Surprisingly, hers was not the only newborn expected in the household. Daisy, their milk cow, was expecting a calf any day, and Mildred was determined to beat her to it. As the morning progressed, so did Mildred's labor pains and the realization she would soon have another baby to care for.

"How are you feeling?" Bill nervously asked as a very pregnant Mildred try to get up from her rocker.

"Oh, shoot. I don't know," sighed Mildred, visibly perplexed.

"Should I take you to the hospital now? We can get in the car and be there in no time. There are doctors and nurses and everything you need," Bill said encouragingly.

"Oh, I don't know," fretted Mildred, rubbing her belly. The fact their dear Patty had died there five years earlier made the thought even less palatable.

"But what are you going to do if the baby comes?"

"Make do, I guess," Mildred said, wincing from a growing contraction.

Bill turned to fifteen-year-old Helen, who was watching with wide, worried eyes, and reached for his coat. "Let's go, Mother. I'll take you."

"No, I think I'm fine," Mildred grimaced, "but it might be good for you to go to the neighbors and call Dr. Boeck just the same."

Bill turned pale at the thought of delivering the baby on his own. "All right. I'll be right back!" he yelled, hurrying out the front door.

"Mother?" Helen asked, full of concern.

"I'm all right, dear," panted Mildred.

A moment later, there was a knock at the door, and an unnerved Helen answered.

"Oh, hello, Helen," said Mildred's sister, Irene, as she brushed by in her long wool coat holding her two-month-old baby. "Hello, sister," Irene smiled, spotting Mildred wedged in her rocker. "Where's Bill going in such a rush?"

Mildred's brow gathered as she eyed her ten-year-younger sister, who had dark, done-up hair and milky white skin. "I forgot you were coming," gasped Mildred, her face red and sweaty.

"Oh dear, how are you feeling?" Irene asked as she realized what was happening.

"I think this baby is coming today," grimaced Mildred. "Billy went to call the do-CTOR!" she grunted as a contraction began.

"Well, who's going to watch Judy if you're having a baby?" Irene asked, looking down at her infant, a little panicked. "I was going to care for mother."

"I surely can't take her!" cried Mildred, shifting uncomfortably in her chair.

"Well, maybe I should just go," Irene said, turning for the door.

"Oh, Irene, it's too late! Don't leave me alone!" exclaimed Mildred.

"But what am I supposed to do?"

Bill burst through the front door, his chest heaving, "I did it! I called Dr. Boeck! He said he'd meet us at the hospital!" Bill caught his breath, then said, "Hello, Irene."

Irene nodded, but her eyes were still on Mildred.

"It's too late for that!" cried Mildred, grasping her belly. "Call him and tell him to come here!"

Bill staggered backward, glanced at Irene, and then bolted back out the front door.

"Helen, get some towels and put some water on to boil," Mildred said, almost out of breath. "Irene, will you help me out of this chair to my bed?"

Irene's eyes swelled. "Mildred, what do you mean? Surely you don't expect me to—Mildred, oh no! You can't do this to me!" she protested.

"I'm sorry. I know it's exasperating, but I'm afraid you're in for it!"

"What about little Judy?" Irene asked, white as a ghost.

"Helen can tend her."

Irene handed her baby to Helen, who had set a pile of rags on the coffee table.

"Oh, I should have gone to the hospital," groaned Mildred.

"Yes! Yes, you should go to the hospital!" exclaimed Irene, seeing a way out of the predicament.

"It's too late for that," panted Mildred.

"Oh, I hope this is a lesson you won't soon forget!" Irene cried, wringing her hands. "Oh, what should I do?"

"Help me to the bed," huffed Mildred, focused on her building contraction.

Mildred was just up from the rocker when Bill burst back through the front door. "I called him back. He said to let him know when the contractions are ten minutes apart!"

"They were ten minutes apart ten minutes ago! They're two minutes now, I'd say," grunted Mildred.

"Oh. Should I let him know?" asked Bill, turning in circles.

"YES!" both Mildred and Irene exclaimed in unison.

Bill raced back out the front door.

By the time Bill returned to the house, he could hear the unmistakable cry of a newborn baby. When Bill pushed open the front door, he saw his daughter Helen standing in the doorway of his bedroom, holding Irene's baby and looking on in awe. "Is Mother all right?" Bill managed, his chest still heaving from his sprints to the neighbor's house.

Helen gave her father a happy nod as she bounced Irene's baby.

Bill's heavy sigh released all the worry and uncertainty he was carrying.

"If that's Doc Boeck, tell him he's late as usual!" complained Mildred.

"It's Daddy," Helen replied as she grinned at her new baby sister.

"Oh, then tell him he has another darling little girl," beamed Mildred.

"Should I come in?" Bill asked, inching closer to the bedroom.

"Just a minute. Let me get the baby cleaned up," replied Irene. "She's all covered in tobacco juice."

Bill grimaced at the image and took a step back. "I'll watch for the doctor," he said, recomposing himself as he looked out the frosted window.

"She's perfect," Mildred strained, her voice weak from exertion. "You should see her! I want to name her Mary, Mary Lorraine."

Bill nodded, but his gaze was far out the window as he realized it was exactly five years since they laid their dear Patty down in the cold earth of Morris Hill. *No wonder Mildred didn't want to go to the hospital.* His heart ached as he remembered the pain of the days, weeks, and months that followed Pattie's death. He still sorely missed Patty, but felt comfort in the hope of seeing her again someday.

Bill could hear his new daughter crying before quieting down to suckle, but his mind was still on Patty and everything that had happened in those five years. Bill thought of the changes in their family with three more children born. He considered the changes in himself. Bill recognized he had come a long way and was now a better man, but he knew he still had a long way to go.

Bill sighed as he thought of how his failings had affected his family. For years, he had made excuses. Bill had told himself he was who he was because of losing his parents or his time in the Army. But he knew what he could become; he had seen it in others. His only fear was his efforts might be too late.

"Come and see your new daughter," called Mildred from the bedroom.

Bill turned from the frosted window. He saw Glen standing behind Helen, looking curiously at the new arrival. "Another girl? Curses," muttered Glen as he turned and left.

Upon entering the bedroom, Bill passed Helen and Irene and paused beside the bed where Mildred was cradling their newest child. "Well, Mother, we have quite a kingdom here, don't we?"

"Kane's Kingdom," Mildred beamed. "Isn't she precious?"

Bill looked at Mary's dark hair and eyes and nodded proudly.

THE HEALING PEN

AUGUST 1938

*S*ummer was all but over, ending the lazy days playing down by the river for the school-aged children. With the eighteen-year-old twins working at the Chinese Gardens delivering produce, Mildred had only Shirley and eight-month-old Mary at home. While Mildred still had plenty of work to do, Bill now helped with her many tasks, making her load lighter. Now in his twelfth year with the power company, Bill had more freedom in his schedule and was taking five-year-old Donna to enroll in school.

The passing air fluttered Donna's short dark hair as she sat on her knees to better see out the open window of their green Chevy sedan. One to think quite seriously about things, Donna turned to her father with her dark, piercing eyes and asked, "Why can't Tuffy come with us?"

"Because I'm tired of dog hair, and I don't want him in this new car," Bill said, brushing his hand over its tan corduroy upholstery. "Besides, we're going to enroll you in school. There's no place for a dog there."

Donna folded her arms and glared forward. "I don't want to go to school if it's no place for dogs," she protested.

"You're going to school, and that's that," frowned Bill. "Now sit down on your behind before you fall out that window."

Donna moved her legs out from under her, but tightened her folded arms as her brooding gaze deepened.

Bill shook his head and smirked. "You don't want to sit in dog hair, do you? The old car was full of it."

"But I *love* Tuffy," Donna replied, looking at her father pleadingly.

"Well, that's fine, but he's not riding in this car," Bill said with finality as they pulled up to the stately three-story Park School, which looked something like a palace with its turret and large arched entry.

After walking inside, memories of Bill's early school days flooded his mind. He remembered his sister Iliene walking him to the Goodrich School. As a first-grader, he had long, curly hair, which was the style for young boys at the time. While it got him plenty of compliments from women, it caused more than one fight with older, teasing boys. Bill remembered little of the classroom, but he recalled sitting in the dark and dank alley near the rat holes where he and his friends caught the emerging rodents, tied strings around their necks, and forced them to fight.

As Bill walked down the worn but newly polished linoleum floor following the sign to enrollment, he passed a pretty young woman in a blue dress with golden blonde hair pulled back and done up. *A school teacher*, he thought. Suddenly, Bill remembered Mrs. Butler, his first-grade teacher and the only teacher to like him. Bill thought it odd she insisted on kissing him on the cheek each day before he went home. Bill's brow furrowed as he remembered her walking home with him several times and helping around the house. Bill came to a stop as the memory became more vivid. *She was after Dad,* he concluded with a wry grin. He remembered her and his father together for a time. *Were they courting?* he wondered as he searched for more details in his mind. *Dad never got over Mother. That's why he never remarried,* Bill sadly reasoned.

"Daddy," Donna whined as she pulled on his hand.

Bill breathed in the musty air as they continued down the dimly lit corridor, but his mind remained on his early school years. He remembered he and his friends getting caught by the police shooting craps with the money his father had given him for the poor and needy. Bill snickered at the memory. At six years old, he was excited to ride to jail in the patrol wagon.

Bill's grin faded as his recollections of school darkened. By second grade, he was out of control, and his father moved him to The Hull House School for Boys in the heart of Chicago. It was a boarding school, and Bill was miserable and lonely there. He remembered begging his father to let him come home, promising he would be good. He remembered his father reluctantly agreeing. Bill spent the rest of his primary years at the Holy Family Catholic School, where nuns scolded and tried to beat him into submission. Bill felt the back of his hand where they slapped him with sticks and horse traces to get his attention. They were dark, loathsome memories that stirred emotions he had not felt in a long time.

"Daddy," Donna whined. "Daddy, I don't like it here. It's dark."

Bill looked down the darkened hallway, forgetting for a moment where he was. He turned back to the lighted area where other parents and children were standing in line. "Oh, we need to go back there," he said, leading Donna back the way they had come.

After a few minutes in line, a ruby-cheeked lady asked, "Name?"

"Kane, William A," Bill said, his mind still in the past.

The woman looked up from her notebook, grinned somewhat embarrassed for him, and said, "No, your daughter's name."

"Oh, of course," Bill laughed. "Donna May Kane."

"Date of birth—your daughter's?" the lady smiled.

"Uh, let's see." Bill scratched under his hat.

"May furth, jus' like my name," Donna said, looking up at her father.

"Of course it is," smiled the woman. "And what year were you born, sweetheart?" she asked, this time looking directly at Donna.

"1933," Bill said, ready for the answer.

The woman filled in the blank, then said, "Continue into that room for the health examination."

Health examination? Bill led Donna by her hand into the classroom where a dozen other parents, mostly mothers, stood with their sons or daughters, waiting to be examined by a man in a white coat. Upon seeing the white-dressed nurse working beside the doctor, Bill's mind went back to his first day in the Army at Jefferson Barracks. His father hadn't been dead six months when he joined. Because Bill was underage and could get no parental permission, he lied about his age and used a fictitious name. His plan worked and got him far away from Chicago and his painful past. Sadly, it also took him far away from his two brothers and sister, whom he had not seen or heard from since.

Bill swallowed as he remembered that day in line at the Army barracks in Missouri. That was the start of a five-year stint in the Army that would take him to the Philippines and beyond. Eventually, it would even lead him to Mildred.

Bill marveled at the course his life had taken. He considered the war in France and how close he had come to going to fight. Bill wondered if he would have returned. He thought of those who hadn't. He remembered his old friend Bill Sharp and how his advertisement in the *San Francisco Chronicle* got him and Mildred together. Bill was thinking of his family and wondering how he deserved them when the nurse in the white dress cleared her throat and said for the second time, "Sir, will you lift your child onto the table?"

Slightly red-faced, Bill hoisted Donna, who was looking at him questioningly, onto the examination table. "There you go," he said, taking a step back.

"Thank you," the doctor nodded before feeling around Donna's ears and jaw. "Stick out your tongue. Say aww," the doctor said for the hundredth time.

No stranger to such feats in a house full of children, Donna stuck out her tongue, put her thumbs in her ears, and wiggled her fingers.

The nurse turned her head and chuckled while Bill watched, horrified.

"No," the doctor said, unamused, "Say aww."

"Aww," repeated Donna.

After the nurse removed Donna's worn and faded blue dress, the doctor continued his inspection. Mildred had made the dress for Helen years before, and each daughter, down to Donna, had worn it. Bill thought nothing of the hand-me-down. It was how they and millions of others had made do during the depression, but when he saw Donna's off-white panties with the words "Gold Medal Flour" printed on the back, he felt a terrible sense of failure. *What kind of father am I that my little girl has to wear underwear made from used flour sacks?*

Bill glanced at the nurse, who pretended not to notice. Embarrassed, he took a step back and, with folded arms, watched the nurse weigh Donna and then slip the faded hand-me-down dress back on. Bill turned back to a mother and son standing behind him and wondered what they thought of him and his poor family. Not usually one to care about such things, Bill was suddenly devastated and felt like a complete failure.

"Thank you," said the nurse, turning to the next child in line.

"Let's go," Bill muttered as he took Donna by her little hand and led her back across the polished linoleum floor and out of the school's grand front door.

. . .

"How did it go at the school?" Mildred asked as she pulled two loaves of fresh-baked bread from the oven.

Donna walked up beside her mother and, with a pouty face, said, "I don't want to go to that school. They're mean."

"Oh, no, they're very nice at that school," smiled Mildred, wiping her hands on her apron.

"I don't want to go," insisted Donna before starting for the front room.

"What happened?" Mildred asked, turning to a still-distracted Bill.

Bill shook his head as he eyed the open flour bin and the twenty-pound sack of Gold Medal Flour resting beside it. "Have I been that bad of a provider?"

"What do you mean?" Mildred asked, closing the oven door.

Bill pointed to the bag of flour. "Donna's panties are made from used flour sacks!"

Mildred straightened up somewhat defensively and said, "I've been doing that for years. It's perfectly good fabric; I can't see just throwing it out."

Bill shook his head, not in an angry sort of way, but more in disillusionment. "I'm sorry I haven't done better for you."

"What do you mean?" frowned Mildred.

"Look at us. We've got nothing! I'm working as hard as I can, but we still have to scrimp by with everything! The twins are already working full time! They should be able to go to college, so they don't have to live like this with their families!"

Mildred sighed. "Billy, that's not true. We have everything that matters. We have a house. You have a job—there are a lot that don't have either of those things! You even have a car! We are never late on our bills. In fact, I got a letter just the other day thanking us for being so prompt!"

Bill shook his head. "I've seen the looks people give us with all of our poor kids, even at church. 'Here comes the Kane clan, poor dumb folks with more kids than sense,'" he scoffed.

"That's not true."

"It *is* true," insisted Bill. "Even your family thinks we're second-class citizens."

Mildred shook her head.

"We can't even fit everyone in the same car when we go somewhere. Some of the kids either have to walk, or I have to make two trips!"

255

"That's all right. None of that matters," insisted Mildred.

"It does matter! I'm a failure!" Bill said, shaking his head.

Mildred reached out to her husband and, with loving eyes, said, "You're *not* a failure. Look at you! Look at how far you've come! You lost your mother when you were just a child. Your father did the best he could, but it was really the nuns and the Army that raised you. Now, look at you. You used to be so hard on the children; you treated them like you were their sergeant, and they were scared of you, but you've changed. You've become more patient and loving toward them, and they're not scared of you like they used to be. You've become a better man, and I love you for it. I don't care about the other things. I don't care if we ever have one new or nice thing. I care about you and our children being happy and feeling loved."

Bill sighed as he considered her words, but he felt no better. Turning, he left the kitchen and went out the back door. Bill stopped on the back step and looked out across the yard from the garden, with its just-harvested corn, across the gravel drive to his dirty green Chevy and roaming chickens. He saw Daisy, their milk cow, grazing on the lawn by the plum tree. They had borrowed her from the Reads years before and had never paid them for her. The thought left Bill angrier and more frustrated. It had been more than two years since Bill had his last smoke, but suddenly he craved the calming effects of the tobacco and wondered why he had gone to such trouble to stop smoking. Turning to the dull green Chevy, he marched to its driver's door, pulled it open, and climbed inside. With a twist of the key and a push on the gas, the car's engine rumbled to life, and in no time, its tires were crunching over the loose gravel as he backed out of the yard.

As Bill started up the alley and turned onto Jefferson Street, his first thought was to go downtown and buy a pack of Lucky Strikes. But by the time he got to State Street, with the fresh air blowing through the Chevy's open windows, he felt less agitated and realized having a smoke would do nothing but make him feel worse about himself. Bill told himself he had made a commitment when he joined the Church, and he wasn't going to become one of those smoking-behind-the-barn jack Mormons.

Bill continued aimlessly driving as he considered his pathetic situation. He considered his few successes and many failures and wondered what actual worth he had. Soon he found himself crossing over the river, driving up Morris Hill.

Bill slowed the car as he saw the inviting lawns and lush green trees of the cemetery. After passing the cemetery's entrance, he brought the car to a stop, turned around, and drove inside.

Bill parked his car just off the grass not far from Patty's grave, turned off the engine, and stared across the well-manicured grounds as the warm breeze washed through the car. It was some time before he heard the bird singing. Soon there was another, and before long, an entire chorus of birds had joined in. Bill stared at the gravestones and markers as the peacefulness grew around him. He wondered about the hundreds of people who lay buried before him. He wondered what their lives had been like—their despair and joy.

After a time, Bill pushed open the door and stepped out of the car. He saw Patty's gravestone thirty yards away. Six years had passed since they buried her. Bill pushed the door closed softly, hoping to not end the birds' happy song. Upon seeing he was alone, Bill started across the grass past the graves of dozens of others he didn't know. Bill's breathing deepened as he approached Patty's simple granite gravestone. Below an engraved flower, it read:

LaRita Kane
Mar. 18, 1925
Dec. 12, 1932

Bill kneeled and brushed away a leaf and some dead grass that rested on its bottom slab and then straightened back up. He remembered that terrible, sad time and breathed in the profound realization that so many of his present concerns didn't really matter. Bill studied the smooth granite tombstone which others, including the Reads, had helped pay for. It had long embarrassed Bill that he couldn't afford to pay for it himself, but he felt none of that shame now. Instead, Bill felt appreciation for the love so many had shown him and his family. He wondered if he had ever properly thanked them.

Bill thought of his sweet little Patty. He wondered what she would be like if she were still alive. Bill wanted to believe she was looking down on him, just like he had hoped his mother was whenever he had done something good. Bill knew Mildred was convinced of it and had long talked about them someday all being together again as a family, but that was after death, something Bill was still uncertain of.

Bill stared down at Patty's grave for a long time as he thought about his family's future and his past. He wished he were a better father. Bill wished he had always done and said the right things to his wife and children—the kind and loving things. He wondered if he could ever make up for it. His mind traveled even further into his past, to his childhood and his father. Bill didn't like to think about it, but he feared his disobedient and wayward ways had led to his father's early death. Bill shook his head at the irony that the life of the very person who might have taught him to be a better father and husband may have been cut short by his delinquency. But unlike before, Bill was not weighed down or discouraged by the thoughts; instead, he saw them for what they were. He was an imperfect man trying to change. Bill wondered if that change was coming too late.

Sitting under the tree and looking across the peaceful graves, Bill reflected more on his father. He no longer felt anger when thinking of him. He no longer blamed his father for his mother's death. Now Bill felt sadness for judging his father too harshly. Bill felt regret for being such a trying son and not allowing his father in.

Bill's heart swelled. He lowered his head, closed his eyes, and said a prayer. It was a simple prayer, as most of his were, but it was heartfelt and pleading.

When Bill opened his eyes, the surrounding green seemed more vivid, more alive. The songs of the birds in the trees seemed even more cheerful, and a warm sense of self-worth filled him. There, under the shade of a sprawling maple tree, looking down on the grave of his dear Patty, Bill knew what he must do.

MILDRED WAS PULLING the last of the fourteen loaves of bread she had baked that day from the oven when Bill returned through the back door. She gave him a wary glance, the same as she had done to determine his mood every day since they had married, and saw not a look of cantankerousness or frustration but a focused calm. "Hello, Billy," she said searchingly. "Did you have a nice drive?"

Bill passed by her, paused as he considered her question, and then looked back and said, "Yes, I think I did."

Mildred smiled and left it at that as Bill continued into the front room and sat at the table where Mildred wrote her correspondences.

After picking up Mildred's fountain pen, Bill adjusted the tip, pulled out a crisp piece of paper, and then turned to the kitchen, where Mildred was still eyeing him. "Do you mind if I use your pen and stationery for a letter?"

"Of course not," said Mildred, wondering why he had asked.

"Thank you."

"Who…who are you writing to?" asked Mildred, wondering what had caused the sudden change in his mood.

Bill looked up from the paper thoughtfully and replied, "My father."

"*Oh,*" Mildred said, taken aback. She wanted to inquire further, but seeing the unusual focus on her husband's face, she returned to her baking, shooting frequent glances at him.

After penning the salutation, Bill stared at the paper for a few moments, then wrote the words he had for so many years wished to express.

Mildred went about her work in the kitchen with one eye on the intently focused Bill.

After a time, Bill set down the pen. With his chest heaving, he reread the letter. The significance of his thoughts put to paper was overpowering to Bill. He wished he would have said these things to his father years before in person, when it would have mattered. Bill shook his head. He remembered Charley Borup teaching him the spirits of the dead were not on a fluffy cloud but living all around them. Bill wondered if his father might be there with him, perhaps looking over his shoulder and reading the letter even now. Bill sighed peacefully at the notion.

Turning to the kitchen, Bill caught Mildred looking away, pretending she hadn't been watching. He wanted to tell her what he was feeling. He wanted to share with her the sudden swell of hope and joy that had embraced him, but Bill was not ready for that yet. *Maybe she'll understand if she reads the letter,* he thought.

When Mildred glanced back at Bill, he caught her gaze and pushed the letter toward her. Sensing the invitation, Mildred dried her hands and approached Bill at the table.

"I wrote it," Bill said, his voice straining with emotion.

Mildred's brow gathered when she saw Bill's pleading face. "May I read it?"

Bill nodded.

Mildred pulled out a chair and read the letter.

Dear Dad:

I am writing this to you though you have been dead for twenty years.

From your seat in the place beyond, I hope you can see these lines. I feel I must say these words to you, things I didn't know when I was a boy in your house, things I was too stupid to say.

It's only now, after passing through the long, hard school of years; only now, when my own hair is starting to gray, that I understand how you felt.

I must have been a bitter trial to you. I believed my own petty wisdom, and I know now how ridiculous it all was, compared to that calm, ripe, wholesome wisdom of yours.

Most of all, I want to confess my worst sin against you. It was the feeling I had that you did not understand.

When I look back over it now, I know you did understand. You understood me better than I did myself. Your wisdom flowed around me like the ocean around an island.

And how pathetic, it now comes home to me, were your efforts to get close to me, to win my confidence, to be my pal!

I wouldn't let you. I couldn't. What was it that held me aloof? I don't know. But it was tragic...that wall that rises between a boy and his father and their attempts to see through it and climb over it.

I wish you were here now, across the table from me, just for an hour, so that I could tell you how there's no wall now. I understand you now, Dad. Oh, how I love you and wish that I could go back and be your boy again.

I know now how I could make you happy every day. I know how you felt.

Well, it won't be long, Dad, until I am over there with you, and I believe you'll be the first to take my hand and help me up the further slope.

And I'll put in the first thousand years or so making you realize that not one pang of yearning you spent on me was wasted. It took a good many years for the prodigal son...and all sons are in a measure prodigal, to come to himself, but I've come. I see it all now.

I know that the richest, most priceless thing on earth, and the thing least understood, is that mighty love and tenderness and craving to help, which a father feels toward his children, for I have ten of my own. And it is they that make me want to go back to you and get down on my knees to you.

Up there in silence, hear me, Dad, and believe me.

"It's beautiful, Billy," said Mildred, tears welling in her eyes. "Your father wasn't perfect, but he loved you and was doing the best he could."

Bill wiped away a tear and nodded. "I know that now. I don't know why, but it was easier to blame him for everything that went wrong." Bill gulped and then shook his head. "It wasn't him."

Mildred wrapped her hands around Bills. "I'm so proud of you for the man you've become. Women used to tell me that husbands don't change.

You get what you get and hope he doesn't get worse. But you've changed." Mildred said, catching a tear running down her cheek.

"I'm trying."

"So am I. I could be a better wife. I could be a better mother. That's all any of us can do. Try to be better and love each other."

Bill nodded, then sighed. "I'll probably still have blowups. I'll probably still yell at the kids from time to time."

"I know, and I'll love you, just the same," laughed Mildred, pushing out more tears.

Bill drew in a ragged breath and smiled. "Thank you. Thank you for loving me through it all."

With tear-filled eyes, Mildred leaned closer and kissed her husband.

~

Bill and Mildred

Bill and Baby Glen. 1929

Patty and Virginia.

Bob and Bill

Alma, Bob, Helen, Alva, Glen, and Tuffy. 1932

Back: Glen, Violet, Helen, Mildred, Donna, Shirley, Bill. Front: Mary and Grant.

The Kane home. Painted by Helen.

I hope you enjoyed *The House by the River*.
I would love to hear what you think about it.
Please leave a rating and a review!

Made in the USA
Coppell, TX
12 February 2023

12682300R00157